THE WITHERING TRIALS OF GWENDOLYN GRAY

THE WITHERING TRIALS OF GWENDOLYN GRAY

Being the Third Volume

In

The Chronicles of Gwendolyn Gray

B.A. WILLIAMSON

For my Father.

And for those seeking an escape—may you find it here.

A TABLE OF CONTENTS

PART ONE: VIOLET

CHAPTER ONE

OH, THE TIMES...

Once upon a time, in the City of No Stories, Gwendolyn Gray was all alone. This little girl did not mind being alone, most of the time. And the deserted Hall of Records was as good a place as any to be alone. She felt less lonely when surrounded by books than when she was surrounded by people.

Books can be great friends. But the shelves that towered over young Gwendolyn Gray held little more than casual acquaintances. The Hall of Records was a building-sized filing cabinet for official documents and instruction manuals and encyclopedias of things that no one cared about.

She didn't mind. These were some of the only books in the entire City, and whatever they lacked in interest or excitement, she would fill in with her own imagination. An imagination as untamed as the bushy red curls that fell into her face as she read, sitting cross-legged on the floor. She blew at a strand of hair, but succeeded only in knocking a few more loose. She brushed them back and shifted positions on the cold tiles. Her legs were falling asleep, and the book she was holding was laughably large in her petite hands.

No sooner had she found a more comfortable position than she felt someone tap her on the shoulder. She cried out, whipped around, and toppled over in the process.

Mother stood there, hands on hips, foot tapping. "Well. It looks like Father was right. He was sure we'd find you here."

Gwendolyn scrambled to her knees and gathered up the book. "I'm sorry, I was just, umm... reading."

Marie Gray cocked an eyebrow, her face serious, but not stern. "How many times have we told you to ask permission if you're going further than our block? I was worried you had run away again."

"No, I was going to come back this time, I promise. It's just that Mr. Tompkins mentioned something in class called an aeroplane, so I came here and found this book about it, see?" She held up a picture of a sleek winged contraption with a propeller on the front.

A flash of white flickered in Mother's eyes for a moment, as it always did when Gwendolyn talked about such things. It was the same light that steered most Cityzens away from the Hall of Records in the first place. Instead of looking at the book, she scrutinized her daughter. "You're getting your new overalls dirty."

"How can you tell, they're already grey..." she muttered under her breath.

"What was that?"

Gwendolyn hung her head, hiding her face behind a curtain of hair. "Nothing. Sorry, mommy."

"It's *Mother*, if you please. Eight-years-old is too old to be calling me 'mommy.' Now where's your hair ribbon?"

Before she could stop them, Gwendolyn's eyes darted guiltily toward one of the books on the floor beside her, where a black silk ribbon had clearly been used as an impromptu bookmark.

Mother sighed. She got down on her knees next to her daughter, taking extra care not to get a run in her hosiery. She tugged the ribbon out from between the pages and motioned for Gwendolyn to turn around.

Gwendolyn did, sitting cross legged once more, and Mother began running her fingers through her daughter's fiery tangles. A pleasant shiver ran through Gwendolyn at the gentle touch, tingling over her scalp and down her spine. She wriggled a little.

"Hold still, please."

She did her best. "When did you stop calling your mommy, mommy?"

"Oh," Mother said in surprise. "I suppose I was a little older than you, if I'm honest."

"And did you ever run away?"

"Certainly not! I was a very well-behaved little girl. Even as a teenager, I would always tell your grandmother exactly where I was going and what I was doing."

"That's not what Daddy says."

Mother peeked around and gave Gwendolyn a pert little grin. "Well, your *father* is not to be trusted." She wagged a finger. "Obeyed, yes. But never trusted."

Gwendolyn giggled. When she stopped, the two of them sat in pleasant silence as Mother finished tying back her daughter's hair.

"I wish I'd gotten to meet them," Gwendolyn said. "My grandparents."

Mother came around and sat down next to her, both legs to one side. "You did. But you were too young to remember." Her tone grew wistful, and she gazed absently at the blank stretch of wall at the end of the row of shelves.

"Do you miss them terribly?"

Mother nodded. "Every day."

Gwendolyn nodded as well. "I wish I knew them enough to miss them. And Daddy?"

Mother did not correct her this time. "It's even worse for him, in a way. He lost his parents when he was still young. Just old enough that he didn't have to go to the Home for Unclaimed Children, thankfully..." Her voice trailed off, and Mother fidgeted with the hem of her skirt. "Anyway. That's enough talk for now. Come on, I'll take you home."

"Can I bring the book with me?" Gwendolyn said, holding up the enormous tome.

"You're not really allowed to, but..." Mother frowned and looked around the deserted space. "I don't suppose anyone will notice. Just this once," she said with a wink. "And don't tell Father, I'll never hear the end of it. Now, help your dear mother up, I don't think I can manage it in this skirt."

Gwendolyn got to her feet, tucked the book under one arm, and took her mother's hand. But Mother gave her a playful pull and she fell forward, both of them laughing as they sprawled on the tile.

Suddenly, there was a thump that knocked the wind out of her, and she opened her eyes. She lay on the floor, yes, but she was no longer in the Hall of Records. And she was no longer with her mother. And she was no longer eight years old. She was in her apartment, lying on the floor next to her father's chair. She was alone. And at fifteen, she felt that she was getting entirely too grown-up.

Once upon another time, Gwendolyn Gray saved the world.

The City had been a dull grey place of rules and regulations and no ideas whatsoever, without enough imagination even to give it a proper name. It was simply the City, and it was the way it was, as it had always been for five hundred years. Gwendolyn's riotous red hair had been the only speck of color in the entire world, and likewise, her daydreams had been the only speck of imagination. Until one day, she had daydreamed a little too *hard*, and made Missy Cartblatt grow a pair of rabbit ears, and brought furry orange creatures to life, and created underground aquatic tunnels full of monsters.

These sorts of changes brought her to the attention of the Faceless Gentlemen, the men in bowler hats who erased everything *new* in the City, preserving the precious status quo. Gwendolyn had only escaped with the help of Sparrow and Starling, two imaginary friends that sprang to life and whisked her away. They showed her the portals between worlds, and they escaped the Faceless Men, hopping from story to story, world to world, and fighting the forces of darkness that threatened to drain them all of their magic and color, until every world was as dull as Gwendolyn's.

With the help of heroes from various other stories, Kolonius Thrash and his crew of airship pirates, the mystical inventress Cyria Kytain, and an army of faerie folk, Gwendolyn had freed the City from the clutches of Mister Zero and his mind-draining

Lambents. She had sent imagination coursing through her world again. She had saved her own story.

But it had come at a cost. And with every day that passed, she wondered if it had truly been worth it.

The image of Mister Five and Mister Six dragging her parents through a portal to another world was permanently etched in her memory. She pictured the Blackstar, the inter-world agent of darkness, leading them through. And Sparrow and Starling, her only two friends in the world, leaping in after them.

"Don't worry, Gwendolyn, we'll find them!"

"We'll be back, I promise!"

She believed in her friends. But she wished they would hurry it up a little. Two years was an awfully long time to wait.

Two years since the battle with Mister Zero in the Central Tower. Two years with no parents. Two years living alone in the big, empty apartment. Feeding herself. Fending for herself. Hiding and lying and living in constant fear that someone would discover her secret. That someone would find out that Gwendolyn Gray was on her own.

And then the men would come.

Not the Faceless Gentlemen, of course. They had not been seen since they had disappeared with her parents two years ago. No, the men Gwendolyn feared were all too ordinary. They would politely knock with their polished nightsticks, politely tip their caps, and politely pack her away to the Home for Unclaimed Children.

She looked around the empty apartment. She must have fallen asleep at the typewriter again and toppled right out of her desk chair. Was she really that tired? She supposed she must be. It was hard to tell. These days, she was always tired. The constant nightmares of the Wastelands beyond the City hardly helped.

She climbed back into the chair and stared at her father's typewriter. The page remained stubbornly blank. The panic welled up in her stomach, the familiar fear that the ideas would no longer come, and then the paychecks would no longer come, and then her freedom would be taken away. She tamped down the fear, and focus ed on the page again. Start with a title, she told herself. Her fingers clacked out a few words and banged at the return, hearing its reassuring chime.

Criminy and the Borpulus Beazle
By Marie and Danforth Gray

"Borpulus?" she read out loud. "What a terrible word. And I haven't the slightest idea what a Beazle is, anyway."

Her publisher, Mr. Mason, would throw a fit if he could see this drivel. Then he'd throw an even larger one to see that his two bestselling authors were, in reality, one freckle-faced fifteen-year-old girl. Her parents had saved enough money that she'd managed to get by, until she had the brilliant idea of trying to sell one of her stories. Of course, that meant writing under a pseudonym and impersonating her own parents, as no one was going to hire a newly orphaned thirteen-year-old girl.

Not an orphan, she would say to herself. *They're missing, not dead. They'll be back.*

She tore out the blank page, crumpled it up, and threw it away. "Fat lot of good you are," she scolded the typewriter. "You could do your part, you know."

The typewriter remained frustratingly silent.

She banged her head on the desk a few times, hoping that might shake a few ideas lose, but no luck.

Gwendolyn looked at her watch, and felt an altogether different kind of panic. She was late for the School.

Very, *very* late.

How long had she been asleep at the desk? She'd be lucky to make it in time for lunch. That's what she got for trying to get in some writing before school, especially after the cruel irony of another sleepless night.

She dashed for the bedroom. Getting dressed was a quick affair, the only benefit of the School's uniforms. Not having any hair to care for saved time as well. Looking neat and well-cared for was another important step in avoiding attention.

She ran a hand over her bare scalp. There wasn't any point in trying to hide it. She hated wigs. Wigs felt like a lie, and they all looked terrible. So she collected hats. Hats were fashionable. And the City actually *had* fashion these days.

There was a mirror in the hall, which Gwendolyn studiously avoided. She knew what she looked like. She had grown, as her trips to the store for new clothes reminded her. Buying her first bra on her own had been the most embarrassing moment of her life, and the last two years presented many strong contenders for that title. The way the salespeople had looked at her...

And anyway, she didn't have time to gaze at her reflection, mentally reciting every detail of her appearance. The last thing she needed was to be reminded of the hair she had lost. Her fiery red hair, her pride and joy, sacrificed to the faeries for their help to save the City. She threw on a yellow bell-shaped cloche and grabbed her satchel.

"Goodbye," she said, as always. And as always, she got no reply.

She stepped out into the hallway of the apartment building, and something furry brushed against her bare legs. She jumped, let out a little squeak of surprise, then looked down.

"Oh!" she said. "Hello, kitty."

A little black cat rubbed its face against her leg.

"Where did you come from?" She reached down to pet it. There was no collar around its neck. She looked around, but there wasn't anyone in sight. "You know, an apartment building is hardly the natural habitat for a feline."

It arched its back and purred.

She was late. Spectacularly so. But she couldn't leave a kitten wandering around on its own, and a few extra minutes wouldn't get her in any more trouble that she was already in. "Do you belong to Mr. Blythe and Mr. Reginald downstairs? They'll be terribly worried about you. Though I suppose they'll have left for work already. Come inside, and when I get home we'll take you down and sort this out."

She opened the door, and the cat bounded in like it was the host and Gwendolyn the guest, rather than the other way around. It hopped up on the counter and meowed a demand.

"All right, fine, here you go." She poured a bit of water into a saucer and set it on the counter. The idea of leaving a strange cat unsupervised seemed a questionable one at best, but another glance at her watch told her she had little choice in the matter. "I've got to run. Please don't get up to any mischief while I'm gone. I've never had a pet before, so you'll want to make a positive first impression, or I might judge your entire species poorly. I know that's unfair, but those are the stakes. Be good." And with one last stroke of its silky fur, she darted out the door.

It was raining. It would be, on a day like today. Since the Change, the City's weather had grown more unpredictable. Some days it was cold. Some days it wasn't. Some days it rained. Some days it didn't. Today was one of the worst—cold and rainy together. You could hardly see the tops of the towering, blocky skyscrapers. She kept meaning to buy an umbrella, but *meaning to* and *remembering to* weren't exactly the same thing, and she reached the monorail platform a bit soggier than she would like.

The wait was painful. She tapped her foot, glancing anxiously down the tracks. A splash of color drew her eye, bright and bold against the dreary day. At the end of the platform was painted a wide arch of various colors, which she now recognized as a *rainbow*. It made her smile a little. Actual *color*, in the *City*. It was unheard of before, but these days, if you turned the right corners and went down the right alleys, you could find colorful murals painted by guerrilla artists in the middle of the night.

Or gorilla artists, she supposed. But that seemed highly unlikely.

A monorail tram arrived, and she grabbed her bag. Then she noticed that the wall behind her was papered with several large black posters that proclaimed **A RETURN TO VALUES** in blocky white text. The sight of it was like a punch to the gut.

For five hundred years, the City's "values" were to drain all your thoughts into the Lambents, leaving you feeling happy, and stupid, and dull. And apparently there were still quite a few people who would prefer it that way. No matter how hard she tried, no matter how much she sacrificed, it hadn't been good enough. *She* hadn't been good enough.

She tore one of the posters off the wall, ripped it in two, then stormed onto the tram.

It was empty, a sign of just how late she was. Since she couldn't make the train go any faster by wishing and worrying, she took out her diary to calm her increasing anxiety. It was blue, with little white flowers on it. A present from Sparrow.

She flipped through the pages, full of sketches, story ideas, notes, and regular journal entries. She'd read somewhere that journaling was an effective way of managing her emotional state, which Gwendolyn could certainly use, given her bipolar swings of ups and downs, mania and depression. But this particular morning she settled for doodling her initials, two looping G's that curled around each other. The repetitive movements helped settle her from a state of trembling panic to mere leg-bouncing tension. She forced herself to move her hand as slowly as she could.

She'd heard of people trying out this new tattoo trend. Maybe she'd get one, her little symbol in green, on the inside of her forearm. It wasn't as though she had any parents to stop her.

She snorted a bitter laugh. Laughter was better than tears. But she still found herself pulling her knees in close, huddled in the back of the train, and wishing she had someone to give her a hug and tell her that everything would be all right.

Everything will be all right, she told herself.

A tattoo was out of the question anyway. It would draw too many questions, and the thought of needles made her shudder. At least, that was how she explained her trembling. Or maybe it was the cold. Or the wet.

But she was fine. Really. She just hugged her knees even tighter to her chest to make the shaking stop.

CHAPTER TWO

That Kind of Day

Gwendolyn reached the school. She stopped at the foot of the steps, the way she did every day, even when she was running late.

This was the last place she'd seen her mother. Before Mother's memories had been erased. Before she had been turned into a Faceless Gentlemen and kidnapped by the Blackstar.

They had argued. "I've had quite enough of this new attitude of yours," Mother had said.

"Good," Gwendolyn shot back. "You won't have to deal with it anymore, and if you like, never again! I'll vanish, and you won't have a freak for a daughter."

The memory did not improve her mood.

The School's corridors were deserted. All of which made her feel painfully exposed. It is remarkable how you can feel as though everyone is staring at you even when no one is around.

At least she got an elevator to herself as she rode up to one of the higher floors where all the fifteen-year-olds were taught. Peeking through the door to her classroom, she saw no sign of

Miss Sahida. The teacher must be out for lunch, leaving the students huddled in groups and chatting amiably. None of them had ventured out into the courtyard in this rain.

Gwendolyn snuck inside, trying her best to remain unnoticed. Though she couldn't resist bumping Cecilia Forthright's desk with her hip, just a little.

Cecilia glared up at her. "Leave me alone, oddling."

Gwendolyn just smirked. Cecilia Forthright had made Gwendolyn's life miserable for years, but ever since Gwendolyn had returned from Tohk, her old bully seemed to have lost her power. Even cronies like Vivian Coleridge and Janette Tice-Nichols had abandoned her.

As Cecilia had lost her friends, Gwendolyn had gained a few of her own. Tommy Ungeroot, Missy Cartblatt, Ian Haldrake, and Jessica Tawny sat at the back of the class.

"Heya, Freckles!" said Tommy.

Gwendolyn sank into her usual chair. "Stop calling me that," she said, more out of habit than anything else.

"Nope!" He grinned. Tommy had grown into his features, and his front teeth didn't stand out so much. That was about all that had grown. He was shorter than the rest of them, with the last traces of baby fat visible in his cheeks. He had taken to wearing the same yellow bow tie every day, which he thought very funny.

Ian arched a delicate eyebrow. "Someone's late again."

"Yes, I know, sorry."

"You missed maths." Jessica said. "It's all right, I took notes for you."

"Is your mum angry?" Missy asked.

Gwendolyn tried not to squirm. "She... doesn't know. Too busy writing."

Ian scoffed. "Wish my mother were that oblivious... she's got her nose so far up my business she can smell my—"

"Did Miss Sahida notice?" Gwendolyn said.

He rolled his eyes. "Of *course*. She always notices when one of her precious pupils goes missing."

"You know she likes you," Tommy added. "Just use a little sob story to get out of trouble." He reached out and gave her hat a playful tousle.

"Stop it!" Gwendolyn shouted, smacking his hands away. "Don't. I mean it."

Tommy looked instantly mortified. "Oh, cripes, I'm sorry... Dunnow what I was thinking."

Ian snorted. "I heard Miss Sahida raking *you* over the coals yesterday for your poor marks. I bet your mother won't even let you out this weekend."

Tommy simply grunted. "Who says I care what she says? I'll be there, whether mum likes it or not."

"Good." Ian slicked back his ultra-stylish hair. "Could today *go* any slower? God, if I can just *make* it to tomorrow night, it'll be a miracle."

"I know," Jessica said. "Tomorrow's Revels are supposed to be exceptionally good. I hear rumors that Zelda has some new singers lined up."

The Revels. Her friends were always talking about them. Secret gatherings that had sprung up all over the City since the Change. Parties where people would share their music, or poems, or art, or whatever other creations they could think of. They were full of young people bursting with ideas. Her friends went nearly every weekend, and it was all anyone in class talked about.

Except for her. She couldn't afford to stand up in front of a room full of people and share her stories, no matter how much the thought made her toes tingle with excitement. The risk of exposure was too great.

"I'm gonna get up and tell my jokes!" Tommy said, tweaking his tie.

The others shared a look. Jessica wrinkled her nose. "Do you mean the jokes you were telling us yesterday?"

"Yeah!"

They all looked at each other again, then looked away. Ian coughed.

"Aww, whatever," Tommy scoffed. "None 'a you'se appreciate real comedy."

"Are you coming this time, Gwendolyn?" Jessica said. "The Revels aren't the same without you."

"Yeah," Ian said. "We've all seen what you've been writing in that notebook."

"You know I can't," Gwendolyn said, cringing. The fear of missing out grew more painful every time they asked. "My... my parents don't approve."

"That don't make no sense," Tommy said. "Your parents are writers. They create new stuff all'a time, how can they be down on the Revels?"

"They just..." Gwendolyn searched for an excuse, but she'd been running out of them recently. "They think I'm too young. It's terrible, they still treat me like a little girl." It would be nice if that were true. She wouldn't mind being a little girl for a while.

"You could sneak out," Tommy said. "S'what I always do."

"Yes, but my parents aren't so busy with my dozen brothers and sisters that they don't notice I'm gone." It came out sharper than she'd meant it to.

"All right. I get it. I'll leave you alone." He got up and went to another desk across the room and put his head down.

Ian nudged Gwendolyn's shoulder. "Good grief, girl, could you *be* a little more sour?" He lowered his voice to a whisper. "Anyway, I heard a hot bit of gossip on the mono. Bernard Finkmeyer told me that Armand Barbington has been talking to Jannette Tice-Nichols—"

"But they talk all the time," Missy said.

Ian rolled his eyes again. "Yes, but there's talking, and then there's *talking*—"

"Oh, please, Ian, no one cares," Jessica said. "Can't you ever talk about anything important?"

He grinned wickedly and leaned back in his chair. "No, I'm utterly incorrigible. Anyway, I guess Janette got all bothered because Armand sat next to Cecilia the other day, which is a *huge* no-no. None of them have hung out with her in ages. Not that I can blame them." Ian and the others looked over at Cecilia, who was sitting with her nose in the air as though everything in the room were beneath her notice.

But she must have noticed something, because she looked back at them all and gave them a dirty look. Gwendolyn and Ian returned it in kind.

The buzzer sounded, and more students filed back into the room. Miss Sahida ushered the last of them in, went to the front of the class, and clapped her hands, "Desks away! Chairs in a circle everyone!"

Several students groaned. Gwendolyn didn't blame them; there was nowhere to hide in a circle, and she would have much preferred to stay in the back row. But they pushed the desks to edges of the room and rearranged the chairs, just as they did every afternoon.

Missy pulled her chair up next to Gwendolyn's and leaned close. "Are you all right?" she whispered, brushing back stringy blonde hair that always seemed to be in her face. "What kind of day is it?"

Gwendolyn shrugged. "A normal one. It's fine."

Gwendolyn may have been a clever noticer, but Missy was as well, and she had noticed what the others never had. Namely, that Gwendolyn struggled with being pulled between two poles: a manic energy that made her dangerously impulsive, and a deep depression that could leave her stuck on the couch for days at a time. Missy had made a habit of checking on her friend. Usually Gwendolyn was touched by this, but today it just irritated her, which was a warning sign itself that she wasn't as all right as she pretended.

Missy seemed to sense *this* too, and she frowned, but didn't have time to press the point.

"Good afternoon, class," Miss Sahida said, wheeling her creaky wooden chair over to the circle.

"Good afternoon, Miss Sahida," the class responded in unison.

"Gwendolyn, thank you for joining us," she said with genuine warmth. "What kept you?"

"Uh... doctor's appointment," she said, her imagination leaping to the rescue. Again, she felt as though everyone was staring at her.

"Well, I do hope everything is all right. Just give me your note at the end of class."

Gwendolyn stiffened. *Stupid,* she thought. Her breathing sped up. *Stupid, stupid.*

Why hadn't she just said she'd overslept? Now she was going to be caught in an obvious lie. Miss Sahida might even want to call her parents.

One little slip, she reminded herself. That's all it took. One mistake to ruin everything. Everything she'd worked so hard to build, all the secrets she'd kept, all crumbling down around her. Her breathing sped up. Darkness crept in at the edges of her vision—

She felt someone squeeze her hand. She looked to see Missy, who was giving her a knowing look. Missy took an exaggeratedly slow breath, nodding at Gwendolyn to do the same. She did, breathing slower and slower until Miss Sahida's voice came back into focus.

"First things first. Who has a book they'd like to share with us today?"

No one said anything. There was a lot of fidgeting in seats and avoiding eye contact.

Miss Sahida leaned back in her chair and crossed her arms. "I see. Perhaps you're all the worthless snot-nosed brats the other teachers have been telling me about," she said with a wry smile.

Jessica raised her hand. "I've got one. I've been reading Edward

R. Newsome's *Philosophy of Change—*"

There was a fresh chorus of groans, but Jessica silenced them with a fiery stare. "—and he puts forward a compelling argument that it is up to the younger generation to shape the society that we're going to inherit, since the older ones don't have any incentive to do so."

"Interesting," said Miss Sahida. "And how do we make those changes?"

"He says that the best thing for change is art. Art shapes culture, culture shapes the way we think, and the way we think shapes the world we live in."

"A novel argument, if you'll pardon the pun," Miss Sahida said. There was another round of grumbling, but Miss Sahida only smiled. "So to that end, let's say we analyze some of these new art forms that have flooded the City since the Change."

For the next several hours, they looked at the creations of the Cityzens from the past two years. When Gwendolyn had freed the City from Mister Zero and his army of faceless men, the Lambents had changed. The glowing baubles had been draining the Cityzens of their imagination for centuries, but now they dazzled everyone with shared ideas and information and all the stories from before the Whyte Proposal had banned them all. All of which you will doubtless know if you have been fortunate enough to have joined us throughout Gwendolyn's *Marvelous Adventures* and *Fantastical Exploits.*

And as for the rest of you? Well, who's to say you cannot start a story in the middle? Such is life, is it not? We are always in the middle of some story or other. Life offers few clear beginnings or endings. There is simply change, shifting from one moment to the next, whether we like it or not. This story is a different story than the last, just as you and I are different than last we met.

Gwendolyn had changed as well. She once would have been thrilled at a discussion of the City's brand-new clothing, art, and literature, but instead her mind was frantically searching for a way to explain her phony doctor's appointment. She didn't even *have* a doctor. Where did one get a doctor? Perhaps she could forge a note...

"Gwendolyn?" Miss Sahida said.

"What? Yes?" She glanced up.

Miss Sahida gave her a tiny smile. "Daydreaming again?"

"No..."

"Ah. Well then, perhaps you'd like to answer the question I asked?"

"Um, also no. No *thank you*," she added.

Miss Sahida gave her a measured glance that said *I know you don't want to participate, and while I respect your feelings, I'm going to call on you anyway*. It was a very specific sort of glance. "We were analyzing metaphors in literature." The teacher wagged the book at her. "And *you* know this book better than anyone else in the room. After all," and she held it up to point at the cover. "It was written by your parents."

And sure enough, there it was.

On Wings of Splendour

by

Marie and Danforth Gray

All eyes turned toward Gwendolyn. It made her want to pull her hat down until it swallowed her whole head.

"You have read it, haven't you?" Miss Sahida prompted.

Gwendolyn took a breath and tried to clear her head. "Yes, of course I have. I don't know if the author meant to put in any metaphors. I think she just sort of... wrote it."

Miss Sahida blinked. "She? Do you mean your mother? I thought your parents were collaborators."

"No! I mean, yes. They. They wrote it. Together."

"Ah. Well, what did you think of their follow up effort, West of the Wilds?" She reached into her bag and pulled out another book.

"I liked that one better," Gwendolyn said, almost immediately. "It was much easier to write."

"The first one's better," said Michael Anders.

"No one asked," Gwendolyn muttered, sinking back into her chair again.

Miss Sahida noticed and moved on, sparing Gwendolyn any further attention. "Jessica, yes, I see your hand. Can you tell us what this one is about?" But Gwendolyn couldn't shake the feeling that Miss Sahida was still looking at her a bit more than usual. Fortunately, she was saved by the end-of-day buzzer.

"All right, students, that's all for today. Put the desks back into rows before the Headmaster sees our little circle and throws a fit. And make sure you've done pages ninety-seven through ninety-nine in your math books by Monday."

The class broke into a cacophony of raised voices and screeching desks.

Missy gently took Gwendolyn's arm. "Are you *sure* you're all right?"

Gwendolyn sighed. *But a good friend is there for us whether we like it or not.* "This morning *was* a bit of a struggle. Don't worry, I'll hold together."

Missy gave her a sideways hug. "We can always help with the holding."

Gwendolyn squeezed her back, smiling to think of the shy little girl Gwendolyn had once given a pair of rabbit ears. "Thank you. I saw *you* struggling with your math yesterday. What if I came over this weekend and helped you puzzle it out?"

They disengaged, and Missy brushed her hair out of her face. "That would be nice. But I could come to you, you don't have to come all the way to the Outskirts," she said, with a hint of embarrassment.

"No, don't come over," Gwendolyn said hurriedly. "I really don't mind the trip. It's always nice to get out of the house. And here..." She took some money out of her bag. "For the Revels." She knew that Missy's family had even less than Gwendolyn.

"No, I couldn't—"

Gwendolyn pressed the bills into her hand. "Yes, you could. Make sure to share some with Tommy. Don't let on where it came from."

"I won't. Thank you," Missy mumbled.

They were about to join in rearranging the desks, but Miss Sahida caught Gwendolyn's eye, and made a subtle gesture to come forward. Gwendolyn's heart skipped a beat. She eyed her friends, who were already packing up their things.

"We'll wait," Jessica said, catching her look.

Gwendolyn waved them off. "No, go ahead. No sense missing

your mono on my account."

Ian sidled up to her. "Look, if you need me to forge a doctor's note for you, let me know. If your parents won't let you Revel, the least we can do is get Miss Sahida off your back."

Gwendolyn forced a smile. "It's fine, really."

He shrugged. "Suit yourself. But next time you decide to skip, let me know so I can join you." He grinned and the four of them headed for the door.

Gwendolyn crossed to the teacher's desk much as a condemned man crosses the courtyard to face a firing squad.

Because teachers asked questions. And the questions they asked during class were very different than the ones they asked after. Questions like, *Where are your parents? Who have you been living with? Who has been taking care of you?*

So many questions. She wished she had a moment to close her eyes and slow her breathing. It had gotten very fast all of the sudden.

Gwendolyn walked up to face her doom, keeping the teacher's desk between them. But Miss Sahida motioned for her to come around beside. "Gwendolyn," she said, letting the name hang in the air.

Gwendolyn forced herself to make eye contact, as if nothing whatsoever was amiss, even though her insides were melting. "Yes?"

Miss Sahida sighed and took off her glasses. "Gwendolyn, Gwendolyn. What am I going to do with you?"

CHAPTER THREE

CATASTROPHES

Every muscle in Gwendolyn's chest suddenly clenched. "I... I'm not sure what you mean."

Miss Sahida gave her a stare that could pierce plate armor. "I think you know exactly what I mean. You're terribly bright. But you're holding back. You come in, sit in the back, only participate when I force you to, and talk to no one except your four friends. But all your written work is fantastic. I have to ask... how is everything at home?"

All Gwendolyn's other muscles tensed as well. "Fine... it's fine. Why do you ask?"

"Well, it's just that I've never seen your parents around here. They've never dropped you off, never checked up on you, and they didn't attend my parent night. Most of the other students' parents were thrilled at the idea, but I never heard back from yours."

Gwendolyn tried to keep a calm expression while her carefully tended world crashed down around her. "They... they're very busy. Deadlines and all."

"Yes, I suppose it must be terribly embarrassing to have such famous parents at your age." Of course, saying so out loud didn't make it any less embarrassing, and Gwendolyn suspected that Miss Sahida knew it. "They are quite prolific. They must spend a great deal of time writing. I take it that's the *real* reason you were late today? Parents getting swept up in their imagination?"

"Yes!" Gwendolyn blurted, anxious to seize on this line of thought. "They can be ever so forgetful. Constantly losing track of time."

But Miss Sahida's expression grew no less concerned. "And... are they able to make time for *you*?"

None at all, she thought, the comment springing unbidden from the darker parts of her heart. She felt an all-too-real swell of emotion. She used it to her full advantage, looking dejectedly away, twisting her foot nervously. And she had another idea. A little sympathy went a long way, so she may as well go all-in. "Can I be honest with you, Miss Sahida?"

Her teacher raised an eyebrow. "Have you been dishonest so far?" she teased.

Gwendolyn forced a laugh. "Funny. No, nothing like that. But it's rather personal, I'm afraid. Not something I'm comfortable talking about much." She trailed off, pausing for just the right amount of time. Then she took off her hat, exposing her bare, freckled scalp. "It is a bit embarrassing. The others haven't always been the nicest to me. I just... I'd rather stay out of the way. So if I act a bit shy, I'm sure you'll understand."

Miss Sahida looked suddenly and exquisitely uncomfortable, as Gwendolyn had hoped she would. "Oh. That's right, I'm sorry, I hadn't considered—"

"As I said, it's fine." Gwendolyn put her cloche back on. "Is that all? I've got to go, my mother's waiting for me." She'd told such lies so often, they hardly hurt anymore.

"Might I ask what happened? You've never said."

I sacrificed it to a faerie queen in exchange for her army, to defeat the evil ruler of our world. And magical sacrifices don't grow back.

Not that she could say any of that, even if she wanted to. "I'd really rather not talk about it."

"Yes, yes, right. I don't mean to pry. Go ahead. I'll see you tomorrow. Only..." Miss Sahida leaned in conspiratorially. "Do try to speak out once in a while. You're a lovely girl, and don't let anyone tell you different. I'd hate to think that everyone would miss out on the wonderful thoughts going through that head, just because there isn't any hair on it."

"I... I'll think about it. Thank you, Miss Sahida."

"Thank *you*, Gwendolyn." The teacher began straightening papers on her desk, and Gwendolyn turned to go.

"Oh, and have your parents give me a call, won't you?"

Gwendolyn froze in mid-step, just for a moment. "Umm, yes. I'll do that." And she hurried to the back of the room.

That was one disaster avoided. For now. Somehow she'd have to fake a phone call from her parents. A surge of anxiety tightened her stomach. So she pictured a door marked *Things To Worry About Later,* and shoved that anxiety inside with all her other worries like cramming laundry into an overstuffed closet. She exhaled slowly, and struggled to close the door on her emotions again.

She took another slow breath and began packing up her things, hoping Miss Sahida hadn't noticed her trembling hands. But she had handled it. That's what she did now—she handled things. And lied. Lying was what she did now, too.

She hated lying. Lately it seemed that lying was all her imagination was good for. Using her lack of hair as an excuse felt dirty, but necessary. Gwendolyn had no problems with standing out or being different. There had been enough teasing when she'd *had* hair. The bushy red mane had made her a target all her life. If anything, it was easier not to have it, though not at all what she'd prefer.

Miss Sahida's words ran through her head as she packed up her satchel, grabbed her notebook, and headed for the door. It would be nice to let herself be herself, rather than holding back all the time. Quiet and control were hard-learned skills, and could be quite exhausting. But her grown-up voice reminded her what was at stake.

Then it reminded her that she had bills to pay, and deadlines to meet, and laundry to do, and she still didn't know what she was going to make for dinner tonight, and...

She was so wrapped up in those thoughts that she failed to notice the foot that shot into the aisle. She tripped, hard, and went sprawling on the floor. Gwendolyn whirled, furious, and saw Cecilia Forthright, her mouth open in feigned shock. Cecilia threw a glance to her right. "Vivian did it."

"Save your breath." Gwendolyn got to her feet and into Cecilia's face. "Why don't you grow up sometime? You might accidentally become a decent human being." She picked up her satchel, and stormed out of the classroom.

Normally, we don't stray too far from Gwendolyn and her story, and we shall catch up to her in a moment, but it is important for you to see what happened next. For after Gwendolyn left the room, Cecilia rose from her chair, and picked up a book from the floor. A blue notebook, with little white flowers on the outside, and all the secret thoughts of Gwendolyn Gray on the inside.

Cecilia flipped through the pages, and a mean little smile crept across her face.

~~~

Some time later, Gwendolyn arrived home, a soggy bag of groceries in each arm. There had been the usual odd looks from the clerks at the store, but Gwendolyn assured them she was only running errands for her sick mother. Nonetheless, she was careful not to visit the same store too many times in a row. It meant a lot of extra travel, but that was what it took.

She pressed the grocery bags against the door to keep them from falling while she got the keys out of her satchel and unlocked the door. It swung open, and she tumbled inside, but one of the bags split open, its contents crashing to the floor. She groaned in frustration, bent down to gather them, but stopped mid-reach.

The apartment had been destroyed.

Not literally, of course. And it wasn't as if the apartment had been all that clean to begin with. Living alone meant she could leave the apartment however she pleased with no one to nag her about it. When she had left that morning, there had been discarded clothes on the floor, plates of half-eaten food everywhere, and I dare not even mention the state of the bathroom.
~~~

Now, however, those plates had been thrown to the floor and the stale food batted about. Picture frames had been knocked off the wall. A roll of toilet paper had been dragged from the bathroom, shredded, and scattered like confetti at some wild party. The black leather furniture had been mauled and their innards leaked out through dozens of rips and tears.

And sitting amongst a pile of stuffing, licking its paw as cool as you please, was the little black cat.

"ARGH!" Gwendolyn shouted in wordless fury. Groceries forgotten, she lunged at the cat, which leapt gracefully away. She ran after it, chasing it around the apartment. It ran into the kitchen, leaping across the tops of the kitchen chairs with playful ease, knocking over each chair as it did so. Gwendolyn climbed over the table to get at it. The cat leapt again, but Gwendolyn managed to grab its tail in mid-air. The cat yowled in surprise, and Gwendolyn got it by the scruff of the neck.

She held it up to eye level. "You horrid thing! What do you have to say for yourself?"

The cat cocked its head, scrunched up its nose, and yawned.

Gwendolyn glared at it. "There's not enough cute in the world to make up for the mess you've made. I should take you out to the street and leave you there."

Which, of course, she didn't. Instead she shut it in the bathroom. She gathered the groceries and put them away. Then she sorted the mail that had come through the postal tube and spilled onto the counter. A bill from City Power stood out by dint of the large red stamp on the front that said *PAST DUE*. Gwendolyn had brought color back into the City, but that didn't make the red block letters any less menacing.

She groaned and slumped against the wall, sliding to the ground. If you have ever forgotten an important homework assignment, you may have some inkling of the mixture of shame and frustration Gwendolyn felt, though the consequences here would be much more severe.

Why? Why couldn't everything go back to the way it was before? She shouldn't have to deal with this. She shouldn't have to worry about anything but her drawings and her stories and her friends. Why couldn't she just be herself for a change?

Gwendolyn took several deep breaths to calm herself, remembering the lessons that Tree had taught her during her time in Faeoria. Though the woodland realm of the fairies seemed impossibly dreamlike in the face of such mundane problems as paying bills.

She tossed her sopping wet cloche on the couch and scratched her head, which always itched after wearing a hat so long. Still, she felt an unusual bit of gratitude. It would have taken hours for her hair to dry.

She went to the desk and pulled out her parents' old checkbook, tearing out the last one. Somehow she'd have to trick the bank into sending her more. Then she wrote out the payment and sent it whooshing off through the postal tube.

Paying the bill reminded her that she needed to get something written soon, or she wouldn't have much left to pay them with. She sat at the typewriter, but all the frustrations of the afternoon made her mind such a mess that it was impossible to wrangle anything like an idea. It was the same feeling as staring down at a blank page of homework that simply must be filled, but without the faintest clue as to how.

That reminded her. She also had homework.

So, rather than deal with any of that, she went upstairs and changed out of her school uniform and into a simple, comfortable purple dress. Then she went back downstairs, into her parents' room, and flopped down on the large bed.

"I'm home," she said to the empty air. She lay on her back and stretched out her arms and legs, taking up as much space as she could.

"How was your day?" said Father, sitting on the edge of the bed and gently moving a lock of red hair away from her face.

"I got a cat," she told him. "It... hasn't gone well."

He chuckled, his mustache quivering. "For as much as you love animals, you've had precious little experience with them. Remember the time you tried to feed the pigeons outside the store? They kept flying away from you, wouldn't touch a bite. You got so flustered that we found you running at them and screaming. I'd swear you were flapping your own arms as if you thought you could chase after them."

Gwendolyn piled her hair over her face, hiding behind the bushy curls. "It wasn't my fault. I tried to give them some of Mother's biscuits."

He laughed again, the sound warm and familiar. "Well, they were quite smart to fly away, then, weren't they?"

That made her chuckle as well, but it was forced, and unconvincing. She put her hands behind her head, feeling the bare skin there. There was no hair. There was no Father. And not even *her* imagination could keep up the illusion for long. The mundane world was too strong, too heavy and real. It seemed hard to believe that she had once had the power to bring things to life with the merest thought, even without meaning too. And it got harder to believe with each passing day. Childlike wonder was hard to maintain in the face of all-too-adult responsibilities.

With plenty to do and no motivation to do any of it, she picked her parents' Lambent up off the bedside table. She was exhausted. Not from the physical exertions of the day, but by the endless stream of thoughts that looped in her head, all of the tasks she had to remember if she was to keep her life running smoothly enough that no one would notice the fifteen-year-old girl living on her own.

The Lambents had once been tools of Mister Zero, the Collector who drained the thoughts and ideas of the Cityzens until they were peaceful and compliant. Now they did quite the opposite, sharing pictures and stories and information with everyone all over the City. Gwendolyn browsed through postings for lost cats, then articles on cat ownership, before eventually finding herself watching a nearly endless stream of cats doing amusing things, the Lambent's flickering colors creating the images right before her eyes.

She supposed she should get up and make dinner for herself at some point. But that would require getting out of the bed, and washing enough dishes to cook with, and she didn't have the brainpower to think of anything to make anyway. Some days it was enough that she almost wished she would be sent to the Home for Unclaimed Children.

No, she thought, slamming the door on such thoughts before they could let out all the feelings in her anxiety closet. She didn't *need* the Home. She had been doing just fine on her own the past two years. Hadn't she taught herself to cook? And clean? Well, occasionally.

There had been a few bumps along the way, of course. There was the laundry debacle, the fiasco with the self-cleaning oven, a mortifying first trip to the pharmacy on the corner, and many more incidents besides. But two years of experience, and all the parenting books she could get her hands on, had taught her quite a lot.

Like being on time for school? said the unhelpful but ever-present voice inside her.

This isn't right, she thought back. Wallowing in her inadequacies wasn't going to help her. This was her depression rearing its dark head. She needed something to shake herself out of the gloom, and zoning out in front of the Lambent was just as bad as if they were still draining everyone's minds. She needed to get out. She needed to have some fun.

She needed to go to the Revels.

It was stupid. It was reckless. The Revels were questionable at best, and she knew there was talk of the City Council shutting them down. There were plenty of grown-ups who did not like the changes Gwendolyn had caused, restoring life and color and imagination to the City. Many of them liked things just the way they were, thank you very much, and wanted things to go back to the "good old days," whatever those were. *A RETURN TO VALUES* floated through her mind in white block letters. Putting herself on display at a gathering of delinquents was the best way of getting sent to the

Home for Unclaimed Children she could think of. And from what
she had heard, the new Childkeeper was not a woman to be trifled
with.

But she didn't care. She couldn't be a grown-up *all* the time.

Yes—the Revels were what she needed. She would go up to her
room, find something that wasn't a school uniform and was at least
somewhat clean. She could put on a dark wig, and call herself
Wendy, she had always liked that name. She would read one of her
stories to a room full of attentive listeners, and everyone would
know that it was *her* story, they would drink in her words like no
one ever had before Gwendolyn saved the City, she had *saved* the
City, didn't she have the right to at least *enjoy* it once in a while,
and—

The phone rang, and she squealed in surprise. She sprang out
of bed and dashed into the ruined living room, but she tripped
over something dark and furry, and fell flat on her face.

The black cat rubbed itself against her cheek, purring softly.

"What?" Gwendolyn shoved it away and got to her feet. "How did
you get out of the bathroom?"

The cat bounded away and she started toward the phone in the
kitchen, but at that moment, there was a knock at the door.

She froze, torn between the competing sounds of ringing and
knocking. But it wasn't a hard choice—the phone would have to wait.
An unexpected knock was almost certainly a sign of trouble, the kind
that made scratched up furniture seem tiny in comparison.

Oh, how right she was.

For Gwendolyn opened the door to see a man in a grey suit and
black bowler hat.

CHAPTER FOUR

AN UNEXPECTED PARTY

Instinctively, Gwendolyn threw herself backwards and crouched with her hands up, ready to... to what? She had no powers anymore, no way of fending off another attack from the Faceless Gentlemen—

But this was no Faceless Gentleman. He had a face, and a rather puzzled one at that. "Excuse me... Gwendolyn, is it?"

Gwendolyn froze. Upon closer inspection, this seemed to be merely an ordinary Cityzen. His choice of hat seemed to be nothing more than an unfortunate coincidence of fashion. "Yes? Can I help you?" She straightened up out of her guard position.

The man took off his hat and held it in front of his chest. He had thinning hair and round features. "My name is Mr. Mason. I'm here on your mother's invitation. Might we come in?"

An icy rush of terror swept over her. Mr. Mason was her publisher, and one of the richest men in The City. Well, he was her *parents'* publisher, or so he thought. Gwendolyn had never actually met the man before. All their correspondence had been by mail (and one awkward phone call where Gwendolyn had done a passable job of imitating her mother's voice). If he was here, he would know that his star authors were really a fifteen-year-old fraud, and would find out that her parents were missing, and he would call the police, and the Childkeeper would come and take her away—

But a word tripped her racing thoughts.

"Did you say invitation? What invitation?" She darted into the hall and closed the door behind her, blocking his view of the wrecked apartment.

Mr. Mason took a startled step back, and produced a card from the inside pocket of his coat. "Your parents' dinner invitation. I would have RSVP'd earlier, but I didn't see it in the mail until a few hours ago. I'd have overlooked it completely if my daughter hadn't found it just in time, thank goodness."

He stepped aside to reveal Cecilia Forthright. Tall, blonde, pretty, and standing at the door with the posture of a gladiator who has scored a lethal blow on her opponent, and is preparing to feed them to the lions. It was a very specific sort of posture.

"Ce—Cecilia, what are you doing here?" Gwendolyn's hands decided that this was the time to start trembling violently, and persuaded her legs to join in. "Mr. Mason, I didn't know... I mean, my parents never mentioned that you had a daughter."

A wicked gleam shone in Cecilia's eyes. "Silly Gwendolyn, I'm *sure* I've mentioned him before. After all, he knows your parents *so* well."

Mr. Mason nodded. "I must say, I was quite flustered when Cecilia brought me your invitation. I hope you'll excuse the state of me." He gestured to his wardrobe, which was perfect in every respect as far as Gwendolyn could tell. "And since the two of you are such good friends from the School, I didn't think you'd mind if I brought her along. She did quite a bit of begging, and I can never seem to say no to her."

He gave his daughter an adoring smile, and Cecilia beamed up at him, as innocent as a baby. Then she turned back toward Gwendolyn, innocence melting into malicious glee.

"But..." Gwendolyn murmured. "Your last name is Forthright, not Mason."

Cecilia grinned even wider. "Oh, *Mason* is just the name he uses for business. Daddy *hates* it when people make a fuss over him. Always pestering him to read some manuscript or other."

Mr. Mason shifted his weight. "Er, may we come in? I'm quite anxious to meet your mother and father. They're so terribly secretive. Between you and me, I was hoping to convince them to do some book signings. Did you know they've never made a public appearance?"

"No!" Gwendolyn shouted to absolutely everything he had just said. "Father isn't feeling well. I'm sure they wouldn't want company just now, I'm sorry—"

"Oh, pish-tosh. Go and fetch your mother darling, Marie and I can sort this out."

"No, but—"

His tone turned hard. "Stop. I will not have my business dealings dictated to me by a child. Go and get your mother."

"I can't! I mean, not yet. Mother's not done straightening up, and I know she wouldn't want you to see an untidy home. So, forgive the awkwardness, but if you could just wait out here for one moment..."

"It's no trouble, we're more than happy to wait in the living room—"

"Take your time, Gwenny!" Cecilia said, voice dripping with sickening sweetness. "Believe me, we're in *no* rush. We're looking forward to a *very* enjoyable evening. Oh, and here. You dropped this at the School today. I begged Daddy to let me come along just so I could give it to you in person."

Cecilia held up a notebook. It was blue, with white flowers on it. "I know how important it is to you. I couldn't *wait* to see the look on your face when you got it back."

The phone rang again.

"Oh! Excuse me, I have to get that." Gwendolyn snatched her notebook, darted back inside, and slammed the door before either of them could get a good look. She pressed her back against the door and tried to slow her breathing.

The notebook. Gwendolyn flipped through the pages, noting her drawings, her stories, and more importantly, her journal entries. No doubt Cecilia had read every word of it. And likewise there was no doubt as to who had written this "invitation."

Knowing all of this did nothing to fix the situation. Gwendolyn looked at the apartment. The place was an utter disaster. The torn furniture bled stuffing, the dining room was in disarray, and the kitchen wasn't so much cluttered as it was downright unhygienic. She hadn't exactly been the best housekeeper *before* the cat had ripped the place to shreds.

But how long could she stall them? And what sort of dent could she make in this war zone? And that blasted phone just wouldn't stop *ringing*.

She dashed into the kitchen. Maybe she could whip something together. She'd just gone to the store, so she could pretend both of her parents were sick in bed and send Cecilia and her father away after a quick bowl of oatmeal—

"Oh, poor Rosecap, what have we here?"

Gwendolyn whirled to see someone sitting on the counter. A man, barefoot and clad in tight black trousers and a tight black jacket over an orange tunic that was open nearly to the naval. He was androgynous and beautiful, the very picture of eternal youth, with rich brown skin and a tousled mop of dark hair. He glowed, quite literally, filling the kitchen with a soft orange light. His pointed ears twitched as he casually flipped through a green leatherbound book-- Gwendolyn's copy of *The Annals of the Fae*, containing all the stories of the faeries she'd encountered. He looked up, cocked one eyebrow, and gave her a fox's grin.

"Dost mischief come and pluck my ear?"

Gwendolyn could not have been more surprised if a dozen dwarves had shown up on her doorstep. She stood frozen, with nothing but the incessantly ringing phone to break the silence.

"Puck Robin!" she cried out when she had found her jaw and picked it up again.

"A fellow now, as you can see, so Goodfellow is what I'll be." Robin gestured to indicate that they were currently in their male form, when they went by Robin Goodfellow. When in their female form, they preferred Puck Robin. Of course, there were those times when Robin was somewhere in between, but everything about Robin was fluid and unpredictable. For example, turning up uninvited in Gwendolyn's kitchen.

"Where did you come from?" Gwendolyn asked. Then she noticed the book of faerie stories he was holding. "Did you come out of the book?"

Robin hopped down from the counter. "No, I've been here since the break of day, you brought me in and bade me stay."

"What? You certainly have not, I... No, no, no, you were the *cat*, weren't you?"

"You've seen that I can change my shape, it's not just human forms I take." He started rifling through the cabinets and plucking out all the dishes.

"Stop that!" Gwendolyn snatched a plate from his hands. "You ruined my apartment!" She slapped him on the arm, which she knew was only possible because he chose not to dodge the blow.

Robin grinned again. "A bit of fun is all I've had, and what's more fun than being bad?"

"Is that why you're here? For *fun?*"

The faerie began juggling a dozen cups and plates. "A favor, I recall you owe. It's time to pay, so off we go."

Gwendolyn paused. A favor. Two years ago, she had asked Robin for a favor, to help her save Kolonius Thrash from Tylerium Drekk and his airship pirates. She had very nearly forgotten. But the faeries never forgot a debt.

"I can't leave now! This is a very inconvenient time for me to have a faerie in my kitchen, and—oh, for heaven's sake, hang on—" She picked up the still-ringing phone and slammed it back down again, silencing it.

Robin stopped juggling, and the dishes crashed to the floor. "An inconvenient time? Do tell. Have I the chance to raise more hell?"

"I don't have time for this, I have to..." But Gwendolyn had a sudden idea. "Robin Goodfellow... How would you like to help me play a little trick? A game?"

Robin crossed his arms. "A trick, you say? A game to play? On whom shall we this mischief lay?"

Gwendolyn put on a somber face. "On a girl most foul and loathsome. She has brought her father here to trap me and take me from my home. You say you can take any shape you wish. So how about my mother?"

"I'm no ones' mum, you little sprite. That is not my kind of night."

"But think it through! You can pretend to be my mother, help me with dinner, and play a grand game of pretend to fool these... uh, foolish mortals. *Such* good fun. And then, once our trick is played, I'll take you to the Revels."

Robin put a finger to his chin. "A revel, eh? That just might do. Show me a good time, and I'll help you."

"And then we're square, yes?" said Gwendolyn. "No one owes anyone anything?"

"If I have a night of fun, then we'd be square, our bargain done."

Gwendolyn was about to clarify what Robin's idea of *fun* was, but there was a sudden banging at the door. She groaned in frustration. "Just... stay here! I'll see if I can stall them a little longer." She dashed out of the kitchen and through the living room. "Though I've no idea what we'll do for dinner..."

But no sooner had she turned the handle than Mr. Mason burst through the door. "Young lady, I won't be made to stand in the hall like some common salesman. I demand that you fetch your mother, and—" He stopped, glancing around the room.

"Let me explain—" Gwendolyn whirled around. Then she nearly fell over in shock.

The apartment was clean. More than that, it was immaculate. It hadn't looked this good since Gwendolyn's mother had been here to clean it. And maybe not even then. The black leather upholstery had been restored, the glass topped coffee table was clean enough to be nearly invisible, and all the chrome furniture legs had been polished to a high sheen. Pictures hung on the walls again. The carpets were free of the stains that had built up over the past two years. Even the air was fresher, carrying a hint of the magical woodlands of Faeoria.

And then Gwendolyn's mother came out of the kitchen.

"Oh. Hello there. I wasn't expecting you."

Of course, it was merely Robin Goodfellow under some glamour, the image of Mother no doubt plucked from Gwendolyn's mind by magic. But knowing this did nothing to stem the impact of seeing her mother for the first time in two years, standing right *there* in a red evening dress with white polka dots, her platinum hair styled up and sculpted into large curls that framed her face.

Gwendolyn felt as though she'd been hit in the gut by the monorail. She couldn't breathe, her throat tightening, her eyes stinging.

I don't have time for that, she thought. She had to stay in control.

Yet, she still found herself throwing her arms around the

woman and giving her a fierce hug. "Mother. You look lovely." And even if it wasn't really her mother, it still felt wonderful to hold her, to feel her, to *smell* her. Good lord, she even smelled right. If it was all an illusion, she might as well enjoy it while it lasted. But if she wasn't careful, she would slip into a manic phase and start glowing as brightly as Robin.

Mr. Mason and Cecilia traded an awkward glance. He cleared his throat. "Yes. Right. Er, did you say you weren't expecting us? I have your invitation right here—"

Robin-Mother pulled away from Gwendolyn and swooped toward Mr. Mason. "No, I only meant that I wasn't expecting you so *soon*. What a pleasant surprise."

Mr. Mason looked down at the phony invitation Cecilia had made, then at his watch. "But you said to be here at six, and—"

"And you are right on time." Robin-Mother took him by the arm and patted his elbow. "But punctuality is such a rarity that I'm surprised when anyone is on time for anything. There is an appalling shortage of manners these days, don't you agree?"

Gwendolyn marveled at the speed and cleverness of Robin's lies. Of course, to Robin, lies were as natural as breathing. Faeries couldn't tell an outright falsehood, but they could bend and twist the truth in ways that would make a contortionist blush.

"Too right," Mr. Mason said. "I see these young people, all running around in their gaudy colors and spouting these new-fangled ideas. A bunch of uncouth ruffians, the lot of them. Of course, that dress looks positively lovely on *you*, my dear. And I dare say we've each made a bundle on this new literary fad, so one can't complain overmuch."

Robin turned toward Gwendolyn. "Darling, you haven't properly welcomed our guest." She raised an eyebrow and gave a subtle nod at Mr. Mason.

Gwendolyn took the hint, and prepared to drop some names. "Thank you for coming, Mr. Mason. Mother, I don't believe you've met his daughter, Cecilia."

"Charmed." Cecilia gave a snarky smile that was anything but charming.

Robin shot back a look of mocking disdain, one that was safely hidden from Mr. Mason's view. Then she led him to a door in the hall. "Come, Mr. Mason, I'll show you around and we can give the girls a chance to catch up."

"This is a coat closet."

Robin shot a glance at Gwendolyn. "Of course it is, I was only offering to hang it up for you."

"But I'm not wearing a coat."

"And yet it is still polite to offer, isn't it? I pride myself on being a gracious hostess..." And their voices trailed off down the hall.

Cecilia whirled on Gwendolyn and planted a finger on her chest. "All right, oddling. What are you playing at?"

Gwendolyn swatted her hand away. She wanted to snap back, to shout at Cecilia for starting all of this, but now that she knew Cecilia was her boss's daughter, shouting hardly seemed wise. "I don't know what you're talking about," she said haughtily.

"Yes, you do!" Cecilia seemed to have no problem shouting. "I read your diary! I know that's not your mother. Your parents are missing. You've been living here, all by yourself. Playing house, pretending to be a grown up, living off my daddy's money, you lying little—"

Gwendolyn forced a laugh, which stopped Cecilia mid-rant. "Oh, that! A bit of fiction. All those stories of monsters and men with no faces kidnapping my parents. Surely you've wished the same thing sometimes." She put on a look of mocking concern. "You didn't think it was *real,* did you? Silly Cecilia. Though I can hardly blame you, fiction is such a new concept for you."

Cecilia's eyes flicked side-to-side and she bit her lip. "No. You weren't making that up. You... it was too real..."

Gwendolyn laughed again. "Don't be so gullible." She leaned in close, right into Cecilia's face. "But making up fake dinner invitations? Whatever it is you're planning, it's not going to work." At least, Gwendolyn hoped it wouldn't. There was no telling what Robin might do. And she hoped Cecilia hadn't noticed how her hands were shaking.

Cecilia narrowed her eyes. "You think you're so clever, don't you? Well, you're not the only one who's clever. Just you wait and—"

Laughter interrupted the two girls' argument, and Gwendolyn's not-mother came back into the room, leading Mr. Mason by the arm. "What an amusing anecdote. I had no idea that a publisher's accounting practices could be so funny!"

"Thank you for that... little tour," he said. "It was a very interesting, er, hallway."

Robin shot a withering glare at Gwendolyn that looked all too much like her actual mother. "Yes, this place *does* have much fewer rooms than one would expect... hard to imagine how one could live in such a cramped little hovel. Now, if you could all have a seat in the living room, I'll get dinner on the table."

Robin went into the kitchen, and Gwendolyn followed. "What are you doing? We don't have anything to feed them. Do we?"

"Double, double, toil and trouble, cauldron burn and cauldron bubble," Robin said with a wink. She did entirely too much winking for Gwendolyn's taste.

"Is that a yes?"

Robin rolled her eyes. "Please, child. Who do you take me for? So far, this night has been quite a bore. Your revels best be quite the show, or my displeasure you shall know."

Gwendolyn frowned. "You're speaking in rhymes again. You weren't doing that a moment ago."

"That would ruin the trick, wouldn't it? I've told you before, I can speak however I please."

Gwendolyn gave a groan of exasperation. "Then why do you do it at all?"

"Because I'm terribly clever. Now, go care for our guests, young lady!" And she pointed to the living room.

"All right. Don't get *too* into character."

CHAPTER FIVE

What Happened After Dinner

Gwendolyn sat in the living room, across the coffee table from Cecilia Forthright. Each of them stared at the other as though blinking would be a sign of full surrender. Even Mr. Mason seemed to notice the tension.

"So... Gwendolyn, yes? Where is your father? I assumed he'd be dining with us."

Gwendolyn glanced at Father's typewriter in the corner. "He's ill, like I said."

"Well, perhaps, I'll just pop my head in and say hello—"

"No!" Gwendolyn wished she was as skilled a liar as Puck. "I mean, he's at a friend's house. He... he didn't want to disturb the meal."

Mr. Mason frowned. "If he's so sick, why would he go to—"

"Dinner!" called Mother's voice, and Robin swept into the living room.

"Excuse me, Marie, but will Danforth be joining us? Gwendolyn seems a bit confused, says he's sick at a friend's house or some such rubbish."

"That *is* what she said, yes. Enough of that. Come on, everyone, before it gets cold! Or warm, depending." And she giggled girlishly.

"That's laying it on a bit thick..." Gwendolyn grumbled to herself as she stood.

"Excellent!" said Mr. Mason, heading into the dining room. "I'm positively famished!"

Cecilia crossed her arms and stormed after him.

Gwendolyn followed as well, but froze as she stepped into the dining room. The sight that met her eyes was simply too much for her to handle after the evening's events thus far, and all she could manage was a stunned, "What... the... devil..."

It was a feast. An utterly unfathomable feast. A fantastical, fantabulous feast.

The glass topped table was loaded with so much food it was like to shatter. The sideboard tables groaned under the weight of countless dishes. Summer salads, stuffed mushrooms, wheels of cheese, glistening berries, plates of turkey and ham, strings of sausages, joints of mutton, pots of oysters, slices of lavender bread, cakes and candies and sweets of all kinds, and even a box of iced cookies that said EAT ME in large, friendly letters, all of it gleaming with goodness.

The room practically steamed, and a warm wave of delicious smells wiped away any trace of thought.

Eventually, Mr. Mason found his voice. "What... What is all this?"

The faerie in the polka dot dress swept around the room, though there was scarcely space for sweeping among the towering piles of food.

"We have lembas, ambrosia, rainbow fish sprinkled with melange, golden goose eggs, roast beast, diamondfruit marmalade, deeper'n'ever beetroot pie, sweet cream, heavy cream, honey cream, nevercream, a couple gargle-blasters for us grown-ups and fizzy lifting drinks for the girls, and then for dessert there's treacle tart, butter pie, strawberry glimmer pudding, Turkish delight, whistling sweets, and a little hot soma for after dinner sipping. Good for the digestion."

Gwendolyn shot Robin a look of wordless, mortified shock.

"Where did you get this?" Mr. Mason said.

"Oh, you know. Lots of places. Here, there, and everywhere." She winked at no one in particular. "Now tuck in! It's positively scrumdiddlyumptious!"

Mr. Mason opened his mouth again, but there was no room for words amongst all that food. So instead he nibbled a piece of maple-glazed bacon. Cecilia, clearly against her better judgment, tried a sip of punch.

Their eyes lit up, and they traded a look of utter bewilderment and joy. Then, abandoning all manners, they leapt into their chairs and attacked the mountains of goodies.

Gwendolyn eased into her usual chair and glanced at Robin. The faerie was staring hungrily at the pair as they aggressively stuffed their faces.

"This is…" grunted Mr. Mason between bites of venison. "This is stupendous! I've never had food like this."

"No," Gwendolyn said through clenched teeth, glaring at Robin. "No one has. We don't *have* food like this here."

"Well, it's not *my* fault you live in such a wretchedly dull story,"

Robin growled back, using Mother's own exasperated tone. "Do you know how many other stories I had to pull this from? Ungrateful child." She snorted. "I'd like to see some mere Christmas Ghost do better."

If Mr. Mason noticed anything odd about the comment, he could hardly be bothered to mention it. Cecilia could hardly be bothered to *breathe*, given the way she was inhaling her pepper cheese popovers. Her face and fingers glistened with juices. All thoughts of ensnaring Gwendolyn seemed to have fled somewhere around the first bite of lobster roll.

"I didn't know there was so much food left in the whole City," Mr. Mason said, spluttering bits of peach across the table. He reached out and tore the leg off a chicken. "What with the shortages and all. We're hardly destitute in the Central, but even we've seen a bare shelf or two since the Change. Darling, could you pass those little pastries over there?"

Cecilia did, in between mouthfuls of lemon-spiced almonds.

Gwendolyn wondered what sort of spells might be on this food to reduce those two to little more than ravening animals. Then again, maybe it was just that good. It smelled absolutely heavenly. Her stomach rumbled. The past two years had involved a *lot* of macaroni. She reached out and tried a jeweled pomegranate seed, which looked like a tiny ruby.

The sugary crust crunched with a delicate sweetness, followed by a burst of juice. The tartness of it made her mouth tingle and pucker and water. Her eyes shot open, and she let out an involuntary moan of delight. She was just about to jam a handful of them into her mouth when she was startled by a loud *bang*.

She looked up to see Mr. Mason, face down in a plate of abbey cake. He didn't move.

Gwendolyn leapt back from the table just as Cecilia dropped as well, her head hitting the table with a heavy thud.

"You've killed them!"

"Did I?" Robin said, looking up. She was peeling an apple with a wickedly curved knife that was very out of place in her mother's hand. "Oh. That. Seems they've found the twilight forest truffles. It does tend to knock mortals out for a while."

"They're not dead?" Gwendolyn asked.

Robin poked Cecilia hard in the cheek, who muttered and turned her head away. "Merely sleeping. It could be worse. At least I didn't serve them the pansy blossom juice. We could hardly have them falling in love with us at first sight. Though what fun that could be..." She twirled around, and suddenly Gwendolyn's mother was gone. Puck Robin stood in her place, now in her own voluptuous female form.

"That's my *boss*. You've knocked out my boss. In my house. And his daughter. What are they going to say when they wake up?"

"I imagine they'll thank you for the best meal of their lives." The faerie pulled back one of Mr. Mason's eyelids. "What does it matter what they say? These two were dullards anyway."

Dashing around the table, Gwendolyn pushed Robin up against the wall, upsetting a tray of fig tartlets in the process. "Because I needed them to go away! I needed them not to know I've been living here alone! And I needed Cecilia Forthright to stop trying to ruin my life!" She didn't know what gave her the nerve to shove the faerie about, but Robin seemed too surprised to react.

"Do you think it's easy, pretending to be your own parents?" It all came rushing out in an unstoppable flood. "I've been doing *everything* on my own the past two years, and I wanted you to pretend to be my mother so that Mr. Mason would go home happy and keep paying me, only I haven't been able to write anything in weeks, and now I—"

"Gwendolyn?" came a voice from behind her.

Gwendolyn spun around.

Miss Sahida, her teacher, stood in the hall, staring into the dining room with eyes as wide as saucers.

The three of them stood in silence for a moment. They all glanced at one another, and back again.

Robin clapped her hands and disappeared with a loud *pop*. The feast vanished with her.

Of course, seeing a grown woman and a room full of food vanish into thin air didn't exactly help matters. Miss Sahida gasped, and stumbled back against the wall. "The... the door was open, so I just... I just..." Her knees buckled.

"Miss Sahida!" Gwendolyn rushed to her teacher.

"I—I need to sit down."

Gwendolyn led her into the living room and away from the bodies slumped over the dining room table. She sat her down on the couch, then went to get a glass of water. Gwendolyn's mind whirled for something, anything she could say to explain what the woman had just seen.

Gwendolyn gave the glass to her teacher, and Miss Sahida took it. Her eyes were glazed, staring off into the distance.

"What are you doing here?" Gwendolyn asked.

"Huh?" Miss Sahida said, turning toward Gwendolyn. She shook her head, and her expression cleared. "Oh, I, uh... You called me. Invited me over for dinner."

"I most certainly did n—oh," said Gwendolyn, burying her face in her hands. "Cecilia."

"What? Miss Forthright? Is... was that her I just saw, unconscious in there? With her father? Are they all right?" Miss Sahida shot up and went for the dining room.

Gwendolyn followed, coming in as Miss Sahida checked Cecilia's breathing.

"She'll be fine," Gwendolyn said. Or at least, she *hoped* Cecilia would be fine. Or at least, she hoped Cecilia wasn't *dead*. Or... to be honest, at this precise moment, Gwendolyn wasn't even sure she could say that much.

"But what are they doing here at all, let alone sleeping on your table? I... I can't even... Where was that water..."

A dark weight settled on Gwendolyn's shoulders. Her breathing quickened. "What did you hear?"

Miss Sahida's tone grew firm. "Well, I heard Cecilia do a convincing imitation of your voice over the phone, it seems. I mean, it was all a bit suspect, so I called the number we have on file for you, multiple times in fact, but when no one answered, I got worried, and I don't live very far from here, and—"

She closed her eyes, and took a deep breath. Then she turned toward Gwendolyn. "But yes, I heard you. I came in somewhere around the *'knocking out the mortals'* bit, which I'm not even going to *pretend* to understand—"

"Miss Sahida, I can explain—"

"Oh yes, please explain. I would so dearly love an explanation. I would love to know where all that food came from, for example, or where that woman went, and why she seemed to vanish into thin air?"

Gwendolyn opened her mouth, then closed it again, then opened it again, looking very much like a fish.

"I see." Miss Sahida put her hands on her hips. Her usual sweetness and warmth were nowhere to be found. "Then let *me* explain. You've been living here on your own for the past two years, if I heard correctly. Your parents are gone—

"Yes, but—"

"—but Cecilia somehow found out, and invited me over for dinner tonight. So you managed to hire that... that *person* to pretend to be your mother. Does that about sum it up?"

All Gwendolyn could manage was her fish imitation again.

"I see. But that still doesn't explain all that food, or the vanishing woman, or..." But she stopped. Her eyes glazed over, and her speech grew slurred. "And... it's a good thing she scarpered out the door as quick as she did, or I'd be calling the authorities on her. Honestly, a charlatan in a cheap disguise? A room full of fake food? Well, she ran away quick enough."

Gwendolyn was confused for a moment. Then she saw the glazed look in her teacher's eye, with a twinkle of blue. It was the same one her mother had gotten whenever encountering something magical. Something was altering her memory.

"Miss Sahida, please listen..."

But Miss Sahida shook her head, eyes clearing, and stormed into the kitchen. She glanced around, spotted the phone on the wall, then picked it up and spun the dial.

Gwendolyn ran over and snatched the phone away. "Stop! What are you doing?"

Miss Sahida seemed taken aback, not used to having students snatch things from her. "Gwendolyn Gray, you give me that phone back right this minute."

"Who were you calling?"

"I'm calling the authorities, obviously."

"No, my mother's here, you just missed her," Gwendolyn said, panicked. "If you wait, I'm sure she'll be back—"

Miss Sahida glared at her, having regained her usual piercing gaze. "And how long would I be waiting? Two *more* years, from what you said? Or just long enough for you to hire another impersonator? You..." She closed her eyes and massaged her brow in disbelief. "You hired someone to pretend to be your mother, I don't even know how you would go about *doing* such a thing, are there ads in the paper for it, or—"

"You can't tell anyone. You just have to trust me, I promise..."

"Trust you? You've been lying to me all year. Not to mention that little act today, playing on my sympathies for your..." and she waved a hand in the direction of Gwendolyn's bare scalp, "...condition."

"But I'm fine, truly, just look around." Gwendolyn gestured to the immaculate apartment, even though she couldn't exactly take credit for it.

Miss Sahida did look. And Gwendolyn saw a flicker of uncertainty. But it vanished as quick as Robin had. "So, I should just go home, and leave a poor little girl all alone, with no one to look after her? And with your condition, to be under so much stress? Just look at the lengths you'll go to when left to your own devices. How could I live with myself? How could I come to the School, and face you each day, knowing you were out there own your own doing god-knows-what? No, I'm sorry, I know you don't like it, but it's for your own good." And she took the phone back from Gwendolyn.

Gwendolyn didn't resist. Instead, she made her eyes as big and sad and adorable as she could make them, even trying for a tear or two. "You'd really send me to the Home for Unclaimed Children?" she said, pitifully.

That struck a blow. The Home's reputation was well-known, as was the new Childkeeper's. The flicker of uncertainty on Miss Sahida's face grew into full-fledged doubt. She sagged against the counter and dropped the phone, letting it dangle from its cord. "I don't know—"

"I've got it all under control, I can take care of myself."

Miss Sahida put her hands on Gwendolyn's shoulders. "That's just the point. You shouldn't have to." She sighed and let her arms fall. "What would you have me do, Gwendolyn?"

Gwendolyn knew it was an honest question. But she had no idea how to answer. "What if..." And oh, if only her magic words still worked. If only she still had the power to create things, and make her imagination real. But she didn't know what she could make that would do any good. She needed her parents, not a furry orange Falderal.

"What if you came to check on me? You could come every day, just to make sure I'm all right. Or..." She had an even wilder idea.

"Or I could come with you. I could stay with you. If you'd have me."

Miss Sahida looked at her. Gwendolyn looked back, and her teacher's gentle face made her melt a little. She had meant it as a ploy, to buy her more time, but was the idea really so bad? Wouldn't it be nice to have a... to have someone to look after her? To not have to do the shopping, or the laundry, or the bills, to not have to be a *lady*, and just be... Gwendolyn?

Miss Sahida was silent for a long, long moment. Then she wrapped Gwendolyn in an enormous hug.

And this time, Gwendolyn's tears were real.

When Miss Sahida pulled back, her eyes were wet as well.

"No," she said. "I can't."

"But Miss Sahida—"

The words seemed to hurt her teacher as much as they were hurting Gwendolyn. "This isn't like one of your storybooks. I can't just go around adopting orphans at the drop of a hat."

Gwendolyn pushed her back, and Miss Sahida stumbled against the counter. "I'm *not* an orphan," she spat.

If Miss Sahida was upset by this, she didn't show it. "Nevertheless. You are alone. And no one should have to be as lonely as this," she said, gesturing around them.

"You're as lonely as this," Gwendolyn said, putting some bite into her words. "Maybe you need someone more than I do."

Miss Sahida flinched. "Well, that's... that's different. I'm an adult. Just look at the mess you've gotten yourself into." She pointed at the dining room. "Consorting with shady characters. Poisoning two innocent people, or whatever you've done to them. No. You'll thank me when you're older. The Home won't be as bad as... as everyone says. You'll see." She picked up the dangling phone and spun the dial again.

"You can't tell me what to do," Gwendolyn said, as firm and angry as she had ever been.

Miss Sahida fixed her with an equally firm stare. "Someone has to."

Gwendolyn knew her attempts had backfired. Miss Sahida certainly wouldn't listen now. She raced to the front door. She would escape, and no one could stop her. She'd faced much worse than the police, after all. Hadn't she fought Mister Zero and Misters One-through-however-many-there-were? Hadn't she done the impossible, quite literally, on several occasions? She might find another home out there. On another world, in some other story.

Except... all the portals to the other stories were closed. She couldn't get into the Library of All Wonder.

She could still run, though. She could live on the streets of the City, staying one step ahead of the police and the Childkeeper, always running, always fighting... for the rest of her life...

Instead, she collapsed face-down on the couch, burying her head in a pillow. She didn't even cry. She had no energy for tears. She'd been battling her depression all day, and was there really any point in fighting it anymore?

At least Miss Sahida seemed to have forgotten the more magical elements of the evening. Gwendolyn didn't know what that blue flash in her eyes had been, but it seemed to cloud her mind against magic the way the Lambents once had.

It didn't matter. Gwendolyn's secret was out. She hadn't been good enough to hide it, and there was no going back. She was tired of fighting. She was tired of being the one in charge all the time. A voice inside her screamed at her to get *up*, to get *out*, to get *away*. And there was a time when she would have listened.

But she was not the girl she used to be.

So, who am I? she wondered.

CHAPTER SIX

THE HOME FOR UNCLAIMED CHILDREN

Gwendolyn stood outside a wrought iron fence, one perfectly polite policeman at her side, as though she were some sort of criminal. She stared at a two-story brick of a building. The narrow windows seemed to be squinting at her in suspicion. At the top of the black gates, words were written in black bars: *The Home for Unclaimed Children.*

A slight breeze chilled her scalp, as they had not let her take any of her hats. Or any of her clothes at all, save for the violet dress she had been wearing, and it was a touch too cold for the thin fabric and short sleeves.

She had been permitted one last night in her own bed, though the policeman never left the apartment. Miss Sahida had stayed as well, all night long, right until they carted her off the next morning. The gloom had settled so thick on Gwendolyn's shoulders that she hadn't even resisted. Miss Sahida had insisted that Gwendolyn be allowed to pack her satchel, with her copies of *Kolonius Thrash and the Perilous Pirates*, *The Annals of the Fae*, and her notebook.

The doors of the Home opened. A woman emerged, and strode purposefully toward the gates. She did not open them, but spoke through the bars.

"Is this the one?" she said. She was clad all in grey tweed, with a silk ribbon round her throat like a choker, and she peered at Gwendolyn over a pair of cat's-eye glasses that perched on her nose. She was as thin as a rapier, her features were sharp as glass, and her voice was as hard as granite. Despite all that, Gwendolyn had to admit that she was quite stunning, with raven black hair, full lips, and a complexion like cool milk.

The policeman immediately removed his hat. "Yes, this is her. Been on her own for quite a while now, but here she is, Ms. Childkeeper, ma'am."

"And her assets?"

"What, the apartment and all that? Nicely taken care of, and at your disposal. All her things have been transferred to you and the Home."

The Childkeeper nodded and smiled prettily. "Very good. Thank you, officer. You're a credit to our City."

The man grinned and fidgeted. "Just doing my job, ma'am. And you as well. Might I say, you're a darn sight prettier than the old Childkeeper. Things have been runnin' much smoother on your watch the past couple a' years."

The woman inclined her head. "Indeed. Now, if you don't mind, the girl must be made suitable. We'd hate for her to burden you any longer."

"Oh, she's no burden at all," he said. "Her place is on my beat, and she's always seemed like a nice young thing. Thought it was only right to look after her m'self." He looked down at Gwendolyn and smiled, but Gwendolyn was in no mood for smiling, and she glared at him hard enough to disintegrate him with the heat of her gaze. But the policeman only flinched a little.

The Childkeeper pursed her lips. "Hmmm. Nice. I always say, nice is *nice*, but *useful* is better. We will do our best to make her into something productive." She opened the gates. As the policeman stepped inside, she put a hand on his shoulder. "And thank you again, officer. I can take her from here."

The policeman blushed. He gave Gwendolyn an almost pitying glance, then left.

The Childkeeper knelt down to Gwendolyn's level. "Hello. I am the Childkeeper. I would say that it is nice to meet you, but I'm afraid I don't much care for orphans."

Gwendolyn opened her mouth to correct her, but the Childkeeper put a finger against Gwendolyn's lips. "Don't trouble yourself. There will be no need for you to speak. I've been told all about your situation. I respect your commitment to remaining a contributing member of society, even in the face of your loss. Few children make such good use of themselves. Still, we have rules, and children must always follow the rules." The Childkeeper stood, headed up the walk, and flung open the double doors.

Inside, Gwendolyn found herself at the head of a single enormous room. Long tables ran down the center, and several dozen children sat at them. Each was dressed in a uniform shade of grey, the boys in slacks and shirts buttoned up to the neck, the girls all in dresses with a sash and bow at their waist.

There was a bowl of porridge in front of each one, and the first thing Gwendolyn noticed was the way they ate. They dipped their spoons and brought them to their mouths in perfect unison, the sound of spoons on bowls making a dreadful rhythm, like the relentless drumbeat on a ship of enslaved rowers.

The Childkeeper clapped twice. The children turned to face the door in one unsettling motion. "Children," the Childkeeper called, though she hardly raised her voice. "Welcome our freshest unfortunate. She's come to stay with us."

The Childkeeper clapped again, and the children stood with a loud screech of benches being pushed back. Music came from somewhere, rhythmic pounding chords from what sounded like a piano, and perhaps an accordion, though Gwendolyn could see no such instruments.

And then, all the children began to sing.

Welcome to the home for those like you.
Worthless retches finally put to use.

It was a dreary song, nearly a funeral march. They banged their spoons and bowls to the beat.

Gwendolyn was speechless.

Here in the Childkeeper's Care
We learn that life can be fair.
If you look to your work
and you don't ask questions.

In what was clearly a choreographed routine, the students began passing bowls to the left and right, sliding them across the table, all in time with the rhythm of the music.

Gwendolyn finally found her own voice. "Why are they all singing?"

The Childkeeper surveyed her charges with obvious pride. "Because this is a happy place. And happy children sing."

Which did not reassure Gwendolyn in the slightest.

The children rose from the long benches and began to dance. Some twirled around the floor, others stood on the benches and tables, stomping and jumping to the relentless beat of the song.

We're happy, healthy, well-adjusted youth.
We labor daily like good workers do.
And when we come of age
We won't be such a drain
We'll be Cityzens who
can be pro-duc-tive.

"Don't worry, you'll catch on soon. Although they do seem rather excited today..."

If any of the children were excited, Gwendolyn certainly couldn't tell, despite all the singing and dancing.

"They don't get much chance to sing this particular song. It is so rare that we receive new arrivals."

"But where is the music coming from?"

The Childkeeper waved dismissively. "We have no time for

frivolous questions. You must be acclimated."

Before Gwendolyn could respond to that rather unsettling statement, a group of children pirouetted up to her. They grabbed at her satchel. Gwendolyn tried to resist, but there were too many of them. They snatched it away, and tossed it into the dancing crowd, where it quickly disappeared.

Then they grabbed her by the arms, and pulled her through the chorus of dancers to a smaller room off to one side, a sort of large closet. The three girls pulled various dresses from cabinets and danced around the room with them. They spun Gwendolyn in circles, holding up each dress in turn to see what would fit.

You will become just like one of us.
Proper clothing simply is a must.

A dress was selected and Gwendolyn was pushed behind a screen, then rather roughly helped to undress. She tried to protest, but lost her breath as a sash with a large bow was cinched tightly around her waist.

If we are seen by the rest
The Cityzens are distressed
So inconspicuous dress
keeps us unnoticed.

The children marched her out of the dormitory and back to the central dining room. Which was no longer a dining room at all. The tables and benches had been pushed against the walls. The

Childkeeper stood in a wide central aisle, tapping her foot in time to the relentless rhythm of the song.

Learning keeps us always occupied
Training, taming, all our restless minds.

Beside her was a Central gentleman in a black suit who gave off a sense of power and authority the way a radiator gives off heat. He eyed the orphans with approval as they danced around the adults and took their seats.

The Home turns us all into
Workers ready to do
Whatever it takes to improve
our kind City.
Oh, our Great City.

With one last, mournful note, the children sat. There was a rustle of skirts, the screech of benches, and all was silent. The girls stared across the central aisle at the boys, all arranged in neat and quiet rows.

The Childkeeper inspected her charges. "Very good. As everyone knows, all orphans sing and dance. Your pathetic situation in life makes those who look upon you sad, so it is important to put on a positive attitude to cheer up any visitors, a service to the City that so kindly takes you in at other's expense. Now that our newest unfortunate has been properly acclimated, let us begin our lessons."

Back and forth the Childkeeper walked, looking over the children but never truly looking *at* them. "We have a visitor this morning. I would like to introduce you to Mr. Pump, head of the City Council. He has taken valuable time out of his day to come speak to us on pressing matters. Please do not disturb him." She turned to Mr. Pump with a beaming smile.

Mr. Pump coughed and adjusted his tie. "Ahem. Yes. You are most welcome, Ms.... erm, Ms. Childkeeper."

The Childkeeper giggled. "Oh, please. Call me Charlotte."

Several children gasped in shock.

Mr. Pump coughed again, his confidence tempered with a hint of bashfulness. "Charlotte, then. I assure you; it is entirely my pleasure." He pushed his horn-rimmed spectacles further up his nose and straightened.

"I will be blunt. New developments are at hand. Resources are quite scarce since the Change. The factories on the Edge that have been producing our food, and water, and clean air are running down. Food shortages are occurring. Power shortages as well. Your wonderful caretaker has presented the City Council with a marvelous opportunity for you all to be of use." He smiled at the children. "You should be very grateful for her."

The Childkeeper put a hand to her throat and waved dismissively with the other. "Oh, do stop, Mr. Pump. You are too kind." Then she turned to the children with her usual business-like demeanor. "You will be used to boost the power of these factories to maximum efficiency again. Isn't that exciting?"

"Hardly," Gwendolyn grumbled. The girl next to her turned and shushed.

The Childkeeper paced the aisle, heels clicking on the polished floor. "You know that as orphans, you are of no worth to the City. You will now have the chance to prove that you can be more than a drain on society's resources."

Gwendolyn scowled. "Horrible woman."

She was shushed again, this time from both sides.

Mr. Pump cleared his throat. "The Change has wreaked havoc on the Cityzens. Our normal way of life has been shattered. Misinformation is being spread through the Lambents—wild stories that defy logic or sense. Even vicious deceptions about our own City. There is some poppycock about a wasteland beyond our borders. Rumors of some tremendous war."

"Lies, of course," said the Childkeeper. "The City is the way it has always been."

Gwendolyn stood up. "That's not true!"

Every eye turned toward her. Mr. Pump was taken aback. The Childkeeper stopped pacing and pivoted. The eyes behind those cat-eye glasses glittered, though her expression was kind and patient.

"Sit down, child."

"I'm not 'child.' My name is Gwendolyn! And you're the ones who are lying!"

The Childkeeper's tone was gentle, but firm. "You insult our guest. Please, sit down."

"No!" Gwendolyn was building up steam. "The Change has been wonderful. We have stories, ideas, and imagination! Our world is full of color! Even the sun has started to come out, and people are happier—"

The Childkeeper nodded, and an older girl on the bench in front of Gwendolyn turned and smacked her on the hand with a short wooden stick.

"Ow!" Gwendolyn cried. Her knuckles stung. The girls on either side put a hand on her shoulders and shoved her down onto the bench.

"Please continue, Mr. Pump." The Childkeeper rested a delicate hand on his shoulder. "I know the sight of these orphans is quite distressing. I shall keep them as pleasant as possible, to alleviate any discomfort."

Gwendolyn tried to stand, but the other girls held her down, and the older girl smacked her across the knuckles again.

Gwendolyn glared at the girl and rubbed her hand, but this time she stayed put, forced to listen as Mr. Pump and the Childkeeper continued to lecture them.

Their speech on the City's "values" dragged on through what should have been lunchtime, but there was no stopping to eat. The Childkeeper informed them that, due to the shortages, no lunch would be provided. Gwendolyn groaned. She hadn't had breakfast, and had only eaten a single bite of pomegranate for dinner the previous night.

As much as Gwendolyn hated to admit it, she wondered if Mister Zero had been right when he said the loss of the Lambents would hurt the City. He claimed to have been using their power to keep things running smoothly. Had the Change been a terrible mistake? The idea gnawed at Gwendolyn's insides. So she shoved it into her mental closet where she wouldn't have to think about it. Which was easier to do as her rumbling stomach distracted her.

Eventually Mr. Pump took a seat to observe the Childkeeper at work, and the lessons shifted to maths. The students were forced to stand and recite sums and multiples. Then they recited philosophy, extolling the virtues of tradition and consistency by rote memorization.

Gwendolyn lost track of it all, drifting in a dreary haze. She did not even have her usual imaginings to comfort her. The dreariness and droning made her too drowsy for daydreams, and she didn't have any ideas anyway.

Endless hours later, Gwendolyn was shaken from her stupor by the sudden silence in the hall as the final recitation ended. The Childkeeper tucked her arm into the crook of Mr. Pump's own and walked him toward the door. "Mr. Pump. I can't thank you enough for devoting an entire day of your valuable time to us. I have additional plans, if you'd like to hear them. Working with these children has given me much experience in the cleansing of contaminating ideas."

He patted her arm with his free hand. "I would be absolutely delighted to have the pleasure of your company once more, Miss, err, Charlotte. And might I say, what lovely company it is."

The Childkeeper giggled again. "Oh, Mr. Pump, you are too much. I can see why such a charming man has gained control of the council." She opened the door, led him out, then closed it behind them.

There was a whirl of activity, and the benches and tables were rearranged for dinner. Several children disappeared into what must have been a kitchen, for they soon emerged with bowls and spoons. The girls sat on one side of the table, the boys on the other, and the bowls were plunked down in front of them. The children ate in unison again, spoons scraping bowls in the same relentless rhythm.

Gwendolyn's stomach clamored at her to join in, until she looked down at the grey goo in front of her. She poked it with her spoon. It jiggled.

She and her appetite struck a hasty truce, and it retreated.

"This is disgusting. Even for the City. What is this?" she whispered to the girl next to her.

"Nutrient glue. The most efficient delivery of all essential calories and nutrients. They wouldn't waste valuable food on the likes of us." Then she smacked Gwendolyn's hand with her spoon. "Now be quiet, new girl."

"Fine," Gwendolyn scowled, rubbing her hand and wiping grey goop on her dress. "Not exactly friendly, around here, are you?" She looked around at the others, and moved her spoon up and down without actually eating any of the disgusting slop.

But disgusting as it was, she hadn't had to cook it herself. She hadn't planned the meal, hadn't done the shopping, hadn't had to think at all. She had simply been *taken care of.* And that was a very tempting feeling indeed, one with hints of *home* and *cozy* and *safe.* She could just be a child again, if she wanted, and undo all the growing up she'd been forced to do. She merely had to stop struggling and let it happen. It would almost be easy.

These thoughts were interrupted when she noticed the boy sitting across from her. Gwendolyn Gray was a clever noticer, of course, and she realized with a shock that she recognized him.

"Bill!"

CHAPTER SEVEN

MORTIFICATION AND MISCHIEF

The boy looked up at her. The boy who had tormented Gwendolyn as Mister Zero. He was no longer withered and frail, and his long white hair had been trimmed, but there was no mistaking his fragile features, or his pale grey eyes with that haunted, fidgety look.

"Quiet," he said.

Gwendolyn didn't know what to say anyway. Bill was the child who had been plugged into the central spire of the City, absorbing all of the energy the Lambents drained out of its Cityzens, using that power to keep the City unchanged for five hundred years. But despite such a larger-than-life history, here he was, sitting amongst the other unclaimed children, looking small and pathetic.

Was he dangerous? It seemed unlikely, given the sad, slow way he ate his nutrient glue. Gwendolyn had only spoken to him briefly, after the collapse of the O.R.B., and he had seemed like a completely different person than he had been when trapped in the spire. Even his voice had been different. Though to be honest, Gwendolyn had been heavily concussed at the time, and had been fairly convinced she'd imagined him. But here he was, bleary-eyed and blissfully ignorant.

She leaned across the table and hissed at him. "Bill! What are you doing here?"

He leaned in as well. Then he whacked her on the head with his spoon.

"Ow!" Gwendolyn roared.

"Quiet! I don't wanna get sent to the Consequence Closet."

She tried to wipe the glue off her scalp. "Well, that sounds particularly horrible. And I'm getting awfully tired of everybody hitting me." But she forced herself to sit back down, and wait for another chance.

After dinner, the children queued up for the evening bathroom routines, boys on the left and girls on the right. Gwendolyn grabbed Bill by the arm and pulled him to the back of the line.

"Bill!" she whispered. "Do you remember me?"

He gave her a dazed look. Then he blinked a few times, and his expression seemed to clear. "I... I think so. You're that girl, ain't you? The one from that place. From when I woke up."

"Yes, that's right. What do you remember about it?"

"I remember... waking up. Like I'd had a long dream. Something about men in funny hats, and a lot of white light."

"And what are you doing here?" she said, careful to keep her voice low.

"The police found me in that tower. They didn't know what to do with me. I told them to go get my father, but when they went to the house, he wasn't there. Nuffin' was there." His expression grew sadder, if that was possible. "It was all gone. So they brought me here."

"So you don't remember anything that happened while you were in... that place?"

He sniffed, and wiped his nose on his sleeve. "No. And I don't want to, neither. Just... just leave me alone."

Gwendolyn knew he wasn't lying. He didn't remember his time as the Collector. Come to think of it... Bill's voice was so different from Mister Zero's. And Gwendolyn had never seen the Collector's mouth actually *move*, had only heard an eerie voice resonating through the O.R.B. Had Bill only been some puppet? If so, who had been pulling the strings, dangling this poor boy inside that crystal spire?

Suddenly, she was separated from Bill and sent into a tiled room with metal lockers and long benches. She watched the other girls to see what was expected of her, and was horrified to see them stripping off their clothes and marching into a large room where she could hear water running.

There was no way she was going to get down to her altogether in front of all these people. But two of the older girls moved in behind her, and Gwendolyn decided it was better to do it herself before they did it for her.

What followed was the single most mortifying experience of Gwendolyn's life. She was grateful she had no hair to wash. She had been the last one in, but made sure she was the first one out.

They were ushered back into the changing room to dry off with scratchy towels that were far too small. Thin grey nightgowns were provided at one end of the room. Gwendolyn put one on, and scowled in disgust at the sash and bow around the waist. She hated

that sort of thing. It was almost more embarrassing than wearing
nothing at all.

Back in the dormitory area, the boys and girls were reunited,
and silently crawled into their beds. Gwendolyn found herself
going along with everyone else and climbing into her own.

The Childkeeper gave them all one last inspection. She chose
children at random and checked that their fingernails were clean
and their area was in order. Then she nodded, satisfied.

"Good night, children. Rest well. You have more work to do
tomorrow."

The children sang back—

Yes, Childkeeper,
Good night to you as well.
We owe you for your time,
and thank you for your care.

Gwendolyn grunted. "It doesn't even rhyme..."

The Childkeeper went to the large double doors that led to the
street. There was the *click* of a key turning, and the massive *thunk*
of a heavy lock. Then she turned out the lights, and exited through
a small side door.

Gwendolyn lay in her bed, absently running a hand along her
freshly-scrubbed scalp. A depressive fog was creeping up on her.
Her limbs were heavy. Her thoughts were slow. Not since her
breakdowns in Faeoria had she felt like this. She had been stripped
of her home, her belongings, even her dignity. All her energy had
drained away with the water in the showers.

She craned her neck and tilted her head back to look upside-down out the barred window. Moonlight broke through the clouds. Its pale glow seemed to caress her.

And Gwendolyn sang her own song, barely above a whisper.

Sparrow and Starling, Darrow and darling
I miss you terribly so.
Come to me here, I need you my dears,
For I'm terribly all alone.
Hey ho, here we go,
I'm...

But she couldn't finish. Her voice choked off, and she rolled onto her side. She wished they had let her keep her books. She would have read *Kolonius Thrash and the Perilous Pirates,* and seen the crew going about their familiar adventures. She would reread how Kolonius and Brunswick and Carsair had stopped Tylerium Drekk from robbing the Archicon bank. Back on their world, she was sure the crew was getting up to newer, stranger adventures without her, filling up more volumes in the Library of All Wonder.

But she didn't have anything. Not even any ideas. So she ran her finger along the sheets, invisibly doodling her initials. Two capital G's, a larger one wrapped around a smaller one. The special symbol she'd drawn since she was a little girl.

But suddenly, it wasn't imaginary anymore. Glowing green ink trailed from her finger, staining the sheet. Her initials shimmered up at her.

Gwendolyn's eyes went wide.

Then the letters began to move. They twisted and morphed and multiplied until new words glittered up at her, written in an elaborate flowing script.

Come and find me.

Gwendolyn touched the words, smearing the wet ink. An electrifying jolt shot up her arm. Suddenly it was as though an invisible hand had lifted a weight from her shoulders; one she hadn't realized was there. She felt lighter. Stronger. A glowing after-image of the words still danced before her eyes.

Come and find me. She could practically hear the words echoing in her head.

Her feet hit the floor.

She glanced around at the rows of identical beds. *I'm getting out of here,* she thought. There was magic out there, somewhere, and she was going to find it. Someone was calling her. Someone wanted her. And her heart leapt to think who it might be.

Well, she wouldn't keep them waiting. She was Gwendolyn Alice Gray, and this place could not hold her.

But first...

I'll need my things. She looked to the front doors. Locked tight. She wasn't getting out that way, anyway.

So she turned and went the other way, to the door the Childkeeper had left through. It was unlocked. Gwendolyn opened it and headed into the dark hallway beyond.

There were a few doors on either side. But the one at the end of the hall had a frosted glass window with the words *Administrative Office* printed on it. It was locked, but hadn't closed completely, and Gwendolyn was able to open it a crack and glance inside.

The room was empty. Moonlight filtered in through a transom window. There was a desk with a large chair behind it, and a tiny chair in front of it. It wasn't hard to picture the Childkeeper looming over whatever poor soul happened to be sitting there.

There were doors on either side of the room. But the one on the left drew her eye. There was nothing remarkable about it, but Gwendolyn felt a strange pull somewhere inside her. She'd had a similar feeling years ago, in the caves of the Crystal Coves. A subtle nudge that drew her closer. Was this what she was supposed to find?

The door opened onto a series of steps that spiraled downwards into darkness. Every ounce of common sense she had screamed at her not to go down a darkened stairwell in the middle of the night. But those ounces of common sense were vastly outweighed by a ton of curiosity.

Which was disappointing when all she found was another door at the bottom, this one emblazoned with the words *KEEP OUT* in very unfriendly letters. Even more unfriendly were the three gratuitously large padlocks that held it shut. It made her curiosity scream so loud she was afraid someone would hear it urging her to *Get Through That Door!*

She pressed a hand to it. It seemed to be humming, like some enormous machinery were running somewhere behind it.

Curiosity alone wouldn't cut through cold steel, though. No matter. This wasn't why she was here. She headed back to the office and looked around for her things. She found her satchel behind the desk and bent to snatch it up, but the sound of feet on the basement stairs made her stop.

Gwendolyn threw herself under the desk and scrunched up as small as she could.

Footsteps entered the room and clicked across the floor. It was the unmistakable sound of the Childkeeper's stiletto heels. Followed by the *sight* of those heels. Gwendolyn pressed herself even harder against the back panel of the desk.

Please don't sit down, please don't sit down, please don't sit down...

Fortunately, the Childkeeper did *not* sit down. Instead, Gwendolyn heard the sound of a phone being lifted from its cradle, and the rotary dial spinning.

"It's me," the Childkeeper said. "I have performed the evening checkup. All is going well, but we will need new recruits soon. There are only so many orphans, after all."

Gwendolyn's eyes widened. That was not a particularly comforting statement.

There was a pause before the Childkeeper spoke again. "I concur completely. These Revels have been going on for quite some time now. The children there would make perfect candidates. Perhaps tonight?" She paused again. "Yes. We must create a return to values."

Gwendolyn's eyes were quite a lot wider now.

"Yes, the girl did make some mischief today. She tried to cause a fuss in front of Mr. Pump. Attempted to rile up the other children... No, they are well trained and drained. They dealt with her on their own. This is undoubtedly the safest place for her. She cannot be allowed to roam the City on her own. I will see that the troublemaker is made quite at home here. If that is all?"

The person on the other end of the line seemed to think so, as Gwendolyn heard the sound of the phone being set down. The Childkeeper's shoes disappeared and Gwendolyn heard them clicking away. A door opened, then closed.

Gwendolyn moved as slowly as she could force her panicking body to go, and peeked around the desk. The room was empty. The Childkeeper must have gone back down to the basement again. Gwendolyn tiptoed to the door to the hallway, snuck out of the office, careful to close the door softly behind her—

Only to come face-to-face, to face, to face, with two girls wearing gray pajamas and cruel smirks. The Childkeeper stood behind them.

Uh-oh, Gwendolyn thought. *Wrong door.*

"See?" said the girl on the left. "We told you she was out of bed."

"You were quite right to do so." The Childkeeper was calm as ever. "Please escort her to the Consequence Closet."

Before Gwendolyn could so much as blink, the girls grabbed her by the arms and dragged her back into the office.

The Childkeeper went in and opened the third door in the room, but it was too dark to see what lay inside.

Gwendolyn was hurled inside, where she slammed face first into the opposite wall. She cried out and spun around, readying herself for a fight.

"I am not as lax as my predecessor. The rules must be followed. I'll see you in the morning," the Childkeeper said. "Well, some morning, anyway. I haven't decided which one, yet."

Gwendolyn lunged at her, only to have the door slammed in her face, hitting her already abused nose. The lock clicked.

And then it was dark. And quiet.

"Ugh," Gwendolyn said. The sound was close and muffled. She felt around, and the room was small enough that she could touch all the walls without moving. She sank against the wall, sighed, and slid to the floor.

"The Consequence Closet," she said, dabbing at her bleeding nose with the hem of her dress. "Well, I suppose it could be worse. There could be spikes in the walls and rusted nails through the door and broken glass underfoot."

There were times when her imagination was less than helpful.

I can't stay here, Gwendolyn thought. *Obviously*. She had to get to the Revels and warn her friends. No doubt they were there right now, partying the night away, with no inkling that a squad of policemen was coming to round them all up and bring them to the Home. To be "trained and drained."

But while her imagination had plenty to say on the subject of the potential tortures that could be inflicted on her, it had precious little to offer in the way of getting *out*.

Think, she told herself. What did she have?

Her satchel. She still had her satchel!

Hurriedly, she flipped it open and dumped its contents on the floor, then felt her way through them. All she had were her three books: her journal, *Kolonius Thrash*, and *The Annals of the Fae*. Though in the dark, she couldn't even read them. Useless.

No, stupid girl, she scolded herself. *What could be more useful than books?* Because, as books often do, they had given her an idea. And if past experience had taught her anything, it was an extraordinarily bad idea. But she had no choice. Not if she was going to escape the Childkeeper, and warn her friends.

She picked up the larger of the two books.

"Robin Goodfellow," she said. "Robin Goodfellow. Robin Goodfellow." She knew the power of names, and the power of threes.

But nothing happened.

She tried again. "Puck Robin. Puck Robin. Puck Robin. I would speak with thee."

The book in her hands began to glow. The edges of the book glimmered, filling the closet with a ghostly green light.

The glow seemed to be coming from one page in particular. Gwendolyn opened to it and found a beautifully painted page, with all manner of faeries and creatures frolicking in the margins and twining around the text. The first letter was an enormous illustrated "R" that took up fully half the page.

It was the "R" that was glowing. The hole in the upper space of the letter was filled with a picture, and if Gwendolyn was not mistaken, it was the inside of Cyria Kytain's laboratory. And into the picture stepped Puck Robin.

The faerie folded her arms. "Oh look, once more the orphan calls my name. Dost thou call me to break your oath again?"

"I'm *not* an orphan," she spat. "And I've come to fulfill the terms of our agreement, actually."

"Such honeyed words I've heard you speak before. But I expect you'd have my help once more."

"Well, *help* is a strong word. You see, I would love to take you out on the town, as we've agreed. There will be singing and dancing and oh, just *so* much fun. I simply need help *getting* there." She tried not to let on how desperate she was.

Puck Robin squinted. "You say you'll take me to these Revels of yours? But how do you strengthen the oath you swore?"

"I don't suppose I could talk to Cyria instead? Is she in there somewhere?"

"The inventress is likewise indisposed, and cannot aid you, little Rose." The imp smirked.

Gwendolyn searched for something she could offer. Robin's use of her faerie name, Rosecap, gave her an idea. "Then, I... I swear by... by my real name." She didn't know what that meant, but it sounded good.

Robin's eyebrows went up, but the surprise disappeared behind a mask of indifference. "For collateral, that will have to do. Give it me, from your lips, and speak it true."

Gwendolyn sighed. Nothing *but* bad ideas today. Cyria would throw a fit. "Gwendolyn. Gwendolyn Alice Gray."

The faerie shrugged. "Fine. I admit, this night has been a waste. Stand back, dear child, and I'll appear post haste."

Robin snapped her fingers.

Nothing happened.

She frowned, and snapped again. And there was just as much nothing as before.

Robin looked shocked and slightly embarrassed. A part of Gwendolyn was glad to see the smugness wiped off her face. But the rest of her was worried.

"What is it?"

Robin kept snapping her fingers. "I swear, this never happens."

"There must be something wrong with your magic!"

Robin glared daggers that nearly tore the page. "My magic is *fine*," she growled. She clapped her hands and turned into a badger, an eagle, a snake, and a lion, in rapid succession. "See?" she said when she had a normal mouth again. "The problem is yours."

Gwendolyn huffed. "I don't see how."

"I feel the problem coming from your end. Or rather, not feel. It's completely dead."

"What does *that* mean?

"That... *place* prevents my attempts to appear."

Gwendolyn glanced around the Consequence Closet. She thought of the heavy numbness that had haunted her since her arrival. Of the Childkeeper's use of the word *drained*. "I suppose it *is* rather more horrible than usual. What do we do?"

"We merely need a *smaller* trick, don't fear. Puck Robin shall get you out of there, oh yes, and then what mighty fun we'll share"

There was a soft *click*. The handle turned by itself. And the door opened.

"Yes!" she hissed, quietly.

Stuffing her books back in her bag, Gwendolyn crept into the empty office and looked around. She certainly wasn't going to try the door again. Instead she eyed the transom window. She wheeled the office chair over to it, climbed up, and sprang the latch. The window opened smoothly, and Gwendolyn squeezed through.

A chill wind cut through her thin grey pajamas, and she crossed her arms for warmth. Not wasting any time, she darted across the concrete courtyard to the front gate. She scrambled up it, which wasn't easy in the pajama dress and dropped down to the other side. She landed awkwardly, fell, and scraped her knee on the asphalt.

"Graceful," said a voice. Gwendolyn looked up to see Puck Robin, clad in her usual black suit and revealing orange tunic.

"Oh, so *now* you pop up."

Robin shrugged. "The magic's not so thin out here. I will not be barred from this mortal sphere. Now, time for fun, to pay your debt. Though my dear, you're not dressed for it yet."

"No, wait—"

"I shall not and won't, not one minute more. A party was promised, so to the dance floor!" Robin clapped her hands, and Gwendolyn found herself once again subjected to a faerie makeover.

There was a blast of wind, and her pajamas were gone, replaced by her violet dress from the previous day. But now it was sleeker, sleeveless, embroidered with glistening silver vines and flowers, and sporting several inches of sparkling fringe around the hem. A hem that was a bit higher than Gwendolyn remembered. A silver circlet wrapped around her upper arm. Delicate silver flats snuggled themselves around her feet.

She also felt a rather unfamiliar sensation on her head. Tentatively, she reached up to find a sequined headband around her forehead with a small feather sticking up from the side, and...

Hair. She had hair. She could feel a mop of sculpted waves, much smoother and tamer than what she'd previously had. She managed to pull some down to see that it was, in fact, a shining platinum blonde.

She shot a withering glare at Robin. Though she was not

entirely sure how she felt about this new development, she definitely did not appreciate it being done without so much as a by-your-leave.

"What?" Robin said. "You can't be seen so bare of head; the sight would stop these Revels dead."

Gwendolyn did not lessen her glare. "Just don't forget who took my hair in the first place. Wait... Where's my bag?"

Robin winked. "It's quite safe and sound, your little pack. And when my fun is done, you can have it back. So let's be off, my violet dear, some distant music plucks Puck's ears." Robin twirled, and her own outfit turned a deep crimson, her plunging orange blouse now jet black. She wore white spats, though her feet were still bare. She was also smaller now, looking more of a teenager, but no less alluring or mysterious for it.

"Fine. Are you finished? We have to get to the Revels before the Childkeeper does. Not that I've any idea where they'll be tonight, they move them every time. I don't know how we're going to find the place."

Robin winked. "With a bit of magic, and a bit of luck. And *no* party can escape the Puck." The fairy clapped again, the world whirled around them, and they disappeared.

CHAPTER EIGHT

THE REVELS

"**A**nd here we are, it wasn't far."

Gwendolyn blinked. They were in the Central City. Skyscrapers towered around them. Streetlamps created puddles of light.

Gwendolyn looked around. "Are you sure we're in the right place?"

Robin rolled her eyes and jerked her thumb at a stairwell across the street. "A revel is as revels be, but it ain't no party without me."

Gwendolyn nodded. "Fine. Follow me. I've heard my friends talk about it enough that I think I know what to do." She dashed across the street. "Come on, faerie boy!"

"Faerie *girl*, if you do please, I—"

"And no rhyming. Not if you're going to blend in." Gwendolyn took them down a set of stairs to an alcove below street level. There was a door with a slitted peephole, which slid open at her knock.

A pair of eyes peered through the slit. "Yeah?"

She vividly remembered her friends' conversations about the

Revels, given how jealous they had made her. She remembered the code phrases they'd talked about. "We're here for a *real sock-dollager*,"

The eyes moved up and down, taking in the pair's colorful attire. "Ain't gonna drop a dime?"

"We're all jake here," Gwendolyn replied, finishing the passphrase.

"Swell. Welcome to the Revels."

The door opened, and the two of them were stunned into silence by a wave of color, music, and light.

It was a large storage room, full of wooden crates that had all been shoved against the walls. Strands of colored lights were hung along the ceiling, and the whole place was bathed in a warm orange glow. Round tables dotted the floor, but the center was left clear for the dozen or so dancers who seemed to be having a fantastic time. A makeshift stage had been placed at one end, where a band was playing a jazzy tune, with instruments and music that had no doubt been found through the Lambents new trove of information.

Vendors had set up displays on top of the boxes that lined the walls. They showed off new artwork, new clothing, even new foods, though the fare was much more limited than the feast Puck Robin had conjured. Everyone wore the most eye-watering colors they could find. The whole place seemed to be a competition to see who could be the brightest, most exuberant, and most full of life. Five hundred years of pent-up energy and imagination all trying to get out at once.

"Now this is more like it," Puck Robin said, eying the room with unbridled glee.

"Don't get into any trouble just yet," Gwendolyn said. "This isn't one of Lady Fen's balls. These are real people, who aren't accustomed to magic, so keep it in your pocket."

Puck rolled her eyes. "Yes, *mother*."

Gwendolyn rolled her eyes right back. "You're so terribly ironic. There they are!" she said, spotting her friends across the room. "We've got to get them out of here before—"

Robin grabbed her arm. "You promised me *fun*," and her tone was anything but. "Break your word to me again and I'll flay the skin from your bones with a cocktail fork."

Gwendolyn blinked, stunned. "No, no, I just meant 'there they are, come on, I'll introduce you.' Well, I'll try, I'm not sure how I'm going to explain you to anyone..." Gwendolyn gulped, forced a smile, and tried to put on a casual air. If Robin wanted a good time, she'd *give* Robin a good time.

How hard could it be? After all, she was out of the Home. She was out of her stifling apartment. She was wearing a pretty dress on a pretty night full of pretty people.

She approached the table where Jessica, Ian, Missy, and Tommy all sat, chatting and sipping fizzy concoctions. Seeing them all, out on the town and having a good time, made her smile anything but forced.

"Hello, my mollys," Gwendolyn said, using one of Cyria's phrases.

"We've already got our drinks, thanks," said Ian, turning around. Then he froze, squinting. "Gwendolyn?"

"Gwendolyn!" Missy exclaimed then rushed over to wrap her in a hug, which Gwendolyn happily returned. It did a lot to repair some of the damage of the day.

"You made it!" Tommy said.

"It's about time," Jessica added. "Those parents of yours are positively tyrannical."

"Yes, I, um... managed to sneak out."

"And *what* a sneaking!" Ian said. "Just *look* at you." He grabbed her hand and twirled her out of Missy's embrace. "That fringe is to die for. You should doll up more often."

"Why, thank you, Ian. You're all quite... uh, smashing... as well."

And indeed they were. Ian was decked out in a bright blue suit with a gold paisley shirt. Jessica wore a pair of high-waisted red trousers and suspenders, a short sleeve shirt of white and blue horizontal stripes, and a red neckerchief tied around her throat, the knot at a jaunty sideways angle. Her dark hair was done up in a bun of braids on top of her head.

Missy and Tommy wore their usual Outskirts clothes, but had managed to scrounge a piece or two of color. Tommy had a green pinstriped vest and his trademark yellow bow tie, and Missy had an orange bow that nearly glowed against her almost-white hair.

"Isn't it all just the bees knees?" Missy said.

"The what?" Gwendolyn said, straining to hear over the music.

"It's an expression." Missy shrank, embarrassed. "I'm just trying it out."

"Oh," Gwendolyn said. "Well, I suppose I should introduce you all. This is... Robin."

"Another imaginary friend?" Tommy said, grinning.

Gwendolyn turned, confused. "No, what—" But Puck Robin was

nowhere to be seen.

No, that wasn't true. Puck was quite easily seen, a whirl of red out on the dance floor. She was dancing with three boys at once and easily keeping up with all of them.

Gwendolyn turned back to her friends and sighed. "That's her. In the red."

"Wow," Tommy said, mouth agape. "Where's she from? I haven't seen her around the School. And believe me, I'd have remembered *that*."

Jessica slapped Tommy's arm. "Don't you dare objectify her."

Ian grinned. "You better tell that to those boys out there."

"Yes, she's..." Gwendolyn tried to think of what Puck would say, lying while telling the truth. "She's home schooled." Which was probably true, in a sense.

Ian raised an eyebrow. "What the devil is a home-school?"

"It's exactly what it sounds like. She doesn't get out much." Which was obviously *not* true. Puck was a lot of things, but shy wasn't one of them. But this was Gwendolyn's chance. "Listen, you aren't safe here, you—"

"I find nontraditional education fascinating," Jessica said. "Not many people work outside the City's structures like that. Did she start before the Change, or after?"

"Oh no," Ian said. "We can talk politics later. The music's keen, so let's cut a rug!"

Tommy took a long sip of his drink and slammed down the empty glass. "Yeah, it's Freckle's first time. No sense standing around."

"You don't understand, you all need to leave, right now!"

"Nothin' doin', old mum, you just got here, and we're not letting you off that easy." Tommy grabbed Gwendolyn's hand and pulled her toward the dance floor, just as the lights above changed to a bright green. Ian and Jessica followed. Missy stayed behind, looking content to watch the spectacle with a dreamy smile on her face.

The music was indeed "keen." There was a pounding piano, brassy horns, and jazzy drums that kept everyone moving.

And now that Puck Robin was in earshot, she couldn't risk trying to warn her friends. She'd have to play the party girl, and no holding back. If she did, the consequences did not bear thinking about. This was officially a life-or-death situation. She wouldn't *enjoy* it, she told herself, but what other choice did she have? She would just have to *force* herself to have a good time.

Ian and Jessica lost themselves in the music, showing off the dances they had learned from the Lambent. Tommy seemed intent on staying as close to Gwendolyn as possible. Gwendolyn tried to keep a little space.

She moved with the tune, grateful that her faerie dancing skills had not deserted her, and soon found Puck Robin alongside her. Well, if the faerie wanted a party, Gwendolyn would give her one.

Wordlessly, the two of them slipped into step. They twisted low, kicked high, held hands and twirled and dipped, all in perfect unison. Puck picked her up and swung Gwendolyn's legs to one side, then the other, then tossed her feet up into the air, fringe flying.

When the music stopped, Gwendolyn was surprised to hear a roar of applause. The other dancers had all stopped to watch, and were now clapping and cheering. The music shifted to something slower, the lights went a pale pink, and the crowd drifted apart. The five of them headed back to the table and Puck took Gwendolyn's elbow. "Rosecap, I must say, you do know how to show a girl a good time."

"Rosecap?" Tommy asked.

"My little nickname for her," Puck said with a flirtatious wink. "An inside joke. You had to be there."

"Be *where*?" Ian said.

"I can explain—" Gwendolyn began.

"Don't bother, I am *entirely* inexplicable." Puck interrupted.

"Ooo, I *like* her," Ian cooed.

Jessica nodded. "Yes, I think it's important to reject labels, so we can create our own identities rather than be forced into the roles society has chosen for us."

"Is it bad that most of the time I have no idea what you're talking about?" Tommy said.

Ian grinned. "That says more about you than it does about her. Jessica's got more good ideas than you have bow-ties."

Tommy sank a little. "That's not hard, I've only got the one..."

"Besides, Jessica's the only one of us delinquents who might actually amount to something," Ian said. "I'm thirsty. Come on, new girl, let's get some drinks. I'm *dying* for a little girl talk, and these three are all *terrible* at it..."

Ian whisked Puck away, the two of them getting much more friendly than Gwendolyn would like. But this was her chance. She leaned across the table. "Listen to me, you all have to go, right now!" she said in an urgent whisper. "There's going to be a raid tonight!"

"Oh, *that*," Jessica said. "We already know."

"No, you don't underst—wait, you do?"

"Of course," Jessica said. "Zelda got wind of the whole thing. She's the organizer. That's why she changed the location last minute. We're completely safe."

Tommy grinned. "I'd like to see their faces when they bust onto an empty rooftop."

"But... but... how can you be sure?"

"We *have* been doing this for a while, you know," Jessica said.

"Still, I think we all better—"

But at that moment, Ian and Puck returned with a tray of colorful drinks. The music ended and a poet took the stage. He was dressed all in plaid with a black beret. He read from a crumpled sheet of paper in a flat, expressionless tone.

"A tree. A tree. I never see. A single tree. I've seen them of course, in my mind, in the shimmering light of the Lambents shine. Where have they gone? Where are they now? Their roots no longer grip the ground."

"That boy up there dost hurt mine ears, is he supposed to bring on tears?" Puck said.

"No more rhyming, I mean it," Gwendolyn hissed.

"Anybody want a peanut?" Tommy said, digging into the bowl on the table.

"*He* gets to rhyme," Puck grumbled and crossed her arms petulantly.

Missy scrunched up her nose at the poet's dreadful recitation. "You're right, he's not very good, is he?"

"At least he's putting himself out there," Jessica said.

"Challenging the system."

"Which is what *you're* going to do, old gal." Ian got up and pulled Gwendolyn out of her seat.

"What are you doing?" Gwendolyn said, digging in her heels.

"Anyone can get up there," Jessica said. "That's the beauty of the Revels. As long as you have something new to contribute, you get to share with everyone."

Tommy nodded. "And we know your stuff is better than most anybody else here."

"But... but... I don't have my notebook!" she said, by way of excuse.

"You mean *this* notebook?" said Puck. She whipped Gwendolyn's journal out of thin air, and tossed it like a disc.

Gwendolyn caught it. "Thanks," she grumbled. "But... what if someone recognizes me?"

"I don't think anyone will recognize you with that wig on," Missy said.

"That settles it. Up you go, Gwendy-girl!" And Ian pulled her toward the stage.

"But it isn't my turn," she tried, reaching for one last excuse. "I'm sure there's a whole line of people waiting. We'd be here all night."

"Oh, Martin and I have an understanding, *don't* we, Martin?" Ian said as they reached the side of the stage.

Martin was an older boy holding a clipboard and guarding the steps. He raised an eyebrow at Ian, but smiled. "She can't be worse than him," he said, jerking his head toward the stage. He went up and whispered something in the poet's ear. The poet gave an offended gasp, threw his beret down on the stage, and stormed off, bumping hard into Gwendolyn as he passed.

Martin came back down. "All right. Your go, girl."

Ian gave her a nudge. "You've got this."

Well, Gwendolyn reminded herself, *Puck wants a show.* Again, she supposed she had no choice. She clambered up onto the stage.

All eyes were on her. The lights above changed to a low red.

"Umm... hello," Gwendolyn said. She was met with a wave of expectant silence. She had fought monsters and pirates and suchlike, but this was an entirely new sort of terrifying. "I'm, er... Wendy. Yes. So..." She flipped through her notebook, looking desperately for something worth sharing. But everything was either too childish, too personal, or had already gone into one of her books. And she hadn't had any *new* ideas in weeks.

But then she looked out at the crowd. She looked at them, dressed in their brightest colors. Artists and poets and musicians, all here together to share whatever they could imagine.

This was the world she had created. This was what she'd worked for, sacrificed for. Her hair. Her parents. Her happiness. She had given it all up, for this.

This was her world. *Hers.*

And she was bloody well going to *enjoy* it.

She smiled. And her imagination, which had given birth to the whole thing, rose to the occasion.

"*Once up a time,*" she said. Though it did not create any visible magic, a ripple went through the audience. She closed her notebook. She would not need it. And the story she told went something like this:

"There was once a man named Giacomo. He was a barber. But in his day, a barber did much more than cutting hair. He wandered the countryside as a jack-of-all-trades, and in the course of his business he might be asked to pull teeth, mend clothes, tend to sicknesses, or shoe a horse or two. And of course, he could give the finest shave of a man's life. And a woman's as well, though most were too embarrassed to present their legs to a stranger. But Giacomo was rather handsome, so it was not unheard of."

The crowd chuckled. And that was it. They were under her spell. For the first time in her life, she had an appreciative audience, a spotlight shining on her, and a stage to stand on.

She told the story of how Giacomo had come to a small village in distress, torn apart by rival gangs. Giacomo, of course, was as skilled with large blades as he was with small ones. Using his many manly skills, he turned the gangs against each other and united the townsfolk to rise up and drive them out. There was action, intrigue, excitement, and even a hint of romance. And the audience loved it.

"Thank you," Gwendolyn said when she'd finished, stepping down to raucous applause. She went back to the table with her head down. Her whole body was shaking.

"All right," Gwendolyn said. "That *was* fantastic."

"Brilliant. Way to go, Freckles," Tommy added.

Missy gave her another hug. Gwendolyn beamed so hard she thought she might be glowing, which was a legitimate possibility. When she got manic, she glowed as bright as the faeries. That thought brought a sudden worry. "Where's Robin?"

"Over there," said Jessica, disapprovingly. "Making quite the spectacle of herself."

Puck Robin was at another table, holding court among a group of boys. She was sitting in the lap of one, had another one's tie around her neck, and had her bare feet propped up on the table. Gwendolyn thought about going over to stop her, but she didn't dare interrupt the faerie's fun.

"Come on, Freckles," Tommy said. "There's some art I want to eyeball. This one bloke's got a bunch of landscapes based on these orchard things he saw in the Lambent. It should be *peachy*."

Everyone groaned.

"I think I need to sit down for a minute," said Gwendolyn.

"Oh," Tommy said, crestfallen. "All right."

"Don't look so glum, chum, we'll tag along." Jessica gave Gwendolyn a knowing look, and her three friends headed for the art displays. Missy stayed behind and scooted her chair next to Gwendolyn's.

Gwendolyn propped her elbows on the table and rested her chin in her hands. "This is amazing. I can't believe it took me so long to come. I mean, just listen to her up there." She nodded toward the stage. There was a singer with a slinky dress and a smoky voice. The music was soft and slow and seductive.

> *A girl like me can't be too careful,*
> *The squares will say I'm rotten.*
> *But if music and dance are dis-respectable,*
> *Let's rot from top to bottom.*

Missy nodded. "Yes. She's one of my favorites." Then she turned toward Gwendolyn. "So where were you?"

Gwendolyn twitched. "What do you mean?"

"It's just us, Gwendolyn. You didn't come over yesterday to work on our math, like you said. I thought I must have mixed things up, so I went to your apartment. You weren't there, but police were going in an' out, taking all your things away. They put tape over your door."

Gwendolyn didn't answer. She just stared into her drink.

"You got sent to the Home for Unclaimed Children, didn't you?"

That got her attention. "What? Why would you say that?"

Missy gave her a steady but gentle stare. "Because your parents are gone and you've been living on your own."

Gwendolyn's shoulders slumped. "How long have you known?"

"A little while. It wasn't that hard to figure out," Missy said. "Don't worry. I didn't tell anyone. And the others don't notice things so much."

Gwendolyn exhaled. "Thank goodness for that—"

But that was when Cecilia Forthright stormed up and slammed her hands down on the table. "What are you doing here?"

CHAPTER NINE

ABRUPT EXITS

Cecilia was resplendent in a daisy-yellow top with white floral print, a plaid skirt, tall yellow stockings, a large yellow purse to match, and a bright red face. "That terrible wig isn't fooling anyone, oddling. You can't hide those freckles," she said, voice dripping with disdain.

Gwendolyn glared at her. "What are *you* doing here? This isn't the place for *proper* girls like you. Run on home to Daddy."

Cecilia scoffed. "Daddy doesn't care what I do. You're the one that should be in the Home with all the worthless cases. Don't they lock you up at night? Like animals?"

Gwendolyn stood up so fast she knocked over her chair. "Stop it! I am sick of your bullying! It won't work anymore, I've faced much bigger things than you—"

"Me?" Cecilia screeched. She threw her hands in the air. "You've been bullying me ever since the Change! I've been ignoring you, keeping to myself, but you just won't leave me alone!"

Gwendolyn stopped. That was *not* the response she'd expected. "What are you even talking about?"

Cecilia scoffed. "As if you didn't know. You're the worst."

"I'm not a bully!"

Cecilia came round the table and got right up in Gwendolyn's face. "Do you think I'm stupid? I hear all the nasty little things you and your friends say behind my back. And I don't know how, but I *know* you're the reason Vivian and Janette won't talk to me anymore. And then there's that *look*."

Gwendolyn was shaken. There was a kernel of truth in what Cecilia said. "What... what look?"

"You know exactly what look. The one that says you think I'm worthless. Like I'm nothing. I'm not *nothing*!" Cecilia said, her voice a hysterical shriek.

"I... I don't..."

Cecilia scoffed again and crossed her arms. "You can stop pretending, no one is buying it."

"You've been teasing me since our first year at the School! You call me oddling, and freak! You're horrid to Missy as well!"

"Please, stop fighting..." Missy said, trying to edge her way between them.

But Gwendolyn wasn't done. "Not to mention how you held me down and tried to cut off my hair!"

"And *you* scratched me! You made me bleed! Look!" Cecilia leaned in close, and sure enough, Gwendolyn could see faint scars on her cheek. "We were twelve. Grow up. Besides, you cut it all off yourself anyway. Poor little Gwendolyn, desperate for attention, wanting everyone to feel *sorry* for her. Wrapping all the grown-ups around your little finger so no one notices how you bump my desk every morning. How you knock my books to the floor. How you say nasty things about me to anyone who'll listen—"

"You tripped me! You stole my diary!"

"I never did! I told you, Vivian tripped you! You're the one who left your diary laying round."

"Stop it!" Missy shouted, uncharacteristically loud.

Cecilia's face twisted into an expression of disgust. "It was about time you got what you deserved. Oh, how my daddy loved your *famous* parents, he could never stop talking about them. And it was you all along. As if tormenting me wasn't enough. Lying to Daddy, stealing his money--"

"I didn't steal anything!"

"But now you're in the Home, where you belong, *orphan—*"

Gwendolyn slapped her across the face.

The three of them stood there in shared shock.

"Gwendolyn..." Missy whispered.

"I... I'm *not* an orphan," Gwendolyn stammered.

"Whatever," Cecilia said, rubbing her cheek. "Precious, innocent Gwendolyn. Don't make me laugh. Just leave me alone, freak." Cecilia turned and stormed away, losing herself in the crowd.

"Are you all right?" Missy said.

"I... I don't know," Gwendolyn said. She truly didn't. Cecilia's words had rattled her. Most of what she said had been true. Was she really the bully here? Gwendolyn shook her head. *No*, she thought. *Cecilia deserves whatever she gets.*

But she couldn't help noticing Cecilia across the room, sitting by herself at a table with a single untouched drink. She looked very small and lonely, and Gwendolyn couldn't help but remember how that felt.

Meanwhile, Gwendolyn's own friends sidled back up to the table.

"See anything good?" Missy asked, trying to lighten the mood.

"Loads!" Tommy said. "There's this new artist who's making animals entirely out of scrap metal, painting them in bright colors, and—"

"Shh!" Jessica said, waving for him to sit down. "Zelda's starting."

A woman stepped on stage, a beautiful brunette somewhere in her early twenties. Even amongst the Revelers she stood out, clad in a dress with layers of shimmering rainbow fringe that shifted color with the slightest movement. She wore one of the sequined bands around her forehead that seemed to be the hottest style. When she mounted the stage, the entire crowd went quiet.

"What a posi-toot-ly splendorous party! It's good to see all you dappers and dames, you sweets and swells, all dolled up in your glad rags and coming out to tap your toes and wear out your dancing shoes." She spoke in a rapid-fire patter, with a confidence and strength in contrast to her high-pitched, girlish voice. "Thank you all for sharing your lovelies. Your stories, your music, your art and your fashion. It's people like you who are pushing our City forward, showing the stodgy old codgers what a glittering future might lay before us if we swing to a new beat."

The crowd cheered. Jessica leaned forward in her seat. "She's amazing."

Gwendolyn had to agree.

"I'm pleased as punch to see so many new faces pop up around here. Where's Wendy? Stand up, Wendy."

Everyone craned their necks to look around the room.

Tommy nudged Gwendolyn. "That's you, remember?"

"Oh! Right." Tentatively, she stood and waved at the Revelers. There was a fresh burst of applause, and a few whistles.

Zelda gestured to her. "That story of yours was real jake, darling, the cat's pajamas. The rest of you better watch out or these little flappers might show you all up. Take a bow, sister."

Gwendolyn did, and eased back into her seat.

"But it ain't all giggles and glamor, gang. Have you seen these posters pasted up? 'A return to values,' they say."

A chorus of boos rippled through the room.

"We all know what that means. Back to way things were. Back to grey and dull and dreary and dumb. For the first time, we're awake, and they'd rather us go back to sleep. Well, we've had enough of their 'values'! If there's to be any returning to be done around here, it's us, taking things back to before the old-timers fouled everything up, to the days of color and bright and bubbling!" Zelda threw her hands in the air, and the crowd rewarded her with a raucous cheer.

"But it won't come easy, you pretty things. The council wants to take away your books. Your stories. Your music. Your art. They want you chained to a desk, doing the same pointless work your parents did, and your grandparents, and so on and so forth into boring antiquity. But we want more than some drowsy, dreary, day-to-day!"

Her tone grew serious, and her sparkling eyes traveled across the room, making contact with each Reveler in turn. "We've seen their world and it's a milquetoast metropolis of mindless mediocre men, and women with no more to do than clean the house and care for the babies." She pointed a bejeweled finger. "But we can show them the possibilities. We can show them the wonderful things you've all created. Change isn't coming, it's already *here*, and we—"

But Zelda's fiery speech was interrupted by a shout from a young man who ran into the room and jumped up on a table. "Beat it! It's a raid!"

The crowd burst into a frenzy. Several headed for the exit, but were met by a group of uniformed men with nightsticks. And right behind them came the Childkeeper.

"This is an unsanctioned gathering of delinquent activities." Her voice was as calm and controlled as ever. "Gentlemen. Round them up. And bring any unsupervised minors to me."

The men fanned out through the room and started grabbing Revelers, hauling them roughly toward the door. Zelda was suddenly nowhere to be seen.

"You can't do this!" Jessica shouted. "There's no law against it!"

"A new policy, directly from Mr. Pump and the City Council. All unsupervised minors engaged in delinquent activity are to be detained and sent to the Home for Unclaimed Children. There we can teach you to be of service to your community." The Childkeeper gestured to a policeman and pointed at Missy. The man stepped in and grabbed her by the arm.

"Let go of her!" shouted Tommy. He pounded on the officer's arm, but the man just shoved him aside.

More policemen approached. One of them darted forward and

snatched Gwendolyn's wrist. "You're coming with us, little girl."

She tried to pull away. "Let go of me! I'm not going back, I won't!" Even living on the street would be better than going back to the Home. She struggled, but the man was too strong, and she fell.

She hit the floor, the policeman's hand still locked around her wrist. When she looked up at him, time stopped. The man's tall hat cast his face in shadow, making him seem every bit as faceless as Mister Five and Mister Six. A wave of memory roared up inside her, triggered by the sight of this man with a face she could not see.

She saw her mother, standing over her in the O.R.B. just as the policeman stood over her now, grabbing her wrist the exact same way. She heard the sickening crunch again as her own mother broke that wrist. She saw her Mother's face vanish into the nothingness of a Faceless Gentlemen.

"Get away from me!" she shrieked, the last word stretching out into a furious animal scream. She screamed, and she screamed, completely out of control. But when she stopped screaming, the sound continued. It grew louder and higher until it was an ear-splitting whine, as if the very air was screaming in pain.

Everyone stopped and covered their ears, including the policeman. Gwendolyn kicked him in the knee. He stumbled to the ground, still holding his ears, and Gwendolyn scrambled to her feet.

But a surge of exhaustion knocked her back down on all fours. She gasped, struggling to catch her breath. Darkness clawed at the edge of her vision.

Then she saw why. A hole had appeared in the air, filled with a shimmering white haze. Gwendolyn recognized a portal when she saw one. A portal she had created.

Tommy took his hands from his ears. "What the flip is th—"

"Quick! Inside!" Gwendolyn shouted over the shrieking that filled the air. She summoned whatever energy she had left and stumbled into Tommy, shoving him toward the hole in the air. He hit it, and disappeared.

"What is that?" Ian said, the children recovering faster than the adults.

"No time! Do you want to get arrested?"

"My parents would murder me if I was arrested, so death's not much of a risk, I suppose," Ian quipped.

"Gwendolyn, are you sure?" said Missy, barely audible amid the noise.

"Just go!"

"Let's bail," Ian said. He dragged Missy inside, and they vanished as well.

"Jessica, come on!"

The policemen were starting to stir, taking their hands from their ears and shaking their heads.

Jessica looked from the men to Gwendolyn, then nodded. "Fine. I trust you." And she jumped through the portal.

A policeman lunged at Gwendolyn, but suddenly Puck was there. She dealt a blow to the back of the man's head and he crumpled. Another officer appeared, but Puck kicked him so hard he flew through the air and slammed into a stack of crates. Sculpted metal animals and bits of splintered wood flew everywhere.

Now it was Puck who grabbed her arm. "You promised me a night of fun, but the night is not yet done. These men's sport gives me much delight, I've longed to have a proper fight."

"You're own your own," Gwendolyn said. "I'm not going back to the Home, and I'm not leaving my friends out there."

Puck Robin's expression turned hard, and her eyes flashed with fury. "If you leave, your debt is unpaid. A steeper price I'll make you pay."

"Rhyming *paid* with *pay*? You're losing your touch, faerie," Gwendolyn sneered back. The hole in the air was already shrinking. Gwendolyn tore herself free of Puck Robin's grip and flung herself through the portal, just as it sealed itself behind her.

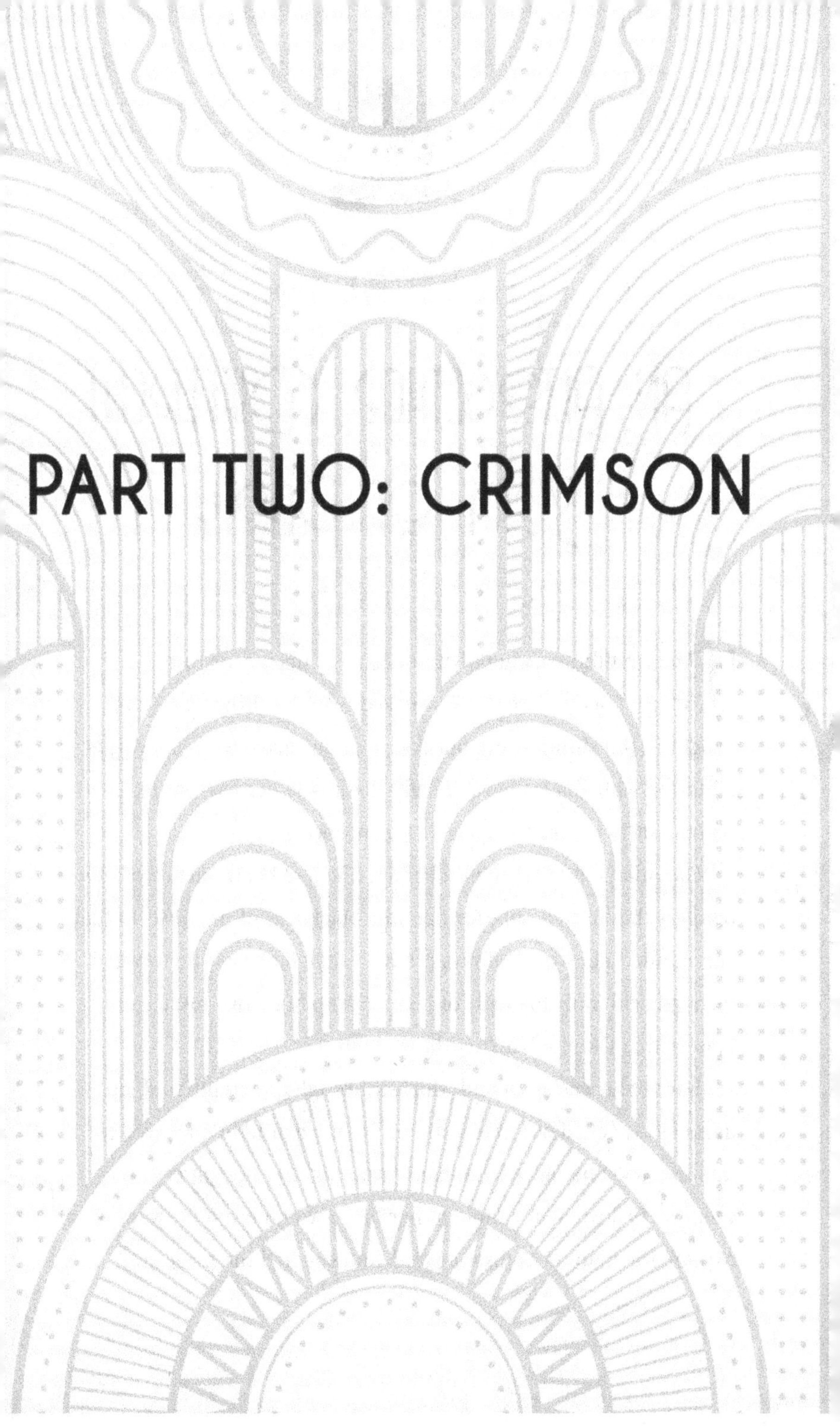
PART TWO: CRIMSON

CHAPTER TEN

AN ALTOGETHER DIFFERENT SORT OF PARTY

The first thing Gwendolyn noticed was the air, or rather lack thereof, as the breath was sucked from her lungs. She was caught in the shimmering not-colors of the space between worlds, glittering with shades beyond sight that made her eyes swim. This was the In-Between, the space between worlds.

Gwendolyn had been here before. She had been warned of the dangers that lurked here for her—the blackness of the Abscess that surrounded her world, always ready to snatch her as she traveled through, with only the Lady of Light to stop him. Two mysterious powers that Gwendolyn knew little about.

But as she was spun and whirled through the empty void, no darkness reached out to tear at her. No wave of light appeared to fight it back. She merely tumbled headlong into the glittery vacuum. Just when she thought her lungs would burst for want of oxygen, the blankness disappeared, and she had the briefest glimpse of a foggy street before her knees gave out, and she fell. She was unconscious before she hit the ground.

~~~

When she came to, she felt hard stones beneath her. She lay there for a moment, sucking in great heaving breaths, and managed just enough to groan in pain. She couldn't see anything through the thick fog. Her skin was damp and clammy.

Here she was again. The last time she had ripped open a portal between worlds, she'd had a complete depressive breakdown. She'd woken up curled into a ball, shaking uncontrollably. Compared to that, a little nap wasn't so bad. It had been an accident, but intentional or not, tearing a hole in reality really took a toll on a girl.

She struggled to her feet and looked around. The sky was dark. Thatch-roof cottages lined either side of the street. The fog hid everything below her knees. A bolt of lightning split the air, and a boom of thunder made her jump.

"What in the..." came Ian's voice.

She spun around to find him behind her. He and Missy and Tommy and Jessica were all staring around in slack-jawed wonder. They'd either been too stunned to notice her fainting spell, or hadn't seen her through the fog on the ground.

"Where are we?" Missy said

Gwendolyn wiped the wetness from her bare arms, and tried to shrug off the last of the fatigue. "Well, umm... I think we might be on another world."

Her four friends turned to look at her as though she'd grown an extra head.
~~~

She gave a nervous shrug. "Well... I *did* tell you about them."

"Yeah," Ian said. "You may have undersold it."

"All that stuff..." Jessica spun, drinking in their surroundings. "Everything you said about pirates, and monsters, and faeries... that was all true?"

Gwendolyn frowned. "Of course it was true. You didn't believe me?"

Ian shrugged. "I thought it was just another one of your stories. It's hard to tell with you, you've got so many."

"I'm sorry," Jessica said. "I knew *some* of it must be true, but I thought you were exaggerating. It *was* a good story."

Gwendolyn turned to Missy and Tommy. "But... you believed me, right? You were there for part of it."

"If I'm honest, it's all a bit hazy, inn'it?" Tommy said. "It was so unbelievable, it was easier just not to think about it."

"I think I knew it was real," said Missy. "But I hoped it was just in my nightmares." And she shuddered.

"Well, now you know," Gwendolyn said in a bit of a huff. She knew she should cut them some slack. This would be a bit of a shock for anyone.

Someone grabbed her and spun her around. Cecilia was there, fuming, shaking her by the shoulders. "What have you done, you horrible little freak? Where are we?"

"Cecilia!" Gwendolyn gasped. Then she glared. "How did you get here?"

Cecilia glared right back. "I jumped in after your stupid gang. I certainly wasn't going to let myself get arrested. Daddy would have kittens. Where are we?"

"Yeah, what is this place?" Ian said, looking up at the stormy sky.

A very good question, Gwendolyn thought. She looked down the street, which ran to the foot of a mountain. On top of the mountain was a tall, turreted castle. A bolt of lightning split the air and lit it from behind.

"I suppose there's only one way to find out." Gwendolyn pointed at the castle.

"It doesn't seem like the kind of place that likes visitors," Missy said.

"We've got to find a way to get back to the City, don't we?" Jessica asked.

"I'm in no hurry," Tommy said.

Gwendolyn clapped her hands together, trying to seem like a confident leader. "In my experience, adventures don't happen while you're standing still. Somewhere is better than nowhere, so off we go."

"I'm not going anywhere with you," Cecilia said.

"Fine," Gwendolyn snapped. "You can stay here." She turned and headed down the street, and her friends followed.

Cecilia crossed her arms and tapped her foot petulantly. Then she took another glance at the misty street around them, at the dark and silent cottages, and hurried to catch up.

~~~

The long walk up the mountain gave Gwendolyn plenty of time to think. The others were too busy marveling at everything to say much, clearly still adjusting to the idea of being stranded on another world.
~~~

As I have mentioned before, children are much more adaptable than grown-ups. But these children were now half-grown, and not quite as accepting of the new and fantastic as they used to be. Eventually, though, a childlike wonder spread over the faces of Tommy, Missy, Jessica, and Ian, and they looked much as they had when they had played at pirates with sticks in the Schoolyard.

Cecilia just looked sullen, and a bit scared.

The road was easy enough to walk. It was well maintained, and not too steep. Gwendolyn's thoughts began to pick up speed. She was out of the City. That meant there was a very real chance of finding Sparrow and Starling, and... her parents. All she needed to do was get back into the Library of All Wonder, which existed between the worlds and held a door to every conceivable story.

We're all in a story, Gwendolyn remembered. *The question is, what sort of story are we in now?*

This wasn't Tohk, or Faeoria. But now that she had a moment to think about it, it did look rather familiar. If she wasn't mistaken, she had seen this world in one of Cyria's tapestries. And again, in an image the Blackstar had shown to King Oberon and Queen Titania. This was the world he offered them as a prize for the duel Gwendolyn had lost.

It had been two years, but the memories felt so close now. She felt more like *herself* again. Gwendolyn Gray, imagination explorer. An adventure always brought out the best in her. And she noticed with a little thrill that there was an energy to the place, a slight tingle like a comforting old friend, a sensation she hadn't felt since she'd reversed the Lambents and filled the City with ideas.

It was *energy.* Creation energy. *Magic.*

Gwendolyn held out a hand. "*What if...*" she whispered. And she imagined a brilliant globe of light, illuminating the dark road around them.

A shower of sparks shot from her fingertips.

Not quite as strong as she'd like, but she *was* a bit out of practice. Or maybe the magic just wasn't as strong here. It was different on every world, and there was no predicting how it would work. In Faeoria, magic was so abundant everyone was literally glowing with it, but in Tohk, using magic was like drinking a milkshake through a straw.

Still, some power was better than none. A little magic could go a long way. She focused again, and managed to produce a few more sparks, all in different colors.

"Whoa!" Ian shouted. "How did you do that?"

Jessica nodded thoughtfully. "So that part was true too. You *do* have magic."

"Yes, it appears I do."

"You are *so* weird," Cecilia said.

"Better weird than normal," Gwendolyn replied. "My advice? Stop expecting things to make sense, and just roll with the punches. Besides, this is usually the fun part of the adventure."

Cecilia shook her head. "This is a dream," she muttered. "It's all some mad dream. I'm going to wake up, and be back in my own bed, and it'll be Sunday, and time to go back to mum's house. There's no such thing as... whatever this is."

"You just keep thinking that," Tommy said. "Now shut up and don't ruin it for the rest of us."

They finally reached the castle and a pair of enormous wooden doors. Black stone walls towered over them.

"So, uh, what do we do?" Jessica asked, a slight tremor in her voice.

"Ain't it obvious?" Tommy said, and ran for the door.

"Tommy, wait—" Gwendolyn said, but it was too late. Tommy was already banging on the wood.

"Oy! Open up! It's cold out here!"

Gwendolyn shook her head. Not exactly the best first impression.

There was a booming noise from inside, and the grinding of heavy machinery. The gates creaked open.

Behind them stood a man, though "man" might be a rather generous description. He was more like a slab of granite, over seven feet tall, with gray skin and hard, blocky features. He wore a black suit with long tails, and a frilled shirt with a silk cravat, all of which seemed ludicrously out of place on his monstrous frame.

He rumbled wordlessly in a questioning tone.

"Oh my god," Cecilia said.

"Hello," Gwendolyn said, trying to sound as though they knocked at the door of strange castles every second Wednesday. *And after all,* she thought, *one shouldn't judge by appearances.* "We are... travelers. We are new to this land, and looking for shelter and hospitality. And possibly directions."

The doorman merely groaned, turned, and headed back inside. The six of them followed him through a flagstone courtyard up to the ornate inner doors, five of them muttering to themselves in wonder and disbelief.

The doorman knocked once, and they swung open of their own

accord.

Light washed over them, warm and cheerful. Music drifted out as well. A gentlewoman stormed up to them in a rustle of crimson skirts. Her hair was black as night, and her skin was pale as the moon. She was ornamented in a dazzling array of diamonds. Her expression was one of annoyance bordering on fury, but as she examined them, her features softened, and she smiled.

"Oh my, it seems a gaggle of guests has tumbled onto my doorstep." Her voice was rich and sweet as cream. "Greetings. I am the Contessa of Stokerly." She curtsied.

Gwendolyn had some experience with courtly manners, and she returned the gesture, then motioned for the others to follow suit. Missy curtsied, and Tommy curtsied as well, a bit confused, while Ian had sense enough to bow. Jessica also bowed, refusing to curtsy. Cecilia just stood there, arms crossed, squeezing her eyes shut as though she could make it all go away.

Gwendolyn spoke first. "Pardon us, your grace—"

"Your *lady*, if you please, I am not quite so noble as that. As for my pardon, that would depend on your offense." She gave them all a toothy smile.

"I suppose..." Gwendolyn thought quickly, trying to get back into the dance of words she had learned from the faeries. "Our offense would be to impose upon the hospitality of your house, and ask for assistance in the ways of this place. We are travelers, from far away."

"Ridiculously far away..." Ian added.

"I see," said the Contessa with a hint of pity in her voice. "Castaways, perchance? Passers through the portals? My poor dears. The lost ones are sad cases indeed. No one to care for you, no one to protect you. I am not without a heart, nor have I forgotten my manners! I welcome you to my house, to the county of Bronteshire, and to the glorious kingdom of Umberland." She took in their colorful clothing with a measured glance. "Normally the castaways we meet are rather more ragged, but you seem to be dressed quite festively."

"Yeah, we just came from another party," said Ian.

Gwendolyn motioned for him to hush. *Though I do seem to be careening from one to the next,* she thought.

"I would be pleased to have you. You must have rather... unique stories with which to entertain my guests. We are always in search of new curiosities. What a treat you are. Follow me!" The Contessa went back inside.

"Of course," Cecilia muttered. "Strange children from other worlds just pop up all the time."

"From what I hear, yes," Gwendolyn said. "Now get a hold of yourself and play along. Tell yourself it's a dream if you have to, and keep your mouth shut."

Cecilia glowered, but stayed silent. For which Gwendolyn was glad—she didn't want anything spoiling her fun, and what could be worse than hearing someone whine about how unbelievable it all was while you were trying quite hard to believe it yourself?

They followed the Contessa into a spacious entryway, lined with marble columns and enormous portraits of stern looking people. Lush red carpets covered the wooden floors. Uniformed attendants in white gloves stood on either side of a grand staircase.

Gwendolyn watched her companions spin in circles to take it all in. "Honestly, if you're going to stand around gaping at every new thing, we'll never get anything done."

"Oh, not to worry." The Contessa swept past them and down the stairs. "I find their curiosity quite amusing. Come along, children."

"We're not children," Cecilia said. "I'm sixteen."

She smiled again. "Ah, yes, of course. I'd forgotten how old such youth can seem to the young. So refreshing."

The staircase led into a sunken ballroom with a polished wooden dance floor. Warm light dripped from hundreds of candles in crystal chandeliers. Couples twirled gracefully across the floor, the women in full-length gowns, the men in tailcoats and lace-trimmed shirts. Gwendolyn rather hoped the clothing Robin gave her would not vanish as faerie gifts often did, as she did not relish the thought of appearing bald and pajama-ed in the midst of such finery.

"And how should you be introduced?" The Contessa said as they stood upon the bottom step.

Gwendolyn knew this dance as well, and remembered its steps. Revealing your true name was a potentially grave mistake. "You may call me Rosecap."

"Lovely. And your title?"

"Title? Oh. Rosecap, the... Princess of the Library." After all, Cyria *had* said the Library of All Wonder was hers now. And if one had to be something, why not a princess?

"Princess of the Library? How delightfully odd. Perhaps I'll show you my own library sometime. And who are they?"

"These are my friends..." she paused for a moment to allow her imagination to catch up. "Blossom, Sorrel, Zephyr, Caspian, and, umm... Radish," she said, pointing to Missy, Tommy, Jessica, Ian, and Cecilia in turn.

Cecilia scowled.

The Contessa waved a hand. "Well, I shan't remember all of *those*. Worthouse, if you please?"

An attendant nodded, and stepped out onto the ballroom floor. The music stopped, and dozens of eyes turned toward them. "Assembled majesties, graces, lords, and ladies. I present to you, Rosecap, Princess of the Library, and her Castaway court, the children Blossom, Sorrel, Zephyr, Caspian, and Radish, of no known house or rank."

The nobles clapped enthusiastically. Cecilia scowled again.

Gwendolyn turned to the others. "All right, gang, here's the rules. Don't tell anyone your real name, don't eat any of their food, just in case, and be absolutely polite. And don't forget, we have a mission."

"We do?" Tommy said.

"Yes. I have friends out here, somewhere, and I intend to find them. And after that..." she paused, thinking of her parents. "I have... something else I need to find." She traded a significant look with Missy.

Cecilia scoffed. "The only thing I'm finding is a way back home and out of all this weirdness."

"I don't want you around anymore than you want to be here, so I'll help get rid of you as quickly as I can. This isn't my first trip, after all. Follow me." And though she sounded stern, she was struggling to hold back a wave of joy. She was on another world again. And that meant Sparrow and Starling could not be far behind. Things could hardly *be* more wonderful.

She noticed that her hands were glowing just the tiniest bit, but decided it wasn't a problem. She deserved a bit of happiness. She'd held herself so tightly in check the last two years that it felt good to let loose a little, as long as she didn't get *too* out of control. In an adventure, you had to keep your wits about you.

Channeling that glowing energy, she closed her eyes and *imagined,* conjuring an image in her mind with an ease she hadn't felt in she-didn't-know-how-long. There was a brief flash of light, and her glittering silver headband was now a dazzling tiara, adorned with swooping wings and set with a shimmering blue sapphire, sitting neatly atop her platinum blonde wig.

The others looked at her in astonishment.

"Well... if I'm to be a princess, one must look the part." And she winked at them.

"Hurry, children!" said the Contessa. "I must present you to my guests. I guarantee, you will be the taste of the ball." And she led them onto the dance floor.

The room was spacious. Through the columns, Gwendolyn saw identical ballrooms on either side, though they both appeared to be empty. On an upper balcony, an orchestra played, strings and violins and all the usual instruments one would find at a fancy party. The band itself was less traditional—the musicians were all skeletons, impeccably dressed in black formal wear. Their empty eye sockets surveyed the floor below.

They struck up a waltz and the courtiers danced, all of them much fleshier than the musicians. Ladies stood on the sidelines with bits of paper tied to their wrists, and gentlemen would come and mark a spot on their dance cards.

The Contessa continued across the room and the others followed, hypnotized by the grandeur of the party. Except for Tommy, who pulled Gwendolyn aside. "Uh, Freckles… Is it me, or is something weird goin' on here?"

Gwendolyn glanced around. "No weirder than a normal hop between worlds. Why do you ask?"

"It's just…" He gestured to the archways between the columns, and the empty ballrooms they led to. "All that."

"I suppose it is a very large house," she said. "They can't have enough guests to fill three different ball rooms."

"Those ain't rooms," he said. "Look closer."

She did. And she saw that the spare ballrooms on either side were not *entirely* empty. In both, she could see two people. Two people that looked very much like Gwendolyn Gray and Tommy Ungeroot.

"Oh, the walls are mirrored. Clever."

"Yeah. And if those are mirrors… then where's all the people?"

Gwendolyn paused. The mirrors were empty, save for her and Tommy, and if she looked around she could see Missy, Jessica, Ian, and Cecilia as well. But none of the courtiers were visible. "All right. That is strange." She scrunched up her nose in thought. "Still, a little strangeness is to be expected. At my last ball, everyone had wings, and went barefoot, and glowed in the dark. It's rude to judge people's customs. Come on, let's catch up." And she headed after the others.

"If you say so…" said Tommy. "I dunno. I think I remember reading about something like this…"

CHAPTER ELEVEN

A DANGEROUS DANCE

The Contessa of Stokerly was introducing the rest of the gang to a pair of nobles, one in a black suit and one in a black dress made entirely of sheer lace. They had shaggy hair that hung into their faces, and seemed to be putting a lot of effort into looking smug and bored. And if Gwendolyn was not mistaken, their pale skin was actually, literally, *sparkling*.

"These are the Baron and Baroness of... I'm sorry, what was it again?" the Contessa said.

The two of them glared at her, not so much with daggers as with entire swords. "We are from the Barony of Stefanaeum, my Lady," the glittering man said.

The Contessa waved a hand. "I'm always losing track of the smaller provinces."

"Well, *that* was rude," Jessica said. "Is Stefanaeum a nice place? What's the tax structure like? What do the peasants think of propping up this aristocracy?"

The Baron shrugged. "Oh, we don't have peasants."

The Baroness gave a smug, sparkling smile. "We ran out of

those decades ago. It is *so* hard to find good peasants these days."

"Come along, my dears," the Contessa whispered. "My glittery cousins are such a bore. None of them have any semblance of personality, and so they suck the life from others. Speaking of..."

The Contessa pulled out a tiny golden box, opened it, and dipped a pinkie into the red powder inside. This she dabbed under her tongue, the inside of her mouth shockingly red in contrast to her pale skin. She sighed in pleasure. "Ah, yes. But not as fresh as it could be. I do so miss it, but powdered is all we have at the moment. Oh, there's the Marchioness. Mina!" The Contessa waved, and dashed away in a whirl of red.

Missy fidgeted with the hem of her skirt. "Are you sure about this, Gwendolyn?"

"Of course. Why?"

"This is all... *strange.*"

Gwendolyn paused. Of course, this whole thing would be taking a toll on Missy. She tended to get kidnapped or erased or transformed whenever magical things started happening. Gwendolyn reached out and gave her hand a squeeze. "Don't worry. We won't stay long. The Contessa mentioned a library—we'll use that to get out of here, and then I can... I can find my parents."

Missy nodded sympathetically "That's right. They were... taken, weren't they?"

Gwendolyn looked down. "Yes. Do you remember?"

Missy shrugged. "More and more, the longer we're here. I'm trying very hard not to."

Gwendolyn took her other hand as well, clasping them both. "Don't worry," she repeated. "I won't let anything happen to you.

Now, let's go have some fun."

She looked around to see where the others had gone, and saw that Ian had struck up a conversation with a dark-haired boy. Tommy was at a buffet table that Gwendolyn hadn't noticed before, stuffing himself.

A shock went through her. She sprinted over and slapped a canape out of his hand. "Tommy! What did I *just* say about the food?"

Tommy gave her a wide-eyed puppy dog look. A droplet of purple jam dangled off his lower lip. "I forgot. Sorry."

Gwendolyn sighed. "Well, hopefully you aren't trapped here forever."

"Wait, what?"

But he was interrupted by the boy that Ian had been speaking to. "Excuse me, princess?"

It took Gwendolyn a moment to realize he was talking to her. "Oh! Yes. Princess, that's me to a T."

He bowed low, swirling his red half-cape around himself, his dark hair falling into his equally dark eyes. He straightened, and held out his hand. "May I have this dance?"

Gwendolyn blinked in surprise. The boy was handsome enough. He was not one of the sparkling kind, but there was a twinkle of cleverness in his eyes. One had to be careful not to get swept up into a magical ball that lasted for all of eternity, but...

"I'd love to," she heard herself say, not entirely sure where the words had come from.

Tommy grabbed her wrist with a sticky hand. "I don't think that's such a good idea, Freckles."

Gwendolyn wrenched her hand away. "My name is *not* Freckles. I am the Princess Rosecap, if you please and thank you very much. Do not forget it. As you were, Sorrel." She glanced down at the jam smeared on her wrist, and wiped it away on her fringed dress. At least the purple would match. She reached up to check that her wig was still in place, then took the boy's hand. "Lead the way."

He smiled. "With pleasure."

He took her by the elbow and escorted her out among the dancers. Then he faced her and raised his arms in a dancer's frame.

Gwendolyn stepped in and took his hands. She felt a sudden shiver at the touch of his ice-cold skin. The skeleton band struck up a waltz in a minor key and the boy led Gwendolyn in a graceful one-two-three around the dance floor.

"I didn't catch your name," Gwendolyn said.

"I did not give it. For then you would have known that I have no royal title, and since a lowly gentleman like me is unworthy to consort with a princess, you would have left me stranded at the buffet." He lowered his head in mock shame, but his dark eyes never left hers. "Please forgive my deception."

Gwendolyn had to fight back a giggle. "So what do I call you?"

"Jack Lazarus, at your service."

"And, Jack, how did a lowly gentleman such as yourself get into such a fancy party?"

A wicked grin spread across his face. "Can I tell you a secret?"

Gwendolyn shrugged. "I suppose you won't know unless you try."

He grinned wider. "I *snuck* in. I'm not supposed to be here, and would be in terrible trouble if anyone found out. Truth be told, I'm not even a lowly gentleman. I am, in fact, something of a scoundrel, and have come on a secret mission." He turned his head and gave a slight nod at the buffet table. Gwendolyn couldn't be sure, but she thought she saw a pair of eyes peeking out from under the tablecloth. He nodded up at the musician's balcony, and the lid of a timpani opened a bit, then closed again.

Gwendolyn smiled. "And why tell me this? Aren't you afraid I'll give you away?"

"Honestly?" he said. "I'd like to have a little fun first. And you are terribly pretty. And pretty girls like secrets."

Gwendolyn stumbled a little, but caught herself. "Well, you're quite the rascal. Can I tell *you* a secret?"

Jack shrugged. "I suppose you won't know unless you try."

At the next turn of the waltz, Gwendolyn pulled him close, her lips next to his ear. "I'm not really a princess. And I'm on a secret mission as well." Then she pulled back and gave him a look that she hoped radiated a sense of aloofness. She'd never tried to look 'aloof' before, and hoped she was doing it right.

Some part of her was shocked by her behavior. Was she actually *flirting*? Well, why not? What was the point of pretending to be a princess on a magical new world if one couldn't enjoy oneself? For the first time in years, she could completely let herself go without worrying about a sudden avalanche of consequences falling on her head.

The shocked part of her thought this all seemed very reasonable, and bid her carry on.

"How about this, Mr. Jack Lazarus. I'll tell you my secret mission if you tell me yours."

He cocked his head in exaggerated consideration. Then he nodded. "Very well. As the gentleman, I shall lead." He sent her out into a twirl, then pulled her back in. "I'm going to steal the queen's prized brooch."

"I see. Is it a special brooch?"

"Oh, very much so," he said in an exaggerated whisper. "It is said to possess all sorts of magical powers. Powers one might even use against the queen herself."

"Why would one do such a thing?" Gwendolyn said, matching his conspiratorial tone.

"Perhaps one is tired of seeing her prey upon the people of Umberland. Perhaps one is tired of watching his crew go hungry every night. And perhaps one is fond of pretty things."

"Well, fortune favors the bold. If I get the chance, I'll be sure to distract her for you." Gwendolyn twirled herself this time, and Jack graciously spun her back in again.

"Since it is boldness you prefer, then I say that you look positively radiant. Literally radiant, in fact," he said, admiring the hand he held and its faint golden gleam. "Does everyone glow where you come from?"

"No," she said. "I'm utterly unique." She knew she was acting out of character. She knew that she wasn't entirely stable at the moment. Glowing skin was always a sign of a manic episode. Of impulsiveness, recklessness. And it felt *delightful.*

"Thankfully you're not as dreary as the sparkly lot we get around here," Jack said. "And we certainly don't see many freckles in Umberland."

Gwendolyn looked away, though the corner of her mouth seemed to know its job, and pulled up into a wry smile.

"Ah, but now you're blushing. It only makes you more beautiful. No one here has blushed in centuries."

"What do you mean?" Gwendolyn asked, but then the music stopped. Jack Lazarus bowed, which Gwendolyn returned with a curtsy. She stood and brushed her hair back behind her ears. The wig's straight hair felt unnatural. Her own hair had never behaved enough for mere ears to hold it back.

"But wait," Jack said. "We had a deal. I told you my secret, but you didn't tell me yours."

Gwendolyn shrugged, with a bit of extra wriggle. She desperately wanted to find Mother and Father, but her parents were suddenly the last thing she wanted to discuss with this boy. "No, I didn't. I suppose you'll just have to live with the disappointment."

Jack clutched a hand to his chest. "And die unsatisfied. A miserable fate, but worth it for the pleasure of a dance with you. Come, I'll escort you to your companions." He held out his arm.

She took it, and he led her back to Ian and Cecilia, who were standing with the Contessa.

Ian was pouting. "Well, at least *somebody* got a dance."

"I'm sorry," said Jack. "The next spot on my card is all yours."

Ian made a show of batting his eyelashes.

"You're not the only one in want of a dance, young Caspian," the Contessa said to Ian. She stared longingly across the room at a man in a crimson military uniform who was engaged in conversation with other similarly dressed gentlemen.

Cecilia scowled. "I don't get it. Why don't you just go talk to him?"

The Contessa clutched her pearls. "I couldn't possibly! The Duke of Austensus is far above my station. His family's wealth greatly exceeds my own, and the gentlemen *always* approaches the lady."

Cecilia rolled her eyes. "Everyone knows that if the man is rich *and* single, then you *know* he's looking to mingle."

"There has to be a better way to say that," Ian said.

Cecelia ignored him. "Just go ask him to dance. He's been shooting dopey looks at you every few minutes."

"No!" The Contessa said with an honest-to-goodness stamp of her foot. "He declined to come to my last ball. And neglected to send me an invitation to *his*. Of course, I attended anyway, and he only danced with me once, *and* he called me a Viscountess instead of a Contessa! The *nerve* of that man. I positively cannot stand him. Oh, is he looking this way?"

Cecilia looked baffled. "But you just said, and I quote, 'I can't possibly live without him.'"

The Contessa blinked. "Well, of course. I'm madly in love with him. I just can't *stand* him. Even though his eyes are like the depths of the enchanted lake on a starless midnight—"

Cecilia threw up her arms in frustration. "Oh, for flip's sake, I'll do it." And she stomped across the dance floor and up to the handsome Duke.

The Contessa gasped. "I can't watch," she said, and covered her eyes with a hand.

The Duke stopped his conversation and looked in shock at the fiery blonde teenager tugging on his coat sleeve. Words passed between them.

"What are they saying?" asked the Contessa, peeking out from between her fingers.

"I don't know, the music is too loud," Gwendolyn said.

"Ugh!" Ian put his hands on his hips. "I wish I could read lips. I'm always missing the juicy bits..."

"Them's the breaks," Tommy said, sidling up next to them.

Whatever was said, it was enough to get the Duke to look over at the Contessa. She hid her face behind a fan she produced from who-knows-where. The Duke excused himself from his conversation and walked toward them, Cecilia in tow.

"Good evening, Lady Stokerly," he said, his voice mellow and rich.

"Your grace," she said, curtsying and flitting her fan.

He took one of her lace-gloved hands and kissed it. Then he inspected the small card that dangled from her wrist. "I see that your next dance is not yet spoken for."

"Why, no, it isn't," the Contessa replied.

The Duke straightened and clasped his hands behind his back. "Well... I... that is to say..."

Cecilia elbowed him in the side.

He coughed. "Right. I know we haven't had the... erm... the most *civil* of encounters thus far. But if I may, my unmanly behavior comes from the strain of concealing my... *passion*, and I apologize."

The Contessa lowered her fan. "I accept your apology, Duke. And I must offer my own in return. I confess, an excess of such passion has made my cold heart run hot as well. If you would accept someone of my station, I would be most pleased to accept a dance from you."

"I'm afraid a dance alone shall not be enough. I can accept nothing less than your hand in marriage."

The Contessa placed a hand at the base of her throat. "Oh, Duke, do you truly mean it?"

The Duke took both her hands in his. "With all my heart. Were it still beating, it would be stilled once more at the sight of your beauty."

"But what of my dowry?"

"You, my dear, are a rich enough jewel to compensate for any difference in our material fortunes."

Cecilia crossed her arms. "Oh, please. 'Ooo, I'm rich, but not rich enough.' Spare me."

"But..." The Contessa stammered. "But what will the queen say? Surely she will not approve."

"We shall not know unless we ask her," the Duke said. "Shall we?"

"Well..." The Contessa looked over at the rest of them. She bit her lower lip in thought. "Yes! Yes! A thousand times yes!"

"Wonderful!" the Duke said. "We must tell the queen at once."

The Contessa took his arm. "Come, children! This happy occurrence is your doing, and in token of my appreciation, I shall present you to the queen. Please, call over your companions."

"We'd be delighted," Gwendolyn told the Contessa. She caught Missy's eye, and waved her over. Missy extracted Jessica, to the relief of the glittering aristocrats. Then the Contessa led the Cityzens to the far end of the ballroom, to a small, raised platform surrounded by uniformed guards.

Upon the platform sat a petite throne. Upon the throne sat an enormous pile of black ruffles. Upon the ruffles sat a barely visible head. And upon that head sat a blackened and twisted crown.

Gwendolyn recoiled. The queen was little more than a child, but her face was withered and wrinkled, as though she'd dried out and crinkled up like a raisin.

But after the initial shock, Gwendolyn noticed a glowing purple jewel set into a brooch at her throat. One that looked a lot like the glowing blue Figment that Gwendolyn used to have. And she knew why someone would want to steal it.

Gwendolyn looked around for Jack Lazarus, but he seemed to have disappeared. She craned her neck and scanned the room, but the Contessa was gesturing them forward.

The six of them approached and Gwendolyn curtsied for what felt like the dozenth time that evening. Missy and Cecilia followed suit, as well as Tommy, who still didn't seem to have grasped the thing properly. Ian bowed, and after a warning glance from Gwendolyn, Jessica rolled her eyes and bowed as well, mumbling something about "imperial oppression."

"Your majesty," the Contessa said. "I would like to introduce you to some rather unusual guests, an assortment of Castaways who have washed up on my doorstep. This is Rosecap, Princess of the Library. The rest of them have rather a lot of names, which I have already forgotten."

"Pleased to make your acquaintance, your majesty," Gwendolyn said, remembering the manners she had learned at the faerie court. This was not her first queen, after all.

The Queen of Umberland scowled. "How unmannered, to speak to us without first being spoken to. But we suppose we can make an allowance for such... *lively* guests."

"Uh, thank you?" Ian said.

"Your majesty," the Contessa said. "The Duke of Austensus has offered me a proposal of marriage."

The queen's crusty eyes turned toward the Duke. "Is this so?"

The Duke straightened to attention. "It is, your majesty. With your permission."

She pursed her cracked lips. "This is a most unsuitable match. Have you any reason we should give such permission?"

The Contessa gestured to Gwendolyn and her companions. "These children."

"We are *not* children," Cecilia blurted.

"Will you shut up, for once?" Gwendolyn hissed.

The Contessa continued as though they hadn't spoken. "I offer them to you as a gift. A boon to purchase your blessing."

"I gotta bad feeling about this..." Tommy said.

"What does she mean by 'gift?'" Jessica whispered, her outrage palpable.

"Don't worry," Gwendolyn whispered. "It's fine. It's just the way they talk. They can't actually give us away without our permission. That's the rules."

"They're rather rude little chatterers, aren't they?" squeaked the queen. "Hissing like tea kettles. You there. Rose-thing. Step forward and show a little manners, if royalty you truly are."

"Trust me," Gwendolyn whispered to her friends. "I've done this before." She stepped forward and took the hand the queen presented to her. It was proportioned like that of a small child, but as wrinkled and dried out as the rest of her. Still, Gwendolyn bent and kissed the top of it. It was like kissing crumpled parchment.

"Very good," the queen said. "Now, present your own hand. We have manners too, and you are a princess, after all."

Gwendolyn gave her friends a reassuring glance that said everything was going completely to plan and they had been silly to worry in the first place. It was a very specific sort of glance. Then she offered her own glowing hand to the queen.

The queen took it. Then she opened her mouth, bared an impressive set of fangs, and bit her.

Gwendolyn shouted in pain and surprise. The fangs sank deep into the soft flesh between her thumb and forefinger. Gwendolyn tried to yank her hand back, but the queen was surprisingly strong. Behind her, the others shouted, but the guards on either side stepped in and blocked their way.

Gwendolyn could feel the queen sucking on the wound. Some of the glow faded from her skin. She pulled again, but that just made it hurt worse. She gritted her teeth and twisted, managing to jerk herself free. She stumbled back off the dais, clutching her wounded hand.

"What the flip is going on?" Ian shouted.

But Gwendolyn's eyes were still on the queen. The little thing on the throne wriggled in her pile of ruffles. A bit of color came back to her cheeks, and some of the wrinkles left her skin, as though someone were re-inflating a crinkled old balloon. She licked her lips, and Gwendolyn could see the inside of her mouth glowing with stolen power. "Mmm. Quite strong for one so small. Oh, it has been too long since we had proper guests. This lifts your fortunes considerably, Contessa. We approve your marriage. What a fine meal they shall make. And we do believe there's enough to share."

Around them, the guards, the Contessa, and the Duke all bared enormous fangs. Their eyes turned black, and their fingers became long claws. They snarled and hissed and grinned.

Tommy snapped his fingers. "Oh! Now I remember! They're vampires!"

CHAPTER TWELVE

GET THEE TO A LIBRARY

"**W**hat's a vampire?" Missy asked, her voice trembling.

"Those are!" Tommy pointed.

"Fair point..." Ian muttered.

"It seems they don't play by your *rules*," Cecilia snapped, but fear showed through the bravado.

"To be fair, the last queen made my hand bleed too," Gwendolyn said. "Though I realize that's not entirely helpful at the moment..."

The vampires closed in around them, snarling in a mixture of anticipation and glee. But suddenly, a troupe of dirty-faced children appeared behind them. They wore motley clothes in various states of shabbiness. They shouted a childish battle cry, and attacked.

A girl no older than ten jumped on the Contessa's back and started yanking at her diamond necklace. Another one crouched behind the Duke's legs, and a third appeared and shoved him. The Duke stumbled backward, tripped over the crouching urchin, and sprawled onto the floor. The one who pushed him jumped onto him and sat on his chest while two more swooped in and rifled through his pockets.

The two guards snarled and went for their swords, but found only empty air. A pair of twins stood on the dais behind them. They brandished the stolen blades, and shouted as fiercely as they could.

Jack Lazarus popped up beside them. "Run!" he shouted, pointing toward one of the mirrored walls. He dropped into a spinning kick that felled one of the guards.

Her friends didn't hesitate, and they ran through the opening Jack had created. Gwendolyn held back.

Jack leapt for the dais. The queen let out a terrifying screech as he tore the brooch from her throat, while Gwendolyn and the twins held off the guards. He whooped with triumph and leapt off the dais.

"Get them!" hissed the queen.

The Duke scrambled to his feet and pounced at Gwendolyn, but Jack rammed a shoulder into his side and knocked him away. "Go!" Then he took off across the ballroom, his red half-cape streaming behind him.

Gwendolyn sprinted after. He led her towards the mirrored wall, rather than brave the crowd of angry vampire courtiers between them and the ballroom door. In a few steps, they reached one of the false archways. "Where now?"

Jack walked to the edge of the nearest mirror, and disappeared. Gwendolyn blinked. This particular mirror was not actually flush with the wall, but was set a couple of feet back from its frame, leaving a cleverly concealed opening to either side. Jack poked his head back out. "Coming?"

"What about your friends?"

He grinned. "What friends?"

She looked back. There were a lot of angry vampires, but the crafty urchins were nowhere to be seen.

"Wow," she said. Of course, that just meant more angry vampires for them.

Jack beamed with pride. "They have a good teacher." He tossed the brooch in the air, pulled open the pocket of his waistcoat, and it dropped neatly inside. Then he disappeared through the passage again.

"A nice party favor," Gwendolyn said, ducking through the concealed gap.

"Indeed. But let's not dawdle." And they ran down a brightly lit stone hallway.

"What about *my* friends?" Gwendolyn said as they turned a corner. As they did, she ran right into Tommy. They fell into a tangled heap.

"Hey, I wanted a dance, but that's a bit rough. Didn't even check my card first," he said, grinning.

Gwendolyn let out a disgusted sound and pushed herself off him. "How did you all get here?"

Jessica pointed. "Missy led us to that passageway."

Missy dipped her head and fidgeted with her hands behind her back. "It's where he pointed. I just noticed it, that's all."

"Yes, well done, all around," said Jack. "But this is the part where we run!"

They did, but running wasn't going to be enough. Gwendolyn could hear the vampires coming up behind them. Gwendolyn racked her brains, trying to think of something to keep them from being eaten. Or at least exsanguinated.

"When in trouble, always head for a library!" Gwendolyn said.

"How do you know there's a library?" Cecilia said.

"The Contessa mentioned a library!" she replied.

"I'll show you the library!" Jack said.

"What's a library?" Tommy said.

"Will everyone stop saying 'library?'" Ian snapped.

Jack pointed down the hall. "Two rights, then a left! The Contessa's personal collection."

The hall behind them was filling with fanged vampires. Some bounded on all fours, their animal movements in sharp contrast to their dapper evening dress. They swarmed over each other, mindless in their hunger. They got in each other's way, slowing themselves down, but they were closing fast.

"Jessica, take the lead!" Gwendolyn said. "I'll handle this!"

"Because you've been doing *so* well," Cecilia sneered.

Gwendolyn whirled to face the oncoming pack. "Do you want to do it?" she called over her shoulder.

Cecilia didn't answer, and kept running. Gwendolyn planted herself in the center of the hall, and Jack stood firm beside her.

Facing down an oncoming horde of hungry vampires is hardly the ideal environment for brainstorming. So Gwendolyn reached for familiar ideas, the way a creator will return to a signature style. She stretched out her hands, pictured what she wanted firmly in her mind, and said her magic words. "*What if...*"

Thorny vines sprang from the floor and walls. They cracked the plaster, wrapped around marble columns, and tore through portraits. The vines knocked down several candelabras, setting the branches alight. Almost instantly, the vines formed an impenetrable flaming hedge.

"Well, well, well," Jack said, impressed. "Not just a princess, but a magical one at that."

The first of the vampires ran headlong into the fiery brambles. They earned deep scratches which oozed a thick tarry substance, rather than blood. One of them took a particularly long thorn in the chest and exploded in a puff of dust.

"What was that?" Gwendolyn asked, a little horrified.

"Wood," Jack said. He grabbed her hand and pulled her along. "A stake through the heart. A vampire's traditional weakness."

"I'm pretty sure a stake through the heart is *everyone's* weakness."

"True. But now is hardly the time for banter."

Gwendolyn smirked. "Oh, there's always time for banter. When there's someone worth bantering with, anyway. Try and keep up!" She pulled her hand away and put on an extra burst of speed, but she was hit with a wave of light-headedness, and collapsed.

Jack was there to catch her. "What is it?"

She struggled to her feet. "Nothing. I'm fine."

"You're not glowing anymore. Is that bad?"

"I *said,* I'm fine." But creating that manifestation out of thin air had taken a toll on her. *I'll just have to be cleverer about it,* Gwendolyn thought. Behind them, vampires were clawing through the hedge, heedless of the fire, but careful not to impale themselves on any thorns.

She and Jack careened down the hall, though Gwendolyn slowed them down. Her feet tried to slip out from under her at every turning, and the polished marble floor wasn't helping.

Which gave her an idea. She looked down. *If only this floor was terribly sticky,* she thought, picturing the stone turning soft and gooey behind them.

She felt a twinge of fatigue, but not as strong as before. It was easier to alter something at hand than to create from scratch. She risked a glance backward, and saw the front row of vampires suddenly stick in their tracks. Their feet stopped but their momentum didn't, and they slammed to the ground. Their entire bodies stuck to the floor like flies in a sheet of giant fly paper.

The monsters behind them stopped, considering the situation. Then they leapt onto the walls, crawling like spiders, effortlessly scuttling toward Gwendolyn despite the vertical surface they clung to. The Duke and the Contessa jumped onto the bodies of their immobilized brethren and used them as a springboard onto the ceiling, which they crawled along almost as easily as the floor.

Gwendolyn counted seven skittering monsters, farther behind them now, and slower than before. "That's got a few of them at least."

"We're here," Jack said.

The others were all huddled together outside a pair of impressive double doors.

"It's locked!" Missy squeaked.

Cecilia glowered. "What now, '*Princess*?'"

"Let me through," Jack said. He went to the door and extended a long claw from his forefinger. Then he jammed the claw into the lock and started feeling around.

"You're one of them!" Tommy shouted.

"Very observant."

"Then why are you helping us?" Gwendolyn asked.

"Truly? You seem nice. Besides, I'm a vegetarian."

"What does that mean?"

"It means I'm hungry a lot. Can you slow them down?"

Gwendolyn looked back down the hall. The more carnivorous vampires were only a dozen yards away.

Once again, she relied on an old favorite. She pictured a glowing ball of light to blind their pursuers.

Two of the vampires jumped off the wall, eyes black and claws extended. But when they reached the ball of light, they burst into clouds of dust.

The dust coated them all and set Gwendolyn to coughing. Farther back, the Duke and the Contessa screamed. Their skin blackened and smoked.

Jack screamed as well, the back of his suit crisping as smoke rose from his collar. "Stop! Turn it off!"

Gwendolyn vanished the light. "I'm sorry! I didn't know it would do that."

"It's fine," he grimaced. He jerked his claw upward, and the lock clicked. "In you go."

They bolted through the doors. Tommy and Ian slammed them shut. Jack turned the lock and broke off the handle. "That should hold them for the moment." He eyed Gwendolyn. "Well, magical girl, how many spells do you have left?"

Gwendolyn took stock of herself, forcing a slow, deep breath. She was trembling a little. Tired. Slowing down. "One more, I think."

She surveyed the room. It was an impressive library, a long room with high ceilings and tall shelves on either side. The shelves were filled with important-looking leather bound books. Comfy chairs and small tables ran down the middle, with an enormous black globe in the center. A mural stretched across the ceiling, showing scenes of horror and violence and monsters.

"What are we doing here? This is hardly the time for reading, weirdy," Cecilia snapped. There was a scratching and clawing at the door, punctuated with shrieks of frustration.

"Maybe we can learn some way to stop them," Jessica said.

"Not much to learn. Sunlight, stake through the heart, or chop off their head," Jack said. "That's the trick with us vampires."

"Again, I think *beheading* will stop just about anyone." Gwendolyn turned back toward the door and held out a hand. "Jack, give me that jewel."

"I beg your pardon. This trinket is the whole reason I crashed this party in the first place. I'd hate to get all dressed up for nothing, and—"

"I'll give it back. I don't have time to explain." Gwendolyn said. "But I can use it to open a portal."

"Really?" Jack said, amazed. "I've heard tales of travels to other worlds, but never seen it myself."

"You'll come with us, won't you?" Gwendolyn said.

Jack shook his head. "I'm afraid not. I've also heard tales of people getting stranded. Castaways. My story lies here, with my crew. They need me. So I suppose this is farewell. I hope you enjoyed the party."

Gwendolyn grinned. "I think I've had quite enough of parties just now, if you please and thank you very much. Will you be all right?"

Jack winked. "I'll be fine. I'm as good at getting out of trouble as I am at getting into it. Even now, I've formulated a clever plan to make my escape, full of dash and flair and clever bits."

The scratching stopped. Suddenly, there was a loud bang, as though something heavy were being rammed into the door.

"Just shut up and get us out of here!" Cecilia shouted.

"Right," Gwendolyn said. "Let me borrow the jewel, and I'll open the portal."

"But Gwendolyn!" said Missy. "You told us that opening a portal nearly killed you. You could get hurt!"

There was another bang at the door. And another.

"I'll take 'could get hurt' over 'definitely dead' any day," Ian said.

A short bark of a laugh came from deeper in the library. "I'm not getting a better opening line than that," said a low, gravelly voice.

The seven of them spun around.

The voice came from a tall armchair. It faced away from them, but a black gloved hand came into view and picked up a black fedora from the side table. A man stood and put on the hat.

He was well over six feet tall. His long black coat had two rows of silver buttons and a high upturned collar. His face was mostly hidden in the shadow of his hat, but Gwendolyn could see a pale, stubbled jawline.

Gwendolyn's body tensed, and she had to fight to stop the panic attack that threatened to overtake her, giving the feelings a quick shove into her mental closet. Running from vampires had all been good fun, as far as adventures went, but suddenly things were very real, very serious, and very deadly.

"Hm. The girl again," he said, casually. "Guess I shouldn't be surprised."

"You know him?" Jessica whispered.

"Yes," Gwendolyn said, her tone cold as the grave. "It's the Blackstar."

"That guy?" Ian said. "He's real too?"

"I told you, I wasn't lying!" she snapped, never taking her eyes off the man.

Sure enough, the seven-pointed star tattoo was visible on the back of his ungloved right hand. In it he held a thick paperback book, the spine bent back as only a villain would do. He sighed heavily. "Don't make this harder than it has to be. You know—"

Gwendolyn hit him with a blast of light as bright as she could imagine.

The blast knocked the chair across the room. But it only knocked the hat from the Blackstar's head, revealing slicked-back hair that was shaved on the sides and long on top.

"Fine," he said. "We'll do this quick." And he sent a blast of darkness that mirrored Gwendolyn's bolt of light. All seven children were flung against the wall, hard.

Gwendolyn didn't bother to struggle to her feet—she touched the wooden floor and imagined it growing into a six-foot high wall in front of them. She collapsed back to the floor from the effort just as the crack of gunfire split the air, followed by splintering wood.

Before she could get up again, the center of the wall blackened and burned to ash. The Blackstar strode forward, holstering a gun. Then he picked Gwendolyn up by the throat, effortlessly holding her off the ground with one gloved hand.

Tommy yanked on his other arm, trying to pull him away, but the Blackstar tossed him across the room as if he were no more than a stuffed monkey.

"What is going on?!" Cecilia shrieked. Ian put himself between Missy and the Blackstar.

Gwendolyn made a monumental effort to ignore all this so she could picture more vines, coming up from the floor to wrap around the Blackstar's legs.

The Blackstar was ready. He had already extended a blade of dark energy from the tattoo on the back of his free hand. He sliced through the vines the moment they appeared. "So predictable. Don't you have any new ideas?"

Gwendolyn headbutted him. Apparently he had not predicted *that*, because he dropped her and stumbled backward, clutching his nose. Even though he was twice her size, she charged at him. He was already off balance, and she drove him back several steps until he collided with a coffee table. He fell onto it with Gwendolyn on top of him, and the table splintered beneath them.

"You took my parents!" she bellowed into his face.

The Blackstar casually threw her off and got to his feet. "Yes. I did."

Gwendolyn summoned a ball of light into her palm and pointed it at the Blackstar. Her skin was glowing all the way up her arm, but it was flickering and weak. "Give them back!"

"No." He swung his arm, and a black whip flicked out of his tattoo and wrapped itself around Gwendolyn's legs. He yanked, and she went down hard, losing the ball of light and seeing stars instead.

He towered over her. "You'll never see them again. But they're comfortable. No memory of you to bother them. So go home. Stay there and out of trouble. Your parents will live out their days in peace. Start causing problems, and they'll be a lot more peaceful underground. Your choice."

Gwendolyn opened her mouth to say something vulgar, but she saw Jack Lazarus, scrabbling across the ceiling, looking like just another character in the painted murals that decorated the plaster. He met her eyes, smiled, and held a finger to his lips.

Gwendolyn looked quickly back at the Blackstar, and glared at him. "Go home? So you can come after me again?"

He shrugged. "You leave us alone, we'll leave you alone. It isn't always about you. So just—"

With a wild scream, Jessica leapt onto his back, holding a leg from the broken table. She wrapped one arm around his neck, and hit him with the table leg in the other.

The Blackstar grunted in annoyance. He closed his eyes, and hundreds of tiny black spikes emerged from his coat. Jessica screamed and fell to the ground. He looked at the rest of her friends, who were doing their best to quietly surround him. He flung out his hands, and geysers of black water shot out in all directions. Missy, Tommy, Ian, and Cecilia were hit by the powerful spray and slammed back against the shelves.

In doing so, his whip disappeared. Gwendolyn got to her feet, staggering from pain and exhaustion. But she imagined a vine growing from the floor and wrapping around her wrist. She yanked the vine free from the ground and brandished her own whip, flicking the vine with a satisfying *crack*.

The Blackstar shook his head in disappointment. "Still nothing original. I'm giving you a way out, kid. Take it." He bent down and picked up the broken table leg.

Gwendolyn only smiled. Because that was when Jack Lazarus dropped from the ceiling, fangs bared, claws extended, his red half-cape flapping dramatically behind him.

The Blackstar never even looked up. He thrust the broken table leg into the air and neatly skewered Jack through the chest.

Jack hit the ground, the makeshift stake sticking out of him. His mouth fell open in shock and horror. He met Gwendolyn's eyes. "But... This isn't how it's supposed to..." Then he burst into a cloud of dust.

The Blackstar brushed a bit of dust off his coat. "Like I said, it isn't always about you."

"NO!" Gwendolyn shrieked. She snapped her whip, aiming for the Blackstar's eyes. But he simply raised his right arm, his tattoo coating it in a sleeve of black energy, and caught the whip around his forearm. He yanked the whip upward and Gwendolyn went crashing into the ceiling, then plummeted back to the floor.

The world went white. Her ears rang. Slowly, the white faded to red, and when her vision had fully cleared, she saw the Blackstar across the room, pulling a small metal object from his pocket.

He pressed a button on the device, and a hole opened in the air. It was dark on the other side. A sickly yellow fog drifted through the portal. Gwendolyn tried to get to her feet, but the world spun around her, and she collapsed to the floor again. It was like some horrible echo of the moment he had stolen her parents.

The Blackstar held out a hand, and his hat flew into it. He put on the hat, waved a hand in front of his face, and a puff of smoke congealed into his usual gas mask, the goggles and breathing canister concealing his features and distorting his voice.

"Take my advice, kid. Look out for yourself. Trying to help just gets people hurt. I'd say see you around, but if I do, they die. Be smart. Stay home." Then he stepped through the portal and vanished, the shimmering hole closing quickly behind him.

Gwendolyn pushed herself to her feet. Her head was pounding. Her muscles were shaking. Her insides were like ice.

"Oh my god," Missy said, her hands going to her mouth.

"That guy," Tommy said in shock. "He just killed that kid. Like, poof. He was here, and now he's just... gone."

"What do we do?" Jessica said. "Gwendolyn, what do we do?"

Slowly, the five of them looked at Gwendolyn.

She didn't meet their eyes. Instead she walked over to the pile of dust that had, just moments ago, been a brave young rascal, who had helped them for no other reason than he had felt like doing so. Wherever they were, a gang of urchin thieves was missing its leader.

But there was work to do. Her mind was lost in a numbing fog, but her hands moved of their own accord, brushing away the dust. She found what she was looking for, and picked up the queen's brooch with its violet gem. At her touch, the gem began to glow.

"Stop! That's disgusting!" Cecilia said.

"Shut up, listen!" Ian snapped.

"I don't hear anything," said Tommy.

"Exactly," he said. "Weren't there vampires out there a minute ago?"

They all stopped and paid attention to the unnerving silence. Gwendolyn glanced down at the other end of the enormous library, at the stained-glass window that dominated the far wall. Lightning flashed, highlighting several dark silhouettes on the outside of the glass.

"Whuh-oh," Tommy said.

"Hang on." She had to think fast. Back to the plan. She turned to the door and looked through the jewel, but it looked exactly the same, though tinted violet.

Behind her, there was an enormous shattering sound, then a lot of snarling and screeching.

She didn't look back. This was their only chance. The Library of All Wonder was connected to every library on every world in existence. And it was *her* Library. Cyria had given it to her. She just had to *get* there. But every time she'd used a door to get into another world, she'd had the Figment to help her.

"They're coming!" Tommy shouted.

"Not helping, Tommy," Jessica said. "Grab some wood."

Gwendolyn pictured the Library of All Wonder in her mind. She pictured the door in front of them swinging open, the torch lit entrance hall behind it, the corridor leading to one of her favorite places in all the worlds. A door to all the people she could find. Sparrow and Starling. Her parents. Everything she'd wanted for the last two years was right here in front of her if she could just take it.

Feelings bloomed at the thought. Anticipation. Exhilaration. She focused on them, trying to drive off the exhaustion and fear and despair. This was just another adventure, she told herself, like many she'd had before. She could do this.

All this raced through her at the speed of thought, faster than any vampire. A bolt of violet light shot from the jewel and struck the doors. They crackled along their seams and vibrated in their frames. The jewel vibrated along with them, growing hot in her hand. But Gwendolyn held the image of the library in her mind, shutting out the scrabbling sounds of claws on wood, sounds that were rapidly growing closer.

The jewel brightened. There was a burst of violet light, and the gem exploded in her hand.

But one of the library doors swung open. There was no marble hallway beyond, no pack of monsters. Instead, there was a tunnel lit by cozy yellow bulbs.

"Everyone, go!" She spun around, and was shocked to see the vampires only a dozen feet away, led by the Duke and the Contessa. They bounded over tables and chairs.

"Is it safe?" Missy said.

"Screw safe!" Tommy yelled, and ran for the door. The others took his cue and sprinted after him.

Gwendolyn was the last one through, just in time to slam the door in the Contessa's snarling face.

Then she turned and faced her friends, all of whom were leaning against the walls and panting.

"Well," Gwendolyn said, wobbling a little. "Congratulations. You've survived your first adventure."

"Can they get through?" Jessica asked.

Gwendolyn shook her head. "No. We're perfectly—" but that was as far as she got before she collapsed.

CHAPTER THIRTEEN

BITTERSWEET

"Quiet, I think she's waking up," came a voice from a thousand miles away.

Gwendolyn wished someone would take the weights off her eyelids, as it was making it very difficult to open them. Finally, she managed it.

She was lying on the stone floor, trembling all over. Missy was there, holding Gwendolyn's head and shoulders in her lap. The others stood above her. They all looked worried and confused. Though Cecilia's expression changed as soon as Gwendolyn looked at her.

"Are you all right?" Missy asked.

"Umm... I might be," Gwendolyn said, her voice as shaky as the rest of her. "How long was I out?"

Jessica checked her watch. "Nearly twenty minutes."

Gwendolyn blinked. "And you've just been standing here the whole time?"

Ian nodded at the door. "After that? I'm not wandering off into god-knows-where. What happened?"

Gwendolyn struggled to sit up, and Missy helped prop her up against the wall. "I used too much magic."

"That's a thing?" Tommy said.

"Of course," Gwendolyn replied. "If I use too much, it sends me spiraling out of control. Or it drains me completely. Or first one, then the other."

She looked back at the door they had come through. It was pitch black. Ominous red designs crept in from the edges. Around the door was an ornate frame, sculpted into golden branches. The branches sprouted pages rather than leaves. And stenciled across the top were the words *Egressai Infinitus*.

Gwendolyn got to her feet and went over to it. Tenderly, she stroked the golden frame. It felt like greeting an old friend.

"Hello? Oddling? What do we do now?" Cecilia said.

"Hey, knock it off with that *oddling* stuff," Tommy snapped. "She got us outta' that place, you should be thankin' her."

"She got us *into* that place too. And a fat lot of help you were."

"Didn't see you doing anything either, Miss Priss," Ian said. "You were too busy hiding your face in your hands. Jessica was the one that staked the one who was about to tear your head off."

Gwendolyn's eyes widened. She must have missed that part while she was opening the doorway. "That's enough," she said. She took a deep breath, feeling a bit more steady. "Some... bad things happened. But we can't let that stop us. Rule one of adventuring: keep moving forward." Inwardly, she cringed. She hated to trivialize Jack's death, but they couldn't all just stand around arguing. This was the time for action, while everything was still numb. There would be time for hurting later. She shoved it all into her imaginary feelings closet, and bolted the door.

"Let's go. That way." She gestured to the light at the end of the tunnel.

Tommy, Jessica, Ian, and Cecilia headed down the hall. Missy put a hand on Gwendolyn's shoulder and held her back. "Are you *really* all right?"

Gwendolyn rolled her shoulders back. "I can manage." She gave Missy a tired smile. "Now come on, I've got something to show you."

The others were standing at the end of the entrance hall, all traces of sulk and snipe gone, traded for looks of slack jawed amazement. They stared out at a library that put every other to shame.

Because this wasn't just *a* library. This was *the* Library. The Library of All Wonder.

Twisting shelves of books towered over them, some as high as cathedral ceilings with ladders that slid themselves back and forth. Some were only two shelves high, no taller than her knees. They were arranged at chaotic angles; a forest of shelves, an entire city of books. More books flapped their way through the air like birds, migrating to the correct shelves and nesting themselves next to their brethren.

Tall windows let in cheerful yellow sunlight, and dust motes danced happily in the air. The sunlight was false—through the open windows she could see the flickering whiteness of the In-Between. New books streamed in, every story from every world.

Gwendolyn stepped past the others, then turned to face them. She spread her arms wide. "Welcome to my library." Then she gestured to the archway above the entrance hall, where words were written in towering golden letters.

The Library of All Wonder

Imagination Can Take You Anywhere

The others read the words.

"Curioser and curioser," said Missy.

"Wow," Ian said in an awed hush. "You really *are* a princess."

She blushed at that. But she forced herself to look cheery. "Come on in!" It was her job to keep morale up. Hopefully the spectacular library could distract them from the horrors that had brought them here.

Gwendolyn led them farther in, to the courtyard with its tiled mosaic. Every tile moved like an individual pixel, creating animated images of characters and settings.

Missy gazed around in wonder. "It's just like you said it was. But better..."

"And if what you said is true, this is where all'a the books in the City came from. You took them from here and sent 'em through the postal tubes," Tommy added.

"It's amazing," Jessica said. "And I hate to put a damper on all the amazement, but could we find a place to sit down? We've been walking and dancing and running for quite a while."

Gwendolyn had to admit, they all looked a bit ragged around the edges. "I know a place."

She led them through the mazes of shelves. The library was filled with wonderful smells, of pages and covers and stories and words. It was a very specific sort of smell, one that all the best people know and love. And it was all good as new. There was no sign of the Collector's attack of two years ago.

Eventually, they reached the staircase Gwendolyn wanted, and she led them up to a cozy loft, which was filled with comfy leather chairs, long couches, and lots and lots of cushions.

But when they reached the top, it was *not* the way she remembered it.

It was a mess. Blankets were strewn everywhere. Dirty plates and silverware littered the floor. Books were piled haphazardly here and there. Truth be told, it looked a lot like her apartment.

The mess, however, was the very last thing on Gwendolyn's mind. Because sitting in the middle of it all, poring over a book that lay open on the floor, were two children. One in a red shirt, with a newsboy cap cocked at a jaunty angle. One in a coppery orange vest and shimmering turquoise blouse. She had black hair, but one blue streak had gotten free and hung down into her face as she leaned over the book. So intent were they that neither of them noticed the group's approach.

Gwendolyn motioned for the others to stay put, then walked up behind the pair on the floor.

"Sparrow and Starling, darrow and darling," she sang. "Hello, friends."

The two of them spun around and looked up in confusion. Then their faces burst into expressions of sheer joy.

"Gwendolyn!" Sparrow leapt up so fast his hat flew off. He pounced on her. Gwendolyn was nearly bowled over. She could barely breathe from the strength of his embrace. But she returned it just as hard, burying her face in his curly brown hair.

Then the tears came. Her resolve melted away, replaced by a swirl of emotions so strong her heart literally, physically ached.

She had imagined this moment many times, but it had never involved any crying. She couldn't help it. The strain of the past two years came roaring up all at once.

"You said you'd come back," she sobbed, her tears wetting Sparrow's hair. "You promised. I waited for you. I waited so long."

It wasn't at all what she had meant to say. But she was crashing, spiraling from the exhaustion and terror. She counted out three slow breaths, focusing on the present moment, on her surroundings, on her friends. Her *friends*. Solid and real and wrapped securely in her arms where she'd never let them go again.

Realistically, of course, she had to. Eventually she pulled away and looked at him properly. He was exactly as she remembered him. And she saw that his eyes were wet as well.

"It's... it's good to see you," he said. "We... Starling missed you."

Starling stood up and rubbed at her own eyes, pretending she was only tired. "Don't be stupid. It's only been two weeks, dummy, and you've been talking about her the whole time."

"Two weeks?" Gwendolyn gaped at them. "It's been two years!"

Then she noticed. Sparrow was *exactly* the way she remembered him. A boy just over the edge of thirteen. She was nearly a head taller than him now, and she suddenly realized how easily she'd lain hers on top of his.

Starling hadn't changed either. And Gwendolyn was now much more Starling's age than she was Sparrow's.

Time, Gwendolyn thought. *It moves differently between worlds.*

And it doesn't play fair, said another, more bitter voice inside her.

~~~
~~~

Reunions can be powerful things. They are full of difficult and conflicting emotions. And in such times of profound emotional turmoil, we handle these feelings in a very mature and responsible way.

We absolutely refuse to talk about them.

Instead we stick to safer topics, such as the weather, or if the local sporting boys were able to move a ball around more times than the boys from the town next door.

"You... you look well," said Gwendolyn. "Just the same."

"You don't," said Sparrow. "I mean... You look well, too, just... different. Purple fringe-y dress, new shoes. I like it. And what's this hair about?"

"Oh, this? No." Gwendolyn whipped off the blonde wig and tiara, then tossed them over the railing and off to who knows where. She didn't need them anymore. Still, she couldn't stop a fidgety hand from running over her bare scalp. "So... how have you been?"

"Surviving," said Starling. "You?"

"The same. What's all this?" She gestured to the blankets and food scattered around them. "Where did it all come from?"

"Cyria," Sparrow said with a tiny grin.

"You've been back to Faeoria?" Gwendolyn was stunned, and more than a little jealous. "How is she?"

"Oh, you know," said Starling. "All wrapped up in her work. Always making some new invention or other. We just pass things through the doorway. No sense ticking off the faeries. And she assures us the food is safe." She pulled a necklace out from under her blouse, a glowing red jewel on a fine golden chain. "And we left this in the doorway, remember? We used it to get into the postal hub, and it was still here, just waiting for us."

Gwendolyn vaguely remembered, as the memory was much more distant for her than it was for the other two. "But how did you get here at all?" Gwendolyn asked. "You hopped into a portal after the Blackstar. Without a library to connect to the *Egressai Infinitus*, you should have been thrown out somewhere random."

Starling shrugged, and leaned against a tall wing-backed armchair. "I don't know what to tell you. We hopped through that portal, and woke up sprawled in the courtyard here. No sign of the Blackstar, or your..." Starling looked at Gwendolyn, hesitated, then changed the subject. She glanced around at the others, who all looked reluctant to butt in on what was clearly not their business. "You can all sit down. Sorry about the mess."

They did, gratefully. If there was one thing the loft was designed for, it was comfort. Ian let out a little moan as he sank into a squashy club chair.

"So, uh, who are you guys?" Sparrow said. "You look like you're ready for a party."

"Just came from a couple, thanks," Tommy said.

"We're a little partied out." Jessica loosened her red neckerchief.

"Speak for yourself," said Ian. "I'm *never* partied out."

Gwendolyn chose a sofa for herself. "These are my other friends. And Cecelia."

Cecilia gave a sarcastic little smile. The others waved nervously.

Starling eased into the chair she'd been leaning against. "Gwendolyn has told us... well, pretty much nothing about you. Sorry, we've never had tons of time for talk."

"That's fine. She's told us all about you," Jessica said. "We just thought you were imaginary."

"So did we," said Sparrow. "But that's a whole other thing."

Starling nodded. "You guys have clearly been through some stuff. Care to share?"

There is always a certain amount of awkwardness when you bring together friends from different parts of your life. You hope they get along with each other, but there is always the strangeness of being pulled in both directions. Fortunately, as Starling got the others started on their story, the barriers began to fall. Sparrow took the opportunity to sit on the sofa, and he scooted closer to Gwendolyn until their sides were touching.

"Hey," he said, gently.

"Hey," Gwendolyn said back. It came out weak, and a little trembly.

"It's good to see you." He paused and seemed to notice her exhaustion. "Are you all right?"

"Almost. I'm just paying the price."

He cocked his head. "Of what?"

"Never mind," she said, leaning over and resting her head on the top of his. "As long as *you're* all right."

"We're fine," he said, playfully shrugging her off and fixing his mussed hair. "So... two years, huh?"

Gwendolyn frowned, and nodded. "Yes. Two weeks for you?"

Sparrow nodded back. "Yeah. Sorry it took so long. We didn't mean to."

Gwendolyn's insides clenched. "It's fine."

Sparrow waved at the piles of books. "We've been trying to pick up the Blackstar's trail on different worlds. Starling's tried altering her portal detector to track the Blackstar's energy, but we've been shooting in the dark. We ended up on this one world where *everyone* knew magic, and there was this whole school about it, and all the kids just kept cursing each other all the time, and the teachers were *real* lax about safety. Starling hated it, but I thought it was kind of fun. Then there was this other world with a talking lion, and it was really cold, and then it wasn't, but we didn't stay there long. Starling's favorite was the one with the submarine and the giant squid, but I liked the one with the dinosaurs in the theme park. Do you know what a dinosaur is? I didn't. Turns out they're giant lizardy-bird things that try to squish you, but they were really cool, and—"

Gwendolyn laughed.

"What?" he said.

"You. You're babbling."

"Oh." He slumped. "Sorry. You could have stopped me."

"I didn't want to. It was nice."

"Oh... okay." But he still seemed crestfallen.

"Did you find any mermaids?" she said, as much to cheer him up as anything. "I've always wanted to meet one."

"No, sorry. But I think we've got a lead on your parents." He retrieved the book on the floor they'd been looking at. "Starling picked up some energy from this one." The cover was grey as a storm cloud, with swirling red designs on it.

Gwendolyn took it. "I think I know this one." The crimson letters on the front read *In the Court of the Queen of Blood*. She flipped through it. Sure enough, there was Jack Lazarus and his gang of pickpockets, getting in and out of trouble and generally being a regular scoundrel. Guilt squeezed her belly.

But then the words on the page began to move. Not vanishing, as when the Collector erased things. The words rearranged. The first half seemed the same, but the second half was rewriting itself. The story wasn't erasing—it was changing. There was no longer any mention of Jack's name.

The Blackstar. Had this been his intention? To cut Jack's story short? To stop him, before he could play a larger role in her own? Gwendolyn filed that away for later and closed the book. A girl could only take so much, after all.

The book, however, was not done changing. The letters on the front twisted and shifted, then glowed a bright green.

Come and find me.

She gaped at it. It was the same message she had gotten in the Home.

Then she noticed that the others were all looking at her.

"What?" Gwendolyn said, setting the book down.

"Well?" Jessica asked. "What do we do now?"

"I don't know," she said, the truth leaping out without asking for permission first.

The City kids exchanged sudden alarmed glances.

Fantastic, Gwendolyn thought sourly. They all looked up to her. She didn't want to be the grown-up in the room. She was exhausted enough just trying to manage herself. The thought of everyone relying on her was nearly enough to trigger an anxiety attack.

Missy seemed to notice, and spoke up. "You need to find the Blackstar."

"That guy who attacked us. This Starling girl filled us in," Ian added.

Gwendolyn nodded. Starling would know what to do. "Do you have any idea where he is?"

"Uh, not really. That vampire book was our only lead on the Blackstar. But from what your friends told us, you already met him and he ran off again. There's no telling what story he jumped into."

"Wait," said Tommy. "Jumping into stories?"

"Yeah, that's what all these worlds are," Sparrow said, gesturing to the library around them. "Every book has a code in the back. You dial it into that doorway, and poof, off you go."

"Although the Blackstar doesn't seem to need it," Starling said. "He's got some device that lets him create portals."

"Yes, I saw that," Gwendolyn said.

"I've tinkered with my own portal detector, calibrated it to hone in on the specific energy signature his device gives off. But Gwendolyn, he..." Starling trailed off.

"What?"

Sparrow answered, his tone flat. "He's killing people."

"Yes," Starling said. "Not just people. Heroes."

"What do you mean?"

"We've managed to track him down three times in the past weeks. Each time, he goes right for the hero of whatever story he's in. Each time, he kills them. And each time, we haven't been able to stop him."

"Like that poor wizard kid, the disfigured one. He was only eleven, Gwen. He didn't stand a chance. When we came back... his story had changed, and... everything turned out wrong." Sparrow said.

"Just like in Umberland," Gwendolyn said. *Just like with Jack.*

Starling nodded. "No more heroes. The bad guys win. Remove the hero, before they can complete their missions. Stop the story in its tracks and set it on a different course."

Gwendolyn remembered a conversation she'd had with Cyria Kytain. "The Blackstar is an agent of the Abscess. That darkness between worlds. This must be his mission. This is... this is why he came after me."

"Oh, so you're a *hero* now?" Cecilia said. She snorted in disgust.

"You're darn right she is!" Sparrow shouted, leaping to his feet.

Gwendolyn tried to ignore this, to keep from blushing. "Regardless, we have to stop him. Trouble is, we don't know which book he jumped into."

"So, would this help?" From his pocket, Tommy pulled out a crumpled piece of paper and smoothed it out.

"What's that?" Gwendolyn snatched it from him.

"I dunno," Tommy said. "It fell outta his book when that Blackstar bloke threw me across the room."

Gwendolyn's mouth fell open. "Tommy, you're amazing."

Tommy beamed.

"This must be where he was headed next." Gwendolyn pointed to the top margin of the page. "There's a title. *Tautopolis.*" She smiled. "The page fell out, huh? That's what he gets for bending back the spine."

"That monster," Starling said. "Here, let me see." She took the page and shook her wrist gauntlet free of her sleeve. It was a black leather cuff that went halfway up her forearm. The device was covered in tiny metal gears and components. She pressed a button and a round metal cover flipped open like a pocket watch, but revealing far more hands and numbers than anyone would ever need just to tell the time.

Starling held the page next to it, and the largest hand on the dial spun to point directly at it. The gauntlet let out a soft mechanical chime. One of three tiny bulbs glowed a warm yellow. Starling flipped the cover closed. "This has traces of the Blackstar's energy on it. I think. If I've calibrated this correctly."

"Then we can use this to follow him!"

"But we don't have the code," Sparrow said.

Gwendolyn gestured to the library around them. "Yes, but there must be a full copy in here somewhere! And that will have the code on the back cover. Then we can dial it into the *Egressai Infinitus* and follow him."

Starling frowned. "It doesn't sound like any of the titles we've seen so far. It must be in a part of the library we haven't explored yet."

"We'll help you find it," Missy chimed in.

"Yeah," Tommy said. "How hard could it be?"

Everyone looked out at the near infinite expanse of the Library of All Wonder.

"That's a joke, right?" said Ian.

"I've got it." Sparrow put two fingers to his lips and whistled. For a moment, nothing happened. Then a little book cart came clanking up the stairs, mechanical wheels extending and retracting to get it up each step.

"What's that supposed to be?" Cecilia asked.

"Help." Sparrow knelt down and showed it the page the Blackstar had dropped. "Can you take us here?"

The cart didn't move. Then it started trembling. And then it simply fell over.

"I'll take that as a no," Sparrow said.

"So, maybe tracking down a single random page was too much to ask for." Gwendolyn set the book cart up again. "Can you take us to books *like* this one?"

The cart spun in a little circle and headed back down the stairs.

Gwendolyn looked at the others. "Well?"

Tommy sprang up. "We're ready to go. Just point us."

"Already?" Ian said. "I just sat down."

Sparrow snorted. "Welcome to adventure. Doesn't give you lots of time to rest."

Jessica gave Ian a soft kick in the shin. "Time is of the essence. You saw that man. There's no telling what he might do if Gwendolyn can't find him."

"All right, no need for kicking, I was only kidding."

Cecilia scoffed and kicked her feet up on her couch. "I'm not joining any mystery-solving gangs with you oddlings."

"Suit yourself," Gwendolyn said.

"Oh, I plan to," she replied. She put her hands behind her head and closed her eyes.

And with that, the other six headed down the stairs and into the stacks.

The paths of books wound endlessly through the Library. There were strange turnings and dead ends, ankle-high shelves to clamber over, archways of shelves to scuttle under. Eventually the book cart stopped and spun in a happy little circle. Two paths branched out ahead of them.

"We've never made it this far before," said Starling. She flipped open the dial on her gauntlet. "No signal either way."

"Right," Gwendolyn said. "Then we split up."

Jessica, Ian, and Missy elected to go with Starling, while Tommy and Sparrow insisted on going with Gwendolyn. Then they set off down their respective paths.

"So what are we looking for, Freckles?" Tommy said after they had walked a ways.

"Freckles?" Sparrow said. "Since when do you let anyone call you Freckles?"

"It's only Tommy," Gwendolyn said, eying the changing shelves around her.

"Yeah, it's just me."

"Well, only *I* get to call her Gwen," Sparrow shot back.

"To be fair, I don't actually *let* either of you call me those things, you both just keep doing it. Now stay focused. Remember, we're looking for *Tautopolis*."

This section of the library seemed different than the others. These were no proud and proper leather-bound volumes, but beaten and weathered paperbacks. The books on the shelves leaned haphazardly or lounged lazily on their sides. Some weren't even on shelves, but stacked in enormous, cobwebbed towers that threatened to topple and bury them in mounds of literature. The titles were mostly a single word and said things like *Unwoven, Nighttouched,* or *Obsidious*. They seemed to ooze blackness and discontent.

"We're getting close," Gwendolyn said.

"Good work, *Gwen*," Tommy said, smirking at Sparrow. He bumped him with his shoulder.

"Stop it," Sparrow snapped.

"*You* stop it," Tommy shot back.

"Tommy, stop arguing, he's just a boy—" Gwendolyn stopped in her tracks, but it was too late. The words were out of her mouth. She turned. Sparrow had frozen several paces back, the hurt plainly written on his face.

"Sparrow, I'm sorry—"

"I'm not *just* anything," he said, and stormed off down another path.

Gwendolyn stared after him for a long second. Then she whirled on Tommy. "Why don't you grow up?" Then she ran after Sparrow, leaving Tommy standing there, slack-jawed.

CHAPTER FOURTEEN

THE FOREST OF IDEAS

"**S**parrow!" Gwendolyn called as she jogged along the shelves, pushing the silver circlet up her arm as it slid down. She wasn't sure what had hurt him worse, the *just* or the *boy*. Probably both. The fact that he'd once said something similar to her did not make her feel any better.

After several minutes of wandering around, Gwendolyn had to admit that she was lost. No sign of Sparrow. No book to help her find her parents. She growled in frustration and ran a hand over her bare scalp. Nothing for it but to keep going.

The Library grew even wilder the deeper she went. At one point she reached an actual stream, the water trickling merrily through a channel carved into the stone floor. The bottom of the stream fluttered with pages that sprouted like seaweed. She crossed over it on a bridge made of more book-lined shelves.

She had no idea how far she went. A dreamy sort of haze fell over her. She found herself in a forest of tall cylindrical shelves. She ran a hand along them, and they spun lazily. As they did, words flew off and floated in the air.

Come and find me.

The path led her down a steep hill. It was growing darker, and she could no longer see more than a few feet in any direction. The cylindrical shelves grew taller. They held fewer books, their wood became rougher, and suddenly they were more like actual trees, with books stuffed into their hollows and perched precariously on their branches.

Deeper still, and the books became leaves. The trees grew slender and more graceful. Moonlight glimmered off their silver bark. A pale mist crept along the ground.

And Gwendolyn realized she was no longer in her Library, but in an actual forest. Leaves crunched under her thin silver slippers, which glittered in the moonlight just as the trees did.

More than that—her shoes and the silver leaves and vines on her dress were actually glowing, casting a pale light of their own around her, illuminating the mist.

Above her, twinkling rivers of stars glowed merrily. She saw galaxies and nebulae and clouds of burning starstuff. She could feel the magic in the air, strong, but somehow soft as well.

Eventually she stopped. Though her shoes were magically soft, the feet inside them were tired, and Gwendolyn sat down on a fallen log. This place reminded her of Faeoria, but less wild. Faeoria was fierce and untamed. This place had the feeling of a mother's comforting hand upon your shoulder.

Her breathing deepened. Her awareness sharpened. Thoughts slipped like water from her mind. All became quiet, outside and in.

"Hello, Gwendolyn," said a soft voice.

She whirled.

A woman sat next to her.

She was the most beautiful woman Gwendolyn had ever seen. It was a natural, honest beauty, not the glittering glamour of the faeries. Her features were delicate, her lips full, and everything about her was soft and serene. The tip of her nose turned up ever so slightly, adding a hint of playfulness to her regal air. She had blue eyes, like chips of ice, cool and clear and sharp.

Her long, red hair shimmered like silk. It was perfectly straight, and dark as blood. On some worlds, she might have been a star of the stage and screen. On others, wars would have been fought over her beauty. But here she sat, with no hint of pride or vanity. Just a look of quiet anticipation.

The woman's sudden appearance should have made Gwendolyn shriek or cry out. But the moment she met the woman's eyes, a powerful wave of calm crashed over her. The feeling or peace and comfort was so overwhelming that it made her gasp, and it was all she could do not to lay her head in this woman's lap and bury her face in the soft folds of her lacy white dress. Instead, Gwendolyn took a long breath, drinking in the woman's presence. The crisp smell of the forest filled her up from head to toe.

Gwendolyn exhaled, feeling all her muscles relax. "I know you," was all she could think to say.

"Of course." The woman's lips did not move, but the corner of her mouth seemed to wink at Gwendolyn. *"I have been with you from the beginning."*

"Your voice. It's in my head." The sensation was nearly beyond description. It felt like the cool side of her pillow on a warm night.

The woman nodded. *"As am I."*

More words spilled out of Gwendolyn. "You spoke to me. In the In-Between. And I saw you during the battle with Mister Zero. You were there for me."

"Always." The other corner of the woman's mouth crept up to complete the smile, and it made Gwendolyn smile in return. The woman gestured to the forest around them, and Gwendolyn noticed what she hadn't before. The slender silver trees all had small, emerald leaves. Leaves she was very familiar with.

"The leaves. They're ideas, aren't they? Cyria helped me figure that out. There was always an idea when I needed one. This is... it's a whole *forest* of ideas."

The woman just kept smiling.

"You've been there since the first day, when I made the leaf in my hair."

"And before. When you were a lonely child. When you sat, and you dreamed. When your head was so full of ideas there wasn't room for anything else."

Gwendolyn looked around. "The Forest of Ideas. Are we still in the Library?"

"You are," the woman said. *"But my realm exists within."*

"Within what? The Library?"

"Merely... within."

Gwendolyn didn't know what *that* was supposed to mean. "Who are you?"

The woman gestured to the leaves again.

Gwendolyn frowned. "You're... ideas?"

Pride radiated from her. *"I am creation. I am Cyria's inventions. I am your own first scribblings. I bring dreams to the dreamers, inspiration to the artists, and magic to the children who need it most."*

The words flowed through Gwendolyn's mind like the melody of a familiar song. "But what do I call you?"

The woman's sapphire eyes bored into Gwendolyn's own emerald ones. It was like staring into the Figment again. *"What would you like me to be?"*

"What?"

"All my children must name me for themselves. Am I the childlike empress of the fantastic? Or a good witch of the north? Or a triad of Who, and What, and Which?"

Gwendolyn thought about that for a moment. "I think... I think you're too big for a name." A rhyme sprang from Gwendolyn's lips, one that had come to her once before. "Lady of Light. Woman in White. A gentle whisper in the night."

The woman nodded. *"As good a name as any."*

Gwendolyn frowned. "A bit long, though."

The Lady opened her mouth and laughed, the first real sound she had made, and it was a tinkling of bells that warmed Gwendolyn right down to her toes. She couldn't help it—she laughed as well. They laughed together, and years-old burdens fell from her shoulders. She felt so light she could fly.

The laughter trickled off. *"The Lady of Light, then,"* came the voice in Gwendolyn's head. *"Light gives life. Light, gives. It shines and shares and never takes. I am all who give, who make, who share their light."*

"But..." Gwendolyn said, a thought occurring to her. "You're not alone. Light creates shadows. There's the other. The dark man I saw in the In-Between."

The woman's smile melted. *"Yes. And you already have a name for him."*

She did. "The Abscess. Light and dark. You are creation. He is destruction."

"No," the Lady said. *"He does not destroy. He takes. He collects. He consumes."*

Gwendolyn was puzzled. "But I thought Mister Zero was the Abscess."

The Lady's voice grew sad. *"That poor possessed boy. A puppet. An extension of the Abscess' will. A governor to keep your world in line."*

"But then, in Tohk. The shadows that attacked us."

"The Abscess in his purest form. Feeding on everything in its path."

"I... I don't understand."

The Lady raised her hand to the sky, her sleeve falling away from her milk white arm. *"Look between the stars. What do you see?"*

"I see... darkness..." Gwendolyn kept looking. "There's so much of it."

"Yet there are places that burn bright and keep the dark at bay."

Gwendolyn looked at the glittering stars. "Places like Tohk. Like Faeoria. Those... those are *your* worlds."

"They are the light bringers. My children." She gestured to the stars strewn across the sky like a river of light.

"Like Cyria said. Similar worlds group together. And... then there are worlds like Umberland. Where the vampires just...

consume."

The woman lowered her arm sadly. *"Yes. Those worlds belong to the dark."*

"Like the Blackstar! He takes things for the Abscess. And... and the City. Everyone being drained. All those ideas, all that energy. All of it feeding the Abscess."

The Lady nodded. *"Oh, how he loved your world. It fed him well."*

"But," Gwendolyn said. "What's so special about my world?"

The Lady gestured at the stars again. *"You have seen that there are different kinds of worlds. There are worlds of magic, where the energy of creation is strong."*

"Like Faeoria."

She nodded. *"One of the strongest. And there are worlds of mind, where magic is weak, but invention and intellect rule. Magicians are rare, but artists and creators abound."*

"Like Tohk. It was harder to use my magic there."

"Just so. But your world was special. Your world was both. A place of magic and mind. A place of unusual power and potential."

"I think I felt that," Gwendolyn said. "It would explain a lot about my life the last few years."

"It gave you the power to do what you have done. And the Abscess wanted that power. He brought about the fall of your world. It turned to the dark, and one of my most precious jewels became one of his most potent sources of power."

"Everyone feeding him through the Lambents."

"And the people were more than happy to do so. Easy to manage with his puppet boy, simple to preserve with his faceless men."

Gwendolyn went silent again, trying to process it all. Then she snapped her fingers. "It's like bees!"

The Woman in White arched a delicate eyebrow.

"Yes," Gwendolyn said, the words bubbling out of her. "The Mister Men are drones. They collect the honey, and keep the hive in line. Mister Zero was the queen, running the hive. And the Abscess... he's the beekeeper. All the hives belong to him. And he takes *all* the honey."

The Lady smiled. *"I love you, Gwendolyn."*

The words were sudden and unexpected, but did not seem strange. They felt familiar as her own name.

"That imagination of yours. No one has described the essence of darkness as a beekeeper before. Yet it is simple, and true, my clever girl. Your world no longer belongs to the Abscess. You saved it. Then you changed it."

Gwendolyn fidgeted. "Well, I didn't do it alone. You helped."

"A bit," the Lady said. *"I cannot interfere much. Those are the rules of our story. When the Abscess and I meet..."* She trailed off.

"It weakens you."

"And him as well. When you have traveled through the In-Between, he has tried to take you. Stopping him is... costly. But necessary. He does not always play by the rules."

Thoughts clicked together like puzzle pieces. "That's why I didn't see him on my way into Umberland. He was weaker, because the City doesn't belong to him anymore. And after Tohk..."

"We fought, and we were weakened. You were truly on your own for the first time." That smile again. *"And you did splendidly. You started the change your City needed. You brought Tohk back from the darkness. Had the Abscess been at his full strength, you never*

could have ripped an entire world from his grasp. But he broke the rules, which left me free to act. I gave you the chance you needed."

Gwendolyn nodded. "You did other things, too, I think."

The woman waved a dismissive hand. *"A nudge, here and there. The least I can do. And the most."*

"When I came back from Tohk... you made sure my parents didn't notice I was gone. And you healed my wrist after the battle in the O.R.B. And Sparrow and Starling, you put them in the Library."

She shrugged. *"Safe returns to your own bed... lost items found again... perhaps a whisper in the inventress' ear. Rules can be bent. A little deus ex machina never hurt anyone."* And she grinned a girlish grin, one that scrunched her upturned nose. *"Sometimes you have to be a little bit naughty."*

She paused, and held a finger to her lips in thought. *"It has been some time since I spoke so much. You are one of my chattier heroes."* She stood and took a few steps into the forest.

Gwendolyn sat on the log, uncertain, until the Lady glanced back at her. She got up to follow, and trod alongside, comfortable as old friends. "The City is back to what it was before Mister Zero," Gwendolyn said as the Lady led her between the trees.

"And now they have a choice. To create, or consume. To give, or to take. Dear Cyria was right. People's lives are stories. People who spread stories, ideas, and inspiration... they create hope."

"I thought it created change?"

The lady looked upward at the branches full of ideas. *"What is hope, but the hope that something will change? Hoping for things to be different? There can be no progress without change. Nothing can get better if everything stays the same."* The Lady turned and her stare was so intense that Gwendolyn felt her heart stop beating. *"Bring change,"* she whispered into Gwendolyn's mind. *"Bring hope."*

"But... I'm finished. The City is fixed. Everything is different now."

"There are always those who want things back the way they were. Back when everything was perfect, though nothing ever was. That is why I have you. My changelings. My heroes. Bringing worlds to the light, and keeping them from falling back into darkness. The Abscess will return. Even now, his fingers are creeping back into your world."

Gwendolyn's head was spinning. "This is... this is quite a lot."

"That is why I waited until now."

Gwendolyn thought. And thought. And thought. There was no sound, save for the crunching of leaves under their feet. "So, you are the spirit of creation. The Abscess is the spirit of... greed, we'll say. Taking and keeping, versus creating and sharing. You have different worlds, and you try to win them from each other. My world, in particular. But you can't confront each other directly, so you need pieces you can move around the chess board. You have... me."

The Lady simply looked at her, waiting.

Gwendolyn nodded to herself. "And the Abscess has his own pieces. The Blackstar. He's not like Mister Zero or the others. He's like me. But... a dark me. And you need me to, what? Protect the City? Win you more worlds? Stop the Blackstar from killing heroes, changing stories, and turning more worlds toward the Abscess?"

The Lady gave her another blue stare. *"I need you to be yourself."*

Gwendolyn snorted. "I wish I knew who that was."

The stare did not let up. *"Then you must find out."*

Gwendolyn turned away from the Lady's gaze. "But... when am I finished? When is it over?" Even the peace of the Forest of Ideas couldn't stop a sudden rush of memories. The fear and anxiety and danger. The manic swings, the soul-sucking bouts of depression that kept her glued to the couch for days on end.

"How long do I have to fight? The City doesn't really need me. It has people like Jessica, and that Zelda woman. I... I just want my parents back. I want to be with my friends. I just want to be a normal girl for once."

"If that is your wish. Farewell, Gwendolyn." The Lady turned and strode away, the mist swirling around her.

"Wait, just like that? Where are you going?"

The woman stopped, one hand resting against the silvery bark of a tree. She looked up at the stars. *"I have no use for normal, well-behaved little girls. I need girls of cleverness and courage and trouble and mischief and above all, imagination. Girls who go down rabbit holes, travel yellow brick roads, and tell stories to lost boys. Girls who wrinkle time, and bring lions back to life. And some who simply stay in green houses, but bring change and hope to everyone they meet, simply by being themselves."* And she gave a little laugh. *"Oh, you redheads."*

Gwendolyn frowned and looked away.

The woman turned, her face in profile. *"Normal is not a thing you have ever wanted to be. But if you would give up yourself to be what others want, then that is your choice."*

Gwendolyn sagged against a nearby tree, slumped to the

ground, and hung her head. "It's too much. It's all too much."

The Lady took a long, slow breath. Her voice took on a weariness that matched Gwendolyn's own. *"And you have more to come. Things will get harder before they get easier."*

The words cut deep. She leaned her head back against the tree, closed her eyes, and tried to relax the sudden tightness in her chest. "I'm not sure how much more I can do."

There was a crunching of leaves as the Lady knelt in front of Gwendolyn. *"I cannot change your story. We each must write our own."*

Gwendolyn opened her eyes, and a bit of heat crept into her voice. "That's it? Can you tell me where my parents are? Can you tell me how to get them back? Or how to beat the Blackstar? Fight the Abscess? Can you tell me how to get Sparrow and Starling home?"

And this time it was the Lady who turned away, her expression pained. *"No."*

"So what can you tell me?"

The Lady turned back, meeting her with those piercing blue eyes. *"Be yourself. Do your best."*

Gwendolyn crossed her arms. "That is spectacularly unhelpful."

The woman chuckled. She waved her hand, and a leaf drifted down from the tops of the trees to land in her outstretched palm. *"I didn't say they were all good ideas."*

Gwendolyn sighed. "So I guess I'm on my own."

The Lady took Gwendolyn by the hand.

"Haven't you learned?"

And she kissed the place where the vampire queen had bitten it.

Her lips were incredibly soft, and a warmth seeped into Gwendolyn's skin as it knitted itself back together. Then the Lady looked up at her.

"You are never alone."

For the first time, the Lady's lips actually moved, and Gwendolyn heard the words with her ears as well as her heart. The Lady placed the leaf into Gwendolyn's hand and closed the girl's fingers around it.

"For later." She spoke in Gwendolyn's mind again, and winked like the twinkling of a star.

Then she stood and walked away, drifting gracefully through the forest, caressing each tree in turn and humming a tune that was at once mournful and full of hope. It reverberated through the woods and faded into the mist along with the Lady herself.

CHAPTER FIFTEEN

WITHERING TRIALS

Gwendolyn sat there, soaking in the peace of the Forest of Ideas. Eventually, sunlight began to color the horizon. She enjoyed that feeling of stillness for a moment. The feeling of being just her own self, and nothing more. Inhale. Exhale. And just... be.

As the sunbeams crept between the slender trees, she knew she had to be going. At least she felt a bit better. It had been a while since she'd taken the time to center herself. She had neglected her meditation exercises for quite some time, but now she felt balanced. She felt whole.

"But if I don't get back soon, who knows how long I'll have been away. They might all be older than me when I get back. Or even younger than before."

She stood up, and carefully tucked the Lady's leaf into the pocket of her dress. Gwendolyn looked around, but could not tell which direction she had come from.

But an exceptionally tiny leaf drifted down and landed on her shoulder, and suddenly she knew exactly which way to go. She brushed the little idea from her shoulder and made her way back through the steadily lightening forest until the trees gave way to books, and she was back in the Library of All Wonder.

"Hello?" she called. "I'm back!"

"Didn't know you were gone." Sparrow stood to one side, leaning against a bookshelf.

Gwendolyn went to him, knelt down, then took both of his hands in hers.

"I'm sorry. Really. You're not just a boy. I shouldn't have said that, and I shouldn't have thought it."

He didn't respond. He couldn't meet her eyes.

"I..." Gwendolyn took a deep breath. "I still love you, you know. I could never not."

Even looking away from her, she could see his eyes were glistening. "I know," he said. "And... me too. But you're... it's different now. You've changed."

"I haven't. I really haven't," she said. "I'm still me."

He turned and looked her full in the face, his brown eyes wide and wet. "I didn't need another big sister. I needed you. I wasn't even gone very long, but you did it anyway."

"Did what?" Gwendolyn said. "Whatever it is, I didn't mean it."

He didn't answer. He looked away again, a tear rolling down his cheek.

Gwendolyn spoke as tenderly as she could, searching for the right words, and finding them in a quote from one of her favorite stories. *"Boy, why are you crying?"*

"You grew up." He sniffed. "You grew up without me."

"I'm sorry," Gwendolyn repeated. "I never wanted to. Never. Growing up is no fun at all, and I would take it all back in a heartbeat. But I had to, at least a little. I was all on my own. You don't know what it was like."

"Two years..." he said.

"And then some," she added, sadly.

"That's a long time. You're sixteen now?"

Gwendolyn looked down and away. "Almost." She stood up, pulled him closer, and interlaced their fingers. "Cheer up. Once we get my parents back, I won't be in charge of *anything* anymore. We can find your home, and I can be just as reckless and impulsive and irresponsible as ever. How does that sound?"

He wiped his nose. "Do you promise? You swear on a badger tea party?"

"I swear by all the badger tea parties in the universe. Now come on. We have to find the others. And you're already losing."

"What?"

She shoved him against the shelf and took off running.

"Hey!" he chased after her, laughing.

Gwendolyn ran, looking back over her shoulder, and ran right into a ladder.

"Ow!" She held a hand to her stinging forehead.

"Look out! You nearly knocked me off this bleedin' thing." Tommy was at the top of the ladder, gripping it tightly.

"What the heck are you up there for?" said Sparrow, who had just caught up.

"Beat you," Gwendolyn whispered to him. He elbowed her.

"I found it!" Tommy called triumphantly. He pulled something from the shelf, put his feet on the outside of the ladder, and slid all the way down. "I've got it, look."

It was a black hardback book, with a title in large block letters. *TAUTOPOLIS.*

"This is it," Gwendolyn said. "This is the key to finding my parents. You two, go round everyone up and meet me at the *Egressai Infinitus.*"

"Got it." Sparrow put his fingers to his lips and blew a piercing whistle. Two book carts trundled up to them. "Can you find the others?" Sparrow asked, and the carts trundled away in opposite directions. Tommy and Sparrow fanned out through the shelves, following their respective carts and shouting for the others.

But Gwendolyn had another stop to make. She put her fingers to her lips and blew, but all that came out was a sputtering raspberry. She was glad no one else had heard. Nevertheless, another cart came up and led her to where she wanted to go. To one very specific shelf. With two very specific books.

A green one.

The Marvelous Adventures of Gwendolyn Gray.

And a red one.

The Fantastical Exploits of Gwendolyn Gray.

She shuddered a little just looking at them. It was unnerving to think that all her thoughts and words and deeds had been magically chronicled into these two. Next to them was a book she hadn't seen before, but one she'd been expecting. It had a violet cover, with shimmering black letters.

THE WITHERING TRIALS OF GWENDOLYN GRAY.

Reverently, she took it off the shelf and flipped through it. Sure enough, nearly half the pages were blank, but she found a part where the words were scribbling themselves in, describing Gwendolyn standing in the library and reading a book about herself standing in the library and reading a book about herself standing in the library—

She shut the book. That sort of thing could go on forever. But at least she was holding the correct volume. If she ever wanted to get back home, she'd need the address. And if she wanted to get back at the right *time,* she needed to make sure she wasn't headed into her own past. She flipped to the back of this new one to find the code: *W-T-G-G-1-2.*

"What are you doing?" came a voice.

Gwendolyn jumped, and dropped the book. She spun to see Cecilia Forthright, standing at the end of the row, giving her a suspicious look.

"Nothing," Gwendolyn said quickly. She crammed the violet book back onto the shelf with the other two. "Come on, let's go. We're meeting the others at the entrance." Then she hurried away, not daring to meet Cecilia's eyes. The last thing she needed was Cecilia reading even *more* about her life than she had seen in Gwendolyn's stolen journal.

The entry hall wasn't far. Gwendolyn reached it before any of the others. At the end of the hall, the *Egressai Infinitus* still held black the black and crimson door that led to the world of Umberland. Jack Lazarus' story. A story he was no longer in. Just as Jack would no longer be in her own. She had expected him to play a larger role, like Kolonius Thrash or Cyria Kytain, but the Blackstar had cut all that short.

On the wall beside the door was something like an old-fashioned telephone dial, a circular spinner with letters and numbers. One only had to dial up the right code, and a doorway would appear to take you to any world you wished, provided you knew where you wanted to go. And provided you had a power source. In the center of the dial was a round slot for any one of the magical gems that seemed to be floating around everywhere.

Well, Cyria said that stories had repeated patterns, things that kept showing up on multiple worlds. *Echoes in the ether*, Titania had called it.

Her wait wasn't long. The whole crew arrived: Cecilia, Jessica, Ian, Missy, Tommy, Sparrow, and Starling. They hardly fit into the hallway together. Gwendolyn wondered when exactly she had gotten so many friends. And a Cecilia. Somewhere inside her, a younger Gwendolyn gave a little cheer.

"All right, everybody," Gwendolyn said. "Here we go. Starling, if you please?"

"Sure." Starling took off the necklace and handed her the glowing red gem, Cyria's own stone of power. Gwendolyn put it in the slot and it clicked into place, glowing brighter. She knew what she had to do. She dialed in the code she wanted, and doors began to spin through the frame.

Finally, one door settled into place. It was a plain grey door, with a metal number plate that read *W-T-G-G-1-2*.

"Wait, Gwendolyn, that's the wrong code." said Starling, flipping through *Tautopolis* to the code printed at the back.

"No, it's not." Gwendolyn said. "This is my mission. I don't want any of the rest of you getting hurt. You need to go home. Back to the City."

There was a wave of protest from the others.

"No, stop it, just listen," Gwendolyn looked at Missy and Tommy. These sorts of adventures never turned out well for her City friends. Any one of them could have died right alongside Jack Lazarus.

No, she told herself. *Best to go back to the way things were.* Just her, Sparrow, and Starling.

"It's about to get a lot more dangerous, and I can't very well go traipsing about with a small army of bumbling amateurs. No offense."

"Oh, offense taken," sneered Cecilia.

"You *clearly* don't belong here, and you never wanted to come in the first place," Gwendolyn shot back.

"But we need you," Jessica said. "You fixed the Lambents. You caused the Change, and no one even knows about it! We have to tell everyone! And now the Childkeeper is raiding the Revels. We have to put a stop to it, and you're the best person for the job."

"No," Gwendolyn said firmly. "I've done my part." It came out harsher than she'd meant. But she'd sacrificed enough for the City. It could take care of itself for a while. "I have to find... the Blackstar. Before he kills more heroes." Gwendolyn opened the door, revealing the City's Hall of Records, with its fluorescent lights and rows of books and binders. "In you go."

Tommy crossed his arms. "You can't just—"

"Wait," said Missy. "What's that sound?"

REVELS AND REVELATIONS

They all stopped. Through the doorway they could hear a dull roar, like that of a large crowd. Which was impossible, Gwendolyn reasoned, since there had never been any sort of crowd in the City, and certainly not a large one. It was loud enough to be heard all the way into the Hall of Records and through the magical doorway.

Gwendolyn looked at Sparrow and Starling. Starling shrugged. "May as well check it out."

Gwendolyn's curiosity grew, and she reasoned it might be easier to leave the others behind if she took them outside first, so she led them all out through the Hall of Records and onto the street.

Down the street was the Central Tower. The glass dome atop it was still a collapsed ruin with jagged edges pointing toward the sky. A few dozen people stood at the foot of the tower. They were mostly young, decked out in the sort of clothes she had seen at the Revels, their bright colors screaming for attention.

They wore ribbons and armbands in every color you could

think of. People were dancing, playing music, telling stories. There were artists doing face paintings. A band played on a platform that had been set up near the doors to the tower, and Gwendolyn recognized the singer from her previous trip to the Revels. The atmosphere was like a carnival, which was the strangest thing that had been seen in the City streets since two airships had hovered above this very spot.

"Okay," Tommy said as they waded into the crowd. "What is all this?"

"Why, it's a party, gang!" A young woman stepped toward them. Gwendolyn recognized Zelda, the apparent organizer of the Revels. She wore her shimmering fringe dress and glittering headband again, and had a butterfly painted on her cheek. "This rub is a real sockdollager. And just listen to that canary."

Gwendolyn frowned, and looked at Jessica.

"That means the event is going great, and that lady over there is a good singer," she translated.

"Of course, honey, that's what I said. Is my gab too garbled? I am a bit of a blabber. Can you blame me for fizzing, with all this fantastic fun floating around? It's the very first public Revel!"

"But... isn't that risky?" Gwendolyn asked.

"No better way to stand up to those squares than to show them what a good time they're missing. And no one's more square than the City Council over there." She jerked a thumb toward the Central Tower.

Then Zelda's eyes brightened. "Hey, Wendy, isn't it? Golly, you've had a bit of a haircut. Bold. I like it! I'm just giggled that you came! Your stories are the bee's knees, the ant's uncle, *and* the cat's pajamas. You're going to sling one on us later, right, gal?"

"Uh—"

"Well, can't stand here bumping gums with you gems and gents all day. Somebody's gotta make sure this rip-roaring Revel keeps ring-a-ding-dinging. Ta!" And she left in a whirl of fringe.

Jessica was grinning. "Isn't she the best?"

Gwendolyn tried to regain some sense of equilibrium. "She's something, I suppose."

"Yeah," Tommy added. "I don't know what, but whatever it is, it's a lot."

"Well, enjoy the party, but the three of us have a mission," Gwendolyn said, nodding back toward the Hall of Records. "

"Tell that to the kid," Cecilia said.

"What?" Gwendolyn looked around, but Sparrow had already wandered off. She spotted him talking with an artist who was chalking giant pictures of animals on the pavement.

She sighed. "Don't worry, I'll get him." She started pushing her way through the crowd.

When she reached the edge of the circle of onlookers, Gwendolyn couldn't help but stop and admire the portraits. But more than that, she noticed how... *happy* Sparrow looked, babbling away at the young man with the chalk who was busy adding a trunk to a life-size elephant.

Had she been like that? Darting off into crowds, starting conversations with complete strangers, confident that nothing truly bad could happen?

Sparrow laughed at something the artist said, his expression free from the worries that weighed heavier on Gwendolyn each day.

He had the softened look of someone who would be hungry, but have someone to find food for you. To be tired, and have someone to tuck you in. To make mistakes, and trust that there would be someone there to help you clean them up.

"He's really quite good, isn't he?"

Gwendolyn turned and blinked in surprise as she saw Miss Sahida, standing next to her and watching the elephant take shape. She was resplendent in a vermilion dress and wrapped in yards of heavily embroidered saffron fabric.

"Oh! Umm... hello," Gwendolyn said. "I—I'm surprised to see you here." She suddenly remembered that she was a bit of a fugitive in the City, and as nice as she seemed, Miss Sahida had been the one who'd sent her to the Home for Unclaimed Children in the first place.

Miss Sahida smiled without looking away from the artist at work. "I had to see what all the fuss was about. I may be a Schoolteacher, but we're not *all* Mr. Percival." Her smile faded, and she turned to Gwendolyn. "I'm surprised to see you too. And glad of it. I wanted to say..." She paused, and took a steadying breath. "I wanted to say, I'm sorry. For sending you to that awful place. I had just received quite a shock, and didn't handle the situation as well I should have. At any rate, I can't say I'm disappointed to find you here, out and about."

Gwendolyn was stunned. "I... erm, thank you," was as much as she could muster.

Just then, a roar went up from the crowd, and not a happy one. The band had been forced off their platform, and in their place stood a group of men who clearly thought themselves to be quite important. Gwendolyn recognized Mr. Pump, the head of the City Council.

"Excuse me, please," Gwendolyn said. She darted forward, grabbed Sparrow by the hand, and pulled him through the crowd as it gathered at the foot of the platform. She found the others there.

"What's going on?" Gwendolyn asked Missy.

"I don't know, but whatever it is, I don't think it's going to be pleasant."

"—and these shenanigans are completely out of order!" Mr. Pump was shouting, red in the face. Standing next to him was none other than the Childkeeper.

A group of her charges stood on the ground in front of the platform, looking more like a line of statues than orphans. She had another shock when she noticed Mister Zero, front and center. *No, she corrected herself. Not Mister Zero. His name is Bill, and he was just as much a victim of the Abscess as I am. Even more so.*

"We need to return to the values of the past, where order and discipline ruled the day," Mr. Pump continued.

"We *are* the values of the past!" came Zelda's voice, followed by a chorus of cheers. "You're the chowder heads who mucked it all up!"

"Lies!" Mr. Pump's face reddened further. He adjusted his horn-rimmed spectacles. "The Lambents that used to keep our City running smoothly have been corrupted. They spread misinformation and falsehoods. They put dangerous ideas into your heads, turning all our children into hooligans and hoodlums."

At a wave from the Childkeeper, the children in front of the platform began to sing. It was a wordless song, a chorus of voices providing a somber backdrop to emphasize Mr. Pump's speech.

"Rest assured, we have found a way to repair them. We will return to a time when our School ensured that every child would be a productive worker. I remember a City where everything was calm, and everyone knew their place. The old ways are the best ways."

"Aw, blow it out your nose!" someone shouted, to more cheers.

But Mr. Pump kept right on going, the children's haunting voices adding a sense of great weight and importance. "Productive achievement is man's noblest activity. These idle miscreants who spend their time cavorting and reveling must be stopped, so they can no longer drain our limited resources with their frivolous *art*." He spat the word like it was something filthy that had crawled into his mouth.

"We must be guided by reason, not emotion, and we cannot allow that reason to be clouded by lies about a war and a wasteland. These *creators* create nothing but trouble. To that end, the City Council has voted to outlaw all gatherings of these so-called artists—"

The crowd erupted into jeers and boos, and Mr. Pump spent nearly a full minute sputtering and shouting before he could make himself heard again.

"—anyone found in violation of this law will be privileged to join the new factory effort to replenish our supplies of food, water, and energy. Any children will be taken under the care of the Childkeeper, as their parents are clearly unfit to raise them properly."

The Childkeeper nodded in polite acknowledgment. "I see some very young faces in the crowd," and her gaze came dangerously close to Gwendolyn. "You have been terribly misled, children. That cannot be tolerated."

"Together," Mr. Pump continued, and the orphan's voices rose in a dramatic crescendo, "we can return to an era of peace, prosperity, and productivity. Where every Cityzen knows their place in the machine of our economy, and ensures the future of our great City!"

On his final word, someone close to Gwendolyn hurled a rotten tomato at the stage. It hit Mr. Pump square in the face with a wet *squish.*

The crowd went silent, along with the singing children.

Mr. Pump's face grew even redder than the sickly-looking vegetable. Droplets of juice dangled off the edge of his nose. "Who threw that?" he roared.

No one said anything. The silence was oppressive.

Then, to Gwendolyn's horror, Ian stepped forward.

"Ah-ha! The guilty party!" Mr. Pump shouted. The Childkeeper tutted and shook her head in disappointment.

Ian seemed just as shocked as everyone else. "What? No, it wasn't me, someone pushed me—"

"Mr. Pump, this seems like an ideal opportunity to demonstrate our new policy," the Childkeeper said.

"What? Oh, yes, of course, Charlotte—I mean, Ms. Childkeeper, er—"

The Childkeeper ignored his blubbering and descended the steps.

"Lady, I promise, it wasn't me—" Ian said.

"There will be no need for you to speak." The Childkeeper looked disapprovingly at him over her cat's-eye glasses. She nodded to her group of children, and two of the older ones stepped forward. Then she turned back to Ian. "Come with me, please. You will be taken care of."

Ian shook his head. "No, thank you, I'll just be going home now, enjoy your salad—"

Quick as a cat, the Childkeeper whipped a Lambent from her pocket. There was a flash of white light, and Ian collapsed. The two orphans caught him under the arms as he fell, and dragged him toward the others at the foot of the stage.

The spell of silence broke, and the crowd erupted in an angry roar.

"Leave him alone!" someone shouted, and it sounded remarkably like Miss Sahida. But the Childkeeper gestured at the orphans, and they all headed toward the doors of the Central Tower, hauling the unconscious Ian with them. All except Bill, who stood unmoving, staring at the Childkeeper.

A group of older boys rushed the stage, but the Childkeeper waved her Lambent at them, and they crumpled to the ground as well. Gwendolyn thought she noticed a flicker of white in Bill's eyes.

Jessica screamed in wordless fury, but Tommy and Missy held her back.

"Take a look at them," Tommy said, nodding to the unconscious teenagers on the pavement. "You wanna end up like that? Don't be daft!"

Gwendolyn simply stood there, stunned. That Lambent. It was

just as they had been before the Change. Mr. Pump said they'd found a way to "repair" them. And there was Bill, the former Mister Zero standing at the base of his former place of power. The boy who had unwittingly powered the mind-sucking Lambents in the first place.

"Go back to the School, children," the Childkeeper said calmly. "Or come work for me."

Gwendolyn stepped forward. "No!" she yelled. "We're never going back! And we're tired of fat old men ordering us around! Now give us back our friends, or else!"

Mr. Pump's eyes narrowed as he glared down at her. "How *dare* you. Who do you think you are?"

"She's Gwendolyn Gray!" Jessica shouted. "She stopped the Lambents! She's the one that started the Change!"

A murmur rippled through the crowd. Gwendolyn spun to face them, her own face going as red as Mr. Pump's. She certainly hadn't expected *that.*

Zelda's eyes were wide. "Is... is that true, Wendy?"

Gwendolyn gulped. But there was nothing to be gained by denying it.

"It's true," she said. The crowd had gone quiet enough to hear her every word.

"So *you're* the one," muttered Mr. Pump, his voice low and ominous.

"You're darn right she is!" Tommy said. "Just look up there!" He pointed to the top of the ruined Central Tower. "She shattered the dome! She reversed the Lambents! Remember those airships? That was all her!"

"Yes!" Jessica shouted, looking around at the crowd. "We've seen it! And we can prove it! We can show you our whole story with the Lambents! So listen to her!"

Zelda burst from the front of the crowd. "You heard her, gang! Wendy's the girl we've heard all the rumors about! Without her, we'd be nothing but a bunch'a slack-jawed dull-eyed dopes! Let's hear it for Gwendolyn! Gwendolyn Gray!"

The Childkeeper spoke, her voice calm and steady. "There will be none of that." She looked right at Gwendolyn, eyes narrowed behind her glasses. "Bring her to me."

The orphans moved toward her, but someone grabbed her by the hand and pulled her back into the crowd.

It was Starling. "We've gotta get you out of here."

"But—" Gwendolyn stammered.

"Look at these people. If you stick around, things are going to get real out of hand, real fast. And we've got other places to be."

Gwendolyn took one last look toward the stage. The unconscious teenagers were being dragged inside the Central Tower, just as Ian had been. Zelda was glaring at the Childkeeper, the two of them facing off across a dozen feet of empty space in the no-man's-land between the crowd and the stage.

"This isn't over, kitten."

The Childkeeper met her gaze with an icy one of her own. "It most certainly isn't."

Zelda turned. "Come on, gang, let's ankle on out of here before they bring out the Bruno's to give us the bum's rush!"

But Starling was already dragging Gwendolyn away. The Revellers parted for her like magic. She heard her name ripple through the crowd.

Gwendolyn heard a familiar sigh, and someone sidled up next to her. "It's sad to see a party end, and sadder still to part with a friend."

It was Robin Goodfellow, clad in an orange suit, black shirt, and as barefoot as ever.

Gwendolyn stopped in her tracks so suddenly she was nearly bowled over by the rest of her friends. "What are you doing here?" she snapped.

Robin shrugged. "Can't a boy stop and have some fun? A shame this fun is all but done. But now you're here, so off we go, to claim the favor you still owe."

Gwendolyn's eyes narrowed. "It was you, wasn't it? You threw that tomato at Mr. Pump."

Robin smiled. "I thought that he might like a snack, but he thought it was a foul attack. Which is most understandable, the food here's horrible and dull."

"And you shoved Ian out there to take the blame!"

Now it was Robin's eyes that narrowed. "I felt I'm owed some recompense, your friend's a fitting consequence. Now come with me, my Rosecap dear, we'll turn this City on its ear."

But Miss Sahida burst from the crowd and grabbed her by the shoulder. "Gwendolyn, what are you still doing here?"

Gwendolyn blinked. "Oh, um—"

"I'd have thought you were smart enough to stay out of sight. Unless you want to get caught." She shook her head. "I sent you to the Home once and I've regretted it every moment since. I'd feel a lot better if you were far away from *her*," she said, and nodded back toward the stage.

"She's right, Gwendolyn, we need to go," Missy said.

"Forget that, we have to go get Ian!" Jessica shouted.

"No!" Miss Sahida said, taking in the group of Gwendolyn's Schoolmates. "I'm not letting you put yourselves in danger. You're far too young for this sort of thing!"

"We're not children!" Cecilia called back.

Miss Sahida ignored her. "What happened to Ian was terrible, and I'm going to be having words with the City Council. We can fix this. I won't let one of my students come to harm. *Any* of you. Now go. I'll stay behind, I promise."

Gwendolyn glanced back at the Childkeeper, who was deep in conversation with Mr. Pump. "She's right. We need to make a plan."

"The plan is, we go in there and we drag Ian out!" Jessica insisted.

"That didn't work out so well for those other kids," Tommy said.

"We're all worried, Jessica, but we need to think this through. You're the one who said we should listen to Gwendolyn," Missy pleaded.

Jessica took a breath. "Fine. But just for a minute. I'm not leaving Ian with that witch a second longer than we have to."

Robin grabbed Gwendolyn's arm, and his voice grew sharp. "Oh, you're not going anywhere. My patience has been worn threadbare. I helped you with your pirate mess, I donned your mother's face and dress. And now 'tis time the Puck was paid, or on you shall my wroth be laid."

"I don't have time for this right now," Gwendolyn said, putting some steel into her own voice.

Robin's face twisted into a snarl. Gone was the rhyming and the sing-song voice. When he spoke, it was with the feline hiss of a predator. "Thrice have I asked. Thrice you have denied me my pleasure." He spat on the ground. "So be it. Your word is broken. And I may do as I wish."

Gwendolyn didn't flinch. "You do what you have to do, and so will I." Then she turned and walked away.

CHAPTER SEVENTEEN

You Can Never Go Back Again

And that was how, not a half-hour later, Gwendolyn found herself walking down the hallway of her old apartment building with a rather odd collection of companions.

"We'll be safe in here," Gwendolyn said as they reached the sixth floor.

"And hey, we get to see where you live!" Sparrow blurted.

"Lived," Cecilia gave a sarcastic sneer. Gwendolyn shot her an arch look, and Cecilia grimaced. "Sorry. Habit. That was over the line."

Gwendolyn sighed. It seemed a silly thought after everything she'd been through, but with Sparrow, Starling, Missy, Tommy, Jessica, and Cecilia in tow, this was easily the largest group she'd ever brought home.

Father always did want me to have more friends over. He'd said as much on her thirteenth birthday. The memory brought a sudden stab of grief.

They reached her door, but found it covered in strips of black tape that read *KEEP OUT-CITY PROPERTY*. She ripped them down and tried the handle, but it wouldn't turn.

"I've got it," Starling said. She whipped out a leather bundle and took out some tools. After a couple seconds fiddling with the lock, the door sprang open. "After you."

Gwendolyn nodded her thanks and led the others inside. The apartment had been mostly stripped bare. All that was left was the heavier furniture, the couch and chairs, the coffee table, and Father's desk in the corner.

"Come on in. Make yourselves comfortable," she said. "I—I'm going to change. I'll be right back." Gwendolyn headed to her bedroom, more for some time alone than anything else. She needed to clear her head.

She went inside and closed the door. She was home. But it didn't feel like home. It felt different. Or maybe she felt different. After all, it wasn't technically *hers* anymore. Most of her things seemed to have been taken away by the police, or the Childkeeper. Her room was sparse. The bed had been stripped. Her closet was empty. The only thing left was her drawings, wallpapering the room.

She hunted around for anything else at all to wear. For once, her untidiness came in handy, and she found a skirt from a School uniform wadded up under her bed, stuffed in the far corner. It was a little too big and wouldn't stay up by itself, which explained why it had been shoved under the bed in the first place. So she went across the hall to her parents' bedroom to raid her mother's wardrobe.

Fortunately, this room hadn't been touched yet. Pulling open the dresser, she dug around for something of Mother's, and found a simple white blouse that might fit. She buried her face in it, and she could almost feel herself snuggled against Mother on the couch on a lazy weekend afternoon. It still smelled like her.

She kicked off her shoes, stripped down, and dropped the fringed violet dress in a heap on the floor. Sure enough, the dress and the silver flats promptly dissolved into a cloud of purple sparks. Gwendolyn shuddered, imagining how the faerie clothes could have vanished at any time. Robin was not above such tricks. All that was left was a small green leaf, the one the Lady had given her.

Gwendolyn pulled on her skirt and Mother's blouse, then stuck the leaf in her skirt pocket.

A pair of Father's suspenders were hanging in the wardrobe, and she grabbed those too. Couldn't very well run from mortal danger with a skirt that wouldn't stay up, could she? She snapped them on over Mother's blouse.

There weren't any shoes that would fit her. Of course there weren't. She supposed barefoot adventures were just her lot in life.

She nearly made it out of the room without incident, but she was brought up short by the picture on Mother's bedside table. The yearly family portrait.

Father sat in front, while Mother and Gwendolyn stood behind him. She'd been only twelve, just before her adventures had started, and though her teeth were showing, it was more of a forced grimace. Mother wore the slightly strained smile of all mothers who must corral unruly children to stand still and look nice and not make the kind of faces Gwendolyn had been making moments before the picture was snapped. It was a very specific sort of smile. Father just beamed with pride, willfully oblivious to the tension behind him.

Gwendolyn felt suddenly light-headed, and darkness overtook her.

When she came to her senses, she found herself curled up on the bed, crying. Her breathing was rapid. Every muscle in her torso was tight, and the taste of bile rose in her throat. Some part of her recognized the signs of an anxiety attack, and she forced herself to take slow, deep breaths.

You don't have time for this right now, she told herself. *You can break down later.*

That helped. It was a strategy she'd used before. She'd need to do some more serious work later. Meditation, and exercise, and rest, and food. But those could be in dangerously short supply on an adventure. Before long, the true toll on her mental state would rear its ugly head. Anxiety attacks were merely short-term reactions. A full-on depressive episode could leave her paralyzed for weeks.

Stop it. You don't have time for that either. Her parents needed her. Now.

She grabbed her bag and went back into the living room. Jessica was staring daggers at anything that might give her an excuse for some stabbing. Tommy and Missy sat on the couch, fidgeting awkwardly. Cecilia was deep in the pages of *Tautopolis.* Starling sat at Father's desk, where she'd taken out some tools and was tinkering with her wrist gauntlet. Only Sparrow was upbeat, wandering around, inspecting the place.

"All right," Gwendolyn said. "I'm ready. Let's make a plan."

"Finally." Jessica rubbed her hands together. "I'm pretty sure they're taking Ian to—"

Gwendolyn held up a hand. "That's not what I meant. I'm sorry, but I still have to find my parents."

Jessica frowned. "What are you talking about? Where did they go?"

Gwendolyn sighed and filled them in on the situation of the past two years. Tommy gaped. Missy nodded, her suspicions confirmed. Starling looked sympathetic. Cecilia never looked up from her book.

"So... you've been living alone this whole time? Lying to us about your parents, and the Revels, and everything?" Jessica said.

"Yes." Gwendolyn didn't like to hear it phrased that way, but it was true enough.

"Why didn't you tell us? Don't you trust us? We could have helped you!"

"Of course I trust you. I just..." She felt her cheeks grow warm. "I couldn't tell *anyone*."

Jessica sank back onto the couch. "So you *don't* trust us. We're your friends, Gwendolyn. We would have been there for you. Just like we need to be there for Ian now. You know how horrible that woman is. She must have taken him to the Home for Unclaimed Children. And you know that place inside and out now, so it should be easy to break in there and get him out."

Gwendolyn cringed. "I told you, I can't. My parents are in

danger. The Blackstar is going to kill them. He might even be doing it already. Ian has you to help him, and Tommy and Missy. And even Miss Sahida and that Zelda lady. My parents only have me."

"You don't even know where to find them, or the Blackstar." Jessica said.

"Yes we do," Cecilia said, finally looking up.

"How do you know?" Missy said.

She snapped the book shut and held it up. "This has to be where he's headed next."

"What's it about?" Starling asked.

"Well," Cecilia said, and flipped it open. "It's kind of terrible. There's this place called Tautopolis, and everyone there is just awful. The people who run things are oppressive and restrictive—"

"An authoritarian regime," Jessica chimed in.

"Okay, I guess, if that means they have one guy who runs everything, which they do. They call him the Supreme Executive. And everyone talks like the Blackstar. All that garbage about helping yourself first and not serving others. And there's smoke and stuff everywhere, and people always wear those gas mask things. It's almost like..." and she trailed off.

"Oh," Gwendolyn said, the ideas clicking into place. "You think it's the Blackstar's book."

Cecilia nodded. "It fits. I think the Blackstar is this Supreme Executive."

Gwendolyn raised an eyebrow. "I see. He could be. I mean, we don't know that *Blackstar* is his real name. I think people just call him that because of the tattoo on his hand. Supreme Executive seems like it would fit him. What else?"

"There's this kid, Cato Locke. He's the main character. He's like, seventeen, and his parents were killed in a war that never ends. People keep calling him 'the chosen one,' and he's supposed to overthrow the Supreme Executive or something."

"This is it. This is what we need," Gwendolyn said. She was talking faster now, pacing the room. "If this Cato Locke is the chosen one, then it's his destiny to stop the Blackstar. I certainly haven't had much luck. We need his help. And he'll needs ours. The Blackstar must be interfering in the story, to stop Cato before Cato stops him."

"And what about your parents?" Missy asked.

"If it's his world, he must be hiding them there," Gwendolyn said.

"How can you know any of that?" Jessica snapped.

Cecilia glowered. "I'm a fast reader. You're not the only ones who like books."

"Why are you even here?" Jessica shot back. "Nobody likes you! Just go back to your Central City friends and your precious little life."

"Fine." Cecilia flung the book at them, snatched up her purse, and stomped to the door. "Have fun, oddlings. I've had enough of your weirdness for a lifetime." She flipped her hair and left, slamming the door behind her.

"Whoah," said Tommy.

"So you're just going to leave, too?" Jessica said to Gwendolyn. She looked more hurt than angry. "Just go charging off without thinking? This is one of your manic phases, isn't it?"

Gwendolyn's face grew hot. She'd thought Missy was the only

one who had noticed her illness. *Is it really so obvious?* "I'm *not* manic. I have to do this, you have to trust me!"

"How can I trust you when you've been lying to me? When we never know which side of you we're going to get? Crazy Gwendolyn, or useless mopey Gwendolyn?"

The two fell silent and looked at each other. Jessica hung her head.

"I'm sorry. I didn't mean that. I'm just... I'm worried about Ian. I'm worried about the whole City."

Gwendolyn nodded, and shoved some more feelings into the closet at the back of her mind. "I'm sorry too. And I've no business judging anyone for blurting out the wrong thing. But I have to go. I promise, we'll come right back and do all the rescuing that needs done. I know it sounds harsh, but at least Ian will be alive. I can't say the same for my parents. Or Cato Locke, whoever he is. I'm not going to let the Blackstar kill him like he killed Jack."

Jessica stood up. "All right. You do what you have to do. Find that Cato Locke person and save your parents from the Blackstar. I'll save Ian from the Childkeeper. Someone has to look out for the City." Then she walked out.

Gwendolyn stood up, but couldn't muster the energy to follow.

"It's okay." Missy came up and put a hand on her shoulder. "She's just upset. She'll calm down, eventually. We know you have to go."

Gwendolyn covered Missy's hand with her own. "Thank you. For everything."

Missy just shrugged, her lip curling up into a half-smile. She brushed a stringy lock of blonde hair away from her face. "We're friends." As if that were all the explanation that was required. Then she reached into a pocket and pulled out a small bundle. "Here."

"What's this?" Gwendolyn said. She took it and unfolded it. It was a pair of striped, violet stockings, exactly Gwendolyn's favorite color.

It used to be green, she thought. But then again, so much about her had changed. A favorite color was the least of it.

"They're for you," Missy said. She broke into a rare full smile, which made her whole face light up. "I bought them at the Revels, but you need them more. You can't go around *completely* barefoot. And you need some color."

"I can't, really—"

"Yes, you can. It was your money anyway. Now I've got to go, before Jessica punches the first grown-up she sees. Just remember—you have friends now. We're here to help. Don't be afraid to ask for it."

"Thank you. That means a great deal." And it did. Gwendolyn took the words and tucked them away inside, where they gave off a faint warmth like glowing embers as Missy headed down the hall, waving back over her shoulder.

Tommy came out into the hall. "Well, that's all settled, then. Let's head back to the library, and go find that Blackstar bloke."

"Tommy..." Gwendolyn knew what she had to do, but it wasn't going to be pretty. "I need you to stay here."

"Nah, I'ma stay with you, have adventures and stuff."

Gwendolyn thought about Jack, about the shocked look on his face, and the stake in his heart. She remembered Professor Zangetsky, stabbed by the pirate Tylerium Drekk, wearing a similar shocked expression. Not erased. Not collected. Just killed. And it was all too easy to imagine the same expression on Tommy. "No. It's no place for you out there."

He snorted. "It's no place for me here, neither."

Gwendolyn sighed. He was not going to make this easy. "I know what this is about."

"What?"

"I know why you follow me. I've seen the way you look at me. And yes, I've known for years now."

"I don't know what you're talkin' about." But he looked away.

"Yes, you do. And it's sweet, but... no. It's just not something I'm interested in. I know it's a horrible cliche and it won't make anything better, but we're only ever going to be friends."

Tommy thought long and hard, a storm of emotions flickering across his face. "So, it's Sparrow then, inn'it?"

Gwendolyn glanced back into the apartment at Sparrow, who was snatching his sister's tools and poking her with them. "No, I think that's pretty much over with."

"Then who?"

Gwendolyn shrugged. "Nobody. Why does it have to be *anybody*? I have neither the time nor energy for anything of that sort. I'm perfectly happy on my own, as long as I have my friends."

Tommy didn't look pleased. "Friends, huh?"

"Yes. I'm sorry. But I'll never be sorry to count you among them."

He stared at the floor for a moment, then shrugged. "I like being your friend. I guess that'll have to do, huh? I just... I care about you a lot." Finally, he looked at her. "I'zzat okay?

She smiled. "Care all you like. I care about you too. You were the first one to listen to me, after all. Before any of the others. That means a lot." Gwendolyn gave him a tender, pleading look, with extra wide eyes and just a tiny bit of pout. "I need you to do this for me, Tommy. Please?"

He wavered, the look on Gwendolyn's face having it's intended effect. "All right. S'fine," Tommy said, forcing a shrug. He started to walk away, but seemed to think better of it, and turned back to her. He started untying his bow tie. "Missy was right. Gwendolyn Gray's gotta have *some* color. Wouldn't be right, otherwise." He held out the strip of yellow cloth to her.

"I—I don't know how," she said, not sure what else to say.

"Can I?"

She thought about it for a moment, then nodded. Tommy put it around her neck and tied it for her. "There. That's better."

She looked at him as if seeing him for the first time. "Thank you, Tommy."

"Well, you know, I gotta stick around and look after the others. But now you've got somethin' to remember us by while you're out there hoppin' worlds. Missy was right about that too—we're friends."

"She's right about a lot of things," Gwendolyn said.

"Yeah." Tommy looked off toward the elevator. "She is. But she can be even more spaced out than you, Freckles. Between her and Jessica, they'll need someone with a level head, a right clever bloke like me. Just don't stay away too long, al'right?"

"I'll be back soon, I promise."

Tommy nodded slowly, then stuck out a hand. "Promise."

Gwendolyn shook it, and saw the sadness in his eyes as Tommy accepted that a handshake was the best he was ever going to get. But that's just the way it had to be. No sense letting the poor boy keep wondering. Then he turned and walked stoically down the hall.

Gwendolyn sighed. Jessica was mad at her. Missy felt bad for her. Tommy felt... who knew how Tommy felt, but it couldn't have been pleasant. Why did it seem that none of her friends were ever better off for knowing her?

Maybe Jessica had a point. How could she trust herself, when her own mind betrayed her? Sometimes it was hard to tell who was in control, herself, or her illness. How could anyone trust her?

But she knew an anxiety trap when she saw one. So she shoved those thoughts in her mental closet with the rest, and went back inside.

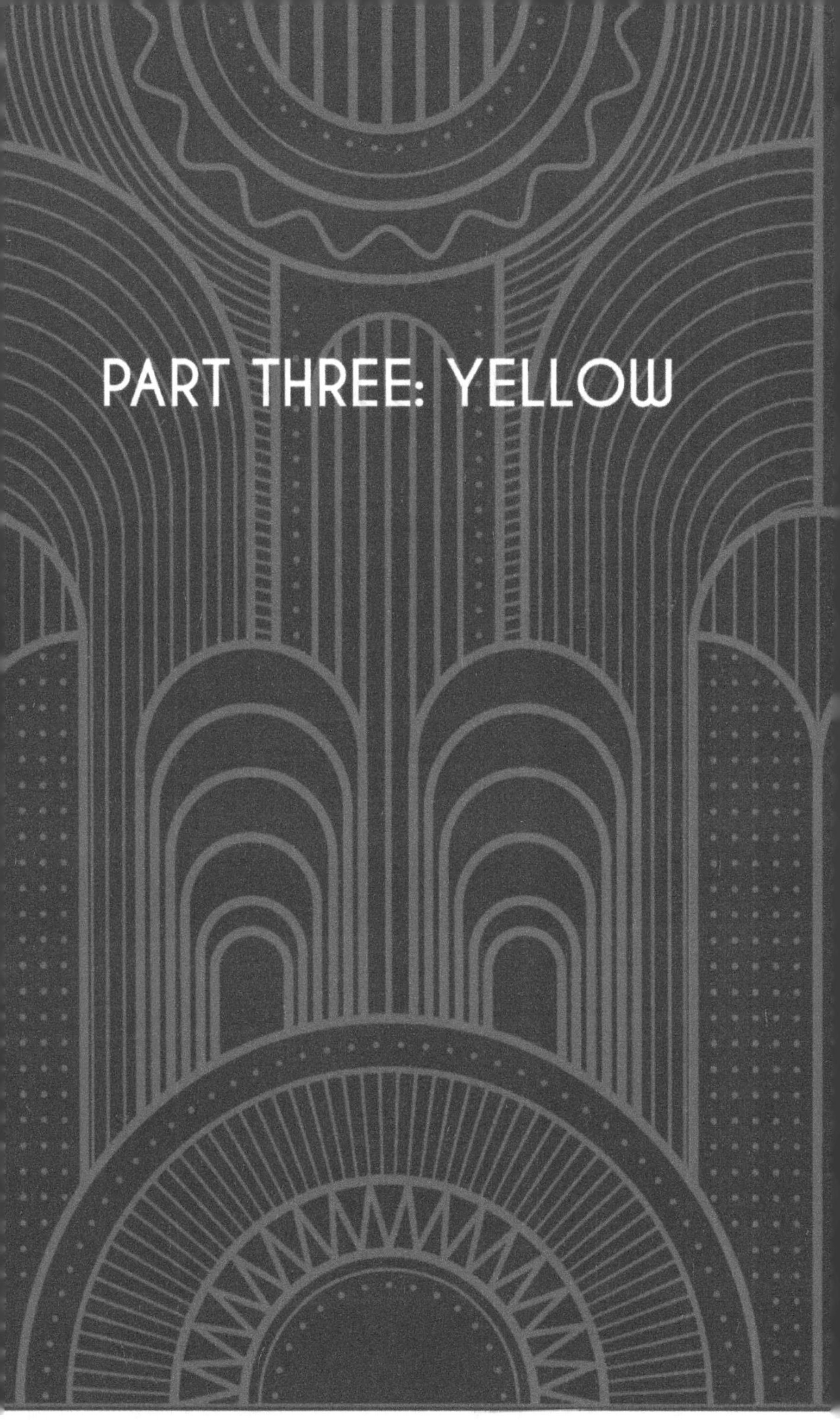

PART THREE: YELLOW

CHAPTER EIGHTEEN

TAUTOPOLIS

"Wow, harsh," Starling said. "Not that I mind. Didn't like that Tommy kid anyway. But they could have come with us." She turned a screw on her gauntlet, waved it at the black book, and was rewarded with a loud chiming from the detector.

Gwendolyn fidgeted. "I know, it's just…" She couldn't explain the feeling she had, the awkwardness of mingling old and new friends. She knew it was unfair, and selfish, but wasn't she allowed to be selfish? At least once in a while? "This is our adventure. The three of us, together. Just like old times."

"Times aren't that old for us. It's only been two weeks since the central tower, and about a month since we fought the Abscess in Tohk."

Gwendolyn was once again struck with the sledgehammer of time lost. Which reminded her—

"Wait, where's Sparrow?"

Starling jerked a thumb in the direction of Gwendolyn's bedroom, then went back to her tinkering.

Gwendolyn headed down the hall and sure enough, she found

Sparrow staring at the drawings on her wall.

"Whatever are you doing in my bedroom?" It shocked her how much she sounded like Mother.

If he'd heard the tone in her voice, he didn't react. He pointed at the wall. "It's us," he said.

He was right. There *were* quite a lot of pictures of Sparrow and Starling on her wall. "Well... I had a lot of time to fill. Most of them are pretty old." She sat on her bed and pulled on the thick violet stockings. They came up over her knees, cozy and warm.

"Lots of time," he said, wistfully. He tapped one of the pictures. "I guess I must look pretty little to you now."

She wasn't sure how much more of this sort of thing she could handle today. "Not as little as I was."

"Yeah," Sparrow said. "Was." He took a breath, straightened, then turned to face her with his usual wolfish grin. "Well, never mind. We've got a job to do, right? Go into the Blackstar's book, find the hero that can stop him, and save your parents."

"You're not worried?"

Sparrow blinked. "Of course not. I'm with you, aren't I?"

That shook her. There he stood, in her bedroom, gazing up at her with nothing but trust and admiration. "Oh. Yes."

He looked back at all the pictures. "You won't let anything bad happen. It's just another adventure. Like with Kolonius, or that Cyria lady, or fighting Mister Zero. And when it's done, we'll use the Library to find a home for Starling and me."

"Of course," Gwendolyn said, hoping she sounded more confident than she felt. She stood up. "Ready?"

He tugged at the edges of his jacket. "Yup. Nice outfit, by the way."

She looked down at herself. Skirt and blouse. Suspenders. Yellow bow tie. Purple stockings. "Yes. Not too bad, I suppose. Though it's a shame there's never a pair of shoes around when you need them."

The streets around the Central Tower were clear. There was little sign of the Revel from earlier, save for some extra litter and smudged chalk drawings on the street. Fresh black posters had been put up, shouting for "A RETURN TO VALUES" in big white letters.

"Gotta be honest, I'll be glad to get out of here," Starling said as they walked down the rows of files and binders inside the Hall of Records.

"I don't think it's going to be much better where we're going," Gwendolyn replied. They approached the Egressai Infinitus. The door to the library was still open.

"Gotta remember to close this," Sparrow said as they went through into the entrance hall. "Anything could get in."

"Too right." Cecilia Forthright darted out from behind the door, slammed it shut, then snatched the gem from the dialing console.

"Cecilia!" Gwendolyn shouted. "What are you doing?"

"Surprise, oddling. You're not leaving me in Dulls-ville while you go hopping around to who knows where, getting all the attention for yourself. I'm following you every step of the way."

"Give it back!" She reached for the red Figment.

"What are you going to do, scratch me again?"

Gwendolyn froze, arm outstretched. The words slapped her

230

speechless.

"That's right. You need this thing, don't you? You're not going anywhere without it, which means you're not going anywhere without me. So can it, Princess."

Gwendolyn narrowed her eyes. "I see what's going on here."

"Yeah, jealous much?" Starling said.

"I'm not jealous!" Cecilia shouted, her voice a hysterical shriek. She took a breath. "Who knows what dangerous stuff you could let in through this doorway? We all remember the airships and the explosions at Central Tower. You cause trouble. Big trouble."

Gwendolyn, Sparrow, and Starling shared a look, holding the sort of silent psychic discussion that true friends can have. Then Gwendolyn turned back to Cecilia.

"All right. You can come."

"What?" Cecilia looked shocked. "Seriously?"

Gwendolyn thought about the things Cecilia had said, and couldn't help but feel just the tiniest bit sorry for her. The very tiniest bit. And if she was honest, she felt guilty about how she'd manipulated Tommy. She didn't have the energy to argue with herself. "Just... let's go. I've got parents to find."

"Yeah, yeah, we've all got parent issues..." But Cecilia didn't argue as she put the gem back in the dialing console. "You. Starling. Give me the book."

~~~

On another world, a series of dull thumps rolled across a dark and cloudy sky. Distant explosions rumbled like a far-off thunderstorm. And a doorway opened the tiniest bit, letting out a beam of warm yellow light. But a fallen bookcase leaned against
~~~

the door, blocking it from opening any further.

The Egressai Infinitus connected to the libraries on other worlds, but the area around the doorway was only a library in a theoretical sense. There were the smoldering remains of what might have once been books. The crumbling walls were doing their best to stay upright, but they looked weary enough to fall down on the job at any moment.

There was a grunting, and the fallen bookcase was gradually shoved clear of the doorway. Four figures spilled out of it.

"Cheerful," Starling said, taking in the scene. The sky was visible through holes in the ceiling, a curtain of featureless black.

"Positively delightful," Cecilia added.

Gwendolyn shuddered and wrapped her arms around herself. "It's cold." Her stocking feet stung with it. And with all the sharp bits on the ground.

Cecilia knelt and ran her finger across one of the books scattered on the floor and it came away soiled with grime. She made a disgusted face. "I told you it wasn't a very nice place. But look on the bright side."

"What bright side?"

Cecilia grinned. "At least there won't be any parties."

"Thank goodness. Where are we?" Gwendolyn asked.

"Not sure. It isn't a part of the story that I recognize."

"Then I guess we go back to the old routine. Time to explore?" Sparrow said.

"*Carefully,*" Gwendolyn told him.

"Who, me?" he said with a grin, then danced away over the mess of books toward the ruins of what might loosely be considered a lobby.

The girls turned to each other and shared a three-way eye-roll.

Outside was no better off. Chunks of concrete and masonry littered the street. It reminded Gwendolyn a bit of the City, but much, much worse. Some buildings were missing their front walls, all their rooms visible from the street, though people still seemed to be going about their business inside. Other buildings had been destroyed entirely and were now nothing more than piles of jagged rubble. The smell of sulfur filled the air, and Gwendolyn felt a layer of grit building up on her skin.

"All right," Sparrow said. "Where to?"

Gwendolyn pointed at a flickering orange glow from an alleyway on the next block. "That's as good a place to start as any. Might as well ask around."

They walked toward the light, but had only taken a few steps when they were deafened by a nearby explosion. The ground shuddered with the impact. And the tired old library, fed up with this constant abuse, finally gave in. The entire front section collapsed. Once the dust had settled, there was no sign of the doorway they had come through.

Sparrow frowned. "Looks like we won't be going back that way."

"Don't worry," Gwendolyn said. "We've got a Figment." She tossed the red jewel to Cecilia. "Here, make yourself useful."

Cecilia caught it, rolled her eyes, and put the Figment in her purse along with their copy of *Tautopolis*.

"We'll find another way out, even if I have to rip open a portal myself." She thought she might be able to do it, too. She could feel the tingle of energy on this world. Of *magic*. It was always strong on the Abscess' worlds, where it was being hoarded and stored instead of shared and used.

Gwendolyn strode purposefully down the street, trying hard to look like the leader they all expected her to be.

The light in the alley came from a fire in a large trash barrel. Books were stacked all around. People in ragged clothing huddled close to it, warming their hands and rubbing their shoulders. One of them dropped a pile of books into the fire. The flames roared up.

"Excuse me," Gwendolyn said, trying on her sweet-little-girl voice for the first time in years, and hoping it still fit. "I don't suppose you could tell us where we are?"

"Whadd'ya mean, where you are?" growled the nearest man. Or at least, something resembling a man, it was hard to say for sure under all the grime. "You'se tryin' to play me? We ain't done nothin', so you can do your spyin' somewhere else."

"No, we're not spies, we're just lost, is all." She didn't get the impression that they'd be handing out any free dresses to cute little castaways. Or maybe she just wasn't as adorable as she used to be.

"Lay off, Benny, they're pro'lly just shell shocked," said another figure, who might have been a woman after a thorough scrubbing. "Don't listen to Benny. He don't know where we are either. We ain't exactly got maps, and the borders keep changing anyway. Who's in charge today, Cotton?"

Cotton adjusted a pair of broken glasses. "Last I heard we was in Corporate territory. The Causists lost it a few days ago."

Benny squinted at them. "And which are you? You'se is all

lookin' pretty fancy. A bunch of Corporate brats, huh? Slummin' down here with the lowlifes?"

"No," Gwendolyn said, trying to sound reassuring. "We just want—" She paused. What did they want? "We're trying to find someone. He's probably with these... Causists."

"Huh," Benny said. "Not Corporate? Prove it. Got any food?"

They all looked at each other. Sparrow shrugged, pulled an apple out his pocket, and tossed it to the man.

"Where do you keep getting those?" Starling asked.

Sparrow just grinned at her.

"An' what exactly is goin' on here?" came a voice from behind them.

Gwendolyn turned to see a woman in a long leather tunic, with shining silver buttons up one side. A squarish, flat-billed cap topped her head, with dark goggles wrapped around it. She wore heavy boots that were made with lots of stomping and kicking in mind. A half-gas-mask dangled from her neck, one that would only cover her nose and mouth.

The woman marched up to Benny and snatched the apple from his hand. "An' where'd ya get this?" she snapped with the air of unquestioned authority.

"'Dat brat." Benny jerked a thumb at Sparrow. "He just gave it to me. For nuthin'."

"Yeah, that's what it looked like he done." The woman grabbed Sparrow by the arm and slapped a metal cuff around his wrist. "You're under arrest."

"Get off him!" Starling shoved the woman, but she grabbed Starling by the arm and twisted it around behind her back. Starling grimaced, and the woman put a cuff on her as well. She kicked the back of Starling's knee, and Starling's leg buckled, leaving her kneeling on the ground.

"Well, peaches, looks like you're coming with me too."

"I don't think so," Gwendolyn said, and she rushed at the woman. But the woman held up a small remote, pressed a button, and Sparrow and Starling cried out in pain. Arcs of electricity crackled up their arms, lighting the alley in flickering blue.

"Stop it!" Gwendolyn said, but she didn't move any closer.

"Why?" the woman said, and hit the button again. And again, her friends screamed, both of them now writhing on the ground. They clawed at their cuffs with their free hands, but it zapped those fingers as well.

"We'll come with you!" Cecilia said. "You can take us too, just stop hurting them."

The woman shrugged. "Works for me." She reached to her belt and unclipped two more cuffs.

Gwendolyn looked down at Sparrow and Starling, who lay panting on the garbage-strewn ground. Then she held out her hand.

The woman slapped on the cuff, and the metal ring clicked into place around her wrist. And again, with Cecilia.

Then she held up the remote and hit the button again.

Gwendolyn and Cecilia fell to their knees, joining Sparrow and Starling in their screaming. The pain was intense. It felt as if her arm was on fire, every nerve screaming louder than her own voice.

"Lucky me," the woman said, bending down to take Starling's tracker off her wrist. She gathered up Cecilia's purse. "Four more for the Bootstrap Brigade."

236

CHAPTER NINETEEN

PULL YOURSELF UP

The four of them were marched down the street. Or rather, they followed the woman who marched down the street, and were given the occasional zap if they slipped on the wet pavement or stumbled over one of the many potholes. The jolts of pain were an unwelcome distraction from the ache in Gwendolyn's feet.

As for the street, it was unlike any she'd walked down yet. Though the buildings grew taller the farther they walked, the devastation did not lessen. Gwendolyn was used to tall buildings, of course. These had clearly been elaborate and beautiful once, but she couldn't see a single one that was undamaged.

There were skyscrapers with holes in them, as though a giant had taken a bite out of the side. A spire had toppled across the road, an immense stone spike that had sheared through the buildings on either side as it fell. The woman clambered nimbly over it, and the others had to hurry to avoid another round of electric encouragement. Gwendolyn tried her best not to cut her feet on the rubble.

The street was not entirely bleak. Quite the opposite. There were cheerful advertisements everywhere. Neon signs blazed, casting colors that danced on the rain-slick asphalt. Yellow lights lit up rooftop billboards, and giant posters papered over gaping holes as though the warzone around them were a passing inconvenience to the sale of new clocks and radios.

In contrast to the ruined appearance of the rest of Tautopolis, the posters and billboards all seemed fresh and in good repair. She spotted a sign with a well-dressed family of four wearing the newest and most fashionable gas masks. A smiling housewife held up a bottle of cleaner that claimed to scrub away pesky toxic residue. One had a picture of a bag spilling out a handful of bright red candies. *New longer-lasting Amnesia Drops! Forget your problems for hours at a time!*

Buzzing neon signs welcomed customers to diners, drugstores, and refugee motels. *Your home for when there's no more home to go home to!* Below this, a bright red NO VACANCY sign belied the cheery slogan.

An extra-large billboard featured an array of kitchen gadgets that ran on something called "Air-Power," with cartoon lightning bolts stretching from an electrical tower to colorful blenders and toasters.

Gwendolyn noticed spindly metal towers on top of some of the buildings, just like those on the billboard. The tip of each tower glowed with a cold blue-white light, and occasionally a bolt of electricity would jump from one to another. Whenever it did, Gwendolyn felt the familiar prickle again. The feeling of *power*.

After a few minutes and a few more shocks from their captor, they arrived at a high chain link fence that stretched down several city blocks, surrounding a massive building. Looking up, Gwendolyn saw that it wasn't just one building, but a cluster of five connected skyscrapers, none of which were in especially good repair. Construction scaffolding covered the first several floors, but it seemed downright puny against the scale of the massive structure.

The woman stopped in front of a gate. A large poster was plastered across it. Big block letters proclaimed *Do your part! No one else will!*

The woman snapped to attention, arms at her sides. "Enforcer Puckett reporting, with three recruits for the Bootsrap Brigade."

A voice crackled through a speaker somewhere. "More, Shauna? That's your third group this week."

She smiled. "What can I say? I love my job. Now open up, Brian, we're burnin' drytime."

"Drytime?" Cecilia mumbled, looking up at the dark sky.

There was a harsh buzz, and two fence panels slid open. Puckett turned back to four of them. "After you," she said, voice dripping with sarcasm.

They exchanged wary looks, but their arms all ached from the stun cuffs, and none of them said a word as they filed in.

As Sparrow passed, the woman gave him a push and sent him stumbling into the fence.

More blue-white bolts leapt from the metal and arced over his body. He gasped and convulsed, then collapsed to one knee.

Starling whirled, murder in her eyes, but the woman just held up the remote. "Ah-ah-ah, kid. Just giving you'se all the orientation lesson. In case you've got any bright ideas of runnin' or somethin'. Almost fog'o'clock anyway. So get moving."

Starling growled, but said nothing.

Puckett nodded. "Better."

She pressed the button, and the three girls shrieked in unison. Puckett strolled inside, past the gasping trio. "That one was just for fun," she called over her shoulder.

Gwendolyn helped Sparrow to his feet while Cecilia restrained Starling from jumping on the enforcer's back.

Inside, they were met by a cavernous open space. A courtyard nestled in the center of the five skyscrapers. A canvas tarp larger than any circus tent formed a canopy that could have fit several smaller buildings under it. Walkways the size of the street outside ringed the second and third floors of the skyscrapers. The edges of the atrium housed clusters of tents and stalls, entire shanty towns springing up in the shadow of the balconies above.

Then Gwendolyn noticed the people. Their clothes were the dull grey of dust, and their faces were equally faded and worn. Several sections of building had apparently collapsed. Teams of workers were hauling the rubble away. Stone, metal, and wood were sorted into various piles. Guards were scattered around, and Enforcer Puckett wandered away to talk to more of her kind.

"What the heck is going on?" said Sparrow. "What is this place?"

"I don't know," Gwendolyn said. "But I think it's high time we get out. Give me a moment."

Cecilia rolled her eyes. "Brilliant. You couldn't have magicked us out of these before all the shocking?"

240

Gwendolyn scowled. "Constant jolts of electricity aren't exactly good for one's concentration."

"Well, if you'd have used your head instead of rushing at that woman in the first place, we wouldn't have that problem."

Sparrow stepped between them. "Could you just stop it before she gets back? You can argue once we're gone. Gwendolyn will get us out of this, so just trust her."

Gwendolyn was warmed by his confidence. She closed her eyes, and *imagined*. She pictured all their cuffs opening so clearly in her mind that she could already hear the *click* they would make and the clatter as they fell to the ground. "*If only* these blasted things would—"

But she was interrupted by another shock from the wrist cuff. The muscles in her arm tightened painfully, her whole left side convulsing. She fell to one knee, teeth gritted against the pain. She looked around for their captor and her remote control. But the woman was still a ways off, chatting and laughing with her comrades.

"What happened?" Sparrow asked.

"I don't think that's going to work..." Gwendolyn gasped.

"Of course not," Cecilia scoffed. "Why would your bloody powers ever work when you needed them to?"

Gwendolyn sprang to her feet. "Give me a minute. I'll figure something out. Starling?"

Starling shook her head. "Sorry. She took my lockpicks."

"Ugh," Cecilia groaned.

"Stop it," Starling snapped. "Be helpful, or shut up."

Cecilia took a breath. "Fine. Involuntary electroshock therapy leaves me a bit *touchy*. What now?"

"Now," came the hateful voice of Enforcer Puckett "you'se get to work." She pointed to a group of haggard looking people across the courtyard, hauling rubble from one pile to another. "E-Crew."

"What are we supposed to do?" asked Sparrow.

Puckett snorted. "What are you, dense? Yer movin' rocks."

"Why?" he whined.

She held up the remote. "'Cause I said so. You gotta real short memory, kid."

"Wait!" Gwendolyn called out. "It's just—We don't know what we did wrong. If you could just explain, we could find a way to make it right."

The enforcer pulled out the apple, took a bite, and let out a little sigh of pleasure. "Oh yeah. That's the stuff." She took another bite and chewed thoughtfully. "You broke the law."

Cecilia snorted. "Yes, we gathered that. What law?"

"What law?" Puckett rolled her eyes. "*The* law. You restricted that man's freedom."

The four travelers blinked.

"Huh?" Sparrow said.

She held up the apple and gave it a little wiggle. "Depriving him of the opportunity to find food for himself. Soon he'll be doing nothing but begging, expectin' other people to do everything for him. Independence is the only freedom."

Sparrow just stared. "Huh?" he repeated.

"And now you've got a nice, hefty fine of one hundred marks—"

"Is that a lot?" Sparrow said.

"Each. And since you don't have the money to cover it—"

"How do you know?" Sparrow said, indignantly.

She stared him down. "Do you?"

He withered. "No..."

"Thought not. Now, shut up ya little brat, and just once, I'll repeat myself for free." She pointed at the four of them. "You." Then she pointed at what must have been E-Crew. "Rocks. Go, before I slap more marks onto your debt for slacking."

Sparrow opened his mouth again but Cecilia kicked him in the shin. "Shut up. Just do what she says."

"It'll be all right," said Gwendolyn as she led them away. "We need some information anyway, and this is as good a place as any to get it."

Starling rammed a shoulder into Cecilia.

"Ow! What are you playing at?"

Starling glared at her. "Don't *ever* kick my brother."

Cecilia opened her mouth, but Starling's glare hit her hard enough to shut it again.

"So we're under arrest for helping a guy," Sparrow said as they approached the pile of rubble.

"I guess taking things is fine," Starling added, shooting a look at Puckett, who was wearing Starling's tracker on her wrist. "It's *giving* them that's their problem."

Gwendolyn nodded. "Definitely one of the Abscess' worlds. Ow!"

An older boy shoved his way through. "Move it." He carried a large chunk of stone, and apparently had little concern for anyone who might stand in the way of moving it from rock pile A to rock pile B.

"Excuse me," Gwendolyn said, getting in step beside him as he deposited his load and went back for another. "I was wondering if you could help—I mean, if you could tell us a little more about this place."

The boy stopped and squinted at her. "What?"

Manners clearly wouldn't work, so she tried another tactic. "We're not really from here. If we knew more about this place, we could do a better job helping you move these rocks. A win-win, if you think about it."

"Don't touch my rocks!" he snapped.

Gwendolyn threw up her hands. "I'm sorry, I won't!"

He stormed off and grabbed another chunk of stone. "Friggin' outsiders," he grumbled, loud enough to be plainly heard as he passed them again. "Comin' in, takin' all our work. They keep draggin' in scum like you, soon there won't be any work left for the rest of us."

"That didn't go well," Cecilia said.

Gwendolyn thought for a moment. "It's this place. If they're all like the Blackstar, no one does anything unless they get something out of it."

"All right, then let's try this again," Cecilia said. "Oy! Prat!" The boy didn't stop, so Cecilia stepped into his path. "Tell us what we want to know, or we'll move *all* the rocks." She put her hands on her hips. "And between the four of us, we can move a *lot* of rocks. Won't be getting paid much then, will you?"

The boy eyed the four of them, doing some complicated internal mathematics, and eventually coming to the conclusion that *four* was indeed more than *one*. "Fine. But I ain't stoppin', so keep up. You're on the Bootstrap Brigade now."

"We're going to need a little more exposition than that," Cecilia said.

"Look, you gotta debt you can't pay, or a crime you doing time for, they send you here. You gotta learn to be productive. Pull yourself up by your bootstraps. Work your way out."

"That's stupid. You can't lift yourself off the ground by your own boots," Starling said.

"It's just an expression."

"Yeah, for how impossible it is to get out of this place…" Sparrow muttered.

"Every man's gotta be free to make his own choices. He's gotta live for his own sake, never sacrificing himself to others," he said, with the tone of someone quoting a well-known phrase.

"We're here because we gave a man an apple. Why isn't he in trouble as well?" Gwendolyn asked.

The older boy gave them a disgusted look. "A hungry man takes free food? He'd be wrong not to. Achievement of your own happiness is the only moral purpose in life. *You* sacrificed what you had, for nothing. That's wrong."

Cecilia rolled her eyes. "Oh my god, where do they get this stuff?"

"It's the same sort of thing the Childkeeper is always blathering about," Gwendolyn said. "Just like the Blackstar. Normally he won't say more than two words, but he won't shut up about all this nonsense. It's definitely his world."

"They can blab all they want, at least it's convenient for us. Who's running the show around here?" Sparrow asked the boy.

He gestured vaguely. "The Corporation. They run everything."

He picked up another large chunk of concrete.

"And why do they have you moving these rocks around?" Gwendolyn said.

"This is just in-between work while we wait for a real recovery job."

"So this is all pointless? That's stupid," said Cecilia.

He glared again. "They're giving us all jobs. And in return, they have a trained work force ready to go the next time the Causists attack. Gotta stay productive."

"Now we're getting somewhere," said Gwendolyn. "Who are these Causists?"

The boy only grunted. But Cecilia knelt down and picked up a fist size piece of rubble.

"Fine, fine!" he said. "They're rebels." The disgust in his voice was palpable. "Tryin' to overthrow the Corporation."

"That's who we need," Gwendolyn said. "Where do we find them?"

"How should I know? I'm just trying to work my way outta here. Just a few more marks and I'll be all paid up, then—"

But he was interrupted by a loud buzz that echoed across the courtyard.

He dropped the rock he was holding. "Finally. Meal break. Now buzz off." And he walked off toward a cluster of stalls.

"Well, what now?" said Starling.

Gwendolyn looked down at the cuff on her wrist. "I suppose we go with the flow. We're bound to find a way to escape sooner or later."

"It's the *later* that worries me," grumbled Cecilia.

They crossed the atrium to the stalls. Just like the street outside, there were signs everywhere, but these advertised things like tools, work clothes, and food. *Available on Credit!* they enthusiastically decreed. *No Marks Required!* Other read things like *Find Freedom in Work!* and *When Everyone Takes Care of Themselves, Everyone is Taken Care Of!*

"This place is *nuts*," said Cecilia.

"I don't know," Sparrow said. "Putting your own happiness first? Doesn't sound so bad to me."

"Of course it doesn't," Starling replied. "You're thirteen. You already think the world revolves around you."

Sparrow grinned. "I'm glad you've all finally noticed."

Gwendolyn rolled her eyes, but couldn't stop a small smile. "I think we've learned everything we can. Let's get our things and get out of here."

"How?" asked Cecilia.

Gwendolyn nodded to a stall full of tools. Its owner was busy in the food line. "We help ourselves. Starling?"

"Got it. Cover me."

Gwendolyn, Sparrow, and Cecilia blocked her from view as she snatched some tools off the table. Gwendolyn held her hands behind her back, and felt Starling working on them.

But there was another electric pulse, and Gwendolyn's muscles seized so hard she bit her tongue, then collapsed to the ground.

"Sorry!" Starling said.

Gwendolyn touched a finger to her tongue, and it came away bloody. "So, not our *best* plan."

"Hey, what're you doin'?" came a voice.

Gwendolyn spun to see Enforcer Puckett charging at them across the atrium, two more enforcers hot on her heels.

"Tryin' to escape, huh?" Get 'em, boys. If they fight, smash the little one."

Gwendolyn glanced quickly at the others with a look that said *this is our chance,* which would have been a very specific sort of look, had it not been interrupted by bolts of electric fire. She screamed, and collapsed.

"I've had just about enough of you, you ugly little brat," Enforcer Puckett said, her hand on the button. She did not let go.

Gwendolyn writhed on the ground in an agony that she had seldom felt before. She'd had cuts and falls and broken bones, but nothing like this. Every nerve in her body screamed, and she screamed right along, her muscles spasming uncontrollably. And it just kept going.

"You're killing her!" Sparrow shouted.

"Good, it'll make the rest of you'se work harder."

"Oh, I have *had* it with you," Cecilia said, and she rushed the woman.

Puckett pointed the remote at Cecilia, but Starling threw a wrench at her. It smacked her in the side of the head, and her jaw dropped in pain and surprise. Cecilia closed it for her with a well-deserved punch. Puckett was rocked backward, and her hat and goggles went flying.

The other enforcers moved in, but Sparrow leapt on the back of one like a crazed primate and wrapped his arms around the man's throat. The man thrashed, trying to dislodge him, but Sparrow held on for dear life.

The other enforcer lunged at Starling, but she ducked his grasp, stepped in closer, and grabbed him by his tunic. Then she spun and flung the man over her hip. He hit the doubled-over Puckett, and both of them went sprawling on the ground.

Cecilia helped Gwendolyn to her feet. "Are you all right?"

Gwendolyn gasped a bitter laugh. "I'm getting quite tired of that question. Let's go!"

Sparrow boxed the other enforcer's ears and leapt off the man's back, and the four of them sprinted toward the door.

They made it across the courtyard, through the skyscraper lobby, and burst through the front doors. The entrance gate was a few feet ahead. A masked guard stood off to one side. Only his eyes were visible above his gas mask, and they widened in surprise as he saw them.

Starling raced forward, then jumped and grabbed one of the support bars of the scaffolding. She swung her feet at the guard and kicked him in the head, and the man went staggering into the fence. Blue-white bolts arced across his body, and the man dropped.

"Thanks, Brian," Starling said, and she slapped the large red button he had been standing next to.

The gate slid open, revealing the darkened street outside. A thick fog had drifted in, the buzzing streetlights tinting it an ugly yellow. The four of them dashed outside.

"All right," Sparrow said, gasping and panting. "Where now?"

"I don't..." Cecilia said, gasping as well. "I don't remember reading about this in *Tautopolis*."

"I knew you were reading too fast," Gwendolyn said, struggling to catch her own breath. She was still recovering from the shock. Her muscles ached, and her lungs burned. She coughed. "But anywhere is better than here."

"Fine with me," Starling said, coughing as well. She took a few steps, then stumbled, dropping to one knee. "What—" she started to say, but she broke off in a fit of coughing.

"Starling—" Sparrow said, but was interrupted by a coughing fit of his own.

The four of them were racked with heaving coughs, each of them gasping for breath. Gwendolyn noticed that it wasn't just her muscles and lungs that were burning. Her eyes stung as well. They were watering, and it was hard to keep them open.

"The fog!" Starling managed to rasp between coughs. "It's gas!"

Gwendolyn tried to speak, but couldn't manage it. The best she could do was flail vaguely back toward the gate. They all stumbled back into the building.

Where they were met by a wall of very annoyed-looking enforcers, gas-masks up and goggles on.

"Well," said Enforcer Puckett, rubbing her jaw. Her voice was distorted through the mask. "What do you know, fog-o-clock, on the dot. Looks like the weathermen got it right today."

Gwendolyn wished she had the breath for a stinging retort, but her lungs weren't cooperating. Toxic gas and electrocution had taken a toll on her witty repartee. The yellow fog was drifting through the open gate. She was coughing so hard she couldn't even stand up straight, and the enforcers were barely visible through her stinging tears.

"Come on, Shauna, can we just kill these kids already? It's time for my break," said a guard on the left.

"Yeah, they ain't worth the fuss. Just push 'em into the fog and close the gate. It's fast, and I won't have to clean my boots afterward."

Gwendolyn's head was swimming. She saw a pair of heavy-soled boots, was grabbed by a pair of heavily gloved hands, and hauled upward by a heavily muscled thug.

"Sorry kid," he said. "I mean, not really, but that's the sort of thing yer s'pposed to say, ain't it?"

She struggled to kick, to move, to say anything, but she could hardly even open her eyes. There was a roaring sound in her ears, and everything went black.

CHAPTER TWENTY

CATO LOCKE

Her vision returned slowly, along with a ringing in her ears. She was on the ground. Stunned, she got to all fours and managed a look around.

There was rubble strewn around her. Smoke, good old fashioned grayish-black smoke, drifted through the air. And she noticed that she wasn't the only one on the ground—all the enforcers were down as well. Masked figures were moving through the smoke, but they did not wear the leather tunics and squared caps of the enforcers.

Focus! Gwendolyn shouted at her addled brain. The roaring in her ears—that hadn't been the effects of the gas. It had been an explosion. The ground was littered with bits of stone and twisted pieces of fencing.

The enforcer next to her began to stir. But he was struck in the head with the butt of a rifle, and went down again.

Someone stood over Gwendolyn, masked and goggled, and six feet tall if he was an inch. He reached out a hand to help her up.

"Come with me if you want to get out of here."

She took hold of his hand. He was wearing fingerless gloves, a high-collared leather jacket, and had jet black hair from what she could see of the few slick locks that fell across his masked face. His whole appearance was tactical in nature, but too cobbled-together to look like any actual military uniform.

Thoughts sluggishly churned their way to the surface. "Cato Locke, yes?"

The boy cocked his head in a look of surprise. "Do I know you?"

Gwendolyn forced a grin through her daze. "No. But who else would you be?"

"Weird thing to say." His eyes flicked to her bare head. "Anyway. Gotta job to do." And he sprinted into the building.

Sparrow, Starling, and Cecilia had all gotten to their feet. The enforcers around them had been dealt with as efficiently as the first, and lay unmoving on the ground. Gwendolyn looked at her companions. "I think we found the Causists." And she led them to toward the battle inside.

There wasn't much battle left. The invading rebels stood, casually holding their rifles, while the enforcers were on their knees with their arms behind their heads in surrender. Fresh mounds of rubble littered the atrium. The surly boy from earlier was cheering now, though it was unclear whether he was glad to be rescued or merely excited at the prospect of more rocks to move.

Workers from the Bootstrap Brigade crowded around their liberators, swelling their numbers to a few dozen. Rifles were handed out. Cato Locke marched around shouting orders. In that moment, he reminded Gwendolyn of Kolonius Thrash, barking commands at his airship crew.

At least something was getting back to normal. This was the sort of adventure she knew the shape of. "That's him," she said. "Cato Locke."

"Great!" Sparrow said. "Now we just have to hope he knows how to stop the Blackstar and find your parents."

"Exactly," Gwendolyn said. "But first—our things." She led them across the atrium to the guard tent and retrieved Cecilia's purse. Then she marched over to the shop area and snatched a few gas masks.

She reached her friends just as Cato's voice boomed over the crowd. He stood on a pile of rubble, easily seen by all.

"Corporate will be here soon. Anyone who wants out, come with us. Join the Cause!"

Some of the workers cheered. Others simply looked bored, and began shifting this new supply of rocks. Cato waved toward the entrance, and Gwendolyn followed.

At the entrance, she found Starling standing over Enforcer Puckett. The woman was on her knees with her hands behind her head. A member of Cato's ragtag militia stood behind her holding a rifle. The strange weapon had a ringed barrel and pointed tip, and clearly was not made for firing any kind of bullet. It reminded her vaguely of the Pistola Luminant.

"Take them off, and give me the remote," Starling was saying.

Puckett spat on the ground.

Starling looked at the armed militia man. "A little help?"

The man fired at the ground, and a bolt of electricity left a sizzling crater in the concrete.

Puckett grumbled, and fished the small remote out of her

pocket. She clicked a button, and the stun cuffs fell off all of their wrists.

"Thanks," Starling said. She reached down and began unstrapping her tracker gauntlet from Puckett's arm.

"Hey! Stop that!" Puckett shouted.

"Just taking what's mine," Starling said. Then she swiped the goggles off the woman's head. "Plus interest."

"And the boots!" Gwendolyn said. "Get her boots." The woman's feet looked pretty small, and Gwendolyn's own ached and stung with tiny cuts.

"Oh, come on," Puckett moaned, but she reluctantly unlaced her heavy combat boots.

Gwendolyn gave the woman a sarcastic smirk and started putting them on. "What's the matter? I thought this sort of thing was encouraged here. Just think of me as a girl achieving her own happiness."

"Girls, plural." Starling gave the Enforcer's goggles to Sparrow.

"Yay! I finally get my own goggles!" he crowed.

"They're for the gas, dummy." She snatched two more from other Enforcers and gave them to Gwendolyn and Cecilia.

Gwendolyn finished lacing up the boots, and donned the goggles too. "We'll need these as well," she said, distributing the gas masks.

"Everyone geared up?" said Starling.

They all nodded, goggles on their heads and masks around their necks.

"Good. Now come on, or we'll lose Cato."

"Good thing he showed up. Just in the nick of time," Sparrow said as they joined the mass exodus.

"Yeah. Convenient," Starling said.

"Not really," Gwendolyn replied, spotting Cato at the head of the crowd. "He's the hero, and we're in his story. He was bound to show up sooner or later. Just like Kolonius in Tohk, and Jack in Umberland…" She choked a little. It was probably just the gas.

She pulled her mask up and lowered her goggles. It felt oddly… safe. She was anonymous. Protected from sight and danger alike. And just in time, as the whole group filed out into the fog.

There was no coughing or watering eyes this time, just a greasy feeling on her bare skin and scalp. It was cold, and she could feel goosebumps running up her arms.

The amber streetlights barely penetrated the toxic fog, and visibility was limited to only a few feet in any direction. The buildings on either side were mere shadowy suggestions. Neon signs were little more than hazy blobs of color, and the metal towers that lined the rooftops created globes of flickering white.

Gwendolyn shoved her way to the front of the crowd. Cato Locke led the way down the street, flanked by armed militia men.

"All right, Mr. Locke. Where are we going?" she said, her voice muffled behind the mask.

"Headquarters," he said.

"Good, good." She tried to sound as though she knew what she was doing. She was supposed to be protecting him, making sure the Blackstar didn't murder him the way he had Jack Lazarus. The idea seemed laughable now. She was small, and unarmed, and so… *soft,* compared with this hardened fighter. "Do I get a gun?" she asked.

"You any good?"

"Umm, a little?" she said, remembering her brief experiences with the Pistola Luminant. "Listen, I can help, and I need yours. I've got to find my parents. And there's this man after us, and we need your help to stop him too, he's going to come after you—"

"Lots of people are after us. Shut up and fall in."

"Corporate incoming. They're closing on our position," said the man to Cato's right, holding a boxy communicator.

"Frak. Our transport?"

"Inbound to the rendezvous point."

Cato grunted in acknowledgment. "How close is Corporate?"

"Hard to say in the fog, but—"

A bolt of blue-white lightning streaked over their heads.

"That close."

Two more bolts crackled past. A neon sign burst in a shower of sparks, and chunks of concrete rained down around them.

"Take cover!" Cato shouted. The Causists returned fire, and the crowd from the Bootstrap Brigade scattered behind automobiles and into alleyways. Gwendolyn and her friends dashed behind a large dumpster, while Cato and two others ducked behind a truck. Bolts shrieked through the fog around them.

"Return fire!" Cato shouted. His men lifted their rifles and sent their own crackling bursts in the general direction of their attackers.

"You wanted a fog-time raid," said a woman with spiky pink hair. "'The element of surprise', you said."

"Rub it in," Cato grunted. "Ugh. If only it were night."

"But it *is* night," Gwendolyn called out.

"What?" Cato said. He leaned out from behind the truck and fired his rifle blindly into the fog.

"It's dark!" Gwendolyn shouted above the crackling blasts.

"What's wrong with you? It's always dark." He ducked back into cover as a lightning blast sizzled through the spot where his head had been.

"Oh," Gwendolyn said. "Umm, we're new here."

"Nobody's that new, weird girl."

Gwendolyn scowled. "If it's always dark, how can you tell when it's night?

"Because it rains at night. Any more stupid questions?" The truck shuddered as more blasts hit the other side.

She considered this. "And you need the rain to deal with the fog." She looked up at the hazy glow of the towers on the rooftops. She focused on that static tingle in the air.

Oh, yes. She could use that. She thought of Faeoria, of the drifting motes of faerie dust, of the magic that filled each breath. She let it fill her up now, inhaling so deeply she thought she might burst. A golden gleam flickered from her hands.

"So *what if* it were raining?"

She infused the words with the energy inside her, picturing the sound of thunder, the patter of rain on the stones, the cold wet droplets against her skin, and the scent of the water washing the dust and grime from the world. She imagined all that energy shooting up into the sky.

And thunder answered her call.

Cato and the others looked up. The rain came in thick, fat droplets. It wasn't normal water at all. It splattered the stones

258

around them in globs much thicker than Gwendolyn had imagined. She brushed at a few droplets on her jacket, then grimaced in disgust. It was thicker than water, greasy and yet slightly sticky at the same time.

"Ugh," Cecilia said, "What is this stuff? It's absolutely ruining my hair."

For once, Gwendolyn was grateful she didn't have any, though the feeling of it on her scalp was particularly unpleasant. It reminded her of her duel with the Blackstar, when he'd made it rain a tar-like substance that tried to bite her ankles. Which reminded her—

She closed her eyes and imagined, which was easier, since this particular image was rooted in her memory. That electric tingle in the air intensified, the hair on her arms stood up, and there was a small *pop* of displaced air.

"Here," she said, and passed each of her friends a cheerful yellow umbrella.

"Thanks," Cecilia said, opening her umbrella.

The greasy downpour came in with a violence that seemed almost personal, and soon the fog was beaten into submission. The air was clear, and the ground was covered in rivulets of sickly yellow muck. The rain splattered against the umbrellas.

"So it looks like you've got your magic back," Sparrow said.

Gwendolyn pointed to the towers. "I think it's those. There's a lot of power in the air."

Cecilia's face brightened. "So, can I do that?"

"Maybe if you spent a decade sitting in a dark classroom every day with nothing but your imagination for company," Gwendolyn smirked.

"Fine," Cecilia said, opening her umbrella.

Cato Locke took off his mask and goggles and held out a hand to catch the rain. "You did this." He gaped at Gwendolyn. "How?"

Gwendolyn took off her own mask and goggles, grinning. "I'm special."

He nodded, as if adjusting to this strange new reality. "Okay. Weird girl is weird, but not useless." He looked her up and down with fresh, almost hungry eyes. Then he took off his jacket and tossed it to her. "Fair trade. You'll want this."

She caught it. "What for?"

He simply gestured to the rain and pulled up the hood on his sleeveless shirt.

Gwendolyn frowned, but it *was* cold at any rate. She juggled the umbrella from hand to hand to shrug into the jacket, then did up the buckles along the front. Their conversation was interrupted by a fresh volley of lightning blasts. Cato nodded at one of his two partners. "Zana? Situation?"

The pink haired woman peeked up over the truck. "Good news or bad news?"

Cato groaned. "Good news first.

"Well, we can see them now."

"Bad news?"

There was a crackling explosion, and the car they were hiding behind shook violently. Lightning crackled over the metal.

"Bad news is, they can see us back," Zana said. The three of them shifted so they were no longer touching the metal of the car. "And they've got crawlers."

"Frak," Cato hissed. "Jax? Alternate routes?"

"Crawlers coming in from the south too," the lanky man next to him answered. "They've got us pinned."

"I think we drew their attention," Zana said, leaning out and squeezing off a few bursts.

"Shut up," Cato said. He popped up from behind the car and fired a few bolts of his own.

"Who's shooting at us?" Sparrow said.

"Good question..." Gwendolyn peeked around the edge of the dumpster, squinting into the gloom.

Wet metal glinted under the streetlights. Heavy treads made a grinding sound. Eight large, bulbous monstrosities rolled toward them, crunching asphalt. They had round metal bodies, squat and stout, with spindly arms, long barreled rifles, and a cone-shaped attachment on one side. A glowing eye dominated the center of the spherical bodies, covered in a crosshatch of metal bars, glaring at them with lifeless mechanical malice. Everything about them was ugly, efficient, and brutal.

Each of their cone-shaped arms began to glow. Blue electricity gathered there, which formed into a crackling ball of lightning. There was a crack of thunder, and the lightning spheres flew at them.

Gwendolyn ducked behind the dumpster again, just as one of the spheres slammed into the other side, delivering another electric shock as the current ran through it. The four of them cried out.

"Don't touch the metal!" Gwendolyn ordered.

"What was that?" Cecilia said.

"Uh... *crawlers*? Like small bathyspheres on rolling tracks."

A ball of lightning blew a hole in the street a few inches from the dumpster.

"Oh, and with weapons."

"Weird girl!" shouted Cato. "Anything you can do?"

"What did you have in mind?" she called back.

"Cover would be nice! We need to get clear and make our pickup before the other squad arrives and hems us in!"

"All right," Gwendolyn said, rubbing her hands together. "I think I have an idea."

She closed her eyes and did her best to shut out the world around her, the constant crackle of electrical fire, the distant grinding of tank treads, the shouted orders and panicked cries.

Instead, she thought of the City. Of the Edge. And the Wall right at the border of it. An enormous, impenetrable wall. She'd spent entire days staring at it, and the image of it was ready in her mind.

Then she opened her eyes and stared out at the street. She took that picture of the Wall and brought it to life in front of her, picturing it rising out of the ground, a wall of concrete as high as the buildings around them.

"*If only...*" she whispered, breathing energy into the words as if it were a sort of prayer.

A section of the street rippled, as though it were liquid rather than stone. A line of asphalt rose. A few inches. A foot. Gwendolyn felt the energy flow out of her. She tried harder, gritting her teeth. Another foot of wall rose from the ground.

But darkness crowded her vision. Gwendolyn staggered and fell over, just barely managing to catch herself, one palm scraped raw on the sticky-slick asphalt.

"Gwendolyn!" Sparrow said.

"I'm fine." But she was short of breath. Her head was swimming.

"Is that it?" Cato called.

Gwendolyn managed to look up. A waist-high wall of stone rose up in a solid line stretching from one side of the street to the other. "Perhaps that idea was a little too big. I *did* just make it rain, you know,"

"Not a great time to be learning your limits," Cecilia grumbled.

Gwendolyn gritted her teeth. "No. I can do this." Creating tons of stone out of thin air clearly took more energy than she had. She tried to think, mind whirling for a solution, thinking of everything she had noticed about Tautopolis thus far.

Cato and his men were trading shots with the Crawlers. One of the mechanical attackers was hit, and lightning crackled over its metal shell. It stopped and sagged forward for a moment, but it seemed to gather itself, then continued rolling inexorably toward them.

They certainly like their electricity. She'd noticed that much. Noticed it a little *too* much.

Then something jumped out at her. She noticed a billboard advertising *"Air-Powered Roller Skates!"* with a picture of a smiling child zooming away. Cartoon lightning bolts streamed into his wheeled shoes from an electrical tower, like the ones that lined the rooftops.

"Air-powered," she murmured. She thought of the electrical tingle on her skin, of the constant flickers of sparks that darted through the air above them. "Cato! Are those machines Air-

Powered?”

“Obviously!” he shouted back. “Everything is!”

“Then let’s try this again...” She closed her eyes again and focused on her tingling skin. She inhaled, drawing in as much of that energy as she could, letting it build and build and build. *“What if...”*

She flung her hands up at the nearest tower. Light poured from her, and the tower exploded. Every tower on the street burst in a shower of golden sparks. The streetlights went out, along with the illuminated billboards, and the neon signs. The street was plunged into darkness and silence. The splatter of greasy raindrops was the only sound.

Gwendolyn looked out again. There was enough ambient light from the rest of the city that she could just make out the crawlers a block away. They were silent and still. Gwendolyn and her friends were lit by the golden gleam from her skin.

Cato and Jax turned towards her, mouths agape. She would never get tired of that.

“There,” Gwendolyn said.

“Oh, no,” Zana moaned.

“*Oh, no,* what?” Sparrow said. “*Oh, no* is bad. I don’t like *oh, no.*”

The silence was broken by a rapid series of cracks, like popping corn and snapping twigs. Metal ricocheted off the dumpster with a clang. Windows shattered. Cato, Jax, and Zana cowered even lower as the car was hit with a hail of bullets. The sound echoed off the walls, building to a crescendo of chaos.

Sparrow stuck his yellow umbrella up above the dumpster. There was a rapid series of cracks, and it was ripped to shreds. He lowered it and looked at Gwendolyn through one of the many holes. "Yep. That's an *oh, no*."

CHAPTER TWENTY-ONE

Bad Ideas

"Frak!" Cato yelled as a chunk of asphalt near his foot exploded. "You call this helping? Whose side are you on?"

"I'm sorry!" she yelled. A sick feeling entered her gut, and her glow flickered. "How are they shooting at us? They should be out of power!"

"Diesel backups!" Zana shouted back.

"Then shoot back!" Cecilia yelled.

"Do I look like I've got a giant diesel engine on my back?" Zana held up her rifle. "These things are useless now."

Cato's face was grim. "Stunners take a lot of power. Guns don't. Looks like we're officially more trouble than we're worth."

"What does that mean?" said Sparrow.

"Means we just went from potential prisoners to potential corpses!" Jax said, fear evident in his tone.

"Relax, Jax," Cato said. "Get Ganner to make a back door for us."

"Already on it," crackled a voice from the communicator. There was a loud boom, and a fireball erupted from a building off to one side.

"Watch it, or you'll bring the whole place down," Jax said into the communicator.

"Inside!" Cato ordered. "Up to the roofs!"

Gwendolyn looked at the hole in the building across the street. "I think... I think I can cover us! Go!"

"You've done plenty," Cato said.

Gwendolyn slumped.

"It's okay," Starling said, placing a hand on her shoulder. "You can do this!"

Gwendolyn nodded and inhaled again, gathering all the power she could. She thought of the neon lights of the now-darkened streets. It wasn't hard to make light, she told herself. Light was nothing, after all. She held out her hands and cast the glow out from her skin, and created a shimmering wall of neon light between them and the crawlers.

The hail of bullets stopped. The roar of them became a muted *pinging* sound as they bounced off her barrier.

"Go!" Gwendolyn said again. "I'll hold it as long as I can."

Cato nodded, then ran. Jax and Zana followed, and others darted out from behind corners and planters and cars and poured into the building.

"You too," Gwendolyn told her friends.

Sparrow shook his head. "We're not leaving y—"

"I'm right behind you." She didn't have time to debate. It was taking every ounce of focus she had to keep that barrier in place. She tried to stand, but wobbled, and would have fallen if Cecilia hadn't caught her under the arms and helped her to her feet.

"Thanks."

There was a crash of broken glass as a bullet pierced her barrier, and the windshield of the car next to them splintered. Gwendolyn inhaled and thought harder. She stared at her shimmering wall and imagined more colors swirling across it, thickening it. "Hurry!"

They started across the street, umbrellas forgotten, but the going was slow. Gwendolyn's knees felt weak. All of her felt weak. It had been some time since she had used this much magic. Had it been this hard when she was twelve? That was no surprise. *Everything* was easier when she was twelve.

More bullets pierced the barrier, and she scolded herself for letting her mind wander. The three of them reached the building. Gwendolyn ducked inside just as a bullet struck the wall next to her head, spraying her with bits of shattered concrete.

They fled inside, into the lobby of an office building. The sound of bullets faded.

Gwendolyn let her focus fade away and drooped, hands on her knees, catching her breath. "Everyone well?"

Starling brushed dust from her turquoise blouse. "Relatively. Not choking to death or getting electrocuted is nice, but getting shot doesn't sound much better. What now?"

Gwendolyn pointed at Cato. "We play follow the hero."

Starling grinned. "At least it's a game we know how to play."

Cecilia grunted. "Just don't run off without us this time."

But Gwendolyn was already moving with the rest of the crowd. "Just try to keep up this time."

They moved through the crowd of wet and frightened detainees until they reached Cato and his team at the front, leading them into an echoing concrete stairwell. It was lit only by the bouncing flashlights of Cato's team. And there weren't terribly many of those left. When they emerged onto the roof, Gwendolyn saw that there was only a handful of Causists, with a few scattered escapees from the Bootstrap Brigade.

"Where are the others?" Cato said.

"Cass managed to split off and get most of them down a side street while the crawlers were focused on us," said the woman with short, spiky hair.

"At least we're good at *something*. Even if it's just getting shot at." Cato shot Gwendolyn a glare that was unmistakable, even in the darkness.

"What now?" Cecilia said. "Or was this the extent of your plan?"

"We've always got Starling's parabrellas," Gwendolyn said, trying to lighten the mood with memories of happier times of life-threatening peril.

Cecilia glowered. "I'm not jumping back down *into* the bullets."

Cato pointed to the next building. "We travel by rooftop until we can get past the drones. Then we'll find a way down and get to the pickup site."

"Can we get a breather?" Sparrow said, panting.

"No time. Won't take Corporate long to follow us up here. Ganner?"

A small, freckled boy smiled gleefully. He was barely older than Sparrow. "Way ahead of you." He pressed a button on some hand-held device, and the building was rocked by an explosion. "There. No more door. It'll take them a bit to shift that."

The Corporation forces seemed to agree. Spotlights hit the roof, creating a sharp line of light and shadow at the edge of the rooftop. A spattering of bullets chipped away at the roof edge. Starling yanked Sparrow back, and everyone edged deeper into the shadows.

"Stay away from the edge," Cato said. He strode across the rooftop, leading his team toward the next building over, which was separated from theirs by a narrow gap.

Gwendolyn, Cecilia, and Starling headed after, but Sparrow lagged behind.

"Keep up, brother," Starling scolded.

"I'm coming, I'm coming. I've just... just got a stitch in my side." But he collapsed to one knee, hand pressed to his ribs.

"Sparrow!" Starling cried. The three girls rushed over to him.

"Look," Cecilia said.

A wet spot had spread across his red shirt. Scarlet blood was seeping out from between his fingers.

"Oh, I... that's not good," he said, groggily. He wavered, and toppled backwards, but Starling was there to catch him and lower him to his back.

"He's been hit!" Gwendolyn shouted at Cato.

Cato had already leapt the narrow gap and was standing on the adjoining rooftop. He looked back at them, then turned to his team. "Jax, Zana, get these ones to the rendezvous. I'll catch up."

The spiky-haired woman pulled him in for a rough kiss. "Stay safe."

"Always." Cato leapt back across to them and knelt next to Sparrow. He whipped open a knife with a fancy twirl, and sliced open Sparrow's shirt. There was a small, puckered red hole in his side. And there was blood. So much blood. A puddle of it was forming on the rooftop.

Cecilia held her hand to her mouth, frozen in shock. Gwendolyn's insides quivered with a storm of emotions she had no time to sort out.

"Help him!" Starling shouted, frantically.

"I don't have a medkit. Weird girl, put pressure on the wound."

Gwendolyn did, pressing her hands against it as hard as she could. She could feel the warm wetness pulsing against her fingers with every heartbeat.

This is the part of the adventure where people get hurt, a bitter voice inside her said. *You always forget about that bit, don't you? But it always comes.*

Cato took off his tactical vest, then his sleeveless shirt. He put the vest back on over his bare chest, zipped it up, and started cutting the shirt into long strips.

"Will he be all right?" Cecilia said. "He has to be all right."

"Can't tell if it hit any major organs. Though if it has, he won't last long enough for us to find out. And I've got no idea how to get him down from here."

"No," Starling said. "There has to be a way. Gwendolyn, think of something!"

"I..." But she had no ideas. How could she imagine anything when there was so much blood? It was slick between her fingers.

What if he dies?

The thought hit her with a dull thud, one she could almost hear. An image popped into her head, vivid and real. It was nearly identical to what she saw now--Sparrow, lying bleeding and motionless. The only difference was that in her imagination, his blood had stopped pulsing against her hand.

Stop it. Don't think that, or it might come true.

She heard another dull thud. It came from that place in her mind, that door where she shoved all her unwanted feelings. They were knocking.

What if we all die? They'd all been hurt, at one time or another. They'd all shed blood. Even Cecilia, and Gwendolyn had been the one to shed it.

If only we'd never come here. Her thoughts were spiraling faster now. *If only I'd been smart enough to stay away.*

No. She had healed him before. Cyria had done it too, and Queen Titania. Magic. You could do anything with magic. Now if only she really believed that, because this wound wasn't from some magical creature, this was cold, hard steel. Even the faeries didn't muck about with iron.

What if I can't? What if I'm not good enough?

And the door in her head flew open. All the feelings she'd been shoving away, all the fears and worries and anxieties and the solid, certain knowledge that she was not enough, that she could never be enough, that all of this was so much more than she could handle. Everyone was counting on her, and she had failed. Couldn't even take care of herself. She started to shake. She couldn't hold it in any longer.

She looked down at her hands, soaked as red as the hair she'd lost. The blood seeped between her fingers and mingled with the greasy rain until she was coated with a slimy crimson sheen up to her wrists.

But... it wasn't crimson. It darkened all the way to black, and thickened until it was more like tar. The blackness crept up her arms, over the sleeves of the jacket, climbing towards her elbows.

A gaping hole opened inside her, dragging her down, until there was no escape, until anything would be better than this, better than here, with her best friend dying in front of her, the darkness literally overwhelming her, and it was all her fault.

"What if it all just stopped?" she said in a soft whimper.

And everything did.

The world went silent. The rain around her froze in midair. The droplets hung, motionless and glistening like tiny diamonds in the spotlights from the crawlers.

Starling and Cecilia looked around in confusion. Starling's wrist gauntlet started chiming, detecting the same dark energy the Blackstar used.

"What the frak..." Cato murmured, awed.

Gwendolyn didn't know. She didn't have any words. She looked down again and saw that the black goop had spread from her hands across Sparrow's chest as well, sealing his wound.

"Gwendolyn..." Cecilia said in a hushed breath. "Your eyes..."

"What?" she said, daring to look away from Sparrow.

"They're... they're black. They're all black."

So what? she thought. What did that matter? Cato elbowed her away, ready to wrap Sparrow's wounds, but stopped when he saw the tarry blackness clinging to the boy. Then the silence was broken by a renewed burst of gunfire from below.

Gwendolyn stood up.

"What are you doing?" Starling said. "Get down!"

But she didn't listen. She never listened. She walked toward the edge. Hovering raindrops bounced off her, and they were not just frozen in midair, but frozen completely, as cold and hard as her insides felt. They made soft tinkling sounds against her jacket as she moved through curtains of ice chips.

She reached the edge. She looked down at the bulbous mechs, all of them belching black smoke. She stared right into their metal eyes. And she thought of Titania, the faerie queen, of her fury, of how her dress and hair and eyes had turned black.

The blackness had spread to her shoulders, and she could feel it in her eyes now too, a thickness that coated her vision, giving her a dark and terrible clarity. A bullet struck her shoulder, but it simply bounced off the congealed shadows.

She held her arms out to the side, gathering that dark power to her, and her feet left the rooftop. The frozen shards of rain drew in around her. Gwendolyn flung her arms at the crawlers, and the rain obeyed.

Thousands of icy projectiles shot towards the mechs. Their weapon arms were sheared clean off. Their tank treads were punctured, the metal slats torn to bits. Their round bodies seemed to be made of sterner stuff, and the frozen darts shattered against the metal, but some slipped between the mesh that covered the glowing central eye and pierced the glass.

The guns fell silent. The bulbous bodies slumped forward, and their eyes went dark.

Gwendolyn floated several feet above the rooftop and surveyed the ruined crawlers. *Good,* she thought. Then the storm of cold fury went out of her, the world went black, and she fell.

~~~

When she came to, she thought she must still be flying. She was suspended, motionless, three stories above the ground. Then she noticed the pain in her armpits and looked up to see Cato and Cecilia, clutching her by the jacket, faces straining with the effort. Together they managed to haul her back onto the roof.

She collapsed in a heap as the weight of everything came crashing down on her.

It was raining again. Fat droplets smacked against her jacket. Black sludge sloughed of her arms. It poured from her eyes as well. Black tears drained out of them, mingled with the rain and ran down her face in tarry streaks. She was down on all fours, trembling furiously.

"How is he?" she managed to squeak out.

"Bleedings stopped," Cato said. "Whatever this stuff is, it's holding."

Gwendolyn managed to crawl over to the roof ledge. The mech drones were below, in various states of ruination. Hatches opened in the back of them and men emerged, stumbling and falling to the street. Some lay motionless on the pavement, some crawled around, a couple stood and pointed at the rooftop, shouting.

"Cato!" Gwendolyn shouted. "There are people in those things!"

"Of course. Who did you think was driving?"

She whipped around to face him. "I thought you said they were empty. You said they were drones..."

Cato's face twisted in disgust. "They are. Drones for the Corporation. They do whatever they're told, without question. Slaves to their next paycheck. Mindless, dull-witted cogs in the
~~~

machine."

"I could have killed them!" The horrible truth of those words stole her breath.

Cato strolled casually over, looked down, and shrugged. "Probably not. See? They're all moving. Plating's thickest on the cockpit. They weren't too concerned when they were trying to punch holes in *us*. Just ask your boy over there."

Sparrow. All other thoughts fled and she raced to his side. Starling was kneeling next to him. Her wrist gauntlet had gone silent.

"He's unconscious, but he's breathing," she said. "He's lost a lot of blood."

A fact of which Gwendolyn was acutely aware, even though rain had now washed her hands clean. Though they never really would be.

"Hey Cato," came a deep, crackling voice from a pocket on his vest. "Heard you could use a pickup."

Gwendolyn heard a new noise, the *whump-whump-whump-whump* of rotors beating the air.

"Ky!" Cato shouted into his communicator.

A shadow became visible in the sky above, a blob of black that was slightly darker than the clouds around it. As it grew closer, Gwendolyn could make out the shape of some sort of helicopter. It was oblong and bulky, the clumsy opposite of the elegant ships of Tohk. The wind from the twin rotors sent a stinging rain into her face. It hovered over their heads, belching black smoke.

Shots came from the street below, smaller pops that pinged harmlessly off the thick metal hull. Gwendolyn was oddly comforted by the sound, confirmation that the men in those mechs were, in fact, alive.

"You're a lifesaver, Ky," Cato said. "Literally. Now get an evac stretcher down here. We've got wounded."

The radio crackled to life again. "You're the boss, boss. But make it quick. These diesel backups won't last long. We need to get to an Air-Powered sector pronto, and Corporate re-enforcers will be here soon."

Cato stared at Gwendolyn as he replied. "Roger that. Don't think that will be a problem. Just get us out of here."

FOR THE CAUSE

The flight was short, yet interminably long. Gwendolyn and Starling knelt by Sparrow in the helicopter. There was little Gwendolyn could do, apart from hold his hand. It felt so small in hers, so oddly still. She was reminded that he was still a child, and though Gwendolyn was a lot of things, "child" didn't seem to be one of them anymore, even if she was only fifteen. How old was old enough to watch his face for the slightest change in breathing? For any sign that his condition was worsening?

But the seal on his wound seemed to be holding. Gwendolyn prodded it. It had dried to a stiff plaster-like substance. Some faraway part of her noticed that her fingernails were still black.

She met Starling's gaze, then looked away. Gwendolyn was supposed to help look after Sparrow, and she could scarcely have done a worse job. Electrocuted. Shot. Bleeding. Nearly dead.

Cecilia tried to speak up once or twice, but she didn't have anything to say, and they wouldn't have been able to hear each other anyway over the sound of the rotors and the wind shrieking through the open sides of the cargo hold.

Gwendolyn found herself eyeing Cato, anything to avoid looking at Starling. He was very tall, and closer to twenty than he was to sixteen. He wasn't particularly handsome. And he was even paler than she was. But his strength and confidence were reassuring.

Good, she thought. *Someone else can be in charge for a change. I certainly haven't been doing a very good job of it.*

Eventually, the helicopter reached an empty parking lot with a large circle painted in the center of it. There was a handful of automobiles, some little more than burned out wrecks. A cluster of trucks stood off to one side: large, militaristic things with tarps stretched over the back of them. People milled around. Gwendolyn recognized the prisoners who had been freed from the Bootstrap Brigade, as well as some of their rescuers. They unloaded boxes and equipment from the trucks.

As the helicopter approached, the circle in the center of the parking lot split open, revealing a gaping hole. The helicopter lowered into it. Concrete walls rose up around them as they descended into some sort of underground silo. She heard a loud *thud*, and the rain outside the helicopter stopped as the hole closed itself again.

The helicopter reached the bottom of the silo and touched down with surprising gentleness. A man in a white coat was already rushing toward them, followed by two people with a stretcher on wheels. "Where's the patient?"

"Here!" Gwendolyn called, jumping down. Gingerly, they all worked to get Sparrow on the stretcher. He groaned and shifted, which made Gwendolyn's heart jerk in a mixture of guilt and relief.

The man pressed his fingers to the side of Sparrow's throat.

"Heartbeat's steady. He seems stable. Won't know for sure until we get..." He took a pen out of his pocket and prodded the hard grey crust on his side. "This *stuff* off him. Get him to the nurse's office." He waved a hand, and they carted Sparrow away.

Starling followed, and Gwendolyn did as well, but Starling held up a hand. "You've done enough."

That stopped Gwendolyn in her tracks. She simply stood there, staring as they carted Sparrow down the hall.

Cecilia put a hand on her shoulder. "He'll be all right. You did the best you could. What nobody else could."

Gwendolyn fought the urge to shrug off Cecilia's hand. "Yes. No one can foul things up quite like I can."

Cato hopped down from the helicopter just as a large black man climbed down from the cockpit. "Where'd you get the chopper, Ky?"

"Jacked it from a Corporate garage. They were so focused on you, they didn't notice until we were halfway through take-off. Glad the diesel was fueled up, didn't know the Air-Power was out in your sector."

Cato shot an appraising look at Gwendolyn. "Yeah. Hadn't expected that. The others?"

Ky shrugged his massive shoulders. "Mostly fine. Cass made it back with two dozen new recruits. They're loading the freight elevators now."

"Good," Cato said. He turned and addressed the rest of the helicopter passengers. "Everyone take a breather. Command team, meet in the study hall in ten. We didn't go to all that trouble to sit on our hands. We've got a mission to plan. Weird girl, with me."

"And what about me?" Cecilia said.

Cato shrugged. "Yeah. Okay. You too." Then he spun and walked off the landing pad and through a set of double doors.

They started to follow, but the spiky-haired woman blocked their way and planted a finger on Gwendolyn's chest. "Watch yourself, baldie." And she stormed off.

Cecilia and Gwendolyn traded bewildered looks, then followed down the long hallway.

The small freckle-faced boy came up beside them. "Hey! I heard about what you did with the rain. Cool trick! Can you teach me?"

Gwendolyn squirmed. Whatever had happened to her, she wasn't ready to think about it just yet. She changed the subject. "Your name is Ganner, right? What is this place? Some sort of military base?"

"Here?" The boy laughed. "No. It's a school, obviously."

"Seriously?" Cecilia said.

Gwendolyn examined their surroundings. The hallway did seem familiar—the long corridor with doors on either side. The tiled floor. She even noticed some scattered banks of lockers. It all bore a striking resemblance to the School back home. "An underground school?"

"Yeah, where else would it be? No one wants the rich kids getting blown up or something. I could never afford any schooling."

"You have to *pay* for school?" Cecilia said.

"Of course. No one's going to just give it away for free, are they? But don't worry," he said, puffing out his chest. "Cato's been teaching me to read. I can do all the street signs and everything.

And being able to read the warning labels on the explosives has stopped all the... uh, well, it's been real helpful."

Cecilia shook her head. "This place, I swear."

They entered what clearly used to be a large classroom, only now, the desks were covered in maps and charts and radios and mugs of coffee gone cold. Grim and grimy rebels hunched intently over the tables, moving figures around the maps, making notes on blueprints. Gwendolyn recognized some of the members of the Bootstrap Brigade. They were being interviewed by members of the Cause.

Cato led them to a large chalkboard at one end of the command center. Two more rebels were chalking in a set of blueprints. Cato studied the map for a moment, then turned to face the girls. "Spill. Who are you?"

"Travelers," Gwendolyn said, who had grown quite accustomed to this particular conversation. "We're here to help."

"Good. That's why we broke you all out in the first place. But there's something different about you."

"We aren't from around here. But what about Sparrow? Is he going to be all right?"

"The boy?" Cato said. "No idea. Doc's got him. We'll let you know when we hear something." He peered at Gwendolyn, and seemed to notice something in her face, because his own softened slightly. "Don't worry. Doc's the best there is. See?" He unzipped his vest to show off his well-muscled torso again, which was marred by several puckered scars. "He's no stranger to bullet wounds."

"Yes, yes, fine," Gwendolyn said. "Just put a shirt on."

"I mean, he doesn't *have* to..." Cecilia said.

"Quiet," she snapped. She was in no mood for banter. "I'm Gwendolyn, and this is Cecilia. You're Cato Locke, obviously. And these people?" Gwendolyn gestured to the bustling room around them.

Cato gave a small nod of pride. "We're the Cause."

"For the Cause!" came a shout from the others.

"Okay," said Cecilia. "And what exactly *is* your cause?"

"We're going to take power from the Corporation," he said with a smile. He pointed to the blueprints on the chalkboard. "Literally. The central power station is where the Corporation generates most of the Air-Power for the city. Without it, they'll be helpless. Once we're in control, we can shut down the Air-Power to critical Corporation sectors, and wait until their diesel reserves are used up. Whoever controls the power, has the power."

He turned back to them. "But more than that. We've got word that the Board of Directors will be touring the central power station tomorrow. We can capture them and take control of the station in one fell swoop."

"Does that include the Supreme Executive?" Cecilia asked. She'd pulled her copy of *Tautopolis* from her bag.

"Of course," Cato replied.

"And is he a tall, pale gentleman, with a long black coat, black hat, and gas mask?" Gwendolyn asked.

Cato shrugged. "I guess. You just described half the people in Tautopolis."

Gwendolyn turned to Cecilia. *"The Blackstar,"* she mouthed.

"We've been planning this for a while," Cato continued. "But now we've got the final pieces."

The spiky haired woman approached with a stack of papers, along with the helicopter pilot and the tall man from the raid.

"Plans are complete," the woman said, handing the papers to Cato. "Internal layout is finalized."

Cato nodded solemnly. He gestured to each of his crew with a jerk of his chin. "Weird girl, sidekick, this is Zana, our second in command. The big bruiser is Ky, pilot and logistics. And that wiry beanpole is Jax, communications expert."

"Hello." Gwendolyn gave a little wave.

The trio stared stonily back at her.

Cecilia scoffed. "Sidekick?"

No one paid her any mind. Cato flipped through the papers. "This looks good." He hung them from metal clips on the chalkboard. "Some of the workers at the Bootstrap Brigade have done time at the power station. We broke them out to get this intel. Looks like it paid off."

"There's a problem," Zana said. "The guard complement is twice what we thought it would be. Not to mention the security detail that will be accompanying the Board of Directors."

Ky nodded in agreement. "With the bootstrappers, we've got the manpower we need. But firepower's in short supply. Hadn't expected to use so much during the raid. If we don't get a resupply, we'll never take the station."

"That's where weird girl comes in," Cato said, pointing.

"What?" she said. "Me?"

"We all saw what you did out there. You can... do things. And if you can make little yellow umbrellas, you can make something useful. Like weapons."

Gwendolyn flinched, taken aback. "Oh, um, I don't know, I..."

"Can you do it?"

"I mean, theoretically, yes, but—"

"You need us to help you save your parents, right?"

She was shocked he remembered. "Right..."

"Our help isn't free. You help us, and we'll help you."

"How exactly do you plan to do that?" Cecilia said. "We don't even know where they are."

But Gwendolyn was looking at the diagrams on the chalkboard. An outline of a boxy structure with a large electrical tower on top. And she was hit with a sudden wave of certainty.

"There," Gwendolyn said. "They're in there. I know it."

"How can you be sure?" Cecilia asked.

"Just... trust me. I can feel it." She had been in enough stories to know the shape of them. This was the Blackstar's world. This was his home. And if her parents were anywhere, they'd be in his very literal place of power. Not that she could explain any of that to Cecilia in front of the others.

"Makes sense. The corporation keeps plenty of high-value prisoners on the work force there." Cato said. "If you're right, weird girl, then we've got a deal. If you get us the firepower we need. Think you can do it?"

Her parents needed her. And from what the Blackstar had said, they didn't seem to have much time. "Yes. I'll help."

Cato gave her an unusually warm smile. "Good. This way."

The boy and his team led them down another hallway. Cecilia sidled up next to Gwendolyn, took her by the hand, and pulled her back, out of earshot of the others.

"What are you doing?" Cecilia whispered.

"Being myself," Gwendolyn said. "I'm not going to sit around thinking. I'm just going to act, like I used to."

"But are you sure this is a good idea? Barging into battle on a hunch? Using your powers to make weapons? It feels... wrong."

"If it helps rescue my parents, I don't particularly care. Besides, this is what's supposed to happen. They raid the tower and overthrow the evil Corporation. Isn't that what happens in the book?"

"I'm not sure, I didn't get time to finish!"

Gwendolyn's expression grew grim. "I'll tell you how it ends. Cato beats the Blackstar. And if he says that he needs my help, then I'll give it to him. So unless you have any better ideas, we'll let Cato do the thinking."

"And what about Sparrow? I bet Cato's not thinking about him."

Gwendolyn tripped over her own feet, stumbling for a moment. Gwendolyn looked at the group ahead, and was struck by how familiar it was. The dashing leader. The ragtag team of fighters. The plans for a daring raid. It reminded her of much happier times, of adventures with Kolonius Thrash and the crew of the *Lucrative Endeavour.* "He's the leader. It's his story. And that's how these stories work. He knows what he's doing."

"It's *your* power," Cecilia said. "If we try to help them, and things go wrong, that's on you."

"Fine. It'll be all my fault. As usual. Which is why you're not coming."

Cecilia scoffed. "Pull the other one. You don't give me orders, *princess.*"

"No," Gwendolyn sighed. "I didn't think that would work. But I had to try. Just don't get yourself killed, all right?"

"Just don't get me killed, all right?" she replied.

"Fair enough."

They entered an old locker room, and though it had clearly been some time since it had been used as such, the smell seemed to have lingered. Stone-faced young men and women were pulling equipment from lockers, checking supplies, loading bags. Cato led them to a table at the far end.

Cato looked at Gwendolyn. "Okay. Go." He gestured to the table.

"What? It's an empty table."

"Exactly. Make something."

Gwendolyn frowned. "Like what?"

Cato nodded at Ky. The big man reached into a nearby locker, pulled something out, and tossed it to Cato, who plunked it down on the table with a *thud*.

It was a gun. A pistol, black and blocky and ugly.

"Go," Cato said. "Make more of these."

Gwendolyn fidgeted. "I don't like guns."

"Oh, I'm sorry," Cato snapped. "Did you think this had something to do with what you liked? Lives are at stake. So make it happen."

"It doesn't work like that!" Gwendolyn snapped back.

"So how *does* it work?"

She stopped in mid-retort. She'd never tried to explain her powers before. How did she make them understand? "It's... I just see things. In my head. I imagine them."

Cato rolled his eyes. "Then *imagine* me some guns."

"No, it's more than that, it's…" She sighed. "It's not just about imagination. You have to *believe.*"

His eyes narrowed. "Believe what?"

"Believe in… whatever you're imagining." The words flowed from her, things she'd never consciously thought, but knew all the same. "You have to *believe* that it could really be real. That it *should* be real. You have to believe it so hard that the world around you can't disagree. Above all, you have to believe in yourself. Believe that you can really do it. That what's in your head is so important that it absolutely has to get out."

Zana looked skeptical. "That's… kind of narcissistic."

Gwendolyn shrugged. "You asked. So it isn't like I can just…" She waved her hand over the table. "Poof."

"But this *is* important," Cato said, pounding the table for emphasis, making the gun jump.

Jax nodded. "If we can't arm these new recruits, there's no way we'll be able to take on the Supreme Executive's security forces."

The Supreme Executive. The Blackstar. Gwendolyn's hands clenched into fists. Cato was right. This was up to her. She had to try.

"All right. Stand back." She pushed up the sleeves on her jacket and held her arms over the table. She tried to conjure the feeling of excitement, of *magic,* of the warm wave of manic energy that coursed through her until she was very literally glowing with it. But the gun on the table was so solid, so *real.* It wasn't an easy thing to get excited about.

No. She could do this. This was one of the Abscess' worlds, one of the dark places where imagination was hoarded, not shared. Her powers always worked better on worlds like this. She could tap into that hoard, steal power from the Abscess.

She closed her eyes and let her mind wander back to Tohk, to Kolonius Thrash and Tylerium Drekk and his pirates, all of them armed to the teeth. She pictured their ornate pistols, artful things with stenciled barrels and pearl grips--

Something clattered onto the table. She opened her eyes.

On the table lay a single object, something somewhat reminiscent of a pistol.

Ky picked it up. He frowned examining it. "What is this?" He turned it over in his hands. "This won't work. The hammers don't move. And look, the barrel's solid all the way through." He banged it on the side of the table. "Makes a nice club, though."

"Well, I don't know anything about guns!" Gwendolyn shouted. She'd failed. She couldn't do it. Her stomach clenched and her breaths came faster. "They're complicated!"

"You didn't know anything about bathyspheres, either," Cecilia pointed out, unhelpfully.

Gwendolyn glared at her. "I was a different girl then. Reality seems a lot less real when you're *twelve*." But the last two years had held a lot of cold, hard reality.

What if I never get that back? she thought. What if she had lost her spark? What if she'd forgotten what it was like to make-believe, and believe it so hard it came to life? And not just to life, but so *much* life that it ran around with its own past, its own memories, its own desires and heartaches and dangers? To make it real enough that he could be dying, right now, back in the medical bay with a bullet in his side? What if Sparrow died, and—

"Gwendolyn," Cecilia said. "Look at your hands."

"What? Why?" Surely they weren't glowing, she—

Her hands were pitch black, all the way to her wrist.

Which only worsened the anxiety in her, the feeling of being squeezed and contracted until she could no longer breathe. This was the opposite of what she needed. She was letting everyone down. How could she protect Cato, or her friends? How could she stop the Blackstar?

He always won. His ideas always beat hers. Because the bad ideas were always stronger, weren't they? They spread faster. Dug deeper. They wormed their way into your head and wouldn't leave you alone, keeping you awake night after night. She'd spent precious little time lost in her imagination the past three years, but had spent plenty consumed by doubt and darkness.

So she reached for that instead. She didn't have to look far. She opened that door in her mind, to the closet where she shoved the feelings she didn't dare to feel. To her sadness, her numbness, her pain.

Her dreams were silly make-believe, but her fears, doubts, and anxieties were all very real. Gwendolyn could beat the Blackstar at his own game. If she was going to make things worse, she'd make them much *much* worse. No one could create a bigger mess than Gwendolyn Gray.

What if this went badly? *What if* someone got hurt?

"What if this is a terrible idea?" she whispered.

CHAPTER TWENTY-THREE

MORE BAD IDEAS

And again, she pictured what she wanted. She placed her hands on the table.

The blackness flowed from her hands like a living thing, coating the table in a slick, tarry puddle. Lumps bubbled up from the puddle, congealing, solidifying into shapes.

In moments, the table was covered with ugly black rifles. They were long, blocky things. Inelegant, and sturdy. They bubbled up from the puddle until they were spilling off the table. Everyone took a step back to avoid the cascade of weapons clattering to the floor.

"Whoah," said Ganner. His eyes gleamed with fascination.

Ky picked up one of the rifles. He pointed it at the wall and fired. A bolt of black energy shot out and splattered against it. It didn't even leave a mark. "Not much good, are they?"

Gwendolyn scowled and straightened. She felt dirty. Greasy. "I tried to make them like your lightning guns. I don't want anyone else getting shot." She wondered where in the base Sparrow was. She pictured him lying on a table, with doctors working frantically over him. *He'll be all right,* she told herself.

Zana took a weapon off the table, sighted down the barrel, and fired across the locker room. It hit an unsuspecting Causist who yelped and dropped. She grinned wickedly. "Yep. Looks good."

Another Causist knelt next to the man and took his pulse. He gave them a thumbs up.

Cato snatched the rifle from Zana. "Enough. Start passing these out. I want everyone armed and ready in the hour. The Board of Directors will be arriving at the central power station soon, and I want us in control before they do."

The locker room was instantly abuzz with activity. Ky and Jax organized the rifles and handed them out. Cato turned to Gwendolyn and Cecilia.

"Good job, weird girl. Now we stand a chance. We'll hold up our end of the bargain and find your parents in there." He clenched a gloved fist. "Then we'll take down the Board of Directors and the Supreme Executive. For the Cause."

"For the Cause!" came an echoing shout.

"Fine," Gwendolyn said. "But where's Sparrow? I have to see him."

Cato nodded. "Ganner, take them to the nurse's office to check on the kid."

Ganner saluted. "Roger. C'mon, girls."

He led them out of the room and through the twisting hallways to a room with a frosted glass door that read *NURSE* in large black letters.

The office had been converted into a makeshift trauma ward. Medical equipment and hospital beds had been crammed in. The sharp smell of antiseptic hit her nose. And there was Sparrow, shirtless, sitting up in bed and sipping a juice box.

Starling sat beside him, looking older and more tired than Gwendolyn had seen her. The look she gave Gwendolyn was not exactly a friendly one. Gwendolyn couldn't blame her.

She rushed over to him. He looked so tiny propped up among all the pillows. She looked at the bandages wrapped around his torso. All white, no sign of red.

"How are you?" Gwendolyn asked, hesitantly. "Does it... does it hurt?"

"Yep," he grunted, staring down at his juice box. "Lots of ouch. But Doc over there says I'll be fine." He gestured to the approaching doctor.

"I'd say this young man is very lucky," the doctor said. "Far as I can tell, the bullet hit a rib and bounced right back out. Cracked the heck out of the rib and tore a pretty big hole on its way through, but didn't penetrate the chest cavity. But that's not the strange part."

He used scissors to cut away the bandages, but underneath, Sparrow looked... fine. There were no stitches or sutures, no sign of a gaping gunshot wound. There was some scarring, but it might have been years old, not hours.

"When we scraped that crust off him, the skin was mostly healed. Never seen anything like it. If Cato hadn't told us the situation, I'd never have believed it. Scans showed no signs of internal bleeding, but that rib won't heal in a hurry. He'll need to take it easy for the next couple of months. Plenty of rest, no running around or other strenuous activity."

Sparrow scoffed. "Pfft. Good luck with that."

Starling gave him a playful swat on the head. "You'll do what the man says."

Relief swept over Gwendolyn and she sank down onto the edge of the bed. "Thank you, doctor."

"Thank me by staying away from bullets in the future." He walked away muttering to himself, checking on various other patients. "Like *that's* going to happen. I don't know why I bother, they all just rush right back out again—"

Gwendolyn looked at Sparrow, who was still fidgeting with the juice box. "Well, that's good news. I'm glad that... stuff... did some good."

He looked up for the first time, and the look in his eyes shook her.

It was full of sadness, and... disappointment? Betrayal? Gwendolyn knew, through some shared special connection, that it was the look of shattered illusions. As though he couldn't believe that this had happened to him. Or that Gwendolyn had let it happen. A look that said that the Sparrow on the bed was a much different Sparrow than the one who had climbed those stairs to that rooftop.

It was a very specific sort of look.

He looked away again. "So what's the plan? I'm itching to get out of here." He scratched at the bandages. "And just plain itching."

Cecilia filled him in while Gwendolyn stared down at her boots. She had let him down. She'd let Starling down. She was supposed to take care of them all, and how long had it taken for Sparrow to wind up in a hospital bed? Who was she trying to fool? She could barely take care of herself.

"All right," Sparrow said when Cecilia had finished. "Get me another shirt, and let's get moving. That was my favorite shirt, too…"

"What?" Gwendolyn said, jerked out of her stupor. "You're not coming. You're going to stay here and rest like the doctor said."

Sparrow snorted a bitter laugh. "Yeah, right. Not a chance. I'm not sitting here while you two go out and save the day. Who knows what could happen?"

"Exactly my point. You've already been hurt once. You're staying put, and that's final."

Sparrow glared up at her. "Just because you're older than me doesn't mean you can tell me what to do. You're not my mom, and you're not Starling." He looked away again. "You're not even Gwendolyn anymore."

The words hit as hard as any bullet. Gwendolyn got up and turned away, leaning against a counter. "Starling, talk some sense into him."

"Oh, no. You're not leaving us behind," Starling said. "What happens when you find your parents, huh? You're going to try to escape that place, and come all the way back here to pick us up? No. We're sticking by you. Believe me, right now, I'd rather be anywhere else. But the library here is destroyed, so whatever happens, you're the only way out of this place."

Gwendolyn stared down at her fingers, splayed on the counter-top. The fingernails were still black. She wasn't numb, or depressed. She just wanted to cry. "It will be dangerous."

Starling snorted. "Of course it will. But someone's gotta be there to clean up your mess. We just need you to find us a way off this world, if you can quit moping around and get it together long enough."

"What?" Gwendolyn said, spinning around.

"You heard me. Lately you're either mopey and sullen, or hyper and impulsive. Sometimes I don't know whether I'm talking to you, or one of your mood swings."

Gwendolyn's face flushed, and her fists clenched. "It's not a mood, it's an illness!"

Starling crossed her arms. "Whatever. At least this Cato kid seems stable."

"That's out of line!" Cecilia shouted. "She's doing her best!"

Gwendolyn was speechless. Starling was attacking her, and Cecilia was coming to her defense? It was enough to make her head spin.

"Guys, come on, quit fighting," Sparrow said. "I'm not looking to get shot again. I'll stay at the back, I promise. But we need to stay together."

"He's got a point," Cecilia said. "It will be a lot easier if we don't have to worry about fighting our way back out again."

"I know." She sniffed, wiped her eyes, and tried to pull herself together. She forced a confidence she did not feel. "Well then. It's not like the 'stay behind and stay safe' conversation ever works. But someone has to say it. It's practically a tradition."

"Great," Sparrow said. He chucked his juice box across the room and straight into a trash can. "When do we leave?"

~~~

Hours later, they were cutting through the water on a collection

296
~~~

of small rubber rafts. The black craft motored through the darkness with nothing more than the muffled hum of the engines.

Gwendolyn sat at the front of the boat, next to Cato. Starling sulked at the rear, Sparrow by her side, while one of Cato's crew manned the rudder. Cecilia was reading *Tautopolis* by flashlight. The light of it sent a rainbow of colors rippling across the surface of the oil-slick water. The neon glow of Tautopolis lay behind them, creating a hazy bubble of light.

The central power station was off-shore, to guard against exactly this sort of attack. But Cato had loaded nearly thirty rafts with Causists armed to the teeth. They had the plans to the station thanks to members of the Bootstrap Brigade who had once worked there.

This was just like her trip to the Crystal Coves with Kolonius, right? A night-time boat ride to a mysterious destination that held the key to their survival.

Except it wasn't. There was no sense of wonder or whimsy. No excitement. Just grim purpose. She would get her parents back. And then she'd be done. No more of this.

No more. She'd never thought that before. Never so seriously. But it was what she wanted, wasn't it? No more adventures? To go back home, to cozy up on the couch next to Mother, safe and sound in her own little world?

She looked back at Starling, who sat with her arms crossed, glaring at the water. Sparrow leaned against her, head on her shoulder, dozing.

Back at the Crystal Coves, Sparrow had put himself in harm's way to save her. He'd been pulled from the water and they had shared their very soggy first embrace. Back when they'd been together. They were only a few feet apart, but two years had put a lot of distance between them. She still cared for him. How could she not? But now she had to *take* care of him, and it was a completely different sensation.

So instead she turned to Cato, who had still not put on a shirt, and was wearing only his combat vest and gloves. "Can I ask you a question?"

He grunted. "Can I stop you?"

"No, you cannot. My question is--why are you doing all this?"

He cocked an eyebrow at her. "What do you mean?"

She gestured to the boats around them. "Helping. You're not like everyone else in this story. They all ramble on about serving themselves, about your own happiness being more important than anything else. But you're risking everything to help them. Why?"

He gave her a quizzical look. "For the Cause."

Gwendolyn sighed. "Of course. For the Cause."

Cato eyed her, and his expression softened. "I never wanted to be a leader, you know. I was just a regular kid. Until they took my parents. I swore I'd never let that happen again." He nodded at her. "You understand."

She nodded back. "I certainly do."

"I spent years living in one of the child camps. On my own. Always dreaming of this day. I would picture it so clearly—"

"You would imagine it?" Gwendolyn said with a smirk.

Cato grunted a laugh. "Yeah. I guess. I swore that I would never live for the sake of another man, or ask another to live for mine. I would make my own life."

298

He stared out at the waves, the light from Cecilia's flashlight casting odd, flickering shadows on his face. "But it's hard. Everyone thinks I'm some chosen one. They all expect me to fix everything." He paused for a moment, then turned to look at her. "Something tells me you understand that too. Because you're not like anyone else, either."

"No, I guess not."

"There's something about you, weird girl. You're so bright. And this world is so dark."

She blinked. "What?"

"Like your eyes. They're green. Like emeralds. No one else's eyes shine like that."

"Um…" She squirmed under his intense scrutiny. "Do you usually spend this much time talking about other people's eyes?"

His gaze deepened. "Only the pretty ones."

"Wow." She rolled her eyes and looked away. "You're even worse than Tommy."

Then she felt his hand cover hers.

She jerked away as though burned. "Eww! No! What are you doing?"

"There's a connection between us. I can feel it."

"You just met me, and you can't even remember my name!"

His voice was low and sincere. "I'd like to learn."

"Oh my *god*. You have *seriously* misread the situation. Firstly, you're a very rude person. Nextly, you're *much* older than me, which is, frankly, disturbing. And finally, I'm far too busy for any of that romantic nonsense, even if I wanted any, which I don't." She crossed her arms defensively and turned back to Cecilia, who was still lost in Cato's book. "You didn't tell me he'd be like this."

She shrugged without looking up. "I don't know, I thought he was kind of hot when I was reading it."

Gwendolyn rolled her eyes again. "You would."

Out of the corner of her eye, she spotted Zana in the adjacent boat, glaring daggers at her. The spiky-haired girl made a cutting gesture across her throat, then pointed at Gwendolyn.

Gwendolyn threw up her hands. "Oh, for heaven's sake! Will you all just shut up, and focus on the mission?"

Cato arched an eyebrow.

Gwendolyn groaned in frustration. "And I am not flirting, or playing hard to get. This is a complete, and unequivocal, no." She glared at Cato. "Got it?"

Cato shrugged and looked back out at the water.

"Now if you can keep from getting distracted by your raging hormones, I need to warn you. The security detail isn't our only concern. We've run into the Supreme Executive before. He has all the same powers I do. So be on your guard.

Cato nodded stoically at the waves. The wind ruffled his hair. "I'm *always* on my guard."

Cecilia whistled in appreciation. "See? Hot."

Gwendolyn clenched her fists to hold back another groan, but was distracted by a light on the horizon. "Is that..."

"Yes," Cato said. "The central power station."

As they drew closer, Gwendolyn saw a structure looming out of the water. Enormous concrete pylons supported a brutal looking building with narrow slitted windows, like giant concrete boxes on thick legs. On top was an even more enormous metal tower, a complicated framework of girders and wires. The whole thing stretched hundreds of feet high. The top of the tower was capped with a large dome, a mesh of crisscrossing steel beams. The dome radiated a sickly light. A haze spread through the thickened atmosphere for a mile in all directions. It looked like a giant metal-mesh mushroom had sprung up, poisoning the very air around it.

"Jax, Ky, Ganner, Zana," Cato shouted to the other boat. "Make sure your gear is prepped and ready to go. Get your harnesses on. Pass word down the line, no radios."

Cecilia turned a page. "You guys know you all have ridiculous names, right?"

The Causist at the tiller chuckled.

Cecilia eyed him. "And what's your name? Xander, or something equally stupid?"

The man sagged. "Yes..." he grumbled.

"Don't let her get to you, Xander," Cato said. "We're here."

POWER

The boats crept up beneath the power station. The massive concrete structure loomed above them like so many giant bricks under that enormous dome. Everything was silent, save for the sounds of the waves that crashed against the pylons. The water slid greasily back down.

"Harpoons," Cato said. The call was relayed from one boat to the next. He lifted a rifle outfitted with a pointed spike, and fired. The spike shot upward and embedded itself in the wall of the building. A long cable trailed back down to the boats.

More cables were fired from the other boats. Cato and Xander got busy preparing the climbing gear.

"Why does this feel unsettlingly familiar?" Sparrow grumbled.

Gwendolyn forced a grin. "Just like the good old days."

"That was, like, a month ago. And it ended with me riding bronco-style on a giant crystal eating monster."

"See? The good old days." Gwendolyn gave him a playful nudge in the side.

He hissed in pain, and Starling shot Gwendolyn a withering look.

"I'm sorry!" she said. "I forgot. But don't worry. I'm reasonably certain there are no giant monsters up there."

"Hey, you never know," Cecilia added.

"Quiet," Cato snapped. "Time to end this." He clipped himself to the line, flicked a switch on his belt, and shot upward with the whine of a small motor.

Gwendolyn went next, soaring high above the waves. It felt exactly like riding the pneumos in Tohk. The cables hauled them up and over an exterior walkway.

An astonished guard was inspecting the harpoons. He reached for his radio just as Cato soared upward and dropped onto the man's back, pinning him to the ground. He socked the guard in the jaw, and the man stopped struggling.

Another guard in a big black coat came around the corner. Cato whipped the rifle off his back and fired two quick bursts of black energy.

Gwendolyn landed and disconnected herself just as a third guard emerged from a door next to her. Without thinking, she dropped into a crouch and swept the man's legs out from under him. He yelped in surprise and fell backwards over the railing. A moment later came the sound of a small splash.

Cato gave her an approving nod.

Sparrow, Starling, Cecilia, and the others flew up over the railing and dropped onto the walkway. Soon dozens of Causists were there. They unstrapped their rifles and readied for battle.

"Where's my rifle?" Sparrow said.

"Here." Starling gave him one of her collapsible swords.

"Aw, man. I want a gun."

Starling looked at the stun rifles, then at Gwendolyn. "No. I don't trust them."

"Come on, let the kid have one," Cecilia said.

Starling's glare could have stopped bullets on its own. "Don't tell me how to take care of my brother."

Cecilia held up her hands. "Fine, don't get all bothered. Just give me one."

Gwendolyn shook her head. "I don't think so. I want you all *away* from the fighting. We'll take care of this."

Cato pressed his back to the wall, out of sight of the windows above, rifle at the ready. The others followed suit. "Weird girl, you and me take point. Ky, Jax, split your squads off to either side and up the catwalks. We take the inside, then make our way to the heli-pad before the Board of Directors arrives with their security detail. Ganner?"

"On it, boss." He held up a strap, which held several dangling cylinders linked by a small cord.

"Good. Once we're inside, you repel up to roof and disable the communications relay. We don't need any distress calls getting out. You remember where it is?"

"Yeah, boss," the boy answered. "One of the Bootstrap Brigadiers we rescued used to work maintenance here. He gave us a good layout."

"Fine." Cato nodded to them all, and lifted his rifle. "Now!"

He threw open the door. Ganner yanked on the cord and lids popped off the grenades. As they began to smoke, Ganner flung the whole strap of them inside.

There was a series of small explosions, and a cloud of smoke burst through the door.

"Go!" Cato barked. He ducked inside, rifle raised, firing blindly.

"Cecilia! Starling!" Gwendolyn called out. "Stay back! Look after Sparrow!" Then she followed Cato as ordered, but she wasn't at all sure what she was supposed to do. She couldn't see anything in the smoke. She heard the others storm in behind her, and two groups split off to the sides.

She ran forward and was suddenly out of the smoke. The room was massive. It resembled the inside of a factory. Machinery was everywhere. The space was dominated by dozens of gigantic turbines, rounded objects with glowing, spinning innards visible through metal spokes. There were coolant pipes, bundles of cables, whirring belts, and enormous levers. A wave of intense heat nearly bowled her over, and the air was so thick it was hard to breathe. The acrid tang of hot metal stung her nose and left a coppery taste in her mouth.

Workers in grimy factory uniforms were running away from them. They scattered between the turbines, fled through doors, or simply sprinted toward the far end.

Black suited guards stood out in the crowd by the simple fact that they were *not* running away, but pushing against the tide and taking up firing positions. Several of them crouched behind turbines, while others flipped over metal tables and ducked behind them. Gwendolyn heard the crack of gunfire, and was hit with splinters of shattering concrete from the wall behind her.

She should have been scared. She should have hid behind the nearest heavy object. But the air wasn't just thick with bullets and heat and steam. It thrummed with *power*. She was flush with it. Her skin was buzzing. So she gritted her teeth, waved her hands, and *imagined.*

And a foot-thick wall of smoky glass materialized in front of them.

Cato and his team ducked behind it. Bullets struck the glass from the other side, but it held.

"Couldn't have made this out of something more durable?" Cato grumbled.

"I thought *transparent* would be more useful."

"Can't argue with that." He took a moment to study the guards visible through the barrier, then ducked around the side and squeezed off a few quick shots with his stun rifle. He didn't miss once. A handful of guards crumpled to the ground. Which still left plenty more to fire back, but it was a good start, and Cato pulled back just as a burst of return fire hit the glass. "But we can't just stay here. Need to find a way to push forward."

"As you wish," Gwendolyn said. She pictured the wall of glass sliding across the floor in front of them, imagining the horrible sound of it scraping on stone. The wall obeyed, though a little more forcefully than she had intended. It flew down the central aisle and smashed into any guards unlucky enough to be standing in the way, flattening them against the opposite wall. The glass wall cracked and crumbled. The guards didn't get up.

"Unbelievable," Cato murmured in admiration.

"Yes, isn't it just," Gwendolyn replied, as though she'd meant to do that.

More black-clad guards were appearing from between the generators. But a shower of black energy bolts came from above, stunning several of them.

Gwendolyn looked up. Metal catwalks ran along each side of the room and crisscrossed over the open space. The two teams led by Ky and Jax were lined along the catwalks, firing at the helpless guards below.

An alarm blared, and lights flashed red throughout the cavernous generator room. Gwendolyn spotted Corporate reinforcements coming from the other end of the catwalks. She reached inside, not for her wonder and excitement, but her anxieties. She found that gut wrenching sensation of failure, and stoked it.

What if my friends got hurt? she asked herself. Darkness flowed from her black fingernails and covered her hands. She felt a wave of disgust, then harnessed that as well, fueling her dark imagination. Then she flung the goop at the catwalks.

Globs of darkness hit the Corporate guards. It stuck where it hit, and expanded, growing over the men as though it were something alive and hungry. It pinned their arms to their sides and wrapped around their torsos. In moments, the men were trapped in cocoons of hard grey crust.

The battle didn't last long. Between Gwendolyn's power and the weapons she had created, Cato's band of rebels easily overwhelmed the last bit of resistance from the Corporate forces.

"Ky, Jax, take your teams and fan out through the building," Cato ordered. "I want full control of the station before the Board of Directors arrive. Their security detail will be a lot tougher than the second-rate drones on guard here. If we can catch them by surprise, we have a chance. Do we have an ETA on them?"

"We won't know until we get to the control room," Zana said. "And we'd better hurry before the radio silence makes them skittish."

"Then that's our next stop. Once we're in position, we'll have Ganner reactivate the comms."

"What about my parents?" Gwendolyn asked.

"What?" Cato looked over at her. "Oh, right." He looked around. "We're set for now. Should be able to take it from here on our own. Go find them, and meet us up at the control room."

"Wait, you don't know where they are?" Cecilia asked.

Cato shrugged. "You're the ones who were so certain they were here. We've done our part. Go find the workers who ran off, see what they know." He made a motion to his crew, and they headed toward one of the doors on the side of the room. "And stay safe! We might need you later."

Starling scoffed. "Nice to know he cares."

"Gwendolyn," Cecilia said. "Your eyes. They've gone black again."

"So?" she snapped.

Cecilia flinched. "Just thought you should know."

"Well, it's not exactly helpful at the moment. Come on," Gwendolyn said. "They're here. I can feel it."

She led them to the far end of the room, where the bulk of the workers had fled when the attack started. Her nerves tingled, both with the danger they might be in, and the sense that they were so *close*. Mother and Father. She hadn't seen them in *years*, and here they were, somewhere inside this building. She hoped.

They didn't encounter any of the workers, just empty concrete hallways. Signs on the wall led them to equally depressing dormitories and a cafeteria, but there were no helpful signs that pointed to Gwendolyn's parents.

"This is hopeless. We aren't getting anywhere," Starling said as they reached the umpteenth fork in the hallway. "Are we even sure they're here?"

Sparrow looked down both hallways. "Gwendolyn, can't you just do that thing you did at the crystal coves, and *feel* which way to go?"

She nodded. "It's worth a try. Give me a moment." She closed her eyes and focused on the sense of power in the air, trying to remember what it had felt like to be a twelve-year-old girl, fresh on her first adventure. But this was a far cry from the fantastic world of Tohk.

Still, she did feel something. The Air-Power that made her skin tingle seemed stronger in one direction. "This way," she said. She took them off to the right, and the feeling grew stronger still. Following the tingle of ever-increasing power, she led them through more winding hallways and down a long flight of stairs.

"This feels... familiar," Gwendolyn said.

"Oh, sure, me too. I come here all the time," Cecilia said. "I just pop by for tea and biscuits with the Blackstar, you know, we're mates, it's no big deal."

"You're really snarky when you're nervous," Sparrow said.

"Shut up," she snapped back.

"You shut up," Sparrow said.

Gwendolyn ignored them, trying to figure out what the stairway reminded her of. She hadn't figured it out by the time they reached the bottom. There was a locked door with a sign that read *Primary*

Generators.

"Sounds important," Cecilia said.

"Starling?" Gwendolyn asked.

"On it." She pulled out her lockpicks and went to work on the door. After a minute or so, it swung open. "Ta-da," she deadpanned.

But Gwendolyn was already stepping through the door. The power here was the strongest she'd felt since... well, since she had stood in the O.R.B. with Mister Zero, flush with the accumulated power of an entire city.

But rather than a giant mirrored dome, they were instead in a long, low-ceilinged room lined on either side with...

People.

Rows of them, strapped onto vertical slabs of some sort, hooked into all kinds of devices. Meters and dials were attached to the side of each station. The needles on the dials jumped, and wavy green lines flashed across black screens.

But all of that barely registered compared to the helmets. A leather band circled each person's head, with a strap that ran under the chin. Wires and metal bits ran over the top of their heads. Electrodes were attached to their temples. Metal eyepieces covered their eyes, and bright white light flickered out from behind them. Each person had some sort of mouth guard in, attached to the chin strap.

None of the people were moving.

"Whoah," Sparrow said. "Uh, we've seen a lot of stuff, but this might be the absolute creepiest."

"There must be hundreds of them," Cecilia said. "What is all this stuff?"

Starling let out a weary, disgusted sigh. "They're the primary generators."

"What?" Gwendolyn said. But then she remembered the sign on the door, and realization hit her with a dull thud.

Starling gestured to the endless rows of people around them, each of them strapped into a horrifying apparatus. Some of them seemed old, with grey skin and gaunt, weathered features. They reminded Gwendolyn of the tiny, withered queen of Umberland.

"The power," Starling said. "It's being drained from these people. This is where all the Air-Power in Tautopolis comes from."

Cecilia recoiled from the nearest person. "Wait. These people are having their brains sucked dry? And the people in Tautopolis are just using it to power their blenders?"

It felt too true to be anything else. "It's just like the crystal spire Mister Zero was in," Gwendolyn said. "Or how the Lambents work. The Lambents were sipping power from thousands and thousands of people. But I guess if you do something like this..." She looked at the flickering light bleeding from the edge of the eyepieces they all wore. "You can draw the same amount of power from a few hundred. You just have to take a lot more from each one."

"And just have to be a total monster, while you're at it..." Sparrow murmured, inspecting some of the dials and gauges.

"This is what the Abscess does," Gwendolyn said, remembering her conversation with the Lady. "It takes, and takes, and takes. Never satisfied." She clenched her fists. "Now I see what the Causists were fighting for. We have to stop this. We have to free all these people."

"We will," said Sparrow, putting a hand on her arm. "But first, maybe we should free them." He pointed to a pair of people at the end of the row.

Gwendolyn looked where he was pointing. And she nearly fell over with shock. She would have, if it weren't for Sparrow's support.

It was her parents.

Mother and Father.

They were strapped to the same upright tables as the other prisoners. Their faces were blank, their eyes covered by those metal disks. But it was them. Real, and in the flesh. Thoughts and feelings overwhelmed her, too fast to pick out any one from the noise.

"What... what have they done to them?" Gwendolyn managed to say.

"The same thing they're doing to everyone else," Starling said. "Draining them."

"But this..." Gwendolyn stammered.

"Let's get them out," Sparrow said.

Gwendolyn clenched her fists. "Right." She hadn't come all this way just to stand and stare at them. She and Starling reached up to remove the helmets and wires while Sparrow worked on the straps.

Her parents stumbled away from their slabs. Father fell to his hands and knees, but Gwendolyn and Cecilia managed to catch Mother.

"Mother," Gwendolyn said, but she could scarcely be heard through the lump in her throat. Mother was here. In her arms. Alive.

Marie Gray stirred. She groaned and put a hand to her head.

"What... where..."

But her words were cut off by Gwendolyn's sudden embrace. She flung her arms around her mother, this woman who had raised her and fed her and scolded her and loved her. It was a feeling she hadn't dared think she'd feel again. The hug was a bit unfamiliar, either because Mother was wearing a soiled factory uniform rather than her usual prim and proper attire, or because Mother sagged weakly against her, or because Gwendolyn was much taller and older now.

Gwendolyn had thought about their last embrace a lot in the past few years. The last time she'd been held in her mother's arms. It had been on her thirteenth birthday, and Gwendolyn had cringed away, not wanting to be touched. How could she have been so foolish? How could she ever want anything more than this moment, than to be held forever and ever and never let go? Her mother seemed too stunned to return the hug, but that didn't matter.

Sparrow helped Father to his feet. He grunted and groaned as well. Gwendolyn heard, and broke away from her mother only to cling to Father with equal force. "Father," she muttered into his chest. She felt the strength of him, his firmness and solidity, in contrast to Mother's softness. But he also felt different. Weaker, somehow. Not as steady. She let go, afraid she might knock him over.

"Are you... are you all right?" Gwendolyn asked.

Her parents blinked and looked around, confused. "I... I think so," Mother said, wincing. "My head... it hurts. Where are we, Dan?"

"I... I don't know," Father said with a hesitancy that was unlike him. "The Outskirts, possibly?"

"Not exactly..." Cecilia muttered.

Father looked around again, seeming to notice the prisoners around him for the first time. The eerie sight of hundreds of people, strapped down and strapped in and drained of their every last thought. "What is this? What happened?"

But Mother looked at the four children. "I think they saved us." She knelt down and took Gwendolyn by the hand. "You rescued us, didn't you?" And she pulled Gwendolyn in for another embrace, and Gwendolyn sank into it, feeling Mother's head on top of hers, Mother's hair falling against her cheek.

"Thank you," Mother said.

And Gwendolyn couldn't hold it in any longer. She cried. Sad, silent tears streamed down her face. Tears that washed the blackness from her eyes, and when she looked back up at her Mother it was with her own sparkling emeralds.

Mother looked back at her and smiled, warm and kind and wonderful.

"Thank you," she repeated. "What is your name?"

Gwendolyn gasped as though she'd been punched in the gut. Her breath stopped, but the tears kept coming. Gwendolyn hung her head, and wished she had a blanket of frizzy red hair to cover her face with. Another jolt of pain shot through her.

They still don't remember, she thought. *And why would they? Mister Zero erased their memories. Why did I think they would remember me?*

"Wait," Mother said. "I recognize you."

Gwendolyn's head snapped up.

314

Mother was squinting, as though struggling to remember. "You're that poor little lost girl that knocked on the door yesterday." Mother winced, and put her hand to her head. "Was it... was it yesterday? How long has it been, Dan? How long have we been in this awful place?"

"I don't know," Father said, stroking his mustache in thought. The gesture was so familiar that it made Gwendolyn's chest ache. "But I think I know *her*."

Gwendolyn's eyes widened, but then she saw that Father wasn't looking at her.

"You're Cecilia Forthright, aren't you?" Father said.

"Yes!" Mother said. "I thought she looked familiar."

Gwendolyn Gray crumpled to the ground. Her knees stung as they hit the concrete floor, but nothing could have been further from her mind. She was far too busy being crushed under a tidal wave of pure, absolute blackness.

She had felt many, many kinds of pain since that day she had imagined a leaf into existence. But this one far outstripped the rest. It struck her in a place so deep she hadn't even known it existed. It knifed through the loss and fear and depression she'd felt before, shredding them and stabbing her until she thought her heart would bleed black.

For a moment, she wished she'd never found them at all. That pain had been so much more bearable. But this? She might never get up again. Her limbs refused all her commands. They simply quivered in absolute, all-consuming grief.

"Wait," Cecilia said, though her words were just meaningless noise to Gwendolyn. "How do you know who I am?"

"Why, from the School, of course," Mother said. "We always heard so much about you. Not very nice things, I admit..."

"But how? You don't remember her." Cecilia gestured to Gwendolyn. "Who did you hear about me from? And what would you have been doing around the School?"

"Don't be silly," Father said, "of course we—ah!" And he cried out in pain, clutching his temples.

"Dan!" Mother shouted.

"Come on," Starling said, crouching down and laying a hand on Gwendolyn's back. "We don't have to do this here. Let's find a portal, jump through the In-Between to some random world, then find a library we can use to get back into the Library of All Wonder."

"No," she said. It came out as a low, animal growl. And this time she could feel it. The blackness filled her eyes, bringing its terrible clarity. The liquid shadows coated her hands and spread across the floor in two small tarry puddles. "I'm not leaving."

"What?" Starling said. "Why?"

"He has to pay."

"Who?"

"The Blackstar," she snarled. "And how lucky for me. He'll be here any minute."

THE BLACKSTAR

"**G**wendolyn, wait, stop!" Sparrow said as she hurried back up the stairs. But as usual, she didn't listen.

He grabbed her by the arm. "You can't just go rushing off like this."

She spun back around. "Watch me. Stay here. Keep my parents safe." Then she tore away and started up the stairs again. "This won't take long."

She darted through various hallways, eventually finding her way back into the generator room, and the door Cato had taken, with more stairs.

The helipad wasn't hard to find. At the top of the staircase, she was met with a rush of cold, salty air. The metal girders of the enormous dome towered above them, with plenty of space for the helicopters to fly in underneath it.

Two helicopters sat on a large stretch of concrete rooftop covered in white paint markings. Dozens of men also sat on the concrete. Or rather, they knelt, hands behind their heads. Most were dressed in long black coats with gas masks and fedoras.

Cato's team stood around them, stun rifles at the ready. Some of the Causists were busy disarming them, taking pistols and rifles and passing them out to the other rebels.

"Cato!" Gwendolyn called out.

"Over here," he said. Gwendolyn spotted him, standing next to a captive group of men who wore dapper black suits, rather than long leather coats, and no hats or masks. They were likewise kneeling, hands on their heads. "What do you think?"

"Is this them?" she asked.

He nodded. "The Board of Directors. Head of the Corporation. Masters of Tautopolis." He turned and gave her a lopsided smirk. "Well. Former masters." Then he raised a fist and shouted to his troops. "For the Cause!"

"For the Cause!" they echoed back.

But Gwendolyn didn't care. She only had eyes for the man at the front of the huddled group. Unlike the other immaculately suited men, he was dressed in a long black coat like his enforcers, done up with a double line of silver buttons all the way to the neck. With his hands on top of his head, his fedora was pressed down until the brim hid his face, but Gwendolyn knew who he was.

The Supreme Executive. The Blackstar.

Gwendolyn looked at Cato. They had done it. "That was quick," she said.

Cato grunted. "It wasn't hard. Got here just in time, as the choppers came in. Ambushed them as soon as they landed. Their enforcers never had a chance to fight. Thanks to you." He gave her a look. "To be honest, I was expecting a bigger battle. All that preparation, months of work, and we just... won. If you hadn't gotten us through those men in the generator room so fast, the choppers would have landed before we could get here. Their security team would have been ready for us, and we'd still be fighting them on the stairs. This would have been much harder without you, Gwendolyn. Your powers bought us a couple of crucial minutes, and... here we are."

A bigger battle. Those words struck her. She'd been part of some of those. *This was the end of his story,* she thought. *This would have been his big moment, the climactic finale, but... I changed things.*

She stepped toward the Supreme Executive, toward the man who would one day ruin her life, the man who now hung his head in defeat. "Then it's over," she said, planting herself in front of him. "For Cato. For me. And for you." She reached forward and knocked the fedora off his head. "No more Blackst—"

It wasn't him.

The man who looked up at her was much older. Weaker. His hair was going gray, and he had a slightly pudgy face with wrinkles around the eyes and a weak chin.

"What?" She whipped around. "This isn't him!"

"It's him all right," Cato said. "I'd recognize that pompous old fool anywhere." The older boy stepped forward and slapped the man across the face. He fell with a cry, then looked up from the pavement with a look of defiance.

"You'll never win," he spat.

Cato kicked him in the stomach, and the man grunted in pain.

"Get them down to the control room!" Cato shouted.

Zana and Ky took the lead, directing the Causists to wrangle the captives. The group of them started down the stairs, with Cato bringing up the rear.

This isn't right, Gwendolyn thought, following Cato down the stairs. Her vision cleared as the darkness retreated again, leaving only her fingernails black.

So much was falling apart around her. She barely noticed when they entered a room filled with control consoles, buttons, gauges with quivering red needles, and screens that showed grainy black-and-white images of the various rooms of the power station. The room was low-ceilinged, but still impressively large. Maps and screens showed images from all over Tautopolis. Gwendolyn recognized one that showed the Bootstrap Brigade.

As the Board of Directors and their masked enforcers were lined up along the walls at gunpoint, Gwendolyn tried to focus on what was important. On what was going to happen next. Cato was the hero of this story, and this seemed to be the end. He'd conquered the villains. But that meant—

"Cato!" Gwendolyn blurted. "You're in danger!"

He whipped around, instantly alert. "Where?"

"Nowhere. I mean, not yet. But you will be soon."

Spiky-haired Zana scoffed. "What are you talking about, weird girl?"

Gwendolyn ignored her and focused on Cato. "Someone is coming. Someone more dangerous than all of these put together," she said, gesturing to the enforcers. "I think he'll be here soon. And he's coming to kill you."

Cato shook his head. "You're not making any sense."

Gwendolyn groaned inwardly. She knew there was precious

little chance of convincing him that a villain from some other world, or some version of this one, was on his way here to assassinate Cato before he could fully take control of Tautopolis. This was the *real* climax of his story. An epic fight with the Blackstar. But she didn't have to convince him to save him.

"The people," she said. "There's people below, in the lower levels. They're prisoners. Hundreds of them, trapped in these terrible devices, draining them of their energy. That's where the Air-Power comes from! They're draining it from people!" She looked at the screens on the wall, then pointed to one. "See? Right there."

"We know." He didn't bother to look at the screen.

"Good. Then we can set them free. If we cut off that power supply, then maybe we'll stand a chance of beating the Blackstar. Not that it's ever stopped him before, but either way, we have to save all—"

"No," Cato said.

Gwendolyn froze. "What?"

He gave her a puzzled look. "Why would we let them go?"

Gwendolyn returned it with equal confusion. "Why wouldn't you?"

"What are you talking about, kid?" Ky said. "Why would we cut off the Air-Power?"

"Because..." Gwendolyn couldn't believe she had to explain this. "Because it's wrong. Those people are prisoners. They're being tortured. We have to let them go!"

"Good god, Cato, I told you she was trouble. We just took this place," Zana said. "I'm not throwing away months of work."

"No," Gwendolyn said, horrified. "That's not... we're here to save people. To free them from the Corporation." She raised a tentative fist and looked to the other members of Cato's team. "For the Cause! Right?"

No one answered her.

She put her hand down.

Ganner, the youngest of the crew, squinted at her. "What exactly do you think the Cause is?"

"To... save everyone?"

Again there was silence, but this time, they all looked to Cato.

"Power," he said simply. He gestured to the Board of Directors. "They had it. Now we have it."

"But that makes you just as bad as they are!"

Zana gave her a look of astonishment. "What is wrong with you?"

"Things will be better with us in charge," Ganner added. "Our lives will be so much better. What's so bad about that?"

"What about their lives?" Gwendolyn shouted, pointing at the screens.

"That's their own business," Ky grumbled. "They're leeches. Draining society of its resources. So now we drain them. They can give back what they've taken. Beggers. Unders. Illegals."

"But..." Gwendolyn stammered, pleading with Cato. "You can't do this." She looked to the others again. "You can't let him do this."

Cato seemed to stand even taller, and his voice took on a commanding tone. "The question isn't who's going to let me. The question is who's going to stop me."

Which was *not* a tone that Gwendolyn responded well to. She squared her shoulders and clenched her fists. "I am."

But as confident as she sounded on the outside, her inside felt as though someone were scraping her organs out with a dull knife. She could almost feel it grating against her ribs.

I helped them do this. Her magic words came to mind, twisted into terrible shapes. *If only I'd said no. I wonder how this story would have ended if I hadn't been here. What if this is all my fault?* She could feel the blackness creeping up her arms again, over the sleeves of Cato's jacket, all the way to her shoulders. The colors in the room shifted as her eyes filled with black.

"You said you were going to stop this," Gwendolyn said, her voice cold. "That after they took your parents, you swore you'd never let it happen to anyone else again."

Cato's eyes narrowed. "No. I won't let it happen to *me* again. No one will take what's mine. You can have your parents, like we agreed. Are you going back on your word?"

"Are you really going to keep all those people captive? Draining them?"

He nodded.

Gwendolyn shook her head. The blackness had completely covered her jacket. "Then you're just as bad as the vampires."

"And you're a lying dealbreaker. Where's your 'good' and 'bad' now?" Zana snapped.

Cato waved a hand and turned away. "Get rid of her."

At once, the Causists whipped up their stun rifles and fired. Surprised, Gwendolyn threw up her arms to shield herself. To her further surprise, the tarry substance on her jacket absorbed the black energy blasts.

She straightened, and smiled. Then she flung out her arms and sent the blasts right back, stunning Cato's entire crew. As one, they dropped to the floor. She saw Ganner, lying motionless, and felt a brief pang of guilt. He was no older than Sparrow.

Cato turned back to face her. "Clever. My own fault. I forgot how strong you are." He raised his own rifle, but Gwendolyn remembered her meditation lessons, and exhaled. She imagined a burst of nothingness in her mind, wiping away all her thoughts, all her creations. The gun in Cato's hand crumbled to dust, along with every other one in the room.

He looked at his hands, then knocked the ash from his gloves. "Only fair. They were yours, after all." Then he spoke to the men who still knelt around the edges of the control room. "Enforcers?"

The men in fedoras and long black coats stood and retrieved their own weapons from Cato's fallen team. Real ones. Then they arrayed themselves behind Cato. The lenses of their gas masks glinted in the lights from the control panels.

"Switch sides quickly, don't they?" Gwendolyn snapped.

"They know who has the power here. Let's see how you do with real bullets."

The enforcers raised their rifles. But Gwendolyn was ready this time—she flung out her left hand, and shadowy vines burst forth, wrapping around the men's guns like tentacles from the Abscess. She pulled, and the guns flew across the room toward her.

She threw out her other hand and sent a blast of black energy at the men, picturing them thrown to the back wall and trapped in cocoons of sticky darkness. But the energy splashed against the men with little effect. They held firm, though their hats were knocked from their heads, and the lead two had their gas masks blown away.

Underneath the masks, the men had no faces.

"What?" Gwendolyn whispered in horror. "No. It can't be." The scraping feeling of hollowness rose in her chest again, and she wasn't sure what insides she had left at this point.

Slowly, ever so slowly, shadows seemed to grow out of the men's bare scalps, shaping into fedoras again, though the faces beneath those hats swam in front of her eyes like heat haze in a blistering desert. She felt the skin-crawling sensation of looking at something plain as day in front of her, but something that was so terrifying her eyes would not deliver the image to her brain.

One faceless man turned to the other. "It seems the girl is familiar with us, Enforcer Three." His voice was similar to the eerie high-pitched whine of the Mister Men from her own world, but rougher, raspier, almost a hiss. Which certainly did not make it *less* disturbing to hear.

"Indeed it does, Enforcer Four, indeed it does. Her power seems equally familiar. Is this the one who has given our brethren so much trouble?"

"It would seem so. Though she is much changed from the reports we received."

"*Change.*" The man spat, with a rare flash of emotion. "How distasteful. Such a thing cannot be tolerated. We must cleanse her infection before it can spread to this world as well."

"After you, Enforcer Four."

"Thank you, Enforcer Three."

"Gwendolyn?" said a voice from behind her. She spun around.

Sparrow, Starling, Cecilia, Mother, and Father stood there, all with shocked looks on their faces.

"Run!" Gwendolyn shouted.

They did. But suddenly Starling's wrist gauntlet went berserk, chiming like an alarm clock, and a wall of concrete grew from the ceiling and slammed down over the door, sealing off the room.

In the center of the control room, Cato Locke stood with his hand outstretched, much as Gwendolyn had a moment ago.

"You're not the only one who can fight for what they believe," Cato said. "But thanks for the lesson."

Gwendolyn roared in fury. She hurled a black fireball at the older boy, filling it with all her hurt and pain and fear.

Cato closed his eyes in concentration and caught the fireball in his hand. It dissipated, just as the stun blasts had on Gwendolyn's jacket. His glove burned away. He examined his hand with a look of approval, clenching and unclenching his fist.

And there on the back of his right hand, Gwendolyn saw a seven-pointed black star.

She gasped. *What?* It couldn't be.

"Oh my god," Sparrow muttered.

Starling checked her chiming gauntlet. "That power signature. It's definitely..."

"You... you're the Blackstar," Gwendolyn choked out.

Cato Locke grunted. "Nobody's called me that in years." He looked at the mark on the back of his hand. "I was born with this. Everyone was convinced it meant something special. Meant I was destined for greatness. Annoying. There's no destiny but what we make and take." He looked around the room. "Greatness. Huh."

Then he clenched his fist. "Maybe they were right."

Cato closed his eyes again. His brow furrowed in concentration. Energy formed around his fist. The top point of the star tattoo grew into a shimmering sword of black energy.

"Maybe it's time to forge my destiny."

Gwendolyn looked at the boy with the black star sword, standing at the head of a line of Faceless Men. Terrifying as the sight was, it was almost comforting in its familiarity. For all the uncertainty and questioning, at least here she knew where she stood. Planted firmly between the monsters and the people she loved. Her family. For that's what they were. Mother. Father. Sparrow. Starling. Maybe even Cecilia. And she would not let anyone hurt them again.

But doubt crept in from the open closet in her mind. *This time, you helped the monsters. You practically gave the Blackstar this world.*

"We *are* in the Blackstar's book," Cecilia said, her voice shaking. "But a lot further back in the story than we thought... I knew I should have read the ending first!"

Gwendolyn knew she was right. *Tautopolis* wasn't the story of how Cato defeated the Blackstar. It was the story of how he *became* the Blackstar.

"This doesn't change anything," Gwendolyn said, talking to herself as much as Cato. "I can't let you keep hurting those people."

He snorted. "You got what you wanted. You're going to give it all up and get yourself killed?"

"No. I'm going to take what I want. And what I want is those people's freedom." She focused on the mess of swirling feelings inside. This whole thing had been a string of terrible ideas. She looked at the tarry blackness that covered her hands.

Fine, she thought. *I have plenty of terrible ideas. He can have them all.* No sense of childlike wonder was going to change this world. No magic leaf would appear. She reached deep inside, not to her imagination, but to her pain, her depression, and the infinitely spiraling thread of horrible *what-ifs* that kept her up at night.

She threw them all at the Faceless Men. The darkness she worked so hard to contain came flying out, and her horrible thoughts struck the men. They were each wrapped in a sticky black cocoon, their arms pinned to their sides. She sent another fireball at Cato.

He batted it away with his sword, and ran at her.

But she had dueled with him before, and this Cato was not truly the Blackstar yet. She waved a hand and thorny black vines sprouted from the floor and wrapped around his legs. He fell hard, slamming into the concrete.

Gwendolyn took a moment to scan the control panels, searching for anything that might help her. But there were so many buttons and switches. She didn't get more than a glance before the Faceless Enforcers broke free of their cocoons. They fanned out, some heading for Gwendolyn, others heading for the entrance and her family, who looked as shocked as the board of directors huddled in the opposite corner of the room.

From the floor, Cato formed a spike of glistening black metal and flung it at her. Gwendolyn pictured a shield emerging from her hand, and the spike bounced off. It impaled one of the Faceless Gentlemen in the chest. The man did not so much as flinch, but kept coming closer.

Gwendolyn turned and ran for the entrance. Sparrow and Starling were guarding the other three, swords drawn.

"What's the plan?" Sparrow said, a slight tremor in his voice, but his face was stern.

She didn't answer. Instead, she pictured an enormous drill. Blocky and brutal, something inspired by Tautopolis technology and the crawling mechs they'd battled before. Reality bowed to her wishes, and the drill sprang into existence. It rolled on metal treads to the concrete wall that blocked the entrance and began grinding into it.

Then Gwendolyn focused her mind on a now-familiar image. One of the stun rifles materialized in her hands. She blasted the Faceless Enforcers, dropping one after the other. "When that drill breaks through, you have to—"

There was a clinking sound. Gwendolyn looked down to see a cylindrical canister with a short throwing handle. It glowed with dark energy. She saw Cato, still trapped in vines, arm outstretched from the throw.

"Grenade!" she shouted. She dropped the rifle and pushed her family away with a blast of energy just as the grenade went off.

The force of the explosion sent them all flying, only saved by Gwendolyn's push. As it was, she and Cecilia were hurled backwards and slammed into a control console. They slumped to the ground.

"Ugh. I knew I never liked him," Cecilia groaned.

Groggily, Gwendolyn saw her family on the other side of the room. Her drill had finished its work, just before it had been blown to pieces in the explosion. She scrambled for her rifle and squeezed off more shots, stunning the Enforcers closest to them. But the ones she'd stunned a moment before were already stirring.

We need a way out, Gwendolyn thought. Not just out of the control room, but out of this world. *If only I had a library,* she thought, *like in Umberland.* But the library on this world had been destroyed as soon as they arrived.

Then she spotted Cecilia's purse on the floor next to them, flung there by the blast. The battered yellow thing had come open, and books had scattered across the floor. There was *Tautopolis.* And three others. Each with her own name emblazoned on the cover.

Gwendolyn's eyes widened. Her *Marvelous Adventures.* Her *Fantastical Exploits.* Even her *Withering Trials.* All spilling from Cecilia's purse. All bathed in a faint red glow from Cyria's jewel.

Gwendolyn had no time to wonder what Cecilia was doing with the books of her life. She snatched up the purse and pulled out the red Figment gem, the one they'd used to enter Tautopolis. Then she looked down at the books again.

A library, she thought. Well, what qualified as a library?

She gathered up the books as well, cradling them in her arms. Cato had reformed his sword and was slicing his way free of her vines. Gwendolyn ran for the door to the control room and closed it. Then she looked at it through the red gem. She *imagined,* picturing the door opening, picturing the Egressai Infinitus, the doorway that connected every other library on every world. She was its Princess, and these four books counted as a library if she said it did.

A spike of pain went through her head, and Gwendolyn dropped to her knees with a cry. The books fell to the floor, and the glowing red jewel rolled away. It rolled right through the now-open door and into the cozily lit entry hall of the Library of All Wonder.

SHATTERED

"**G**o!" Gwendolyn shouted.

"We'd love to!" Starling called. "Little help here?"

She and Sparrow were dueling with two Enforcers, protecting Mother and Father, but the Faceless Men were batting aside the blades with their bare hands. More were surrounding them.

Gwendolyn imagined a bubble of energy which sprang up around her family. The Faceless Enforcers pounded on it, but it held. Each strike sent a burst of pain through her skull. Through the smoky barrier, Gwendolyn saw the terrified looks on Mother and Father's faces. It was a horrible expression, one she had never seen before.

Then she realized she'd lost track of Cato. She turned and saw him with his eyes closed, face scrunched in concentration. A heavy black gun took shape in his hands, one that was definitely *not* made to stun. But it looked rough, more like a hastily scrawled sketch than an actual weapon. He lifted it and pulled the trigger.

Nothing happened.

Gwendolyn smirked, glad that someone *else's* magical weapon had failed for a change. She shot Cato and he fell to one knee.

But the Faceless Gentlemen continued pounding on her barrier, and she felt every blow. She tried to imagine the ceiling breaking apart and crushing the men under slabs of concrete, but the repeated pains in her head broke her concentration.

"Get to my parents," Gwendolyn told Cecilia. "I'll cover you."

"Wait, what about you?"

"Just go!" Gwendolyn said. "I have to free these people!" Five of the Faceless Enforcers were closing in on them. She stunned three of them, and missed two more.

Cecilia grabbed her wrist. "You're coming too."

Gwendolyn pulled her arm away and fired again, but the rifle was losing its effect. "You were right. I shouldn't have helped Cato. I have to stay and fix this." She re-stunned the five Enforcers. "Now go!"

"This isn't your fault! Cato would have taken over anyway! We've got your parents, now come on!"

But Gwendolyn threw out a hand and pushed Cecilia away with a wave of black energy.

The other girl hesitated, then nodded. "Fine. Be that way." Then she ran across the control room. But she wouldn't be able to get through Gwendolyn's barrier. Gwendolyn gritted her teeth and willed the rifle to fire *faster*, fueling it with her anxiety and fear for her family.

The rifle kicked in her arms and spat a rapid-fire volley of black bolts. She swept it side-to-side and stunned all of the Enforcers, struggling not to hit Cecilia, a few of the blasts bouncing off the protective bubble around the others.

Cato and the Enforcers were down, for the moment. Gwendolyn focused and tried to empty her mind enough to dispel the barrier *without* vanishing the rifle in her hands. But there was no way she could quiet her mind enough for that. Instead she fired at the barrier, over and over again, shouting in wordless anger. The barrier shattered into a thousand shards of energy. Cecilia threw up her arms to protect her face, then raced to Gwendolyn's parents.

"Come with me," Cecilia said. Mother and Father nodded, too shocked for questions, and the three of them raced to the door.

"No, what?" Sparrow said. "We're not leaving her!"

"Yes, you are!" Gwendolyn said.

"None of you will be going anywhere," droned one of the Enforcers, pushing himself to his feet. "There is no escape."

"Oh, *do* shut up," Gwendolyn said, and stunned him again. "I'll be fine! I'll find my way back, I promise!"

"No!" Sparrow shouted. "I'm not leaving you again!"

Sometimes there are no good choices, Gwendolyn thought, remembering Sparrow's words from long ago.

"Starling, catch!" She stunned Sparrow, who collapsed into his sister's arms.

Starling gaped at her.

"I'm sorry!" Gwendolyn yelled.

"I'll be you are," Starling growled, and dragged her brother toward the door.

"You know what?" Cecilia shouted at Cato as the others went through into the library. "Your story isn't even good!"

"Just get out of here," Gwendolyn called. She threw a wave of energy at them. Cecilia was pushed through the doorway, the books flew inside, and the door to the Library slammed shut. The Figment skittered away and bounced off a console.

A sudden pain hit Gwendolyn in the chest, but she choked down a sob with a small gasp. She looked out over the bodies strewn around the floor. Cato and his team were still unconscious. The Board of Directors still huddled in a group at the other end of the control room, looking as stunned as if Gwendolyn had zapped them herself.

But the Faceless Enforcers were not so obliging. They got to their feet, too many of them for Gwendolyn to stun, though she blasted one after another back to the ground. Each blast seemed to have less effect.

She wasn't sure how much longer she could keep this up. She had tried to sound confident for the others, but she had no idea *how* to free these people. There was plenty of power in the air, nearly as much as in Faeoria, but just thinking about it reminded her of where that power came from.

She was using energy that had been sucked from all those people. The image of a child flashed before her eyes, one the same age as Sparrow, strapped to one of those upright tables, his head and eyes covered by those awful helmets.

That moment of doubt made her knees buckle. A wave of fatigue washed over her. And that gave the Faceless Enforcers the opening they needed. One of them tore the rifle from her hands while two more grabbed her arms. Gwendolyn shouted and struggled, but their grip was like iron, and they forced her to her knees.

She was forced to watch as Cato stirred and got to his feet.

"I don't understand you," he grunted. "You had what you wanted. You had a way out. Why stay?"

"What if I *wanted* to knock you around a little more?" she spat. But she was rapidly scanning the control consoles.

"Helping them makes them weak. You free those people down there? What would they do once you're gone? No ability to fend for themselves." He gestured to the control room around them. "And what about the rest of Tautopolis? What would it do without the Air-Power? You claim to think of others, but it's all just moralistic posturing."

"What about you?" Gwendolyn said. "You're the same as the Supreme Executive. How would things be any different now?"

"Because now *I'm* the one with the power."

"By keeping people slaves. Draining them like your own personal batteries." *Keep him talking,* she thought. Which wouldn't be hard. They just would *not* shut up about this nonsense. "I thought you were all about freedom and happiness. What about theirs?"

He shrugged. "Nothing is perfect." He closed his eyes and took a deep breath. The black star tattoo on his hand started to glow. "But now?" He opened his eyes. "With this power? I might just come close."

But Gwendolyn wasn't listening. She had spotted something. She was, even after all this time, a clever noticer. One of the screens showed an image of the prison below. And underneath the screen was a big. Red. Button.

She could just make out the label below it. *Primary Generator*

Shutdown.

Gwendolyn smiled and looked back at Cato, black eyes flashing. "That's all well and good. But that power won't help you."

"Oh? Why not?"

"Because I know three things you don't." Her false confidence was helping. "One: I'm better at this than you."

Cato smirked and the sword extended from the back of his hand again. "You sure about that?"

"Afraid so," Gwendolyn said. She focused on the tarry blackness that coated her arms, and the Faceless Men who held her. "Two: I've done this before."

She imagined the blackness on her arms turning from tar to oil, coating the floor around her as well. She pulled, her arms slipped from the men's grip, then she blasted them all with a wave of energy. Cato and the men were knocked back and Gwendolyn went flying backwards across the slick floor, propelled by the force of her own blast. She used another energy pulse to change direction, skidding into the control panel she wanted.

She pulled herself up, nearly slipping in the shimmering oil. There was the camera feed of the prison, and the big red button below it.

She turned back to Cato. "And three? I love buttons." Then she slammed her hand down on it.

Lights flashed in the generator room. On the screen, sparks erupted from the mechanisms imprisoning the people below. But then the screen flickered, and shut down. All the lights in the control room shut down, the buttons and diodes going dark. Even the overhead lights went out.

For a moment, there was silence.

"What have you done?" came Cato's voice in the darkness.

Gwendolyn smiled, though she knew he couldn't' see it. "I've given them the chance at happiness. That's what you're all about, isn't it?" She moved as she spoke, creeping to the side, trying to hide her position.

"This doesn't change anything. We'll put them back."

"I've set them free. They'll just have to take care of themselves, right?" *It's all I can really do,* Gwendolyn thought. *Sometimes there are no good choices. I've done the best I can.*

At that moment, red emergency lights flicked to life. Cato and Gwendolyn spotted each other in the gloom, the world reduced to the simple, brutal shades of red and black.

Cato flung a hand toward her, but nothing happened. He stared at it in confusion. "What?"

Gwendolyn knew that confusion. She knew this feeling. "The power's out, Cato. In more ways than one. But as I said: I've been here before."

She reached a hand toward the rifle that lay on the floor where the Faceless Enforcers had tossed it. She imagined a thin black vine leaping from her hand, and it *did,* the branch bursting from her palm. But she felt thorns tear through her skin, and she gasped in pain.

The vine grabbed the rifle and pulled it back into her hand. She shot Cato with it and he dropped to the floor. Hopefully, he would stay there this time.

Which just left a line of nearly a dozen Faceless Men in fedora hats standing across from her. And her power was almost gone.

"No," she said to herself. The Blackstar had no trouble creating things, no matter what world he was on. "If the Blackstar can do it, then so can I."

Something hit her from behind, sending her flying. She skidded across the oily floor and bumped up against a console chair.

"You're right. I can."

"What?" she groaned, and looked up.

Near the entryway, bathed in red light and standing in front of a shimmering portal, was the Blackstar. The Blackstar as she had always known him. Cato Locke, as he would one day grow to be. All thanks to her.

"Huh. It *is* you." Clad in his black coat, mask, and hat, he looked nearly identical to the Faceless Enforcers. But when he reached up and took off his mask, there was indeed a face underneath. A face that was now more familiar to her. Older, more tired, but just recognizable as the Cato Locke who lay sprawled on the floor.

"I wondered. Didn't recognize you back in Fairyland." He chuckled, a strange sound coming from him. "Of course, you were younger then. And buried in that bush of hair. Never suspected that little kid was the bald teenage girl who'd stepped into my story. But I see it now. The weird girl. The one who helped us take control." He pressed a button on a metal device he held, and the portal disappeared. He slipped the device into his pocket.

Off to the side, Zana stirred, rolling over. The Blackstar held out a hand and a wave of blackness rippled through the room. Everyone stopped moving. Even the Board of Directors stopped their trembling, looks of terror frozen on their faces.

"Should have suspected." He walked over to the side and ran a finger along one of the control consoles. "I sent your parents here. Figured they'd be safe, inside my own story, where I could keep an eye on them. Should have known you'd find your way in eventually."

Gwendolyn's jaw clenched, and she tried to sound casual. Confident. "To be fair, I didn't recognize you either." She nodded at the unconscious Cato.

The Blackstar went and nudged his past self with the toe of his boot. "We all have our awkward phase." Then he looked at her. "I told you to stay home. Little girls should listen better."

That chased away her fear. "I'm not a little girl anymore," she snarled. She crouched into a fighting stance and tried to gather as much power as she could. The Air-Power was gone. No tingles of energy rippled across her skin. But maybe that didn't matter. Imagination might be fickle, but this dark power seemed to be everywhere. *Bad ideas spread faster than good ones, anyway.*

The Blackstar didn't bother with creating anything fancy. He simply threw a blast of raw energy at her. Gwendolyn felt a spike of fear, and the words *What if I get hurt?* flashed through her with the speed of thought. She channeled it into a shield that sprang into existence just in time to block the blast, but it *hurt*. Pain seared up her arm.

She ignored it. With no power from the world around her, she dug into the closet in her mind where she shoved all the things she couldn't bear to think about. The dread wasn't hard to find, and she conjured a sword to match her shield, forging herself into a knight of shimmering darkness and bad ideas. But creating the sword sent a stab of pain through her other arm, as well. She nearly dropped it, but held on.

Smiling, the Blackstar strode toward her. His own sword sprang from his hand. But Gwendolyn was ready. She'd done this dance with him before.

The Blackstar swung his sword at her head, casually, almost lazily, and Gwendolyn held up her own sword to meet it.

The Blackstar's sword sheared hers in half. Metal clattered to the floor. The Blackstar's fist shot out, but Gwendolyn held up her shield and caught the punch full-on. The shield cracked and crumbled, and Gwendolyn fell to one knee from the shock of the blow.

"Pathetic," he growled.

Gwendolyn slapped the ground in frustration, but rather than get back up, she pressed her palms to the floor and *imagined*. Black spikes sprang from the floor, angled towards the Blackstar. She gasped again, as her palms felt like they'd been pierced by the spikes as well.

The Blackstar took an easy leap backwards, out of range of her spiked barrier. He shook his head. Then he kicked at the spikes and they shattered like icicles.

A sinking feeling was growing in her gut, but that only made her stronger. Ignoring the pain in her palms, she imagined a wall of fire. Black flames flared up in front of the Blackstar, but her own hands burned in return. She screamed, and clutched them to her chest.

Ignoring the fire, the Blackstar stepped toward her again. Relentless. Unstoppable.

No, she thought. *I can stop him. I did it before, in the Hall of Records.* She had hit him with cinder-blocks pulled from the wall. Tangible objects hit harder. She tried to picture the ceiling crashing down on top of him, but was met with a wave of exhaustion, as though heavy stones had been heaped on top of her instead.

Her breath came in short, ragged gasps. Black tears fell from her eyes, spattering the floor. She looked up to see the Blackstar still strolling toward her. Desperately, she searched for an idea. What if a giant hand slapped him away?

That's stupid, she thought, but that moment of doubt cost her, and it was all the opening the Blackstar needed to smack her across the room. She flew through the air and slammed into one of the control consoles. She heard a crack, and gasped as she crumpled to the floor.

Gwendolyn managed to lift her head and see him coming toward her again. She tried to focus, but every breath felt like grinding broken glass against her ribs. The monster that lurked in her mental closet stirred. The despair threatened to smother her.

So she let it.

The tarry blackness on her arms pulsed and squirmed. Her skin flared with fresh prickles of pain, but the shadows swirled around her, thickening, until she had encased herself in a hulking monstrous form. She wore it like a suit of translucent armor, turning herself into a snarling beast.

Black fur rippled across its squat cat-like body. She gritted her teeth, and her monster-self bared long goblin fangs. She pushed herself up with one arm, and the shadows that engulfed her hand dug wicked claws into the floor. She growled in frustration and anger and pain, and she felt the monster give a rumbling snarl.

Then she leapt at the Blackstar. The power in her monstrous legs flung her forward with surprising speed. She hit him full in the chest, knocking him to the floor. But he rolled with the blow and managed to fling her away. Gwendolyn came back at him, slashing and snarling.

The Blackstar was already on his feet. He ducked her first swipe, then caught her arm on the second. He twisted to one side and swung her in a full circle, then flung her across the room. She smashed through the wall beside the door and into the stairway.

She fell through open air and crashed onto the landing one floor down. She slumped against the wall. Her shadow monster body vanished. It had offered her just enough protection that it had been the wall that shattered, rather than all of her bones.

Gritting her teeth against the pain, she got to her feet and stumbled up the stairs to the door of the control room.

The Blackstar grabbed her by the throat. He lifted her into the air with one hand. He stared into her solid black eyes. Then he sucked the darkness right off of her. The tarry substance on her jacket flowed into his hand. His glowing tattoo pulsed as it absorbed it all. Gwendolyn's eyes were green once more, and brimming with tears from the pain.

"Why?" she managed to gasp. She struggled for breath. Darkness crowded her vision as her lungs began to scream.

"Why?" he said. Anger flashed in his eyes, the first real emotion she'd seen from him. "You stole my story. *I'm* the hero here. You took that away from me. Made it all about *you*. I owe you a debt for helping me. One I intend to repay."

He has an odd way of showing gratitude, Gwendolyn thought bitterly. "I'll fix it," she croaked. "I'll put your story back the way it was."

He snorted. "You can't go back again. Changed once is changed forever. I'm going to have to live with this story, and you're going to have to live with the consequences."

She didn't know what to do. She needed help. But no faerie army came to her rescue. She had no magic pistol, no surge of energy to revive her. No helpful leaf danced on the air.

All she had was the burning desire to hurt him, in any way she could. And that was all the idea she needed. She imagined a spiky black choker around her throat. The spikes pierced the Blackstar's hand, and he dropped her, roaring in pain, and Gwendolyn screamed as well as a matching pain speared her own throat.

But she sprang up and dove at him. She frantically scrabbled at the pocket of his coat. He tried to throw her off, but she felt a lump of metal through the fabric. She punched it and felt the satisfying *click* of a button.

Across the control room, a rip appeared in the air. A portal. The shimmering nothingness of the In-Between.

The Blackstar flung her off. Gwendolyn went sliding across the oily ground and slammed into Ganner's unconscious form.

With the bandolier of grenades across his chest.

She yanked a grenade from the strap, and heard a small metallic *clink.* A metal ring lay on the floor.

Gwendolyn tossed the grenade at the Blackstar and threw whatever power she had left into a wall of energy. It sprang into place just as the explosion went off, throwing him into the stairwell, and flinging Gwendolyn into one of the control panels. Her back slammed against the metal edge, bringing a whole new kind of pain to her already long list.

She heard footsteps and looked up to see the Blackstar, no longer striding confidently but running flat-out toward her. But she was faster. She sprinted to the Figment, scooped it up, then hurled herself through the portal.

PART FOUR: WHITE

CHAPTER TWENTY-SEVEN

BLEEDING RED

Once more unto the breach. Once more into the eye-watering nothingness of the In-Between. Her head swam.

But she had the Figment. She held it out, picturing where she wanted to go, shaping the Library of All Wonder in her mind, willing the Figment to take her there, rather than stranding her in some random story. The Library existed in the In-Between, after all.

But it was not the only thing that lived between the worlds.

Suddenly, she was yanked off course. She could sense a presence there. A dark presence. The Abscess in its purest form. It hovered on the edge of her perception, as though she might glimpse it out of the corner of her eye if she turned her head quick enough. She felt the tingle of someone right behind her.

"You will fail them, and it will be all your fault." The Abscess' voice rumbled like thunder.

"Go!" came a voice in her other ear. The Woman in White. She was urgent, desperate. *"He is growing. He is coming."*

Then she heard the Lady gasp in pain. A cocoon of white light wrapped around her, blinding her, and the In-Between disappeared.

~~~

She landed face-first on solid ground, banging her head against unforgiving stone. A wave of pain rolled over her. It was so intense that she vomited on the flagstones under her. The heaving sent fresh pain through her ribs. She cried out, a hoarse gasping sound.

Gwendolyn rolled over onto her back and looked dazedly around. She was in the Library of All Wonder, all right. Lying on her back right next to one of the outer walls. She'd never been this way before. Above her was one of the tall cathedral windows. The In-Between glittered madly at her from the other side.

Shoved through the window. *That's one way to get in,* she thought blearily.

She took a deep, shuddering breath, and was rewarded with another sharp stab in her ribs. It hurt. It all hurt. The pain forced a hiccupping sob out of her, which just made her hurt all over again. So she just lay there, sobbing.

She had failed. She had rescued her parents, freed those people, but she had still failed. The Blackstar was still out there. That meant Cato must have taken control of Tautopolis after she left. And the adult Blackstar ruled Tautopolis with the Faceless Enforcers just as Mister Zero had ruled her City with the Faceless Gentlemen. It had all been for nothing.

No matter what she tried, it always made things worse. It just. Wasn't. Fair.

Anger flooded through her, pushing her to her feet, and she managed to slump against the wall. Cyria's crimson Figment lay glowing on the floor, and she scooped it up. She spotted the
~~~

enormous golden letters that stretched above the entryway.

The Library of All Wonder

Imagination Can Take You Anywhere

She grunted, then stumbled as best she could toward the entrance. Her combat boots felt so heavy she could barely lift them, but she trudged forward, gritting her teeth against the pain. Every step made her gasp. One hand clutched her side, and the other gripped the shelves for support. She tripped, and grabbed a ladder to stop her fall, and another jolt of pain made her vision go white.

The thick leather jacket had offered her some protection, but she suspected one of her ribs was broken. Her right eye throbbed from where the Blackstar had smacked her, and was doubtless turning a terrific shade of black. Her legs were scraped, her stockings torn. Her head throbbed. Her arms ached and stung. Every inch of her felt battered and broken. It was all she could do to remain standing. It was all she could do to cry.

Still, she pushed on, her tears washing the last traces of black from her eyes.

She'd never wanted any of this. Never wanted to be the leader, or the hero. She'd just wanted a little excitement. She just wanted to *be* on adventures, not lead armies to save worlds. She would give anything to have her parents back, *really* back, memories and all. To have someone who would tell her what to do for a change. To let her be a child again. To let her *be*. But all that would be waiting for her at the entrance were two strangers.

Except that when she reached the entry hall, the only one there was Cecilia Forthright.

She sat in a cozy little chair outside the entry hall, comfy as you please, reading her way through *The Fantastical Exploits of Gwendolyn Gray.*

"What are you doing?" Gwendolyn shouted.

"Gwendolyn!" Cecilia shot up. She tossed the book onto the chair behind her, her face undeniably guilty.

Gwendolyn spotted the other two books as well, the green copy of her *Marvelous Adventures,* and the violet cover of her *Withering Trials.* The record of all her adventures, everything she'd done and thought and felt since the day she'd first brought that leaf to life.

Gwendolyn's face grew hot. "How dare you. How *dare* you. First my diary, now this? Ruining my life wasn't enough? You have to spy on me? Dig your grubby little fingers into every part of me?"

"No, it isn't like that!" Cecilia said.

"The devil it's not," Gwendolyn spat. "Where are the others? Where are my parents?"

"They're fine! They're safe. They're back up in that loft, with all the couches and pillows and things. Your parents are... well, they're rather shell-shocked. Haven't really said much. Sparrow's awake, and Starling had some bandages and supplies stored up there. His wound had opened again..."

"Is he all right?"

"Yeah, he's doing fine. Starling is royally pissed at you for stunning her brother. And she was already pretty upset that you let him... that he got shot on the rooftop."

That hurt worse than her injuries. Gwendolyn staggered and sagged against a nearby shelf. A thought struck her. "But how? You all only just left—oh." Time playing its little tricks between worlds again. "How long has it been?"

"A few hours..." Cecilia said. "I tried dialing the code to Tautopolis again, but we didn't have the jewel to power the doorway, so they all went to make your parents comfortable, and--"

"And what about you? What are you doing down here, besides violating my entire life?"

"I..." Cecilia fidgeted a toe against the floor. "I didn't really belong up there. With the others. So I came down here to... to read..."

Gwendolyn's eyes flicked back to the chronicles of her life. Her eyes narrowed. "Go," Gwendolyn ordered. Her voice was low and hard.

"Gwendolyn, wait, let me—"

"Just go! Get away from me!"

Cecilia didn't argue. She backed away down the shelves until she was out of sight.

Gwendolyn groaned and staggered into the comforting darkness of the entry hall, lit by its cozy yellow bulbs. She couldn't face the others. Couldn't face Starling's anger. Gwendolyn knew the look that would be in her eyes. Nor could she face her parents. Or at least, the two adults who no longer remembered her. She could picture their faces as well, blank and uncomprehending, and couldn't bear to see them in person.

She found herself stroking the golden doorframe of the Egressai Infinitus. She ran her fingers along the sculpted branches and the pages that sprouted from them like leaves. Absently, she realized she was still holding Cyria's crimson Figment. She clicked it into the slot of the dialing console, just so she didn't have to hold it anymore.

She nearly jumped out of her skin as the Egressai Infinitus sprang to life on its own. She staggered backwards as the doors began to spin. The Figment glowed even brighter.

And with a shock that stopped her heart, she watched a door made of rough tree bark slide into place. A brass plaque in the center read M-S-N-D-W-S-1-4.

The door swung open and cheerful golden light filled the hall.

There, silhouetted against the sunshine and dancing motes of colored light, was a woman's lithe figure. A very familiar figure. A figure sporting clockwork wings glinting with a rainbow of metallic colors.

"Well, sprout," came the husky voice she knew so well, as the figure wiped her hands on a dirty rag. "I suppose it's high time *I* stepped into the story, eh?"

Gwendolyn gaped. She rushed forward, but Cyria held out a hand.

"Stop there. You can't come in, and I can't come out." The inventress rapped her knuckles against the invisible barrier that kept her imprisoned in Faeoria. "Rules are rules, and this seems to be the only rule those blasted faeries remember to follow."

Gwendolyn almost didn't care. The urge to touch her was so strong her whole body shook with it. Instead, she soaked the inventress up with her eyes.

Cyria Kytain, legendary inventress of Copernium, trapped in the world of the faeries for a having a bit of fun and a bit of food that she shouldn't have. Bound, for as long as they would keep her.

There was no invisible barrier keeping Gwendolyn out, but King Oberon and Queen Titania were no longer her biggest fans, and she'd had to sacrifice her hair to escape their wrath the last time she'd trespassed in their realm.

But none of that mattered, because Cyria was here now, and everything would be all right. Her friend, her teacher. Her short bob of snow-white hair was held back by her ever-present goggles, her face smeared with some sort of dirt or grease. She wore tweed jodhpurs tucked into her high-heeled boots, along with a simple collarless blouse and a red necktie at her bare throat.

A slight curl of a grin twitched at the corner of Cyria's mouth, and Gwendolyn felt the warmth of it right down to her toes.

"Hello, Rosy britches. You've grown. Oh, how you've grown. Even more beautiful than before, you ravishing little bearcat, you." Her voice quivered. Her violet eyes sparkled. "Ugh. All this faerie dust in the air. Plays merry havoc with my sinuses." She wiped at her eyes with the rag in her hands, smearing even more grime on herself. "Well? Not even so much as a how-do-you-do? You haven't lost your voice again, have you?"

She grinned. "No. I can talk."

"A whopping understatement, in my experience," Cyria teased.

Gwendolyn barked a small, wet laugh that loosened something inside her. She gasped and clutched her side. "Ow," she moaned.

"You're hurt!" Cyria said.

"Just a little..." She gritted her teeth. "All right, more than a little. I sort of got thrown through a wall."

"Hmm. Sit tight, then." Cyria put her fingers to her lips and whistled. Something small and gold shot out of the doorway.

"Blast it, no, hang on!" Cyria shouted, but the something slammed into Gwendolyn's chest. It was a tiny clockwork faerie, metal wings whirring as she pushed herself against Gwendolyn in a hug that felt much larger than such tiny arms should have been able to give.

Cyria's mouth quirked into a mischievous half-smile. "She always did take a liking to you."

Gwendolyn hugged the tiny faerie back, cradling it gently in her arms as it emitted soft cooing noises. "You... you rebuilt her."

"Yes. Couldn't have you go traipsing around without some decent supervision. Now get over here and take this to her, you flighty fidget." Cyria took a small bundle out of her pocket. The faerie darted over to retrieve it and delivered it dutifully to Gwendolyn. Gwendolyn unwrapped it to find a small strawberry tart.

"Well? Go on, take your medicine."

She didn't have to be told twice. Gwendolyn wolfed it down in three bites. The strawberry was sweet, and there was ginger too, sharp and spicy and so strong it almost stung her throat. The warmth of it spread down into her chest. She took a deep breath to keep her eyes from watering as the spice passed.

Then she noticed that the pain in her chest was gone. She took another few breaths, deep and easy.

"Better?" Cyria asked.

"Much. Thank you."

"You are incredibly welcome. Now, how is my bricky girl?"

Gwendolyn noticed the soiled rag in the inventress' hands and the way her tie was tucked into the buttons on the blouse, as though she'd been working with something complicated that she hadn't wanted to be strangled by. "I'm not interrupting something, am I? I know how you hate being distracted from your work."

"I'd take a thousand interruptions from you any day. It can be so dreadfully dull around here. No wonder the faeries go barking mad for a little entertainment. Above all, I must do my duty. I know a dark night of the soul when I see one, and a magical mentor must be punctual. I couldn't leave you all moping and alone up here, now could I?"

Gwendolyn blinked. "How did you know?"

Cyria flapped the rag at her. "Oh, pish-tosh. I'm certain I know all the goings-on in my own library, thank you very much."

"*My* library, you mean," Gwendolyn said, her face breaking into a smile. "You gave it to me. I don't know if you heard, but I'm a princess now."

Cyria shook the rag at her. "Don't go putting on airs with me. I knew you when you were just a scrap of a thing with more hair than head. Princess of the Library, indeed. I hear everything that happens in there. And I keep tabs on you through my tapestry gallery. I've got my little spinners working on one just for you. Looks as though you've been having a spot of trouble."

Just like that, all the joy and relief came crashing down. "You don't know the half of it." Gwendolyn filled Cyria in on the past few hours. And days. And years. It felt better to talk about it all. And Cyria just listened, leaning against the door-frame with her arms crossed, nodding attentively. The clockwork faerie took her usual post on Gwendolyn's shoulder.

When Gwendolyn had finished emptying herself, she looked back up at Cyria.

The inventress' eyes were wet again. "Oh, my little princess. I want to give you the biggest hug in the world right now."

The inventress sat on the floor and crossed her legs. "That *is* quite a lot. I won't say growing up is easy, because my mother didn't raise any liars, and I've already done enough besmirching of the family name. If only you'd had some sort of exposition-filled nursery rhyme that could have helped you on your way. I don't suppose you're in that sort of story. But as your wise old mentor, I think I know exactly what you need to hear."

Gwendolyn sat as well. "What is it?"

"It's really quite simple. Just remember—"

"Inventress!" came the booming voice of the tree that Cyria lived in. "Trouble."

Cyria spun around just in time to see Robin Goodfellow, bounding up the hallway on all fours like an animal. His fingers were wicked claws that dug furrows in the wood with each bound.

"Oathbreaker!" Robin bared pointed teeth in a gleeful snarl, and leapt at the doorway.

But Cyria was too fast. She jumped up and slammed the door shut, and Gwendolyn heard a loud *thud* from the other side. The Figment fell from its slot and hit the floor, rolling to a stop against her foot, its red light fading to a dull glow.

"No!" Gwendolyn shouted, leaping up and pounding on the door. "No..." she repeated, her voice a low moan. She fell to the floor, her bare knees stinging as they hit the cold flagstones.

The little faerie fluttered up and knocked on the door, then fluttered sadly down next to Gwendolyn.

What had she done? Put Cyria in danger, is what. She should have known that Robin would be out for blood. She should have slammed the door herself as soon as Cyria had opened it. Faeoria had never brought her anything but trouble.

She crawled over to the wall and drew her legs to her chest, resting her head on them, feeling the cool skin of her knees press against her forehead. She did not rock with sobs. She was overcome with a numbing exhaustion which some distant part of her recognized as depression. Not that recognizing it did much good to drive it away.

And why shouldn't she feel this way? What good had she done? She thought of Jack Lazarus, cut from his story too soon by a sharp stab from the Blackstar. She remembered Professor Zangetsky, the kindly inventor from Copernium, skewered on the end of Tylerium Drekk's sword. Also dead, because of her.

Dark thoughts ran through her mind on an endless loop. This was not about paying bills, or making dinner, or forgetting to buy an umbrella. This was life, and death. And death. And death. And it all seemed to fall on her shoulders.

The inventress would be fine, she told herself. Robin was after Gwendolyn, not Cyria, and King Oberon and Queen Titania would likely not permit their puckish servant to harm the inventress. There was no point in keeping a toy and allowing it to be broken, as faerie logic went. At least, that's what Gwendolyn told herself.

She tried to shove the feelings away, to put them in that imaginary room in her mind where she stored everything else she didn't have time to feel. But the closet was already open. And the feelings wouldn't leave her alone.

The little faerie flew over and hugged itself against her shoulder, which comforted her just enough to curl into a ball and cry herself to sleep.

CHAPTER TWENTY-EIGHT

GOING BACK

Gwendolyn noticed that someone was shaking her, calling her name.

She looked up to see Cecilia Forthright.

Gwendolyn jerked away and crawled back against the wall.

"Don't panic, it's just me," Cecilia said, as though soothing a wounded animal.

Which wasn't far off. Gwendolyn panted, her back against the wall, trying to clear her head and slow her racing heart. She squeezed her eyes shut and focused on taking long, deep breaths.

Then she felt a pair of arms around her. She opened her eyes to find the hated enemy of her childhood sitting next to her on the floor, hugging her, and resting her head on Gwendolyn's shoulder.

It felt nice, Gwendolyn realized, after the initial shock wore off. She let her head rest on top of Cecilia's and they just sat there, side by side under the buzzing yellow lights. The metal faerie perched on one of the sconces and watched with a look of concern on its expressive little face.

"What are you doing here?" Gwendolyn said, her voice a weak

whisper. "I told you to go away."

Cecilia gave a little snort. "I don't take orders from you, Princess." She sat up, and her tone softened. "Are you—"

"All right?" Gwendolyn finished for her. "Umm... no. But I will be in a minute." She wiped at her eyes. "This is somewhat normal, for me."

Cecilia nodded. "I guess. You haven't been acting like yourself, lately."

"I don't know what that even means!" she blurted, louder than she'd meant to, but now that she'd started, she couldn't seem to stop. "I've been a fairy and a princess and a hero and an orphan and I've even had to be my own parents, and according to you, I've been a brat and a bully as well, and everywhere I go everyone expects me to know what to do, and I just don't anymore! I just..." She trailed off, finally stopping to breathe. "I was a little girl with big red hair and a bigger imagination who brought furry monsters to life, but I don't know where that girl went, and now it all seems so silly and stupid and I would do *anything* to go back to her again. Now I'm some bald girl who is either hopelessly depressed or dangerously out of control." She sniffed and wiped her nose with her sleeve. "How can I 'be myself' when I can't even trust *this*?" She clutched her head in her hands. "I don't know where the magic went. And I don't think I can do this anymore."

Cecilia gave her a long, slow look. Then she simply said, "I'm sorry."

A lightning bolt would have been less shocking. "What?"

"I'm sorry. For everything. I know things have been tough for you. But you're not alone. We're here for you."

There is a limit to how much strangeness one can take at any given time, and Gwendolyn had finally reached hers. "Why are you being so nice to me all of a sudden?"

Cecilia turned away and stared at nothing in particular.

"Tell me. I've been horrible to you for years," Gwendolyn said, finally admitting the truth of it to herself. "And you've been horrible to me for years before that. If this is some game you're playing, it's the worst thing you've ever done—"

"It's not a game, it's—" and Cecilia let out a long, heavy sigh. "It's hard to be mean to you after you've been through so much. I never realized what it was like."

"What do you know about it? You don't know me. We've barely spoken until a few days ago."

"No, but…" And Cecilia took three books out of her purse, all with Gwendolyn's name on them. "Then I read these."

Gwendolyn snorted. "Yes, so you could find even more ways to torment me."

"No, not like that. Well, I mean, maybe a little at first. I saw you with them in the Library the first time, and you were acting so suspicious, and when I looked at them, there was your name. In big, shiny letters. So… I took them. I couldn't help it. I was…" She bit her lip. "You had *everything*. You had friends. You had all these stories about amazing adventures. Even Miss Sahida adored you. And now you even had books about you. It wasn't fair."

Gwendolyn rolled her eyes. "I'm sure you found them very dull."

"No! I… I got to know you. Like, really *know* you. First I was just flipping through, mostly trying to find *my* name, to be honest. But there was so much I didn't know. So much that wasn't just about me. And I saw how hard it was. With the Abscess, and the Collector, and the Mister Men, and... and... and me." Her face fell, colored with several shades of embarrassment. "I never saw myself that way before. Like that day we tried to cut your hair, it was..." and she stopped, the words choking off. She sniffed. "It was awful. And... and I'm sorry."

"That's no excuse," Gwendolyn said, but all the heat had gone out of her words.

"No, it's not. But I understand now."

"What do you understand?"

Cecilia looked at her, her expression sad and serious and kind, all at once. "Everyone else is struggling too."

Neither of them spoke. Gwendolyn flipped idly through *Fantastical Exploits*. "How far did you get?"

"I finished them."

Gwendolyn blinked in surprise.

Cecilia shrugged. "I keep telling you, I'm a fast reader. Plus time in this place is really weird. I spent a *long* time waiting for you after the protest. Quiet time to read and... think, and... and I'm sorry about your parents. They seem nice. I wish I had parents like yours."

Gwendolyn snorted. "At least yours still remember you."

"I suppose. They never *seem* to remember me." The other girl leaned her head back against the wall. "They got divorced, you know."

That took her aback. Divorce was not unheard of in the City, but it was quite rare, and very much frowned upon. It simply was *not* done. "I'm sorry."

"I'm not. Not really. It's better than them fighting all the time, isn't it? Still, wasn't easy for Mum. We had to move out of Central. She had to find a job."

Something else that the City frowned upon. Gwendolyn could only imagine what that must have been like. Cecilia was the quintessential Central child, wealthy, bratty, and popular. To leave all that... "When did it happen?"

Cecilia looked down at her feet. "Oh, about a month before I cut your hair and chased you onto a monorail."

Gwendolyn had never suspected there might be some reason Cecilia acted the way she did. She didn't know what to say, so she settled for "Oh."

"I suppose I just needed someone to blame. It's no excuse. It was still awful of me. I... I never told the others. Armand and Vivian and the rest. But they found out after a while, when I stopped inviting them over. And they stopped hanging out with me."

"I thought that was my fault," Gwendolyn said, remembering how she'd broken Cecilia's power when she returned from Tohk. She had dethroned the queen bee with a single glance. Or, that's what she had thought.

Cecilia snorted. "It's not all about you, princess."

Gwendolyn nodded. "Yes, I suppose you're right. But if you hated me so much, then why did you come with us? Really?"

"Why would I go back? Back to Daddy, who ignores me every other weekend until he needs to trot out his pretty little dolly at parties? To Mum, who's always angry, when she talks to me at all, since she's always... sleeping." She looked away, unable to say any more.

Gwendolyn fidgeted. "Why are you telling me all this?"

"I read your story." Cecilia gestured to the books. "Seemed only fair to tell you mine."

Gwendolyn picked up the books and handed them back to Cecilia. "Here. You hang on to them for now. I don't want to seem vain."

The other girl grunted. "Not much chance of that, baldy."

Gwendolyn chuckled, which made Cecilia relax and chuckle a little too. Silence fell between them. It was a more comfortable silence than before. It was the silence between two people who could almost be called friends, sitting against a wall, and leaning on each other for support of all kinds. It was a very specific sort of silence.

Cecilia leaned her head on Gwendolyn's shoulder, idly toying with a lock of her own hair. "I miss it, too. I cried when I read that part."

Gwendolyn's nose wrinkled with a little smile. "I always knew you were jealous."

Cecilia gave her a playful nudge. "Don't let it go to your head, oddling." They rested in the silence for a moment more before Cecilia spoke again.

"I don't know what Cyria was going to tell you," Cecilia said. "But perhaps this would help."

Cecilia flipped through the pages of *The Fantastical Exploits of Gwendolyn Gray*, to one of the worst moments of Gwendolyn's life. Titania had been "training" her, which involved trying to kill Gwendolyn in several very creative ways. Gwendolyn had barely survived, crashing to the forest floor and hiding in a tree. She read of her anxiety and depression taking hold, nearly strangling her.

Gwendolyn looked away. "That's not exactly helpful."

"No, not that," Cecilia said, turning a couple more pages. "This."

Gwendolyn read about herself sobbing, coming to terms with a depression that she was only beginning to understand. But when she needed it most, she'd had kind words from a good friend.

Everyone is different. None of us are born to fit in, Cyria had told her. *Trees don't grow in straight lines, and neither do people. You can never tell what direction they'll go, but they're always growing upward, never backward.*

That was true enough. Gingerly, Gwendolyn took the book and skimmed further.

You are wonderful, and beautiful, and kind, and clever. You're stronger than you think.

The trouble was, she didn't feel like any of those things. But it would be nice if she was.

We become what we do, Cyria had said. *Dream enough, you become a dreamer.*

She may not have felt beautiful and kind and clever, but she could try to act it. She could do kind things. She could do clever things. Perhaps that would be enough.

It takes a lot of strength to be yourself.

And that's what the lady had wanted, yes? For her to be herself? Maybe she didn't have to focus on who she was. She could focus on who she *wanted* to be. The others believed in her because they saw something worth believing in. As long as she believed in herself.

"Is this helping at all?" Cecilia said, fidgeting.

"Yes," she told Cecilia. "I think it helped. Thank you."

"I mean, it's fine. Don't worry about it." Cecilia pushed against the wall and stood up. "Let's go home and rescue Ian. Are you ready for another adventure?" She stuck out a hand.

Gwendolyn sighed. "Do we have to? I'm getting a bit tired of adventures," she said with a small smirk. But she took Cecilia's hand, and allowed the other girl to pull her up. She straightened her skirt, then took a moment to take stock of herself. Her plaid School skirt. Mother's blouse and Father's suspenders. Tommy's yellow bow tie and Missy's striped, violet stockings. The boots she'd taken from Tautopolis. Cato's jacket.

Her clothes were a mishmash of her family, her friends, her adventures, and her mistakes. She wore her own history. And she supposed that was who she was. She was a combination of everything she'd been through, each adventure changing her just a little more. Even Cato's jacket. That was part of her now, too. She couldn't ignore what had happened. She'd keep it, as a reminder.

But...

Gwendolyn closed her eyes.

"What are you doing?" asked Cecilia.

"Shh, just give me a moment..." Gwendolyn said. She took a deep breath and imagined. Not with anxiety and doubt and fear and anger, but with curiosity and excitement. With all the wonder of her Library around her.

Fabric rustled, as though in a sudden breeze. She opened her eyes and looked down again. Father's suspenders were now the same yellow as Tommy's bow tie. Her plaid skirt was violet and yellow and black. The rips in her striped stockings had mended. The jacket had shrunk, and conformed itself to her body, rather than Cato's.

Her jacket and boots were no longer black, but a deep, dark purple. And in every fold and shadow, glittering stars and galaxies twinkled at her, like the ones that burned above the Forest of Ideas.

She moved and twirled. "What do you think?" Where the dim light from the bulbs in the corridor struck, the jacket and boots looked purple, but in the shadows and creases in the leather, the stars shone. Even in the darkness, she would remember that there was light to fight it back.

"Neat trick," Cecilia said. "I didn't know you could do that sort of thing in here."

Cecilia was right. She hadn't even thought about it, or realized what she was doing, but she had summoned her powers easily. "Umm... I suppose I've kept the others waiting long enough. I've got to face my parents some time."

Cecilia looked her up and down. "If you're ready. Do you need another hug first?"

Gwendolyn blinked in surprise. She looked inside herself, and was surprised at the answer she found, and equally surprised at how touched she was by the question. "Um... yes. I could use a hug."

Cecilia hugged her, and Gwendolyn hugged her back, and they shut out the world for just a little longer.

CHAPTER TWENTY-NINE

Home Again, Home Again

The trip through the Egressai Infinitus and into the City was a quiet one. Her parents seemed practically catatonic. They said nothing as they boarded the monorail from the Central City to the Middling. Gwendolyn didn't have the energy to strike up any kind of conversation anyway, and what exactly did one say to parents with no memory of you? The most she could manage was to sit next to Mother on the tram.

The silence was exquisitely awkward. Gwendolyn fidgeted with the Figment necklace, then stopped herself and tucked it under her blouse. After a few blocks, Mother gave a little cough. "The others told me what you did. For us," Mother said in a quiet voice. "Thank you again. Your name is Gwendolyn, yes?"

Gwendolyn bit her lip and nodded.

Mother frowned, seeing her expression. "I'm sorry. I... Cecilia says, that I'm... I'm your mother. Somehow."

Gwendolyn nodded again. She didn't trust her voice enough to speak.

"Well," Mother said, and placed a hand on Gwendolyn's knee.

368

"Daughter or not, we were trapped in that horrid place, and you rescued us. Thank you."

Father nodded at them from across the aisle. "Yes. I'm not sure how we can ever repay you."

"It was no trouble, really..." Gwendolyn mumbled. But the silence in the tram was a little less awkward as they entered the Middling.

~~~

"This is all rather unnecessary," came Father's voice from outside the door to apartment 6E. There was the sound of ripping tape, the door swung open, and the Gray family came home.

Mother looked around as they entered the nearly empty living room. She gasped. "What happened?" The heavy furniture was all there, but the room had been stripped of all else.

"The Childkeeper," Gwendolyn said. "She took everything when I was put into the Home."

"Well, we'll soon put a stop to *that*," Father said, stroking his mustache. "But I want to change into something respectable. Can't wait to get out of this filthy thing," he said, tugging at the power station uniform. He went to the bedroom. "At least nobody's been mucking about in here."

"And I'm told you've lived here by yourself for two years?" Mother ran a finger along the coffee table. "You've kept it remarkably clean."

Gwendolyn choked a little. "Yes. Right. I... may have had some help." Hopefully Robin wouldn't come to call with a bill anytime soon. But faeries seeking deadly vengeance seemed trivial when her Mother was right here, standing in their living room again.
~~~

Dirty and haggard, in stark contrast to Robin's immaculate imitation of her. And all the more real for it.

It was overwhelming. But it was so like Mother to seek comfort in normalcy, checking for dust while the world turned upside down. "Regardless," she said. "You must be an extraordinarily responsible young girl."

"Marie." Father came in from the bedroom, still in his soiled uniform, his voice serious. "Look at this." He handed something to Mother.

It was the family photograph from their nightstand.

Gwendolyn's parents stared at the picture for a long moment, then looked back up at Gwendolyn. "It's all true..." Father said. "She really is..."

Mother hissed in pain and put a hand to her temple.

"Marie! Are you all right?"

"I'm fine. Just a headache. I'll go fix us all some tea," Mother said, but she couldn't hide the tremor in her voice. She turned and headed for the kitchen. "Tea fixes everything."

"Of course," Father said, taking another look at the photo, and another at Gwendolyn herself. Then he set the photo down on his desk and began rummaging in the drawers. "Seems there's quite a bit of catching up to do. And from what you tell me, the Lambents can do that sort of thing now, yes?"

"Oh! Umm, yes," Gwendolyn said, fetching it from the coffee table drawer. She handed it to him. "You just... look into it, like before, but instead of nothing, it's full of... everything. It'll show you whatever you want to know."

"Good, good. The City's had a quite a few changes, I hear, and

I'm dying to know all about them." He went over to his desk and set down the Lambent. The small glass sphere started to glow. Colorful patterns danced on Father's face, and he went still.

Gwendolyn turned away and noticed her friends, all staring at her.

"What?"

"It's just weird," Sparrow said.

"Sparrow!" Starling scolded.

"What? It *is* weird. Having to remind your own parents who you are..." His voice trailed off. "Starling, you don't think... Mom and Dad, they're going to... when we get home, they'll—"

"Of course they will," she interrupted, but her voice broke a little. She looked away. "Sorry, I have to go to the bathroom." And she rushed out of the room. Gwendolyn thought she saw her wipe at her eyes.

"Cecilia, don't you think you should be getting home as well?" Gwendolyn said. "You haven't been back since Umberland. Your mother must be worried."

Cecilia turned sideways in her chair and kicked her feet over the side. "Let her worry."

"Fine." Gwendolyn threw up her hands. "It's your life."

"Darn right, it's my life. Besides, it's Ian we should be worried about."

"Yes, and I'd wager the Childkeeper has been stealing more children than just him, from the plans she kept boasting about."

Mother came back into the living room and took a long sip of tea. She sighed in contentment. "Oh, yes. That's wonderful. Would anyone else like some? There's not much to choose from, I'm afraid. Dan?"

But Father didn't answer. He sat at the desk, head resting in his hand, eyes covered. He just held the Lambent out to her. His hand was trembling.

Mother took it. "What? What is it? What's wr—" But she went silent as the light played over her face. She stood there, speechless, her eyes growing wider.

"Oh," Mother said. "Oh, my." She looked up. "Oh, Gwendolyn."

The cup fell from her fingers and hit the floor, splattering tea everywhere. But Mother didn't notice. She crossed the living room and clasped Gwendolyn by the shoulders, looking her up and down, eyes still dancing with the Lambent's rainbow light. "My sweet Bless..." her voice choked off.

Gwendolyn was speechless. *Bless. She called me Bless.* It had been her parents special nickname for her. And then she realized.

The Lambent.

Thoughts raced through her head, puzzle pieces fitting together. When she had battled with Mister Zero, she had reversed the Lambents. Gwendolyn had brought back everything he'd erased. Including all her parents' memories. Mother and Father had been taken before they could look into the Lambents, but their memories had been here the whole time, stored in the Lambents, just waiting for her parents to retrieve them.

But all her thoughts were squeezed out of her as Mother pulled Gwendolyn into an embrace, one that only a mother could give.

Gwendolyn gave in, and let the tears come. Every inch of her melted into her mother's arms.

"I'm sorry," she whispered, face buried in Mother's shoulder.

They were the words she'd been longing to say, the words she'd sworn would be the first she spoke to her parents. The harsh memory of their final moments together was never far from her mind. "I'm sorry. I'm so, so sorry." She sobbed, held in her mother's arms for the first time in over two years. It was everything she'd dreamed of.

"But..." Mother said, pulling away. "What happened to your hair?"

~~~

"So you really remember?" Gwendolyn said. She sat on the couch, a warm mug of tea cupped in her hands, snuggled in between Mother and Father. Mother had an arm around her. Father had a hand on her knee and was absently stroking his mustache. Sparrow, Starling, and Cecilia sat nearby, obviously hesitant to intrude on the moment.

Gwendolyn felt like a little girl again, safe in her parents' arms. And that was fine for now. She'd managed to explain some of the past few hours, and years, and everything was fine. She didn't even hurt too badly. As long as she didn't breathe overly much.

"Of course we remember, Bless," Father said. "Even if it is rather... extraordinary."

"It makes much more sense now, with our memories returned," Mother said. She shook her head. "Listen to me. *Memories returned.* I sound utterly ridiculous."

"But you believe me?"

"What, about how our memories of you were erased through the Lambents?" Mother replied. "Or how we were taken to that *horrible* place, and imprisoned for god-knows-how-long?"
~~~

"And how our wonderful daughter has apparently been gallivanting off on adventures, reshaping the City as we know it, and generally being... well, sort of fantastic," Father added with a sly grin.

"Umm... yes," Gwendolyn said. "That."

Mother took a deep breath. "Well. I'm a modern, well-adjusted woman. I'd like to think that if my daughter can handle it, then so can I." But behind her words, Mother's eyes were just slightly too wide, her body just a bit too tense.

Not that Gwendolyn could blame her. But she had to admit, she was impressed. She had never in a million years pictured a moment like this. Any time she had imagined telling her parents the whole truth, it had involved a lot more yelling.

"But I have to ask..." Father said. "Whatever happened to your hair?"

Gwendolyn choked a little. "It's a long story."

Cecilia held up *The Fantastical Exploits of Gwendolyn Gray.* "Not that long," she said.

"Yes, thank you, Cecilia," Gwendolyn snapped. "But I think there's a limit to how much exposition my parents can handle at once."

"What is *that?*" Mother said.

Gwendolyn sighed, and gave her parents a quick explanation on the Library of All Wonder, and the books that held the story of her life. Their faces showed looks of utter bewilderment.

My life is completely, utterly, bizarre, she thought.

Mother reached for the book Cecilia was holding. "I would certainly like to read those..."

"No!" Gwendolyn said, getting up and stepping between them. "I'm sorry, it's private." The thought of her mother reading every one of her inner thoughts felt so incredibly wrong. "Just... no."

"But it's your life," Mother said. "I want to know everything."

"I'll tell you everything, I promise, but please, trust me."

"Even *she* won't read it," Cecilia said.

"But she let *you* read them?" Father raised an eyebrow.

"Well, she didn't exactly let me, but... yes."

"Hmmm." Father gave the girls a knowing look. "You two must be getting rather close, then. It's good to see you making some friends, Bless."

"And what about you?" Mother asked Sparrow. "Where do you come from?"

"Uhh..." Sparrow said. "From... another world."

Gwendolyn supposed it was true enough. Sparrow and Starling had lost their parents and been stranded in the In-Between, stumbling between worlds trying to find their way home. At least, that was the history Gwendolyn had imagined for them. Because they had come from her, sprung fully formed from her imagination. But at the same time, they had memories of their home and their parents.

Memories Gwendolyn had given them? Where *did* they come from? It was a question that had never been fully answered. Her mind, or another world?

Or maybe both at once, she wondered. If there was anything she knew for sure, it was that ideas could take on a life of their own.

Mother got up, knelt down in front of Sparrow, and gave him a gentle hug. Gwendolyn blinked. Her mother was not the affectionate type.

Mother held Sparrow at arm's length. "Thank you." She clasped his hand, and looked at Starling, who stood awkwardly off to one side. "Both of you. For protecting my daughter. I think..." Her voice broke a little. "I think she needed someone like you."

Sparrow fidgeted. "Of course. She's great. She looks out for us too."

"Well, then." Mother stood and stretched, hands on her lower back. "Tea is all well and good, but let me see what I can do about some proper food."

"And I'm still dying to get out of these clothes," Father added.

Mother put a hand on Gwendolyn's shoulder and looked her in the eye. "We won't be gone long. I promise."

Gwendolyn blushed and looked away. "Mother, you're only going into the kitchen, I'm sure I'll be fine..." But it felt indescribably wonderful to have someone to worry about her.

Mother went into the kitchen, and Father went into the bedroom.

"I suppose that's settled for now," Gwendolyn said. "But we can't sit here long while Ian is—ow!" Starling had crouched in front of her and was poking her in the ribs. "Stop that!"

"Oh, I'm *sorry*, did that hurt?" she said sarcastically. She dumped a pile of bandages and other supplies onto the coffee table. "My bedside manner needs work, I guess. Now be a good patient and hold still."

"Starling, I told you, Cyria fixed me."

"Oh, so this doesn't hurt then?" She gave Gwendolyn another poke in the ribs.

"OW! Fine, fine, it still hurts!"

"Good. Don't you ever shoot my brother again. No matter how much we might want to sometimes..."

"Hey!" Sparrow said.

Starling wagged a roll of bandages at him. "Watch it, you're next. I don't care how much magical healing you've both had, those ribs need wrapped, and you need to take it easy."

Starling was right. Cyria's healing food seemed to have fixed the worst of it, but her rib was still tender and sore.

"Now, hold still." Starling crouched down again and brushed her lock of blue hair out of her face. Then she started applying ointment around Gwendolyn's eye. "You've got some nasty swelling here. This should take care of it."

Gwendolyn winced, but did her best to hold still. "You just keep all of this in your pockets?"

Starling grunted. "Swiped it from the nurse's office in Tautopolis. Knowing the two of you, I figured it would come in handy."

"I'm sorry. I truly am. I didn't know what else to do. I had to get you out of there, so I stunned him. And on the rooftop—"

"I get it. It's fine. It's not your fault. We're all just doing the best we can. Sometimes..." Starling sighed. "Sometimes I wish didn't have to be the tough big sister. That I could just be *me*. It felt nice to let someone else take over for once."

Starling looked away and put the cap back on the ointment. "And when he got shot... He's my brother. It's *my* job to look after him. If it weren't for you, things would have been even worse. So, thanks, I guess. Even if I'm still mad at you for a while."

Gwendolyn put a hand on her shoulder. "Starling? We'll find your parents too. I promise."

Starling brushed her hand away. "Don't. Just... just don't. I'll be fine." Then she started checking her brother's bandages. "Don't suppose there's much chance of us staying put and healing up for a change—"

She was interrupted by a knock at the front door. Before Gwendolyn could get up, the door burst open, and two uniformed policemen stepped inside.

"Oy!" said the younger of the two. "Told you I saw someone sneaking in. I'd know that bald girl anywhere. That's the kid you took to the Home, inn'it Tom?"

"Right you are." The older one gave them all a stern look. "All right, you other three, you clear off right quick and I won't bother reporting you for trespassin'. Come on, girlie." He grabbed Gwendolyn by the arm.

"Stop it! Let go of me!" she shouted.

"Nothin' doin'. We'd heard you'd run off. Back home you go."

"She *is* home," boomed Father's voice from the bedroom doorway. "Now unhand my daughter."

The policeman obeyed and stepped back in shock. Gwendolyn looked at Father, dressed in his usual white shirt and black trousers again, hands on hips, his expression stern and commanding. At that moment he was more of a hero to her than Kolonius and Jack and Cyria all put together.

"Now, wait a minute," the younger officer stammered. "You're not supposed to be here. This is City property and you're all trespassin'—"

378

"We most certainly are not!" Mother snapped, coming out of the kitchen. "This is our home, and you will leave immediately."

"Isn't that right, Tom?" Father said sternly. "You've walked this neighborhood since before Gwendolyn was born. What I'd like to know is why my home has been ransacked by the City police."

"Well... we were told that you were gone, and..."

"Clearly you were misinformed. And it is equally clear that there has been a grievous misunderstanding—"

"Where you *kidnapped* our daughter—" Mother added, furious.

"—but if you leave immediately, I may leave your name out of the many, many complaints I intend to file with your captain and the City Council."

Tom's face paled. "Right away, sir. Sorry, sir. Just following orders, s'all."

"But Tom, that girl's a wanted fugitive—" the other officer said.

"The man lives here, Oscar, and there's no sense in sending the girl back to the Childkeeper when her parents are standin' there, plain as day. There's been more than enough of that goin' on 'round here for my taste anyway. Sorry again, sir," Tom said, and tipped his cap to Father and Mother. "And we'll be gettin' your things back right quick, ma'am. Have a nice day." Then he hustled the other officer out into the hall and shut the door behind them.

"Well," Mother said, dusting her palms. "That settles that. Now we can all get back to *normal* around here."

Normal. The word produced a knee-jerk reaction of disgust in Gwendolyn. The officer's presence had brought back painful memories of the Home For Unclaimed Children. And her friend was still trapped there. "I'm sorry mother, but we can't stay long.

We have to go."

"What?"

Gwendolyn stood. "We can't stay. I'm not the only one who was kidnapped. The Childkeeper took Ian, one of my friends from the School, and we have to save him and who knows how many others—"

"Don't worry about that. As I said, I'll be lodging a full complaint with the City Council," Father said. "We'll get it sorted, I promise. We won't let anything happen to you or your friends again." He looked at Sparrow, Starling, and Cecilia.

Gwendolyn shook her head. "The City doesn't work that way. The City Council is supporting the Childkeeper and her plans. They're trying to put everything back the way it was before."

"I don't see what's so bad about that," Mother said, walking over to Father and putting a hand on his shoulder. "Leave it to us. We're here now, so there's no need for any more heroics on your part."

"I'm sorry," Gwendolyn said. "But you don't know what it's like, you weren't here, everything is different now. I *have* to fix this."

Mother sighed and put up her hands. "I know. You... You're right."

Gwendolyn's jaw dropped. "I'm what?"

Mother took another long breath. "You're right. We weren't here. We weren't here to protect you." She reached out and brushed a hand against Gwendolyn's temple, as though tucking back a strand of hair that was no longer there. "We weren't here when you needed us. And I will never forgive myself for that. And after... everything..."

A pained expression crossed her face, and Gwendolyn could

almost see the memories flash before Mother's eyes. Memories of being strapped to a table in a dark Tautopolis prison. Mother shook her head. "I know that there is so much more that I *don't* know. But I know that you saved us. And if you say that this is something you have to do, then I believe you. We trust you."

"We do?" Father said.

Mother gave him a soft slap in the chest. "Yes, Dan, we do."

Father grinned and winked. "Only kidding, Bless. Of course we do. You're all grown up now, after all."

"Not *all* grown up." Mother took Gwendolyn by the hand. She looked deep into her daughter's eyes, and Gwendolyn melted again. "But tell me one thing. Why does it have to be *you*?"

Gwendolyn thought about that for a long moment. "Because I started all of this. And I have to finish it. And because..." She sighed. "It's who I am. I'm different. I'm... special." It felt strange to say it out loud.

Mother smiled a reluctant smile. "I can't argue with that." She stood up. "But if we're all going to go running off to who knows where, we should have a good meal first."

"What?" Gwendolyn said. "We?"

"Of course," Father said. "We're going with you. We're not letting you out of our sight for one more minute. If there's dangerous doings afoot, then by thunder, we'll be there to protect you."

"But—"

"Either we go with you, or you don't go at all," Mother said. "And that's final. Now, Cecilia, will you be joining us for dinner?"

Cecilia looked shocked. "I... umm... yes?" She shot Gwendolyn a look. "As long as it isn't *enchanted* food this time."

Mother threw up her hands. "I'm not even going to pretend to know what that means, and I'm too tired to ask, so I'll go get cleaned up, and then get dinner on the table." Mother crossed over to the bedroom. "I intend to take the world's longest shower."

Father followed. "If that's the case, then I'm going to take a nap in my very own bed, if you please and thank you very much..."

The four children shared bewildered looks.

Starling shrugged. "Well, you wanted your parents back."

Gwendolyn flopped down on the couch, and her little faerie zipped out of her jacket and perched on her knee. "I suppose I forgot what it was like to *have* parents."

"I'm hungry," Sparrow said. "It couldn't hurt to stay for dinner."

Gwendolyn snorted, toying absently with the faerie while it played with her fingers. "You don't know my mother's cooking." Then she grinned. "Fortunately, I think the kitchen has been cleaned out already."

"Aww, man..." moaned Sparrow.

"But there's something I have to do first." She looked down at her free hand. It was trembling.

"What?" Starling asked.

"Nothing." And it was the truth. It had been a long time since she'd meditated properly. But after the last few days... she couldn't afford to wither in depression, or get lost in a manic episode and make some reckless mistake. She had to stay balanced. "I need to do nothing for a while. Cecilia, can you track down the others?"

"Yeah, I'll make few calls."

"Good. I'll be back in a few minutes."

Starling tossed her a roll of elastic bandages. "And go wrap those ribs."

"Yes, yes, fine..." Then Gwendolyn headed up to her room, to try and find some peace for the trials ahead.

CHAPTER THIRTY

REBELS AND REVOLUTIONS

I shall not even attempt to describe the embarrassment of having one's parents chaperoning a daring rescue, but it is enough to make us cringe in sympathy for Gwendolyn as she rode the monorail with Sparrow, Starling and Cecilia, while Mother and Father sat across the aisle.

To make matters worse, they were being *affectionate*. They held hands, and Mother rested her head on Father's shoulder. Awkward circumstances aside, it made Gwendolyn smile to see them this way.

A little while later, they all stood in front of a restaurant on the other side of the Middling.

"Good!" Father said. "I'm famished."

"I'm afraid we're not here to eat," Gwendolyn said.

"This is where Jessica told us to meet," Cecilia added. "She's got some information on Ian and the Childkeeper. We're meeting her and Tommy and Missy to come up with a plan."

"Yeah, but we can eat while we talk..." Sparrow said, as Gwendolyn opened the door.

They were met with a wave of shouts and applause that nearly knocked Gwendolyn off her feet. The restaurant was filled with people, all dressed in brightly colored Revels clothes. And all of them were cheering.

For her.

"Okay," Sparrow said. "We might have to wait for a table."

"We might already have a reservation. Look." Cecilia pointed to the colorful signs people held. Signs that had Gwendolyn's name on them. *We Believe in Gwendolyn!* read one. *Gwendolyn For The Change!* read another.

"Whoah," said Starling.

"What is all this?" said Mother. She and Father were struck dumb by the noise and color and chaos. A band was playing on a makeshift stage at the other end of the dining room. Food and drink were being passed around, but most of it seemed to have been forgotten as the crowd pressed around Gwendolyn and her family.

"I know that *normal* is a dirty word with you three," Cecilia said, "but I wouldn't mind a little more of it once in a while."

"You're the one who decided to tag along," Starling said.

Cecilia grinned. "Oh, I wouldn't miss this for the world."

"Gwendolyn!" Jessica pushed her way between people and tables. "I'm so glad you're here. Come on, Zelda's waiting!"

"What are all these people doing here?"

"They're here for you! Once Cecilia told me you were back and wanted to meet, Zelda called an impromptu revel."

"You told Zelda I was back?" Gwendolyn asked, but she already knew the answer. Jessica only grinned.

Zelda swooped up to them in a whirl of rainbow fringe. "My little ears were burning." She eyed Gwendolyn up and down and gave a dramatic gasp. "Wendy, is that you? My word, girl, that outfit is ta-da and to-die! So *chic*, so *bohemian*. The designers around here will go gaga trying to make fabric like that jacket. It's practically magical! I'm posi-lutely green all over. Though it's no surprise you're a trend-setter. After all, you're the *original* trend-setter."

"What... what's happening here?" Gwendolyn asked. Every eye in the place was on her and Zelda.

Zelda gestured at all the posters and banners. "*You're* what's happening here, you dazzling dame! You're going on stage any second now! These people didn't dash on down to hear me droning on all day. They want to hear from *you*, Wendy. Although I suppose I should call you Gwendolyn. That's your real name, right? How about Gwendy? Or Gwenny? Can I call you Gwenny? Swell! Gwenny Gray. The girl who saved the City! And with luck, you can help us *keep* it saved. I'm going to go warm up the crowd. See you in a mo'! Come on, you lot, give them some space, you'll all get to hear from her!"

Zelda breezed away as quickly as she came. Gwendolyn wondered if the woman ever took time to breathe. The crowd around them relaxed some and conversation rippled through the room. Gwendolyn turned to Jessica. "But... all these people..."

"We told them about everything," Jessica said. "How you reversed the Lambents and flooded the City with imagination. How you found all those books and shared them with everyone."

"And they all believed you?" Cecilia said.

"We helped," said Tommy, pushing his way through the mob. Missy was by his side, both of them beaming with the energy of the room. "We were able to show them our memories through the Lambent. See?"

He thrust one in her face, and with a flash of light Gwendolyn was suddenly back in the dome atop the Central Tower, battling with Mister Zero. Although this time she stood off to one side, looking at herself, staring up at the boy in his crystal spire.

"Stop it!" she shouted, and she slapped Tommy's hand away.

"Oh, right," Tommy said, cringing. "That was rude. Sorry. I don't suppose you want to go through all that again. But everyone saw what you did. We left out most of the magicky-magic. People can only believe so much at once. But you're a right celebrity now."

She looked around at the rally, taking it all in. "All of this...for me? To help save Ian?"

"Not just Ian," Jessica said, darkly. "The Childkeeper's kidnapping children from all over the City. Not only from the Revels, either, but anyone she thinks won't be missed. Outskirts kids mostly. And she's... she's doing something to them."

"What?" Gwendolyn asked.

Jessica's expression was stony and serious. "There's a place in the bottom of the Home, where they take the children. They've got them locked up down there."

"How do you know this?" Gwendolyn said.

"I, uh..." Jessica squirmed, uncharacteristically nervous. "I sort of snuck in."

"You did what?" Gwendolyn said, more in surprise than disapproval.

"You weren't here, so I just... did. It seemed like the sort of thing you would do."

Gwendolyn blushed. This was going to take some getting used to. "But how did you get in? And back out again?"

Jessica scratched the back of her neck. "So, I *may* have borrowed those clothes they gave you at the Home. I took them from your house, put them on, and hopped the front fence while they were having outdoor time in the rear courtyard."

"You did *what?*" Gwendolyn repeated.

"They didn't seem too worried about anyone breaking *in*. Too busy singing some ridiculous song about chores and exercise or something. No one noticed another good little orphan. I snuck into the Childkeeper's office, and a kid was screaming from down some stairs. I went down to the basement, but the door down there was locked. The screaming... it didn't last long."

"I know that door," Gwendolyn said.

"Ian was in there, I know it." Jessica closed her eyes for a moment, and when she opened them, her expression was fierce. "I was about to find some way of smashing in, but some older kids caught me and dragged me upstairs. They brought me to the Childkeeper, who was outside lining up all the others. I fought them off enough to run and hop the fence again. That was yesterday."

Gwendolyn was speechless. *It seems Jessica has been up to some adventures of her own,* she thought.

"But now *you're* here!" Jessica said. "You can help us, and we can put a stop to it all! We can free Ian and protect the Change. Wait here, I'm going to go help Zelda. I'll let you know when we're ready for you."

Jessica disappeared into the crowd. Gwendolyn was struck by how much Jessica had changed in the past two years. She supposed they all had.

"Is this all right?" Missy said, putting a hand on her arm. "All this attention. And noise. It's all a bit... manic." She gave Gwendolyn a meaningful look, as though asking Gwendolyn if *she* was manic as well.

"It's fine. I'm fine. I've got *you* to keep me balanced, don't I?" She gave Missy a hug, then nodded toward Mother and Father. "Having them helps as well."

Missy put her hands to her mouth. "Oh my goodness! I didn't even notice! Are those your parents?"

"Hello," said Mother, who had hung back with Father, not wanting to intrude on their daughter's social life.

"You must be Gwendolyn's friends," Father said, sticking out a hand.

Tommy shook it. "Yeah, best mates. Pleased to meet ya."

"I'm sorry, excuse me, did you say this was Mr. and Mrs. Gray?"

Gwendolyn spun around. "Miss Sahida! I mean, yes, this is them. These are my parents."

Miss Sahida shook hands with them. "It's nice to finally meet you. I'm Gwendolyn's teacher from the school. Your daughter is... well, sort of wonderful."

Father chuckled. "I've always thought so."

But Miss Sahida's face was serious. "Indeed. Yet you've been away for quite some time, I hear. Leaving Gwendolyn to fend for herself."

Gwendolyn put a hand on her teacher's shoulder. "It's all right. It wasn't their fault. And they're back now." She saw Jessica pushing her way back through the crowd. "Could you sit with them for a little while? I have a feeling I'm about to be very busy. And I'm sure they're a little overwhelmed by... all of this."

Miss Sahida frowned, then nodded. "If you say so. I was a bit overwhelmed myself, at first. It's a lot different to how *we* grew up, that's for sure. And thank goodness for that. Why don't you come and sit, I've got a table over here."

Mother looked out at a sea of faces that were all much younger than her, and seemed to take comfort in the presence of another adult. "Yes, that would be nice." She squeezed Gwendolyn's hand. "We'll be right over there, Bless. We're not going anywhere."

Gwendolyn rolled her eyes. "Mother, I'll be fine..." Then she broke into a wide smile. Feeling exasperated with her Mother was the most excellent feeling in the world.

"I dare say, you're a darn sight better than old Mr. Percival," Father said as Miss Sahida led them away. "I'm sure Gwendolyn's just wild about you."

"Er, yes. Ted has his methods, I suppose..." she replied, and then they were out of earshot.

Jessica appeared and grabbed Gwendolyn's arm. "Come on, we're ready!"

Before Gwendolyn could say a word, she was dragged to a small stage at one end of the restaurant, where Zelda was already addressing the crowd.

"...and it's not enough that they're snatching our fellow Revellers, gang, now we know that they've got some nasty nefarious

390

notions about what to do with the one's they've snatched. We've got one who's laid her peepers on it first-hand!"

"That's right!" Jessica said, leaping onto the stage. "It's all true. They've got them locked in the basement of the Home, and they're doing something to them. The City Council has gone too far this time. They have to be stopped!"

"And we are in loads of luck, kiddos. Because we've got someone here who can make it all happen! She's the reason there's any happenings happening at all. So give it up for the most happening girl in the City... little Gwenny Gray!"

Zelda gestured to her, and the crowd roared with cheers and applause.

Gwendolyn looked up at the stage, and bit her lip. She suddenly felt very small and exposed. Without thinking, she ran a hand over her bare scalp.

"Hey," said Sparrow. "Here." He took off his hat, stood on tiptoe, and put it on her head.

"Really?" Gwendolyn asked.

"Yeah, I know you like them, and the police took all of yours. Go."

She hadn't realized she was feeling self-conscious, but the hat *did* help. She didn't have time to thank him as Jessica grabbed her and pulled her up on the stage.

It was just like the Revels. There she was, in front of dozens of people. Except now she had no wig or "Wendy" to hide behind. Nothing but herself.

Then I'll be myself, she thought with a wry shake of her head. After all, that was who these people had come to see.

"Umm... hello," she said.

More cheers erupted. Zelda waved at them for silence.

And suddenly, she was twelve again, standing on her desk in Mr. Perceval's classroom, Lambent thrust in the air, trying to show her classmates how wonderful imagination could be. She smiled. This was who she was all along.

Gwendolyn took a deep breath, and raised her voice. "That place," she said. "The Home. I've been there. It's just as terrible as everyone says. And what they're doing to the children there..." She thought of the soulless orphans. All of them droning their songs, repeating the Childkeeper's twisted philosophy. Not unlike the people in Tautopolis, really.

"Whatever it is, it isn't good. They have to be stopped. Whatever they're doing, they're trying to put the City back the way it was before the change."

An angry murmur went through the crowd.

"'A Return to Values,' they say," Gwendolyn continued. "But we've seen their values, if you please, and thank you very much. They want everything to be the same again. No ideas. No stories. Keeping the City locked into its status quo for century after century. All built on stolen children."

She spotted Mother and Father in the audience, off to one side with Miss Sahida. They were beaming with pride. If felt strange to be so exposed. She'd spent so much time trying to hide things from her parents, and then two years of lying, keeping secrets, and doing whatever it took to keep from being noticed.

Judging from the posters and banners that bore her name, she had done a spectacularly poor job of it. The crowd hung on her every word. All the people in their colorful clothes, some with brightly colored flowers or butterflies or fireworks painted on their cheeks.

"Look at yourselves. Look how far you've come. You're all creators now. Dreamers. Changers. People who know that no one is born to fit in. That there is no such thing as an ordinary person. That this place can be whatever we want it to be. Our ideas can change the world around us, if we believe in them, and we're brave enough to act." She opened her jacket, and out popped the little faerie. It zipped once around the room, then came to rest on her shoulder, striking a heroic pose. The crowd murmured in amazement.

"Change. Growth. Progress. These are worth fighting for. We have to stop the Childkeeper, and the City Council."

"That's right!" Zelda cried, stepping forward. "We can do it, gang. That's why you're all here. We'll march ourselves over there, storm the place, and take it over. Get whatever weapons you can lay your paws on! The walls are thick, so once we're inside, we can hold out against the city police for as long as it takes, until we can use the Lambents to rally the rest of the city to our cause!"

"No!" Gwendolyn shouted. She thought of Cato, and the raid on the Central Power Station. "Not like that." *Not again.*

But Zelda barreled on. "I know it's a bit shocking, gang, but we can't stop these people with posters and songs. We need some action! Show them that our fists and feet ain't just for drawing and dancing!"

"I said *no!*" Gwendolyn snapped.

Zelda gave her a puzzled look. "What do you mean, *no?*"

Gwendolyn stared her down. "I mean *no*. That isn't how we do things."

Zelda looked her up and down, then gave a small shrug. "You're the boss-girl. What's the plan, Gwenny?"

"Uh..." She hadn't thought quite this far ahead. "We don't want this to turn violent. We need to convince the rest of the City. Make them believe. You can't punch people into changing their minds. Some of us will need to sneak into that basement and set those children free, and shut down whatever it is they're running down there. I'll fix this. Me and my friends."

"How are we going to get in?" asked Jessica.

Gwendolyn thought for a moment. It wasn't easy with so many eyes on her. "We'll need a distraction."

Zelda grinned mischievously. "Oh, I can be *quite* distracting. Right, everyone?"

A cheer went up from the crowd.

"All right, gang, you heard the girl! We're going to take this party over to the Home for Uptight Hussies and make as much ruckus as we can manage. We'll give that Childsnatcher a show she can't ignore."

The crowd cheered again and broke into a flurry of activity. "Do you know what you're doing, Gwenny?" Zelda said.

She nodded. "Yes. I'll take it from here. You get that distraction ready."

"Super keen." Zelda hopped down from the stage and breezed through the crowd, shouting instructions and organizing groups.

"Nice speech," Tommy said as Gwendolyn and Jessica got down from the stage.

"Thanks."

"No worries. So how we gettin' in?"

Gwendolyn blinked. "I didn't mean you, I just meant— "

"We're coming," Missy interrupted. Her voice was small but insistent. "It's Ian. He'd do the same for us. Besides, it can't be worse than that vampire place." She shuddered.

Gwendolyn looked at them. Sparrow, Starling, Tommy, Missy, and Jessica. And Cecilia, of course. Her friends. All looking to her.

"All right, then. Together," she said. "And I think I have an idea. But we'll have to go quickly."

"Aw, man," Sparrow groaned. "So we don't get to eat?"

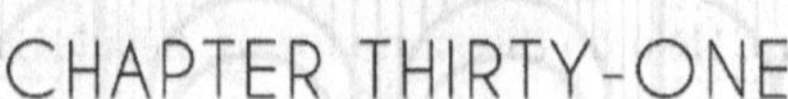

CHAPTER THIRTY-ONE

ECHOES IN THE DARK

"**A**re you sure this is going to work?" Sparrow asked.

They walked inside a crowd of people, dozens strong, marching down the City's streets. It was a rare sunny day, as if the sun itself was reveling in its newness. The colors of their clothes and signs and painted faces shone bright. They looked like a very upset parade.

"To be honest, I'm never sure any of our plans are going to work," Gwendolyn said. "But we've done all right so far." Perhaps a bit of an overstatement, but this was hardly the time for harsh reality.

"I still don't like this," Mother said. "You going in alone."

"Can't be helped, dear," said Father. "It's the Home for Unclaimed Children they'll be sneaking into, not the Home for Concerned Mothers. And she's not alone. She has them." He gestured to her six friends.

"I share your concerns, Mrs. Gray," added Ms. Sahida. "But I must say, your daughter has proved... well, rather capable." She gave Gwendolyn a tender look. "I'm sure she'll do just fine."

The wrought iron gates of the Home for Unclaimed Children loomed over them, met on either side by tall stone walls.

And on the other side stood the Childkeeper. She was as pretty, calm, and composed as ever. She peered at the crowd over the rim of her cat's-eye glasses. She was flanked by two lines of children. These were all older, some even taller than the Childkeeper herself. Gwendolyn spotted the girl who had kept smacking her hand.

"This is an illegal gathering on City property," the Childkeeper said through the bars. "Please leave."

Zelda stepped up to the gate, her rainbow fringe dress standing in stark contrast to the Childkeeper's grey tweed. "You'll have to come out here and make us, sweetie. But you won't, will you? You don't have it in you to stand up to all of us!" The crowd answered her with a loud cheer.

The Childkeeper did not so much as blink. "It is not my place to stand up to anyone. I am here to make the children of this City productive and useful members of society. If you do not leave now, I will summon the authorities." She raised her voice to the crowd. "Those of you who are underage will be placed into my care. Your parents are clearly unfit guardians to allow you to participate in such activities. The rest of you will be taken into custody and await a hearing before the City Council."

"We're not going anywhere, right gang?" Zelda called. "We know what you're up to! You've been taking children from all over the City. Children that you have no right to keep! Set them free!"

The Childkeeper raised one eyebrow. "Or else?"

"You asked for it, cupcake. Pauline! Get the band up here, and strike us up a tune!" Zelda stepped up to the gate until her face nearly touched the bars. "We won't be moved from this spot until you let them go. The people will see us. The people will hear us. And the Cityzens will come to our aid. All the police in the City can't hold a candle to that."

"We shall see," said the Childkeeper, cool as ever.

"Here we go," Gwendolyn said. "The police will be here soon. And if I remember correctly, exercise time is almost over." She gave Mother and Father a quick hug goodbye, then the seven children set off around the back of the compound.

Starling and Jessica helped boost Gwendolyn to the top of the wall, followed by Tommy and Sparrow. Together they hauled up the rest. From there, they could see the rear exercise yard of the home. Rows of children stood there, all of them with their backs to the wall. They faced the Home and performed a sort of calisthenics dance. Gwendolyn caught snatches of a song, something about the benefits of regular exercise, and how fine it was to be a useful hard-working orphan.

"How come none of them ever try to escape?" Sparrow asked. "This wall isn't *that* tall."

Gwendolyn shook her head. "It's this place. Whatever the Childkeeper is doing in that basement is sucking all the willpower out of them. It's how she keeps them in line. Nobody has the strength to think about escaping."

"Whoah. That's dark," said Starling.

"Just wait..." said Jessica.

They took turns lowering each other down the other side. Then they worked their way to the back of the crowd of orphans just as they were filing their way back into the building. Starling sprinted forward and caught the door just as it was closing behind the last of the miserable children.

"Wait until the hallway clears," Gwendolyn said. "They'll all be at mealtime soon." They waited for two silent minutes, then entered. The hallways were as clear as they predicted.

"So far so good," Tommy said.

Missy punched him in the arm. "Why would you say that? Now something's bound to go wrong."

"That's okay," Sparrow said. "Something always goes wrong. That's why we have a plan." He turned to Gwendolyn. "Right?"

Gwendolyn nodded. No one stopped them as she led them all to the Childkeeper's office, and down the dark steps. Starling clicked on the lights of her goggle lenses. Jessica took out a Lambent, and it shone with a thousand colors. The lights bounced around with every movement, adding to the eeriness of the staircase.

"Whoah," Tommy said. "Look at Freckles."

Gwendolyn looked down at herself. In the darkness, her jacket and boots shone with stars, spraying colorful patterns of light around the stairwell.

"Pretty," Missy said.

"Don't get distracted." Jessica held her own Lambent higher, adding even more color.

At the bottom was the door marked *KEEP OUT*. Three large padlocks held it shut.

"I've got this," said Starling. She whipped out her lockpicks and set to work. The little clockwork faerie darted out of Gwendolyn's jacket and zipped over to assist, sticking its tiny metal hands into one of the other locks.

"We're in," Starling said after a moment. She reached up and gave the little faerie a high-five. Then she pushed open the door. A pale, flickering gleam spilled out into the hall.

Gwendolyn went first. The room was a long tunnel-like chamber with a high ceiling, and it was filled with an amalgam of the worst memories of her travels so far.

There were crystal chambers on either side, twenty-foot-tall versions of the one that had imprisoned Mister Zero, arranged in rows just like in the power station in Tautopolis. At the base of each spire was a flickering Lambent. They did not shine with the rainbow of colors that Jessica's did, but were once more empty and white, the way they were before Gwendolyn had changed them two years ago.

Inside the chambers were children, each frozen in time, each giving off a white glow tinged with gold. Their eyes were closed. Their faces were peaceful. The room was filled with a steady thrum like large machinery, and Gwendolyn felt the tingle of *power* ripple across her skin.

"This is... horrifying," Starling murmured, switching off her goggle lights.

"It's just like Tautopolis," Sparrow said. "Although that was worse. At least there's no creepy helmets."

Echoes in the ether, Gwendolyn remembered Titania saying. Similar patterns echoing across multiple worlds.

Cecilia touched one of the crystals. "It's the same thing. They're draining these kids. Stealing their imagination, or life force, or something. All to power the City."

"That explains why the children upstairs are all so lifeless. This place must be feeding on them, too, in a way." Then she remembered her stay in the consequence closet, how Robin had appeared in her book of faeries, but was unable to get out. This place had interfered with his magic.

Jessica peered at the faces in the chambers. "Look! It's Ian!"

Indeed it was. He was trapped inside one of the crystal chambers. His face was so peaceful he might almost have been asleep, save that his eyes were wide open, and glowing white. The faerie flew over and tapped on the crystal.

"Let's get him out," Jessica said.

"Right." Gwendolyn turned to the others, but noticed that Missy was shaking. "Missy? Are you all right?"

She bit her trembling lower lip and shook her head.

Tommy wrapped an arm around her. "It's this place," he said. "It's... familiar. I think we've been somewhere like this before."

Gwendolyn's eyes went wide. "When they collected you. When they turned you into Mister Men." She looked back at Ian, then around at the other crystal prisons. "Perhaps that's what happens after they're drained. They become Faceless Gentlemen. The Childkeeper is making more of them."

"Precisely," came a voice from behind them. And that sort of thing never turned out to be anyone friendly.

The Childkeeper stood in the doorway, flanked by a few of the older children from the Home. Bill stood at her right hand. The former Mister Zero seemed to shrink in fear at the sight of the room.

"Good. You're here. I'm glad you accepted my invitation." The Childkeeper strode into the room.

"What invitation?" Sparrow said.

"To this little reunion with your friend, here." the Childkeeper gestured to the frozen Ian.

Cecilia snorted. "Nice try. Like you just *let* us in."

"Why wouldn't I? You cause far too much trouble to be allowed to run loose in the City. No, you'll be much safer down here, in my little... *collection*." She raised an eyebrow as she said the word. "At least the Change brought something useful. All those tales about the City's past made a useful blueprint for its future. That, and your little friend here." She gestured to Bill.

"What?" Gwendolyn said.

"Yes. The Lambents acted so oddly around him. Or rather, they acted normally again. Taking away all the troublesome thoughts and ideas of these children." Tenderly, she stroked the nearest crystal. "When we have gathered enough energy, we can restore *all* of the Lambents to what they once were, and every Cityzen can contribute a small part of themselves to power the world we share. Until then, of course, these children will have to do."

She tapped the crystal with a fingernail, making a soft *clink*. The light from it reflected in her glasses, hiding her eyes for a moment behind a flash of white. "Children have more ideas than most. More questions and wonderings and what-ifs. More power. And here they can be peaceful and productive. Good little workers, all with a job to do."

"And taking from the orphans in the Home wasn't enough," Gwendolyn said. "You needed more children. And who better than the ones from the Revels, who had spent all their time drinking in new colors and wonders and ideas."

The Childkeeper looked her up and down. "Gwendolyn Gray. The girl who changed the City. How nice of you to gather all those revelers in one place. Now they can be put to use: the older ones, sent to the factories on the edge, to keep the City functioning. The younger ones down here, to give it power."

"You're forgetting the part where we stop you." Gwendolyn kicked a steel-toed foot at the Lambent at the base of Ian's crystal chamber. It shattered, just like when she'd smashed her parent's Lambent years ago.

The crystal spire crumbled to pieces. Ian's eyes fluttered closed, and he slumped forward.

"Ian!" Jessica shouted. She dropped her own Lambent and caught him. The little marble rolled away, still flickering its rainbow colors.

"Is he okay?" Gwendolyn asked, not taking her eyes off the Childkeeper.

"For a very broad definition of *okay*," Ian mumbled.

"He's all right!" Jessica said.

That actually worked, Gwendolyn marveled. *What if this does too?* She drew on the power that filled the air and pictured what she wanted. A half-dozen crowbars clanged to the ground, appearing from nowhere.

"Get smashing, gang," Gwendolyn said. "I'll handle this."

"Hell, yes." Cecilia snatched up a crowbar and tossed one each to Tommy and Jessica, then she smashed the Lambent at the base of the nearest crystal spire. Again, the crystal cracked and crumbled, and Cecilia caught a small girl. She passed the girl over to Missy before moving on to smash the next Lambent.

"That is no way for a young lady to talk, is it children?" the Childkeeper said to the orphans on either side of her.

"No, Childkeeper," the older children sang in unison. Slowly, their eyes filled with liquid shadows.

"Young ladies should be pretty, pleasant, and above all, obedient. Teach them a lesson, please."

"Yes, Childkeeper," they sang. They grinned, and every one of their teeth was pointed and sharp. Shadows congealed around their hands, and slimy black tentacles grew from them and coiled on the floor.

The Childkeeper smiled again. "These crystals weren't the only thing we learned from dear Bill." She placed a hand on the boy's shoulder, and Bill cringed. He hadn't transformed like the others. "He no longer seems compatible with this... technology. From what I understand, we'll need a new primary receptacle. Someone to collect and store all the energy of the Cityzens. And you seem to be the prime candidate, Gwendolyn Gray. Bring her to me."

CHAPTER THIRTY-TWO

FANGS

The fanged orphans snarled, then pushed off the ground with their shadow tentacles, flinging themselves across the room.

"Swords!" Gwendolyn called.

Starling threw up a collapsible blade. The little faerie caught it and brought it to Gwendolyn. She caught it and twirled, just managing to avoid the orphan who flew through the air to tackle her. He landed hard, and Gwendolyn flicked the sword open and severed a tentacle that whipped at her face.

Starling tossed a sword to Sparrow, then dashed to protect Tommy and Cecilia from two more shadow children that landed in front of them. The orphans flung their tentacles out, but Starling whirled her sword and managed to slice off three of the four. "Stay behind me!"

But another orphan got past her and wrapped a tenacle around Cecilia's arm and crowbar, halting her mid-swing. Starling sliced through this one as well, and shared a nod with Cecilia. Cecilia smashed another Lambent, freeing another child, and kept working her way down the row.

"Get everyone out of those crystals!" Gwendolyn shouted. "Missy, make sure they are all right. We'll handle the orphans." She ducked a flying tentacle from an older girl, the one who'd smacked her during her previous stay. The girl's tentacle missed and wrapped around a crystal. Gwendolyn grabbed the tentacle, yanked, and sent the girl stumbling forward. Gwendolyn socked her across the jaw, and the girl dropped.

"Serves you right," she said.

"Gwen!" Sparrow shouted, pointing.

She looked. Two teenage orphans swung towards her, tentacles wrapped around the crystals. Gwendolyn flung her arms out and let loose a blast of light. The shadow tentacles vanished. Untethered, the children went flying, one hitting the wall, the other slamming into a crystal pillar. Neither of them moved.

Gwendolyn took a moment to look around. Sparrow was fighting with a shadow orphan, and Starling dueled two more. For every tentacle they severed, their attackers sprouted more, wielding them like whips from either hand.

Gwendolyn sprinted toward Starling, snatched up a crowbar, and struck one of them in the back of the head. The girl slumped to the ground.

Her partner threw his arms out and caught both Gwendolyn's crowbar and Starling's sword arm. Gwendolyn pulled back, straining against him, stretching the tentacle like a rubber band. Then she let go of the crowbar. It flew toward him and smacked him square in the face. He joined his companion on the floor.

Starling brushed his limp tentacle away, then glanced to her brother, who was completely wrapped in black whips. A fanged girl snarled gleefully as she held him in place.

Starling pulled a metal ball from her pocket, wound up its two halves, then threw it. The sphere exploded with a blinding flash, disintegrating the tentacles, and knocking out the shadow girl.

"Sparkspheres?" Gwendolyn asked, scanning the room for any more attackers lurking in the shadows.

"Yep. I've made some improvements." She hissed in pain and clutched her arm. It was covered in tiny scratches. "Gross. Those tentacles have teeth."

"Are you all right?"

"I'll be fine. Sparrow?"

"All fine here, too," he said. "My jacket stopped the teeth. But how are we going to get all these kids out of here?"

Around them, kidnapped children were stirring. Cecilia and the others had made quick work of the crystal prisons. Missy was helping them to their feet. There were twenty or thirty, all told. Gwendolyn looked back at the entrance, and the Childkeeper. More orphans were pouring out of the stairwell, all fangs and tentacles.

"Not that way. Run!" She pointed to the other end of the cavernous basement. Without the light from the crystal spires, it was completely dark, which made Gwendolyn's boots and jacket sparkle with even more stars.

"What's over there?" Tommy asked.

"Not dark imagination child soldiers, so that's a plus," Cecilia said. She led the way, and the others followed. Gwendolyn, Sparrow, and Starling stood their ground, bracing for another assault. But the orphans seemed content to fan out around the entrance, gathering more reinforcements.

"Guess they're in no hurry, seeing as we're trapped and all," Sparrow said. "Can't you imagine a way out? Make us another bathysphere or something!"

Gwendolyn shook her head. "There's not enough energy to create something that large. Especially not with all the crystals shattered. But look..." She pointed to the ground, where bundles of cables ran from the spires to the other end of the basement. "She has to be sending all this energy somewhere. We've got to be near the City's utility tunnels. Starling, I don't suppose you have any explosives?"

Starling grinned. "One or two."

"What?" Sparrow said. "Since when?"

Starling snorted. "Since that world with all the dinosaurs. You're easily distracted."

"I was almost easily *eaten*..."

"Bicker later," Gwendolyn said. "Come on!" She turned and ran, the other two right behind.

The shadow children let loose a chorus of inhuman screeches, and ran after them. Some pushed off the ground with their tentacles and vaulted over the wrecked remains of the crystal prisons.

"That is all *kinds* of creepifying," Sparrow said.

They reached the other end of the basement and pushed through the crowd of rescued children.

"Here?" Starling said, pointing to a spot on the wall where the bundles of cables all converged and ran into a pipe set into the brickwork.

"Let's hope," Gwendolyn said.

Starling reached into one of her many pockets and brought out a small half-sphere, the size of a Lambent, with a squashy bit on one end like chewed gum. She slapped it to the wall, where it stuck. "Stand back!"

No one argued with her. Gwendolyn turned and imagined a wave of light flying at her pursuers. They were knocked backward, and their tentacles vanished for a moment. There was a large *thud* from behind her, one she felt more than heard, followed by a crashing sound.

Gwendolyn turned to find a massive hole in the wall, beyond which lay a pile of shattered bricks, and the City's utility tunnels.

"There's one," Starling said.

Jessica and Cecilia led the children through the hole and into the tunnel. Gwendolyn sent another wave of light at the shadow children. Again, they were pushed backward, but Gwendolyn's legs wobbled under her. She was growing tired, and running out of energy without the power from the crystal spires.

"Gwen, come on!" said Sparrow. The children were all in, and Gwendolyn clambered over the rubble. When she was through, Starling jumped and slapped another explosive to the top of the hole. Gwendolyn didn't have to be told this time, and sprinted away from it.

There was a flash, another *thud*, and a tremendous crash as the ceiling collapsed, sealing the hole in a mountain of stonework.

"And that's two." Starling dusted her palms.

"Cool!" Sparrow said. "Give me some!"

She glared at her brother. "Uh, no. I'm out."

"I don't think that will hold them for long," Gwendolyn said.

"We've got to find our way up to the streets again. The Childkeeper won't send those orphans after us in broad daylight. That's too much, even for the City."

Gwendolyn darted down the tunnel, lit only by Starling's goggle lights and her glittering jacket, as well as a few flickering utility lights set into the ceiling. They found the group of rescued children in the middle of a four-way intersection, huddled together on the filthy floor.

Missy was moving from one to the next, trying to comfort them all. Tommy, Jessica, Ian, and Cecilia walked over. Jessica supported Ian under one arm.

"What now, Freckles?" Tommy asked.

"Up here," she said. There was a ladder in the center of the intersection that led up to a manhole cover. "Get them up and get them out."

"On it." Tommy scrambled up the ladder and started turning a crank next to the manhole cover, slowly levering it open.

"This is the weirdest dream ever." Ian said, shaking his head. "I'd like to wake up now."

"Wouldn't we all..." Cecilia said, glancing at the eerie tunnels.

Something chimed, a tiny bell-like sound that echoed off the stone walls.

"Starling?" Sparrow said, his tone worried. "Is that you?"

Starling looked down at her chiming wrist gauntlet. "Yep."

"And does that thing still do what I think it does?"

"Track dark imagination energy signatures?" She flipped open the metal cover on the dial. "Yep."

"Like the energy from those kids back there?" he said.

Starling tapped the dial, squinting. "Possibly."

"Aaaand why is it going off *now*, instead of *then*?"

Gwendolyn's fists clenched. "He's here."

From the tunnels all around them came a snarling sound.

"That sounds... *bigger*," Sparrow said.

"The little castaway has found her way home," hissed a voice from one of the tunnels.

"And what a terribly dull place it is," came a reply from another intersection. Shadows moved in the tunnels, darting between the flickering utility lights. And one by one, the lights were going out.

Starling's wrist gauntlet continued to chime. "It's all around us..." she said.

"Rosecap, Princess of the Library," came a familiar voice, closer this time. Gwendolyn spun around to catch a glimpse of the Contessa of Stokerly, standing in the tunnel behind her. If it could be called *standing* when one was on the *ceiling*.

The vampire brushed at her crimson skirts, which likewise defied gravity by not falling down into the Contessa's face. "What a terribly untidy welcome. This is no way to repay my hospitality." The last of the lights went out around her, and the tunnels were smothered in darkness.

"Now this dream I've had before," Ian moaned groggily.

"Tommy!" Gwendolyn shouted.

"I've got it! Come on!" He called down. A beam of sunlight spilled down into the tunnel from the open manhole. The little faerie darted up and waved frantically, gesturing for everyone to climb up.

No one needed to be told twice. The gang of children scrambled to their feet and started climbing the ladder, one by one.

The snarls from the tunnels grew louder. The scuttling sounds grew closer. Missy helped herd everyone around the ladder, into the small puddle of light.

"Let's go everyone!" Jessica helped get the littlest children on the ladder, urging them on as best she could.

Starling screamed as something darted from the shadows and tackled her. A well-dressed vampire with glittering skin pinned her to the ground, away from the small patch of sunlight.

Gwendolyn darted over, swung her sword, and sliced straight through the monster's neck. The vampire burst into a cloud of glitter and dust.

"Eww!" Sparrow shrieked in disgust.

"No time to be squeamish!" Gwendolyn called. She threw herself to the side to avoid two more vampires who lunged at her from the darkness. But a third slammed into her and pinned her to the wall with an arm on her throat. It reared back, fangs bared—

And caught a crowbar to the mouth, swung by Cecilia Forthright. The blow knocked it backward into the beam of sunlight. He burst into flames, his body slowly burning away to dust.

More monsters scuttled out of the surrounding tunnels, crawling on the walls and ceiling, keeping out of the light. Starling had gotten back to the group in the center of the intersection, and she and Sparrow fended off any vampires that got too close. Most of the children had escaped up the ladder, with more still climbing.

"Hold tight," Gwendolyn said. "We have to buy time for the others."

The Contessa darted from the shadows and grabbed Gwendolyn's sword arm by the wrist. "Yet time is something you cannot afford, dear. You have guests to feed."

In one fluid movement, Gwendolyn dropped her sword, caught it in her other hand, and slashed at the Contessa.

The Contessa flared her arms and swooped backward through the air, like a bat with crimson wings. She bared her fangs and hissed.

Gwendolyn threw a blast of light in all directions. The vampires screeched and dropped to the ground, smoking. Then she conjured thorny vines to block the tunnels around them, keeping out most of the vampires, stranding them with only a half-dozen or so who lay squirming on the floor of the junction.

"Nice!" Cecilia said. She broke off a long thorn and stabbed one of the downed vampires, disintegrating it.

"That's all of them! Come on up!" Jessica called down from above.

"Right behind you!" Gwendolyn called, and started toward the ladder, but her knees buckled, and she stumbled.

Cecilia caught her. "Are you all right?"

"When will people quit asking me that? Look out!" She pulled Cecilia away from a vampire who lurched up from the ground. She aimed another burst of light at its face, and the vampire dissolved into powder. Gwendolyn fell again, onto the filthy tunnel floor.

"Careful!" Cecilia said, helping her up.

"Sorry. The energy from the Home is dissipating. I don't have much left."

"Good," came a voice from above. A figure dropped down from

the ceiling, landed behind her, and wrapped an arm around her neck. Then he pulled her toward the tunnel wall, away from the beam of sunlight.

"Gwendolyn!" Cecilia swung her crowbar, but the vampire caught it in his free hand. He tore it away, then swung it back at Cecilia, hitting her in the side of the head. She managed to stagger back into the light before crumpling to the floor.

"Cecilia!" Gwendolyn screamed, but the vampire tightened his grip on her throat.

"Look, my love, I have a wedding present for you," he said.

The Contessa rose from the ground, simply floating upwards without using her hands. She stared at them from the opposite end of the intersection. Gwendolyn saw her sneering in the shadows, keeping away from the patch of light in the center. "Thank you, my precious Duke. It is all my heart desires, apart from yourself."

"Do you mind if we share?" he said, his breath hot in Gwendolyn's ear.

"I mind," Sparrow said, appearing suddenly with his sword at the Duke's throat. Starling likewise popped up beside the Contessa. Gwendolyn looked around to see that all the other vampires had been done and dusted, though she could hear more of them snarling beyond her thorny barricades.

"Let her go," Starling said, pressing the blade against the Contessa's pale skin. "Or you'll need a broom and dustpan to walk her down the aisle."

"And I can tear this girl's throat out in an instant," the Duke said. The hand around Gwendolyn's throat grew claws. She winced as they dug into her skin. "Though it would be a shame to waste so much blood."

"Try it, ugly," Sparrow said.

The Contessa only smiled. "Aren't children precious, my darling?"

"Adorable," he replied. "We should have some someday."

"Well, we can start with these four, then try the dozen or so that ran away. I know how hungry you get when you're working." With a burst of superhuman speed, she grabbed Starling's sword and broke it in half with her bare hands. Then she grabbed the girl by the throat and lifted her from the ground.

"Starling!" Sparrow cried out, taking his attention off of the Duke for a moment, but a moment was all the Duke needed to swat him across the tunnel with his free hand. He hit the stone wall and slumped to the ground.

Gwendolyn felt the Duke's hand tighten around her throat. She watched helplessly as the rest of the vampire courtiers clawed their way through her vines and surrounded them.

"I hope you enjoyed this little party, Princess," the Duke snarled. "Because it was your last."

"Sparrow..." Starling gasped, struggling in the Contessa's grip. "I'm sorry..."

"It's okay, sister," Sparrow mumbled, getting to all fours. "It's not your fault..."

"No, I'm *sorry*." Starling stopped struggling. "I lied."

Then she flung something at the ceiling. A small object hit it, and stuck there.

"What?" the Contessa hissed.

"Gwendolyn, now!" Starling shouted.

Gwendolyn squeezed her eyes shut, and thought *If only...*

But her thoughts were shattered by a deafening explosion, and the entire tunnel collapsed.

CHAPTER THIRTY-THREE

LADY OF LIGHT

When Gwendolyn came to, there was only darkness, and a sense of crushing weight. However, nothing seemed to be actually touching her. She reached out and felt the barrier of energy that had protected her from the blast. It was all she could create before the bombs went off. Now she was snug in her own little stone-covered bubble, with just a hint of illumination from the glittering starlight of her jacket and boots.

Carefully, she imagined the bubble stretching upward, pushing aside the rock and rubble. She saw sunlight, and let the bubble vanish.

An enormous section of the tunnel ceiling had quite suddenly become the tunnel floor. Where the ceiling had been was now a hole ringed with shattered asphalt. Sunlight flooded down from the street above. The sunlight dimmed the stars on her boots and jacket, turning the leather purple again.

As she looked down at her boots, she saw the face of the Duke of Austensus staring up at her from under the wreckage. She jumped back, but the Duke didn't move. With Gwendolyn out of the way, the sun shone on the vampire lord. His skin smoked, turned black, then he cracked and crumbled to dust.

Gwendolyn looked around. Ruptured pipes sprayed water over everything, soaking the rubble, and Gwendolyn as well. Cecilia stirred as it rained down onto her face. She lay under the twisted remains of the ladder, but one of Gwendolyn's energy bubbles had kept her safe. The dusty remains of the vampire court mingled with the water and ran in dirty grey rivulets along the ground.

"You filthy wretch!" screamed a voice from the darkened tunnel across the clearing. Gwendolyn shaded her eyes from the sun, and saw the Contessa. She was luckier than the rest of her kin, and had managed to escape the blast and the sun. She stood in the shadows, eyes black, fangs bared, her crimson gown little more than tatters.

"You've murdered my betrothed! You obstinate, ignorant, ugly little girl!" She stuck out a shaking finger. "I will not forget this. I shall haunt this City. I shall find you in your bed and torture you until you beg me to stop. By day I shall let you live, quaking in fear, with the knowledge that when the sun goes down, I shall come to you again, and again, until I have shattered your very mind and left you nothing more than a witless, trembling sack of meat! And then, and *only* then, shall I feed on your precious blood, you—"

Suddenly, Sparrow burst from the rubble behind the Contessa. He shoved her, and the vampire stumbled into the blinding light.

She screamed, so loud and shrill that Sparrow and Gwendolyn had to cover their ears. The vampire's dress caught fire. Her hair burned and shriveled. Her skin blackened and cracked.

She turned her desiccated face toward Gwendolyn and

screamed even louder. She launched herself through the air. But all that reached Gwendolyn was a cloud of dust and ash.

"Holy crow," Sparrow said. "You don't see that every day."

"Where's Starling?" Gwendolyn said, wiping ash and water from her face.

Off to one side, some bricks shifted, and they heard a muffled chiming sound. The two of them raced over, cleared away the wreckage, and pulled Starling to her feet.

"And that's three," Starling wheezed. "Thanks, Gwendolyn. Wasn't sure that would work."

Sparrow brushed dust from his jacket. "Blowing yourself up is a risky strategy. Next time you're carrying heavy explosives, give me a heads up, will ya?"

Starling smiled, then coughed again. "What? I can't hear you. My ears are ringing."

"Oh, ha, ha. It's your stupid wrist, dummy."

She gave the chiming wrist gauntlet a good smack. "Must have been damaged in the explosion."

Gwendolyn froze. Then she sighed, and shook her head. "No. No, we don't get that lucky." She looked up. "Do we?"

The Blackstar floated in the air above the tunnel. His coat fluttered around him as he hovered over the hole they had blown in the street.

"No such thing as luck." His words were cold and sharp, as was his expression. He drifted down through the hole and landed lightly on a pile of shattered brick. "If there was, I'd be done with you by now. But no matter how many monsters we throw at you, I always have to deal with you myself."

Gwendolyn held out a hand to her friends. "Starling, quick, give me a—"

The Blackstar took off like a bullet and slammed into her. He grabbed her by the jacket and yanked her up through the hole in the ceiling.

The force of it knocked Sparrow's hat from her head and the breath from her lungs. He flew her high over the street, and higher still, up between the skyscrapers. Wind tore at them, stinging her eyes, and the City was a blur as they rose. Her stomach chose to stay with the ground below. She'd had plenty of experience falling from heights, but she didn't find the opposite to be any better.

"Look at this place," the Blackstar growled, his face inches from hers. They came to a stop, hovering effortlessly in the air.

They were above all but the tallest buildings. The City stretched out around them, in all its infinite greyness. The height and the rush of it all nearly made her vomit. Her heart was thundering. Her jacket dug into her armpits as she dangled from the Blackstar's grip. Her feet kicked the empty air to remind her that this was *not* where they should be.

"This place is nothing." He spat in disgust, and Gwendolyn felt an irrational burst of pity for some poor soul below. "We are the chosen ones. But you fight. You struggle. You throw yourself in our way again and again. You come to *my* world, take *my* story from me. For what? For these petty, ordinary people?"

His words made her think of something Cyria had said once. She forced a smug smile. "There's no such thing as an ordinary person."

He grunted. Then he spun her through the air and flung her

away.

She flew across the street, hit the nearest skyscraper, and smashed straight through a window. She slid across the floor until she came to a stop, lying amongst the shattered glass. Around her were the desks and cubicles of some empty office space.

Gwendolyn sucked in a breath, then gasped at the stabbing pain. *So much for that rib,* she thought groggily.

The Blackstar hovered just outside the broken window, wind whipping his coat around him. "We gave you everything you wanted." He floated inside and dropped to the floor. "Your friends. Your family. A doorway to any shiny new world you could want. A happy ending." With each phrase, he took another step toward her. "But you keep. Coming. *Back.*" He kicked her hard enough that she went skidding across the floor and bumped against the floor-to-ceiling windows on the opposite side.

She coughed, and felt another burst of pain, but managed to push herself up. "Then..." she wheezed, "why not just kill me?"

"They tried. Twice. But you're stubborn." The Blackstar's boots crunched over broken glass. "Too stubborn to stay put. We knew if you left your world again, you wouldn't stop until you'd completed some absurd quest. So, we gave you one. I took your parents. I let you find them. I even let you rescue them. Figured the best way to deal with a hero was to make you think you'd already won."

Gwendolyn thought back to the beating he'd given her in Tautopolis. "*That* was letting me win?"

He shrugged. "I may have gotten carried away."

"And their memories? Not exactly a happy ending if my parents have no idea who I am."

"Blame the faceless ones for that. I never liked this plan anyway. Never wanted you on my world. So no more games. No more trying to use you, or turn you, or contain you."

He held out a hand and let loose a burst of energy that shattered the window. Wind rushed in and tore through the office, stirring up papers in little whirlwinds. He reached down and grabbed her by the jacket again. She tried to swat his hands away, but he plucked her off the ground as if she weighed no more than a kitten.

"Now I just kill you. And this world goes back to the Abscess."

He stepped to the edge and dangled her out the window. She stopped clawing at his arm and clung to it instead. She had to *think*. She needed an idea.

Then she remembered. She'd had one all along. But she needed time.

"What about you, Cato?" she said, letting go with one hand to gesture toward him. "Why do you serve the Abscess? What do you get out of it?"

The Blackstar sneered, and started spouting more of his twisted philosophy of self-importance. But Gwendolyn didn't listen. She concentrated on letting her free hand fall to her skirt and slip into her pocket.

Inside was the tiny emerald leaf the Lady had given her, back in the Forest of Ideas. Slowly, she drew it out, not daring to look at it.

But she fumbled it, and the leaf fell. She looked down in horror and saw the leaf, falling between her purple boots, drifting down to the street below.

Time slowed, giving her the cruel chance to notice every last detail. A crowd had gathered. It was quite a colorful one, all the Revelers decked out in their finery, holding signs with her name written so large she could read it from up here. There was a cluster of grey-clad children, the ones she'd freed from the home. Everyone was looking up at her. She lost sight of the leaf as it drifted down into the crowd.

She imagined she saw her parents down there. Her friends. Her teacher. And off to one side, she saw a manhole cover open. Out climbed two colorful figures, who took in the crowd around them, and then they looked up as well. They all saw her. They all believed in her.

She could *feel* it.

And leaf or no leaf, she had an idea.

"And you?" the Blackstar said, coming to the end of his rant.

She looked back at him. His face was twisted with disgust.

"Why come back to this world that you hate? Why can't you let yourself be happy?"

Gwendolyn Gray simply smiled at him. "Because it isn't all about me." Then she raised her arms, slipped out of the jacket, and fell.

She fought back the urge to scream, and forced herself to focus on the people below. The Blackstar could steal power from any world he went to. But Gwendolyn's magic had never come from stealing ideas and imagination. It came from sharing it.

Now these people were sharing theirs with her. Gwendolyn had ignited their imagination, and all that energy was feeding right back into her. She could feel it, filling her up, just like the energy from the Lambents. Or at least, she hoped she could, hoped it wasn't just the wind and the adrenaline. She closed her eyes to block it all out, and concentrated as hard as she could on their energy, on the power of their belief, their wonder, and on her own magic words.

"What if..."

And everything stopped.

Gwendolyn took a deep breath. She didn't *feel* like a smear of paste on the sidewalk. Slowly, she opened one eye. Then the other.

She found herself hovering in mid-air, spread-eagle over a sea of faces a few feet below. They gaped up at the floating girl in slack-jawed amazement.

She wiggled her fingers. She wiggled her toes. Nothing happened. Physics seemed to have forgotten her, at least for the moment.

"Hey, freckles!" she heard Tommy shout. "You're flying!"

She squeezed her eyes shut again. "Yes, now stop talking about it, or I very soon won't be!" Gravity was an awfully hard habit to break. But she could *believe* she was flying, if she didn't think about it too hard.

Gently, she wondered what it might feel like if she floated upward. Wouldn't that be nice? Just an easy little float. She would probably feel a little fluttering in her stomach as she turned upright again, wouldn't she?

She opened her eyes, and found herself standing on thin air.

And she smiled.

The crowd cheered. The sound of it brought a surge of joy, and she felt herself rising even higher, like a balloon filling with hot air. Up she went, trying not to question the fact that she. Was.

Flying.

She squinted upward, into the sun, looking for the broken window amongst all the gleaming glass. Then she spotted it, and the smudge of black standing inside.

Well, if the Blackstar could do it, why couldn't she? She pictured herself going up. She *believed* that she could.

Slowly, she found herself rising through the air, and trying very hard to ignore how impossible it was. She relished the feeling of weightlessness. The longer she did it, the easier it was to imagine herself doing it. She *was* flying, which was surely proof that she *could* fly, and could *keep* doing it, if you please and thank you very much.

Soon she was face to face with the Blackstar again, with nothing but empty air between them. The tiniest hint of surprise played at his face, which he quickly covered with a scowl. But Gwendolyn couldn't stop smiling.

The Blackstar and the Abscess and its minions could steal imagination from others. But Gwendolyn didn't need to steal that power, not when others were so willing to share.

She had spent years avoiding the Lambent's glow, snuggled in a blanket of her own imagination. Those years had changed her. Prepared her for this. Her imagination had protected her from the worst the world had to offer, and it protected her now. She wrapped herself in a comforting cocoon of wonder and amazement, and her skin began to glow.

Rather than resist it, she embraced it. She shaped the glow into a suit of gleaming golden armor, the way she'd coated herself in blackness in Tautopolis. But this felt *much* better. The armor of light was solid, where her shadowy monster form had been transparent.

She closed her eyes and took the deepest breath she'd taken in years, hardly feeling the pain in her ribs. She took a moment to feel the sun on her face. Then she opened her eyes, exhaled, and unfurled a set of shimmering wings. The white-gold feathers glistened in the sunlight, so beautiful that any faerie would turn pink with jealousy.

Gwendolyn looked at herself. A winged knight in shining armor. Cyria would be so proud. Her smile widened

The Blackstar simply shook his head. "Stubborn."

She looked back at him. "Always. You're done, Cato. No more jumping from story to story, killing heroes. I've seen inside yours. And it's time someone brought it to an end."

He snorted. "Nice try. Wings or no wings, you're just a scared little girl."

Gwendolyn's smile vanished. "I'm no 'little girl'. I am Gwendolyn Alice Gray, Princess of the Library of All Wonder, Champion of the Lady of Light. I am Rosecap of the Fae, dreamer of dreams and changer of worlds." Her eyes narrowed. "And I'm the one who's going to kick. Your. Butt."

The Blackstar just waved a hand in front of his face, and his gas mask appeared in a puff of smoke. Then he flew at her.

She swooped out of the way. He tried again, but Gwendolyn was quicker, and she batted him away with a wing. He was knocked aside, and she heard him grunt in frustration.

He held out a hand and fired a bolt of darkness at her. She was caught off guard, but the bolt struck her armor with a shower of sparks. It stung, but not too much. He fired again. She turned aside and blocked the blast with her wings.

Gwendolyn *imagined,* and flew even higher. With each beat of her wings, she flung razor-edged feathers of pure light at him.

The Blackstar conjured a shield to stop them. Gwendolyn flapped again, and again, and each feather sheared off another piece of the shield. She steadied herself and prepared for another volley, but the Blackstar dispelled his shield and rushed at her. His long black blade sprouted from the back of his hand. She fired at him again, but he dodged the deadly feathers, and came at her.

Gwendolyn hardly had time to conjure a glowing golden sword for herself. Their blades met with a crash and a burst of light.

Floating in mid-air gave her precious little in the way of leverage. The force of the blow knocked her back. She flared her wings and stopped her tumbling in time to see the Blackstar coming at her again.

This time she met his charge with one of her own. But she turned aside at the last second, and her sword carved a line of light across his back. The Blackstar cried out in pain.

They turned to face each other. The Blackstar shrugged off the remaining pieces of his trench-coat. "You'll pay for that."

"That makes two coats I owe you," she said, trying to sound confident.

Again he charged, and again their swords clashed. Gwendolyn was knocked back even harder this time, soaring across the street until her back slammed into the building on the other side. Glass crunched, and she had the breath knocked out of her, but the armor protected her.

The Blackstar held out a hand, and concrete tentacles grew from the side of the building and wrapped themselves around her. He clenched his fist. The tentacles started to squeeze. But Gwendolyn took another deep breath, pulling in air and light. Her armor glowed brighter. She flexed her wings, and the feathers sheared through the concrete as though it were tissue paper.

The Blackstar came down on her with a double-fisted blow. She got her arms up just in time and took the blow on her armored gauntlets. It was like someone had dropped a car on her. She went flying toward the street below.

She folded in her wings and let herself fall. Just before she hit the ground, she flared them out again, and soared over the cheering crowd. Her sword glowed even brighter.

"Gwendolyn!" someone cried.

"Starling!" Gwendolyn called back, spotting the girl's signature streak of blue hair. She was holding part of the Blackstar's coat.

"Catch!" She threw something, and Gwendolyn swooped to grab it.

It was a small metal device with a button and a dial. The Blackstar's portal creator.

"Thanks," she shouted. Then she pulled up and flew back at the Blackstar.

He was still high above her. He made a motion, and a twenty-foot metal spike appeared from nowhere, and dropped down at her face. Gwendolyn twisted out of the way. She heard a scream from the crowd. She glanced down and saw people dive out of the way as the spike embedded itself in the concrete.

She looked up again just in time to dodge another spike. The

Blackstar threw one after the other, filling the air with a rainstorm of iron skewers. She spun and rolled, wings a blur. She dodged through the air like she was born to it, ever higher, ever faster, clutching the portal device to her chest.

The Blackstar threw one last spike, but she batted it away with her sword. The impact knocked it from her hand and it went spinning away, vanishing into a golden mist. But Gwendolyn slammed into him and wrapped her arms around his waist.

"You want me to leave?" she shouted over the wind. "Fine! Let's leave!"

She gripped the portal device even tighter, then slapped the big red button against his back. A portal opened above them and Gwendolyn carried the Blackstar through it.

CHAPTER THIRTY-FOUR

...THEY ARE A-CHANGIN'

There was a flash of not-quite-light. Gwendolyn caught the merest glimpse of the In-Between, and suddenly they were hurtling through an impossibly pink sky.

Gwendolyn saw the Blackstar blink. But he managed to spin and fling her away. She soared through the air and face-first into a fluffy blue cloud.

But the cloud was solid. Hitting it was like colliding with a wall of pillows, albeit a slightly sticky one. Gwendolyn pulled her face free and tasted something sweet on her lips. It was a cloud of blue candy floss.

Something grabbed her foot, and Gwendolyn was pulled free from the cotton-candy cloud. The Blackstar spun her around, faster and faster, then let go, flinging her at the ground. Gwendolyn had a brief glimpse of the world below, which was a patchwork quilt of the most garish colors imaginable. Then she crashed hard into a forest of licorice stalks and gumdrop palms.

She closed her eyes and pulled in her wings to protect herself as she plowed through the confectionery forest, hearing the crack and snap of sugar splintering around her. Then there was a splash, and a bone-jarring thump.

She opened her eyes to find herself waist deep in a chocolate pond. Rich brown goop coated her golden armor and dripped off of her in heavy globs.

Dazed from the crash, she shook her head and looked around. Lollipops sprouted like reeds from the shore of the pond. And emerging from the candy forest around her, she saw furry black creatures staring at her, wide eyes blinking.

One of the creatures emerged tentatively from the trees, its flappy feet slapping the ground comically. In contrast to his brethren, his fur was a bright and shocking orange.

"Meep?" it asked.

Gwendolyn's eyes widened. "Criminy?"

But the Blackstar dropped from the sky like a comet. He smashed into her with both feet, driving her down under the sugary mud.

She flailed about and just managed to free herself and break the surface. She sucked in a breath, but the Blackstar wrapped her in a crushing bear hug.

"Nice try," he hissed in her ear. Then he snatched the portal device from her and hit the button.

There was another flash as they entered the In-Between, though this time they were engulfed in a suffocating cloud of darkness. The Abscess, lurking between worlds, always eager to steal her away.

Gwendolyn struggled in the Blackstar's grip, and she felt pulled in a dozen directions as they hurtled through the nothingness between worlds. She fought, beating her wings against him. But just as she broke free, tentacles of darkness seized her. She was hurled out of the In-Between and into a world of pitch-black skies and blinding rain.

Gwendolyn flapped hard, just managing to stay aloft. She scanned the sky for the Blackstar, but it was too dark to see.

Lightning split the air with a deafening crack, and she spotted him off to her left.

He still had the portal device. She needed it if she was going to get home. Hopefully, with him stranded here in the process. Wherever *here* was.

She closed her eyes, concentrated, and re-formed her golden sword. Then she flew at him. Rain spattered her face, stinging her eyes, rinsing away the last of the sticky chocolate. She couldn't see much more than her glowing sword, stretched out in front of her as she flew through the rain.

Something hit her. She was knocked off course, and fell for who knows how long before she managed to get her wings under her again. She turned to see another figure, smaller than her, but with even larger wings.

A blood red moon broke through the clouds, illuminating the figure. No larger than a child, but withered and decayed. Its bat-like wings beat the air.

The Queen of Umberland. Gwendolyn looked down, and sure enough, she could spy a castle and a village of thatch roof cottages. The realm of the vampires.

"I was forewarned of your return," the Queen rasped. Lightning flashed again. The thunder deafened Gwendolyn for a moment, but when her hearing returned, the Queen was still talking.

"—and you stole my brooch. I think it only fair I take your necklace." She bared her fangs. "Before I take your neck."

Gwendolyn looked down. The Figment necklace had shaken loose in all the fighting and lay against her breastplate. She looked up just as the bat wings flared and the tiny body shot toward her.

Someone grabbed Gwendolyn from behind. The Blackstar. Before she could cry out, the queen was upon her, clawing at her throat. Her withered face was inches from Gwendolyn's own.

Gwendolyn willed her armor to glow even brighter. It burned the Queen, who flew back with a hiss. The Blackstar's arms were wrapped around her, and Gwendolyn spotted the portal device clutched in his fist. Gwendolyn slammed a hand down on his hand. She heard a *click,* and a portal opened in the air next to them. She flapped hard and tumbled into it.

They were in the In-Between again. Clouds gathered, blocking out the swirling not-quite-colors. Tentacles emerged as the Abscess reached for Gwendolyn. The Blackstar hit her and clung to her back. She felt something pulling at her leg as well. She looked down and saw the vampire queen, clawing at the greaves that protected Gwendolyn's shin, face twisted in desiccated rage.

But this time Gwendolyn remembered the Figment around her neck. The Figment that could guide her through the In-Between to wherever she wanted to go, rather than some random world or one of the Blackstar's choosing.

And she knew exactly where she wanted to go.

It wasn't hard to picture it. The Figment glowed, there was a burst of red light, and suddenly they were flying through another new sky. An orange one, with russet clouds.

Gwendolyn saw the city of Copernium stretched out below them. Airships drifted lazily around them. And more importantly, the twin suns of Tohk hung above them. The large red one, and it's smaller yellow sibling.

Gwendolyn heard a blood-curdling screech. She looked down to see the queen of Umberland burst into flames. Gwendolyn kicked, and the queen's hand broke off. The queen plummeted. Her scream faded, and she dissolved into a cloud of dust that drifted away on the wind.

That was for you, Jack, she thought. Then she elbowed the Blackstar in the gut, loosening his grip, and dropped.

She tucked herself into a dive, putting as much distance between them as she could. Below her she spotted the very thing she wanted.

Gwendolyn hit the deck of the airship *Lucrative Endeavour* with a hard *thud,* landing in a crouch.

The eyes of the crew all turned toward her, every face frozen in surprise. Gwendolyn glimpsed Burly Brunswick, with his muttonchops and peg leg. Enormous Carsair, reflexively drawing her massive war hammer. And Kolonius Thrash, teenage boy captain, complete with dreadlocks, eye patch, and a look of utter bewilderment.

"Gwendolyn?" he said. "Is that you?"

"The Blackstar's not the only one with friends," she mumbled with a sly grin. "Quick, everyone! I need—"

The Blackstar hit the deck like an ebony comet. A blast of dark energy knocked them all off their feet. "No. No help for you *this* time." He hit the button on his portal device, and Gwendolyn heard the air tear open behind her.

Gwendolyn sprang up to face him, but he thrust his sword at her. The black blade doubled in length and took her square in the chest.

It hit her golden armor, and shattered. But the blow knocked her backward, into the portal.

The Blackstar soared in after her, and they were lost in the noxious cloud that was the Abscess. Its tentacles caught her in a crushing embrace, and she was stuck, caught in the In-Between. Suddenly, a voice cried out. The Lady of Light. There was a feeble burst of light, the tentacles holding Gwendolyn disintegrated, and she managed to flap away and back into reality.

The In-Between vanished again, and again, Gwendolyn found herself in open air, in a sky more blue and more brilliant than the City's could ever hope to be. Rainbow clouds mingled on the horizon. An endless forest stretched out below her.

Hovering in the sky next to her was an enormous floating city. It glistened in the sunlight like some impossibly huge jewel, a giant disc in the sky. Waterfalls streamed from the circular city's edges and dissolved into mist.

She caught a glimpse of crystal domes and silver towers, of metal and glass in every color imaginable. But she looked up in time to see the Blackstar diving at her. He clapped his hands together, then pulled them apart, stretching out a thick strand of black goo like pulling some disgusting taffy.

Gwendolyn dove, flipped over onto her back and shot more feathers at him, but he dodged again, and flung the goo at her. It whipped end-over-end and struck, wrapping itself around her and pinning her wings to her body. She struggled, but to no avail. The goop thickened and spread. It tarnished her golden armor. Her dive became a free fall.

She managed to twist herself around to look down. At this angle, she would miss the floating city and go plummeting to the forest below. Then she remembered—she didn't actually *need* the wings to fly. She closed her eyes for a moment and imagined herself as a leaf on the wind, fluttering effortlessly.

The floating city grew closer and closer, but she had no intention of landing there. Instead, she aimed for one of the waterfalls that spilled over the city's edge. She hit the water and passed straight through.

She *imagined* the water washing the goop away, and it did. Her armor was pure golden light again, albeit marred with a large black scorch mark from the Blackstar's sword. Her clothes were soaked, but her wings were free.

Hidden behind the waterfall and under the city, she took a moment to breathe. She exhaled. She centered herself as best she could and focused her will. Then she opened her eyes and shot forward.

She burst through the waterfall and back up into the air. The Blackstar was there, and Gwendolyn shot upward, over the edge and into the strange shining city.

She flew over streets full of colorful denizens in metallic clothes. There was greenery everywhere she looked, from tree-lined canals to rooftop gardens to plants that seemed to climb up the very sides of buildings. Flying cars whipped past, and people zipped around with rocket packs strapped to their backs. The whole city was a dazzling display of light and life and color, and it shone so bright that it was almost hard to look at.

She darted between gracefully arcing walkways and long glass tubes that snaked through the air. She thought she glimpsed people zooming around inside them. She turned this way and that, darting around corners and between buildings.

A stream of airborne commuters blocked her way, and she barreled through them, bouncing off some unlucky man in an orange jumpsuit.

"Sorry!" she called back. She soared higher and glanced back again, but the Blackstar was gone. She scanned the city. Nothing but jetpack people and flying cars. She spun around. Nothing.

Then something detached itself from the bottom of a hovercar above her. The Blackstar dropped down and landed on her back.

"Playtime's over," he hissed in her ear. A shadow knife appeared and he slashed at her back, cutting through wings, armor, and skin alike. Gwendolyn screamed, and fell.

The silver city blurred around her. She tried to find that feeling of flying again, to focus through the pain, but now that gravity had claimed her again, it seemed that much harder to resist. She slowed her momentum as much as she could, and then she crashed into a park below. She hit soft earth and carved a long furrow in the dirt as she slid to a stop.

Gwendolyn rolled onto her back, groaning in pain. She cried out again as the Blackstar landed on her, stomping on her wrist, pinning her arm to the ground. He held up the portal device.

"Enough games," he panted. "It's over." He glanced around at the city, then back at the portal device. "Huh. What do you know. Isn't that ironic."

Gwendolyn imagined a long wooden thorn and threw it at him. It stabbed through the portal device and the Blackstar's hand. He roared in fury. The portal device exploded, and a hole opened in the air behind him.

Gwendolyn put everything she had into a final blast of light. It hit the Blackstar square in the chest and knocked him backwards, into the In-Between. Then the portal closed behind him.

She lay there, panting, and let her head fall back onto the soft grass. He was right. It *was* over.

She managed to roll over onto all fours and catch her breath. She took a deep breath, held it, then exhaled as long as she could. She repeated this process three more times. The glow faded from her skin, and her armor dissolved into golden sparks that fizzled away on the wind.

When she looked up, she found herself surrounded by a crowd of onlookers in various colored metallic jumpsuits.

"Umm... Hello..." she mumbled. Gwendolyn touched Cyria's Figment necklace, still safely around her neck. "I don't suppose any of you could show me to the nearest library?"

~ ~ ~

A short hovercar ride to the *New Astro Municipal Library* and a trip through the Egressai Infinitus later, Gwendolyn hobbled gingerly into the eerie silence of the City's Hall of Records. Everything hurt. And she knew that the second she stopped moving, she'd probably keel over from exhaustion.

The Hall of Records was just as it always was. But the street outside could not have been more different. She opened the door to the sound of cheering and clapping. A crowd of people, awash in color, was waiting for her. Zelda was there, with all her Revelers. There were the children she had rescued. And a sizable collection of grey-clad Cityzens, drawn from their homes by the commotion.

She gave a nervous little wave from the top of the steps, and the cheers became a roar.

A small mob rushed up the stairs to greet her. Tommy, Missy, and Jessica, still supporting Ian. Sparrow and Starling. Even Miss Sahida.

And her parents. Mother and Father swept her up in a crushing embrace.

"Are you all right?" Mother said, looking Gwendolyn up and down. Gingerly, she touched the scratches on Gwendolyn's throat. "Did he hurt you?"

Yes, Gwendolyn thought, also keenly aware of her freshly broken rib and the cut on her back. "Not too much." She gave Mother a reassuring smile. It felt good to have someone to check on her. "I'll be fine in a day or two."

"Of course you will!" Father said, beaming with pride. "Our girl's a fighter."

"What happened? Is he gone?" Starling said when they parted. Each of her parents kept a protective arm on her shoulder.

Gwendolyn nodded. "Yes. Stranded in the In-Between. Or on some other world. But without his portal creator, I don't think the Blackstar will be a problem for a while. All this, though..." she gestured to the crowd, and the dozens of eyes on them.

Ian looked around. "Yeah, it's all a bit much, isn't it?"

"Well, normally at this point I find myself waking up in bed alone, so yes, it's not exactly normal..."

Cecilia snorted. "When have you ever been normal?"

"Well, what now?" Tommy said.

"Jessica?" Gwendolyn asked.

Jessica held up her glittering Lambent. "I recorded it all. Everything from the basement of the Home. The crystal chambers, the Childkeeper explaining everything, all of it right up until those kids attacked us." She shook her head. "Which is still... super weird. But the broadcast is out there, sent to every Lambent in the City. The City Council won't be able to cover this up. It's time for some *real* changes."

"That's right!" said Zelda, walking over. "Starting with that Childkeeper floozy. Just leave it to us."

"Yeah," Tommy added. "Not to mention how half the City saw you flyin' around up there, Freckles."

Gwendolyn blushed.

Missy stepped forward. "But is it over? Truly?"

"I think so. For now," Gwendolyn said. "Are you all okay?"

"A little banged up, but none the worse for wear," Cecilia said.

"Speak for yourself," grumbled Ian. "You weren't locked in a soul-sucking basement for a week."

"He'll be fine," Jessica said. She looked around at the eager crowd. "Uh, you should probably say something to them."

"No, thank you," Gwendolyn said. Leaning against Father was the only thing keeping her standing. "You do it, Jessica."

"What? *Me?*"

Gwendolyn nodded. "I think you and Zelda have it under

control."

Jessica straightened and squared her shoulders. "Right," she said. "I'm on it." She passed Ian off to Missy, then walked off to confer with Zelda.

"I think..." Gwendolyn said, mustering the last of her energy. "I think I just need to go home for a while." She looked at Cecilia, and Sparrow, and Starling. "We all do."

Cecilia sighed an exasperated sigh. "Fine..." she groaned, and rolled her eyes.

"But... can we just..." Sparrow said, and his voice broke off. He took Gwendolyn's hand.

"Yes?" she said.

He looked up at her with his big brown eyes and a pleading look. "Can't we have dinner first?"

Gwendolyn snorted, and Father barked a laugh.

"Absolutely," Father said. "The more the merrier!"

"Oh no," Mother moaned in horror. "I'll need to go shopping."

Gwendolyn smiled until her face hurt. "Don't worry. I'll help."

CHAPTER THIRTY-FIVE

PARTINGS

Once upon another time, in the Library of All Wonder, a door opened. Gwendolyn, Sparrow, and Starling stepped through from the Hall of Records. The clockwork faerie zipped in after them, flew a quick loop around the hall, then came back to hover in front of Gwendolyn.

Sparrow coughed. "So... uh, this is it, then?"

Gwendolyn nodded. "I think so. Are you sure you won't stay?"

"We're not really the staying type," said Sparrow. "We've got our own parents to find."

"I understand." Oh, did she ever.

"Are you sure you won't come with us?" Starling asked.

"Yes," Gwendolyn replied, though the word felt like a rock lodged in her throat. "My parents need me. Someone has to take care of them. All the changes in the City will come as quite a shock. Oh, and I should probably also explain why they are suddenly the City's most famous authors." She forced a smile, and it tasted bitter. "Either way, I have a lot of lost time to make up for."

"Yeah," Sparrow grumbled. He looked away, fidgeting a foot

against the floor. "Time. Not sure I like the idea of splitting up again. Time wasn't very nice to us last, uh... time."

He looked so dejected and vulnerable, that Gwendolyn couldn't stop herself from sweeping him up into an enormous hug. Starling joined in, and the little faerie too, and they all simply held each other, dreading the moment they would have to let go. She winced at the pain in her ribs, but it was worth it.

Sparrow sobbed against her shoulder.

Gwendolyn pulled away enough to see his face. "Boy, why are you crying?" she said, quoting her favorite story again, and smiled through her own tears.

"Why does it always have to end like this?" he said.

She planted a soft kiss on his forehead. It was a much different kiss than the ones they'd shared before, and all the sadder for it. A kiss that spoke of time lost, opportunities missed, and love changed from one form to another. It was a very specific sort of kiss.

"This is just how our story goes, I think. But we always find each other again, don't we?"

Sparrow sniffed. "Okay," he said, even though it clearly wasn't.

"Here," Gwendolyn said, letting him go. "I have an idea."

Gwendolyn held out a hand for the little faerie. It landed in her palm, its head quirked in question. "I want you to stay with them," and she gestured to Sparrow and Starling.

The faerie nodded solemnly. It gave her a crisp salute, then fluttered up to her cheek and gave her a tiny metal kiss. Then it darted over to Sparrow. He cupped his palms, and the faerie sat in his hands, cross legged. It gave him an energetic wave, as if it were trying to cheer him up.

He looked at it, then looked back at Gwendolyn. He opened his mouth to speak, but couldn't quite manage it, and settled for a nod instead, biting his lip.

"Don't go growing up on us, okay?" Starling said. Gwendolyn had never heard the stoic girl so choked up before. "Give Sparrow a chance to catch up first."

Sparrow attempted one of his wolfish grins, but not terribly successfully.

Gwendolyn gave him an equally forced smile, which squeezed another tear from her. "I'd like that. I think I've had my fill of growing up, if you please and thank you very much. Here." She tossed Starling the crimson Figment. "You know how to use this. Say hello to Cyria for me. I'm the one the faeries despise, so it's probably safe to dial up Faeoria as long as you don't go through the doorway."

Starling nodded and put the jewel in one of her nearly-infinite pockets. "Thanks. We will."

And then there was nothing more to say. *This has gone on too long,* Gwendolyn thought. Any more would do more hurt than help. "I love you both. And I'll see you soon, I promise."

And before she could think twice, she turned back towards the Hall of Records.

And came face to face with Robin Goodfellow.

"My, my, my, what a touching little scene." His voice dripped with disdain and a perverse glee. "It would be so heartless to intervene."

"Robin!" Gwendolyn said. "What are you doing here?" The

444

memory of him rushing toward her through Cyria's workshop, claws and teeth bared, was suddenly very bright in her mind.

"Why, Rosecap, I have come for *you*, of course. The tune has ended. It is time to pay the piper."

"Uh..." she couldn't think of what to do. Robin was blocking the doorway. She had to stall, to come up with a plan. "You aren't rhyming anymore."

"We are well past the time for rhymes and games. I did not come to play. You broke your bond. Your word. Your oath."

"But you got what you wanted! You had your fun!" Gwendolyn said, panicked. Whatever happened, she had to protect Sparrow and Starling. "All of this, because of a little party?"

Robin's eyes narrowed. "A little party? You wretched cur. You witless child. You mewling fen-sucked giglet."

"Hey! You can't call her that!" Sparrow shouted. "Whatever it was—"

Robin raised a hand, and Sparrow's voice cut off. He clutched at his throat. Robin flicked his hand upward, and Sparrow's feet left the floor. He flicked his wrist again, and Sparrow was slammed against the wall. Then he dropped in a heap.

Starling rushed forward, but Gwendolyn threw out an arm to hold her back.

"This is not about your pathetic excuse for a party," Robin hissed. "You *insulted* me. You think some jumped-up mortal can summon my power at will? The sheer, unbridled arrogance, treating me as your puppet, and for what? To save this world? To find your precious parents? You smooth-brained milk-breathed brat. You must be taught a lesson. And it seems to me that the most fitting one would be to take back all that I have given you."

Gwendolyn took a step forward. "Wait, what are you—"

"By your oath you thrice did break: I bind thee."

Gwendolyn was slammed backwards as though she'd taken a hammer to the chest. Images rushed at her—Robin, in her apartment. Robin, at the Revels. Robin, at the protest. Three times, she had refused to repay the favor she had bargained for in Tohk, all those years ago. But years were mere moments to the immortal Fae.

"By the food which you did take: I bind thee."

Another blow. Another image. A single pomegranate seed, red and glistening. From Robin's feast in her apartment.

Faerie food.

Oh, no.

Robin saw the look on her face, and sneered. Then he held up a book. A blue one, with flowers on it. Her journal.

Gwendolyn's eyes went wide.

"By the power of your own true name, from your own lips, of your own will." He moved a finger in the air, trailing fire, until he had drawn her symbol in floating emerald flames. The interlocking double G that was her mark.

"Gwendolyn Alice Gray: I bind thee."

She held up her hands to protect herself, but the invisible force struck her again, and her feet skidded back across the floor.

"Thrice bound, and done. Hence from this world, I banish thee."

"No!" she shouted. She rushed the doorway, but she was too far away. Robin slammed the door in her face. The *boom* of it echoed down the corridor and into the Library beyond.

She was left staring at the pale gray door. The brass number plate on the back fell to the floor and crumbled into dust. The crimson Figment dropped from its slot and rolled across the floor.

Gwendolyn leapt at the door and grabbed the knob. It wouldn't turn. She tried again, and again, with all her strength, but the door wouldn't open, no matter how hard she pulled at it, how hard she wanted it. She pounded on the door until her fists hurt, then pounded some more, until she collapsed breathlessly against it, feeling the smooth gray wood against her forehead.

It was gone. It was all gone. The City. Her parents. All of it. Just when she'd had it all back, when everything had been put to rights. All because of her own foolishness. She was bound. Banished. Just as Cyria was trapped in Faeoria, Gwendolyn was now locked out of her own world.

She screamed. She screamed with every breath she had. She screamed and she screamed until her throat was hoarse. Her screams grew shorter until they were no more than great, heaving cries. Until finally even those were spent.

"No," she whispered. "Not again..."

Pain and anger at the unfairness of it all exploded within her. She had lost so much. First her friends, then her hair, and then her parents. And now her home along with it. There would be no waking up in her bed at the end of this adventure. Whoever was in charge of all of this wasn't playing fair.

Not fair, she thought again. *It's just. Not. Fair.*

Anger flooded through her, pushing her to her feet, and she managed to slump against the wall. She looked at the Egressai Infinitus. Then at her friends.

They stared back at her, mouths agape.

"Gwendolyn. I'm so sorry, I..." Starling said, but Gwendolyn stormed past them and down the entry hall.

Sparrow yelled, "Gwendolyn, wait, stop!"

Gwendolyn didn't listen. She never listened. There was something she had to do. She marched out of the entryway and into the Library proper. Her rib hurt. The cut on her back hurt. All the pain came back to her, amplified by the pain inside. Her boots felt so heavy she could barely lift them, but she fought the exhaustion and rising depression.

She closed her eyes, blindly feeling her way along. As she ran her hands along each shelf, clutching them for support, she imagined. She pictured where she wanted to go. The shelves grew rougher. Shallower. Then they were no longer shelves at all, but the trunks of slender trees.

Gwendolyn opened her eyes. The Forest of Ideas surrounded her. Mist swirled around her knees. Moonlight glittered on the leaves. The colorful kaleidoscope of stars and nebulae burned above her, reflected in the shadows on her jacket and boots.

"Hey!" Gwendolyn shouted, but it came out as little more than a rasp. She hissed at the pain in her side. But she tried again, louder. "Hey! Come out! I know you're here."

"*Of course,*" came the voice in her mind. Gwendolyn spun to see the Lady of Light, gliding through the mist, her sheer white dress little more than an ethereal dream. Her perfect face was marred with care, her expression sad.

It made Gwendolyn furious.

"Why?" she shouted. "Why do you do this to me?"

"I have done nothing," the Lady said.

"Liar!" Gwendolyn shouted, but it hurt too much to shout, and she collapsed against a tree. "You've been behind this all along. Pulling my strings. Sending me your stupid leaves. Pushing me on from one disaster to the next. And no matter what I do, it always ends the same way! Why?"

"I do not control." The Lady gestured to the leaves. *"I inspire. Your story is your own. Your choices are your own."*

"My fault?" The numbing nothingness was creeping upon her. The image of Sparrow, lying bleeding on the rooftop, sprang into her mind. She turned and punched the tree in frustration. "I'm trying my best! People just keep getting hurt! I'm done."

The Lady didn't respond.

"I said I'm done!" she shouted. She whirled and tried to shove the Lady, but she stumbled right through her as though the Lady were made of air. "Send me back! Open a portal, and let me go home!"

The Lady shook her head. *"I cannot. The Abscess blocks my way, and I have not the strength to confront him again."*

"But I've sacrificed everything! My friends, my parents, my life, even my hair! And for what? What's in it for me?"

Those piercing blue eyes took on a hint of disappointment. *"That... is a question you have never asked before."*

Gwendolyn looked away. "Maybe it's time I started." But she knew who she sounded like. She coughed, then gasped again. She sank to the ground with a sob, the tree just barely keeping her upright. She struggled to slow her breathing.

There was a long silence. Eventually, the Lady got down and sat beside her.

She sagged against the Lady of Light, and now the Lady was solid. She guided Gwendolyn's head into her lap, and gently stroked her scalp, as though brushing away a strand of hair that was no longer there. The way her mother used to.

The Lady didn't speak as the last of Gwendolyn's anger burned away, replaced with the familiar exhaustion that follows. The closet in her mind was open, black tentacles creeping out of it to wrap her in the familiar darkness of her depression. Black thoughts ran through her head.

"The Blackstar is still out there."

"Yes."

"And the Abscess."

A pause. *"Yes."*

"When does it all end? I'm just... tired. I'm so tired. I want to go home. I want my Mother and Father. When do I get a happily ever after? When can I stop?"

The Lady's expression was unreadable. *"Do you remember how it started?"*

Gwendolyn frowned. "What do you mean?"

"Think."

Gwendolyn did. She thought back to that fateful day it all began. When the Mister Men first appeared. When her life changed forever.

"Yes. I created a leaf out of thin air. It was the first time I used my power."

"No, not that," the Lady said. *"Before."*

Gwendolyn had almost forgotten. It had *not* begun with her

power. Not when she had created that first tiny leaf out of thin air. Not when she glimpsed Sparrow and Starling in her imaginary woods. Not even when she'd run away from Mother.

It was all started by a mouse.

Nothing more. Just a tiny little mouse that a very not-tiny woman had been about to step on. No one else had noticed. So Gwendolyn had shoved the woman. Then she ran away. The very first line of her very first story. She smiled, remembering how she had fed the tiny mouse her sandwich.

It hadn't been the leaf, or the Lady, or the Mister Men, or her powers. It was her own choices that started it. She had chosen to help, even when it got her in trouble.

That was who she had been. She noticed when someone needed help. And she just... helped. She remembered how it had felt, to help without thinking, without asking why, regardless of the consequences. There was a bravery in that.

Gwendolyn sighed. She thought of her younger self. Free from the pain of the last two years, the loneliness, the constant paranoia, the lies. Always hiding, keeping everyone at arm's length. It had taken a toll. But that other Gwendolyn never worried about who she was. She just... was. She was confident, and blissfully ignorant.

"I don't know. Perhaps I'll just find some world with Sparrow and Starling and stay there. Maybe back in Tohk. I'll settle down and live my life and the adventures can all keep to themselves for a change."

"You could..."

"I could."

"But will you?"

Gwendolyn thought about it for a long moment. "No," she said at last, her voice a choked sob. "Even if I could go home, it wouldn't be the same." She did not know where she found the strength, but in spite of the darkness gripping her heart, she forced herself to sit up on her own. "The Blackstar is out there. And it *is* my fault. I created him. I have to fix it."

"And how will you do that?"

Gwendolyn made a face. She knew the answer. "I'll... have to be myself," she grumbled. "I can't just quit. Can't go back to being a little girl again. That's not..." She took a deep breath. "That's not who I am."

This time it was the Lady who broke the silence. *"Perhaps it is just as my little prince says. Growing up is not the problem. Forgetting is."* She held up a hand, and a leaf floated down into it. *"Do you remember? Do you remember who you are?"*

"Yes." And she remembered what Cyria had said to her, all those years ago. "I am clever. And kind. And brave." The words had helped her when she needed it most, and they still lived within her. They kindled a tiny spark of warmth in her heart and chased away some of the darkness.

The Lady's smile brightened further, and the sky above took on the pale glow of the coming dawn. *"And will it be enough?"*

Gwendolyn thought some more. Perhaps she could get up. Perhaps she could go on. Because she was the kind of girl who would always get back up. The kind of girl who helped the mice and the Missy's of the world.

She nodded. "It will have to be."

The Lady beamed with pride. Literally. *"You have chosen."* Then she helped Gwendolyn sit up, the two of them kneeling across from each other. *"And if I'm not mistaken, you have a family to get back to."*

She snorted a bitter laugh. "How can I? I'm banished. They're all on the other side of the doorway."

The Lady's face melted into an expression of heart-breaking sadness. *"Oh, my beautiful girl. You have more family than you know."* Then she stopped. She cocked her head to the side and scrunched up her nose in thought. *"I suppose..."* She eyed Gwendolyn up and down. *"Yes. I can do that much."*

"What?" Gwendolyn said. But the Lady put a finger against Gwendolyn's lips.

"Close your eyes."

Reluctantly, she did. Gwendolyn felt the Lady's tender touch on both cheeks as she took Gwendolyn's face in her hands, and the coolness of the Lady's skin seemed to spread throughout her body. Gwendolyn's breathing grew deeper, and slower.

"You have been through much, and you have more to come," the woman said in words as clear and fragile as glass. *"You have sacrificed. You have been selfless, and kind, and asked for nothing in return. I think you have earned a reward."* She ran a finger along Gwendolyn's brow and down her cheek. She did it again, caressing the girl's bare scalp, then down behind her ear, and along the side of her neck.

Gwendolyn shivered, goosebumps rippling from her scalp to her spine and along her arms. But the shiver continued, growing more intense. Every muscle in her chest and arms and shoulders tensed as the quiver ran through her. Her eyes shut even tighter. It would have been almost pleasurable if it wasn't so overwhelming. When she thought she could take no more, the feeling passed, and her muscles all relaxed with the release of sensation. Her head hung low, and it felt unusually heavy. Eventually, Gwendolyn opened her eyes.

But she could not see.

Panicked, her hands went to her eyes. But something got in her way. Something frizzy, and familiar.

She parted the hair from her eyes and looked at the locks that tumbled down her shoulders. Fiery, crimson, uncontrollable hair. Her very own. And Gwendolyn shook again, overflowing with shock and relief and excitement, shaking until hot, messy tears streamed down her cheeks and dripped off the end of her nose.

The Lady put a finger under Gwendolyn's chin and brought the girl's face up to her own, fixing her with that sapphire gaze again. She wiped the tears from Gwendolyn's cheek, and playfully tapped the tip of the girl's nose to shake the last dangling drop away.

"I am no cruel queen," she said aloud. "What she can take, I can create."

Gwendolyn shook her head, as much to clear that gaze from her mind as to feel her hair flailing around her once again. It felt so foreign, and so familiar. She sniffed. Her whole face felt wet and stuffy, and she was glad she couldn't see the state of it. Part of her scolded herself for being so concerned with something as petty and vain as hair. But it was hers. And she loved it. And she knew she had missed it, but hadn't realized quite how much.

And if she wasn't mistaken, the Lady had healed all her injuries too. Her breathing was no longer pained. The cut on her back no longer stung, if it was there at all. She managed to squeak out a soft "Thank you." She bowed her head in thanks, losing herself again in the forest of crimson curls.

"You did not need me. You would have made this choice on your own. And so, I have not broken the rules. But every hero is allowed a boon. It is tradition, after all. A sword, a bow, a horn, a cordial. Let this be your magic armor. You have more than proved your worth. Your trials are far from over, your infinite end not yet reached, but may this gift lighten your load a little along the way."

Gwendolyn looked up, peering through her hair again. Her hair. Again.

But the Lady was different now. Fainter. Gwendolyn could almost see right through her to the trees beyond.

"Wait! What did you do? You're fading!"

The Lady nodded. *"There must always be a sacrifice. Everything has a cost. It will be some time before I can see you again. But as I said, you do not need me. You have yourself. I thought it might help if you looked more like yourself again. Goodbye."*

Gwendolyn reached for her, but her hand went right through the Lady's own. "Just like that?"

The Lady smiled one last time. *"Just like that. But remember..."*

Then she was gone. Gwendolyn sat alone in the Forest of Ideas. Except...

"I'm never alone."

The forest was quiet. The stars twinkled softly. And Gwendolyn simply sat and drank it all in, taking a long blissful moment of silence.

Meanwhile...

Her hair.

Her hair.

Her *hair*.

She plunged her fingers into it, ruffling it, shaking it, smelling it, feeling it. She tried to run her fingers through it and they became helplessly tangled. She pulled it in front of her again, admiring the fiery color that had always set her apart in the grey and dreary City. Once again, she stood out like a bonfire.

And she sat there for a while, doing and thinking absolutely nothing. But the world was waiting for her. Her problems had not vanished with the Lady. The sadness crept up on her again, and she had no closet to shove the feelings into.

Nor did she wish to. She would feel her feelings, face them head on. She had faced much worse than herself.

Gwendolyn pulled her hair over one shoulder and wrestled it into an unruly braid. "Curls are all well and good," she said, "but a girl has to be practical." Because if she wasn't, she'd just curl up on the forest floor and cry for who-knows-how-long.

She made her way back through the forest, and into the library. Because the Lady was right. She *did* have a family to get back to.

And there they were. Sparrow, and Starling. Waiting for her between the stacks, faces wracked with worry. Faces that widened with amazement when they saw her.

"Gwendolyn…" Sparrow murmured. "You… your…"

Starling nodded. "It's nice to see it again."

Gwendolyn's hand went to her braid, and she breathed, deep and slow. "It is, isn't it?"

Sparrow took her by the hand, his eyes glistening. "Are you…

are you all right?"

Gwendolyn felt a stab of guilt. Of course; these two knew the pain of losing a home better than anyone. They had likewise been stranded on the other side, with home so close and so far.

She tried to steer her thoughts away from the dangerous path of self-pity. At least her parents were safe. They were home again. They could find some measure of happiness.

And the City itself was no great loss, she told herself. She'd spent most of her life wanting to leave it, anyway. With Cecilia, Jessica, Ian, Tommy, and Missy on the other side, it was in good hands, especially with the Childkeeper beaten and exposed. Gwendolyn had been taking care of herself for some time now, and she knew she could do it again without too much trouble.

These were the things she told herself. She only half believed them.

So she looked at Sparrow and Starling. Her friends. Her creations, in some unexplainable way. They were her responsibility. And if she had to be stranded, there were no two people that she'd rather be stranded with. Starling, the sister she'd never had. Sparrow, a little brother. Her throat tightened, and her eyes prickled.

She closed her eyes, took another deep breath, and opened them again. There was no need for words, and she couldn't have gotten any out if she tried. Instead, she forced a small smile. She would be brave, for Sparrow's sake. The pain would overwhelm her if she let it, but she would not let it show, the way Mother would hide her own worries to protect her daughter from the cruelty of the world.

After all, this was what she'd wanted, wasn't it? The three of them, together, with nothing but time and freedom and adventure? With the library, there were plenty of adventures to be had on an infinite number of worlds.

If those worlds were now infinity-minus-one, she could handle that. She'd have to.

Starling gave a small nod, and forced another smile of her own. The two girls looked at Sparrow. He looked back up at them, and a sad sort of smile spread to his face as well. The little faerie fluttered up and landed on Gwendolyn's shoulder, and Gwendolyn reached up to pat her tiny head.

She walked down the row of books. Her two companions followed. She stopped at the central courtyard and gazed out at the Library.

Her library.

She heard a squeaking sound and turned to see the little book cart rolling its way toward them. Its wheels squeaked as they crossed the mosaic of shifting tiles and it's moving pictures. On top of the cart sat the glittering tiara Gwendolyn had discarded on her last visit. The cart bumped playfully but insistently against her.

Gwendolyn's mouth twitched in the smallest hint of a smile. She took the tiara and looked at it for a moment, admiring the glittering wings and running a thumb over the blue sapphire set into the center. Then she looked back up again.

"All right, children," she said, putting on a confidence she did not feel. "Where to next?"

And the three of them stood there, staring out at the endless shelves, and all the stories that lay ahead of them.

AN EPILOGUE

Doorways have two sides. And on the other side of the door that Gwendolyn could no longer open, Robin turned around and dusted his hands. The door behind him vanished, leaving nothing but a smooth grey wall in the City's Hall of Records.

"Well," he said. "You have kept your bargain. I have kept mine."

Two figures approached the faerie, walking down the row of shelves in perfect unison. One clad in a grey skirt and suit, her raven-black hair pulled tight into a bun. The other wore a dress of rainbow fringe and a dash of glitter on her cheeks.

"The faerie is true to its word," said the Childkeeper.

"A distasteful arrangement, but most advantageous," said Zelda.

Robin snorted. "You two have no use for your glamours now, they do not work on me anyhow."

The two women looked at each other and nodded slightly, ever so slightly. The air around them shimmered like heat haze, and the women themselves shimmered too. The leader of the Revelers and the Keeper of Unclaimed Children vanished. In their place were two men, clad in crisp grey suits and bowler hats. But the shimmering haze never left their faces. Their features were slippery enough to escape even Robin's faerie eyes.

"You were right, Mister Five," said the former Childkeeper. "It seems the Gwendolyn girl will not be who we need her to be. She refused the darkness."

"Nor was she content to settle down, Mister Six," said the man who was no longer Zelda. "Forced isolation is our safest option. Keep her on the Woman's worlds."

"We can continue unopposed."

Robin snorted. "Yes, your sinister plot's all well and fine. You found me the girl, and vengeance is mine. To this world, the girl can no longer come. So are we done? This place is tiresome."

Mister Five waved a gloved hand. "Our transaction is completed. You may go."

"Gladly." Robin snapped his fingers, and vanished in a puff of green smoke.

The men stared silently, ever so silently, at the blank stretch of wall before them.

"A pity," said Mister Six after a time. "She could have won us many worlds."

"Yes," said Mister Five. "But no matter. We still have *this* world. The seeds of the Discord have been planted. The Fall shall begin again. And with its power restored, we shall have a foothold from which to broaden our horizons."

"Indeed. Shall we proceed, Mister Five?" said Mister Six.

"After you, Mister Six," said Mister Five.

The Faceless Gentlemen in their bowler hats began to shimmer, replaced by Zelda and the Childkeeper once again. And together they walked, slowly, ever so slowly, back out into the City.

And So Ends

THE WITHERING TRIALS

OF

GWENDOLYN GRAY

ACKOWLEDGEMENTS

As always, thanks to my amazing wife Kori, without whom none of this would be even close to possible. Thanks to my fantastic children, whose imagination inspires mine every day.

Thanks to the students and colleagues that I pestered for information, which deep and probing questions such as "Hey, what's hard about growing up these days?"

Thanks to Sanjay Charlton, for his amazing artwork and for putting up with my copious cover notes!

And an amazing thanks to all my Kickstarter backers that made this book possible: Allen Hill, Rob Steinberger, Madison, Skye and Caroline Larsen, Thomas Bull, Esa Eriksson, Christine, Jamie, Jordan Murray, Rachel, Fiddlehead Press, Shaun Merida, Eron Wyngarde, Ashley Anne Cook, Keith Turpin, Dan Shockley, Francesco Tehrani, Merridee Brown, Dawnsbrook Press, Debbie Lynn, Leslie, Andrew French, David Wood, Kourtney and William Stauffer, Erin Warner, and Elizabeth Carter. You're all rockstars.

B. A. Williamson is the award winning author of *The Chronicles of Gwendolyn Gray*. When not mining the unfathomable depths of consciousness for new words to sling, he can be found wandering Indianapolis, directing plays, taming children, and probably singing entirely too loud. Direct all complaints and darkest secrets to @bawrites and bawilliamson.com.

www.ingramcontent.com/pod-product-compliance
Lightning Source LLC
Chambersburg PA
CBHW011922300726
48970CB00008B/2540